Blood

Rhapsody

Blood Rhapsody

Nancy Morse

3

ISBN 978-1492275749

Chapter 1

...for they have shed the blood of your saints and profits, and you have given them blood to drink as they deserve. Revelation 16:6

*H*e emerged from the shadows, the ancient hunger gnawing at his belly like a rat in a cold, dark place.

With his head bent against the mist, features shielded from the glow of oil-burning street lights, he wended his way through the honeycombed streets of London's East End, his footsteps making no sound against the cobblestones as they led him to the place of thieves and mischief-makers.

Through the black locks that slanted across his brow and fell into his eyes, he watched surreptitiously as people moved through the streets.

He had been like them once. Bored, disillusioned with life, moving from one day to the next as if waiting for life to happen. With little success he tried to understand the perceptions and principles of men. Although he was acutely aware of how much people needed each other, there were times when he felt that it was equally appropriate to feel nothing at all for anyone, least of all for himself. This life, when viewed from a distance, was meaningless. When viewed from up close, appalling.

What fools, he thought with contempt, *clinging to their petty little beliefs based on clouded perceptions of what they feel is right according to what makes them comfortable, crying over their little tragedies. How can any of them know the true tragedy of my life?*

He possessed all the tragic qualities of men—greed, lust, obsession—but unlike them, he was the dark rebel, trapped in a half-world between the living and the dead, a world they could never fathom save in their deepest, darkest dreams.

He was the outcast, the outsider who did not fit in, the menace of myth and legend who walked among them, a soulless creature with only heartbreak and bitterness to look back on and eons of nothing to look forward to. What could any of them know of this?

The heavy metal wheels of a horse-drawn carriage splashed through a puddle putrid with muck, startling him out of his dismal, defeating thoughts and soiling his woolen cloak, furthering the foulness of his mood as he hurried down the narrow, unlit passageways between the crammed residences. Into his nostrils drifted the dirt and dust of the stinking, airless alleys, the smell of wet horses, and the stench of raw sewage that stagnated in cesspools. Yet there rose above the rank odors that turned his stomach the scent he was hunting. Blood. To him, purity and impurity, sacred and profane, life and death.

With the moon sequestered behind inky clouds and the ever-present shroud of fog, it was a dark and dangerous place to be. But what fear did he have of the peril that lurked all around? What fear did he have of anything, save himself?

With nothing to live for, and no fear of death, the only pleasure he derived was in sating the blood lust, and even that pleasure was perverse and not of his own choosing. He could very well understand why people would hate one such as him. He hated himself for all the same reasons.

"Dead drunk for two pence!"

"Drunk for a penny!"

From the dimly lit alleys came the cries of the gin-hawkers, peddling their cheap alcohol to the drunken masses that gravitated to these dark places to evade the government's attempt to control its sale.

"Some Cuckold's Comfort, my fine gentleman?"

A toothless hag reeking of gin and disease tugged at his cloak. Without breaking stride, he knocked her into the air and hard against the wall of a shadowy building, the crack of her bones lost amidst the clamor of the night.

In his hunt for pure, untainted blood he avoided the prostitutes whose gaunt bodies were riddled with consumption, the drunks saturated with gin, the watery blood of the old and feeble, and the deficient blood of the malnourished. It was becoming more and more difficult these days to find adequate prey. The wellborn were his feast of choice. They were so plump and well fed. Blood flavored with sherry, now that was a feast indeed. Nevertheless, he could not very well knock on the door of a fashionable Mayfair house and drink his full. Unless, of course, he was invited inside, and then woe be to the unfortunate human who made that fatal mistake. Alas, it was not likely he would be feasting in the West End any time soon. Most of the constables were corrupt and scarcely capable of preventing crime, but a death like the kind he inflicted would surely arouse attention and spread panic among the well-heeled populace.

Why tempt fate? And why do anything to draw the attention of the de Veres who, throughout history, had relegated the first born sons of their first born sons to slaying those of his kind? A sneer curled his lip. What a single-minded lot they were with their crucifixes and hawthorn stakes. He had succeeded thus far in staying one step ahead of them. All the more reason to feed on the seamy side of town where death was rampant and no one looked askance at dead bodies in the alleys.

Besides, just because a man wore a fine suit of clothes did not mean he was uncontaminated. Just last month he had followed into a back alley a well-dressed physician who had no doubt been summoned to rid some putrid prostitute of the inconvenient fetus she was carrying. The physician never got the chance to perform his sordid deed, falling prey instead to a much more evil doer. It was only when the blood had been drunk and the physician lay dead at his feet that he realized his mistake. The physician had availed himself of a tincture of opium in alcohol. Having gone undetected beneath the strong aroma of cinnamon and saffron, he had spent the next several days writhing in pain from the physician's laudanum-tainted blood.

No, he had to be much more careful in selecting his victims. Perhaps a young pickpocket only recently initiated into the art, too young to be eaten up by disease. It was convenient to reason that he would be doing the lad a favor by saving him from a life of crime at the end of which was a hangman's noose.

But wait! A footpad was lurking in the shadows, no doubt waiting to murder a passing pedestrian for a few shillings. He lifted his head and sniffed the foggy air. He detected no hint of gin or disease about the intended victim. This was luck, indeed. He snickered to himself, put his head down, and strode into the alley where his prey was waiting.

With every footstep he took he could feel his eye teeth lengthening. It was not a pain really, just a few moments of discomfort, as if he had bitten down too hard on a stale biscuit, until the fangs were fully pointed and ready for the attack.

A mere mortal could never have heard the footsteps that fell into place behind him, but his wolf-like hearing told him his prey had taken the bait.

"Can ya tip me any quidds, mate?"

He kept walking.

"No, eh? Maybe this'll change yer bloody mind."

He heard the blade slide out from beneath a soiled sleeve. *Go ahead, do your dirty deed, and then I shall do mine.*

The knife thrust forward. Its rusted blade caught the glint of a random rushlight as it ripped through the expensive woolen cloak swinging from his shoulders, slicing flesh and muscle. He grimaced, but it was a momentary distraction, the wound healing in seconds.

Drawing himself up to a height that towered over the stalker, he glared down at him with the molten eyes of a pagan creature. The man shrank back and turned to run.

He reached out to stop his flight with a movement so fast that it was scarcely discernible. His fingers closed around the man's neck like talons and dragged him closer. The man tried to scream, but no sound emerged.

Sometimes, when he was feeling benevolent, he induced the catatonic state so that his victims would have no memory of the attack. But not this time. He sank his fangs into the man's throat. The blood was thick and sweet upon his tongue. He could taste the man's fear in every drop. Fear and hatred, and a wild confusion as though he was desperately trying to comprehend that which formed no definition in his small and feeble mind. And then, with the sound of suction, irrational terror took hold as his victim began to understand that someone, some*thing* was drinking from him.

The heartbeat slowed from the rapid palpitations of pure panic to a dull, heavy, thump…thump…thump…

And then…nothing.

The silence of death, accompanied by the exhilaration of warm, fresh blood flooding through his veins lasted only moments before he realized that he still held the dirty dead body in his arms. With a growl of disgust he let it fall to the ground. He whipped the neck cloth from about his shirt collar. Oblivious to the costly lace from which it was made, he wiped the crimson blood from his mouth. Lest he leave any further evidence of his crime behind, he shoved the bloodied fabric into his pocket.

He felt no guilt for what he had just done. No remorse. He was doing humanity a favor, after all, by ridding the streets of vermin like that. As he slipped noiselessly from the alley he was feeling sated. Yes, sated and satisfied, and in smug awe of his own superior powers, if he didn't mind saying so.

He turned his boots in the direction of the Old Bell Inn behind the New Church in the Strand where half a pint of wine was just what he needed to wash away the aftertaste that lingered on his tongue. He could have hailed a sedan and paid the shilling to be carried the rest of the way, but as he was feeling robust in the aftermath of feeding, he opted to walk. Besides, his pedestrian wanderings gave him the opportunity to scour the dark corners of the city for future meals.

He made his way past shop fronts bulging over the cobbled footways, their sign boards creaking overhead. The rough roadway was pitted with holes. Shouting hackney-coachmen and insolent footmen thrust their way through the streets, sloshing mud on unsuspecting pedestrians.

Gradually, the stench of the seedy part of the East End gave way to the sooty deposits of burning sea coal that hung in the air from the hearths of the weavers' houses in Spitalfields.

Pulling his cloak tighter about his body, he put his head down and continued on into the mist, blotting out the sounds of the night, drawing a curtain on his tormented thoughts, until all that remained was the silence within, punctuated by the beating of his own immortal heart.

Presently, there came to his ears a sound that could not be dispelled. Somewhere, a woman was weeping.

He shook his head in an attempt to chase the sound away, but it lingered, stubbornly drawing him toward it. It was coming from the river. It annoyed him, not because he was moved by the sound of a woman's tears, but because of the way in which it captured his attention, much like the sweet scent of blood.

Through the mist he saw a woman standing on the stone bridge that spanned the river Thames. Her anguish was palpable even over the noise of the waterwheels churning nearby. Her cloak whipped about her body, pressing against her legs in the wind. She lifted her head and glanced skyward. As she did, the hood fell back revealing hair the color of dark ale, long and loose, the tips blowing up in the wind off the river. Had it not been for that, he would have turned away, but in that moment he caught her profile etched against the darkness, illuminated by the glimmer of dripping oil lamps. There was something about her profile that gripped his gaze and held it. He caught himself thinking that she looked like an angel, one hell of a thought for someone like him to entertain. Angel, indeed. A deep chuckle rumbled in his chest.

He felt the familiar stirrings of his libido. He'd had more than his share of beautiful women. Immortal though he might be, he was still a man with a man's hungers which grew ever more aggressive with the passing of each century. Unlike his mortal counterparts he did not fear his lust, nor did he feel constrained by any gentlemanly behavior to control it. Others of his kind did not limit their carnal adventures to the opposite sex. So terrible was the magnitude of their lust that they satisfied it with just about anyone. But not he. He had no taste for boys. His passion had always been for women. Blood he could obtain anywhere, but the sating of his sexual desire was a different matter. Of course, the mortal women with whom he coupled more often than not wound up dead owing to his strength and insatiable appetite for their blood. Ah well, it was, he supposed, the price they paid for inhumanly spectacular sex, a price much fairer than that which he paid for being excluded from society and the glorious light of day.

He was about to turn away, when the woman's scent drifted to where he stood in the shadow of one of the Tudor houses on the bridge. The vibrant lifeblood coursing through her veins created a familiar throb from within. She was so vital, so full of life...and blood.

Her slender white throat beckoned. But he had only recently satisfied the blood lust. His face was still flushed from feeding on the footpad. Too much generally made him ill. If he had any hunger at all, it was for the meal waiting for him at home of cold meats, fruit, wine, and perhaps a bit of chocolate stewed and thickened with eggs. No, it was not her blood for which he hungered. The sudden press of his phallus against his trousers aroused a different appetite.

She turned her face away from the sky and back toward the river where a waterman was pulling against the tide. Her weeping was almost musical to his ears, a beautiful sound were it not filled with such deep despair. He carefully approached.

"Excuse me," he said, in a low voice so as not to alarm her.

She turned, startled.

"Have no fear," he hastened to assure her. "I mean you no harm. I see that you are weeping."

She brushed the tears from her cheeks. "You have been watching me?"

A voice like honey, sweet and savory, drifted into his ears as if on a moonbeam. He studied her face, dignified but not at all stern, the eyes round as saucers and ringed with dark lashes, the smooth brow, straight nose, firm little mouth, the chin that turned up as if with a mind of its own. Taking her features together as a whole she was not what one would consider beautiful, yet there was an allure about her that went straight to his loins. But it was more than her unusual appeal that aroused him. For a fleeting moment he imagined that having this young woman would instill in him a tranquility that had vanished from his being on the night he was made. That her soft, demure body might somehow transport him from the savage reality of his existence to a higher place. That burying his face in the plump breasts that strained at her cloak could make him forget centuries of dreams ruthlessly crushed.

The pulsing in his trousers intensified.

"No, not at all," he lied. "I was just passing by."

Sensing the ebb of her suspicion, he edged a little nearer. "This is a dangerous place for you to be. The pickpockets that filch so boldly during the day make no scruple to bludgeon people from Fleet Street to the Strand. A woman alone, here on the London Bridge, can offer little resistance against such evil." And if anyone knew just how evil a man could be, surely, it was he.

She glanced around, as if becoming aware of her surroundings for the first time. "I rushed from the house and ran so fast, and found myself here."

"Were you being threatened?" he asked.

"No, not at all. It's…" Her voice cracked. "It's my father. He's dying."

"Ah, that is sad, indeed," he said, affecting a tone of false concern.

"Each day he grows weaker. It's as if the life is slowly slipping away from him. We have tried everything. Rosemary-flavored brandy to bring the color back to his cheeks. Treacle water from the apothecary. Charms and amulets. Even astrology. To no avail. The doctors are mystified by his growing decline." Tears misted her eyes. "And it is not even of himself that he thinks. It is of his pupils."

"Your father is a schoolmaster?"

"He is the music master."

His green eyes brightened, then narrowed as he inquired, "May I ask your father's name?"

"James Hightower."

"But of course. Permit me to introduce myself. My name is Ambrus Nicolae Tedescu. I am one of your father's pupils. Forgive me, but I did not know he has a daughter."

"I only recently returned from Paris where I have been residing with my aunt since the death of my mother last year."

That would explain why he had never glimpsed this dainty little prize during any of his lessons with the music master. He thought back to his last several visits. "That is odd indeed," he observed, "for I had not noticed your father looking ill. More to the contrary, he seemed extraordinarily vigorous for a man of his age. Fifty, I would venture to guess." And looking oh so hale and hearty, with all that clean, healthy blood pumping through his veins. On more than one occasion it had crossed his mind to partake of that blood, but music being the inspiration of his soul, so to speak, for in reality he did not have a soul, it would have defeated his own musical ambitions to cause the man's demise.

"It began soon after my return," she said. "At first, he complained of being tired and cancelled several of his lessons."

That explained why the music master's servant called at his home to inform him their lessons were being postponed indefinitely.

"You say he grows weaker. Does he also grow paler?"

Could it be that another such as he was on the prowl in London? They were everywhere, in every dark corner of every city and hamlet. Foolish mortals, not even aware of the bloodthirsty evil that lurked in their midst. Not that his kind were all created equal. Some possessed super human strength but were exceptionally addlebrained. Others had vastly superior intellects but were little more than mesmerists. Was the music master the victim of a common blood drinker?

"No," she said. "Just weakened a little more each day, as if the life were slowly slipping from him for no good reason."

His cool outward countenance did not register his inner alarm. It was possible that the music master was not the victim of a blood drinker, but of something much more insidious. A life drainer, subsisting on the energies of their victims, leaving them feeling drained and fatigued without ever having to draw a single drop of blood. In all his years on earth, in all his wanderings, he had come across only one such creature. Lienore. Red-haired, fiery-eyed, beautiful beyond words. Born of a black magic blood ritual at a time when the Druids inhabited the ancient land of Dubh Lein and the Goddess ruled the earth. A ghostly presence that moved from host to host, a dangerous and enigmatic foe of the living, seducing her victims and slowly daining them of vitality, a cunning and devious mistress of deception.

He suppressed a fiendish chuckle to think that not even the scurilous de Veres, with their centuries-old vendetta against his kind, could know what they were up against in such a diabolical creature as she.

A hulk passed beneath the bridge with its cargo of prisoners bound for the North American colonies. The wherries were busy shuttling passengers to Gravesend. A punt thudded against the bank, the waterman hauling his baskets of fish on shore, the smell wafting upwards on the breeze.

The river traffic drew him away from his murky thoughts and toward the river itself. It was fitting, he supposed, that the Thames should derive its name from the Celts' word for "dark". That Lienore was a product of a Celtic ritual. That he and his kind roamed in darkness. All bound together by a fate which mere mortals could not possibly comprehend.

His thoughts returned to the music master. In all the centuries since his making, music had become the only source of pleasure in his shadowy and lonely existence. The instrument of his choosing, the violoncello, had become a life source for him. No other instrument could rival the mournful longing, the deep lament, the plaintive sorrow or the fierce rage of his own heart.

It was only when he was seated behind his instrument that he was able to keep the stark reality of his existence at bay. With its maple body suspended on its endpin, holding it much like a lover between his knees and against his chest, drawing the bow stick across the strings with his right hand while the fingers of the left depressed the bridge, the sound he created filled him with an incomparable depth of emotion.

The music master had taught him how to draw the most out of his instrument, to make it come alive in his hands as he himself would never be alive, to make it sing as no earthly voice could ever sing and draw the heavens down to where earth abides, and for those few moments of rapture, for him to feel almost human.

It was with his own selfish motives in mind that he caught himself thinking aloud, "If only there was something I could do."

She turned to him then. The glow of the oil lamps danced across her face. Her complexion was dewey from the mist off the river. Her eyes glistened with tears, and for the first time he realized that they were blue, like the silent clarity of a sky that was almost beyond recall, until now. Her smile was luminous despite her pain. Into his nostrils came the scent of her, fresh and clean and sweet.

He felt an animal power surging through his loins, and he knew with almost cruel certainty that he would have her. But not now. The time would come. If there was anything a man who had lived for centuries learned, it was patience.

"My father told me about one of his pupils who shows remarkable accomplishment," she said in that soft voice that fanned the flames of his desire.

"I am sure it was one of his other pupils to whom he was referring."

The modesty of his reply was matched only by the swelling of pride from within. Yes, he was a superior musician. Unmatched in raw talent and emotion. Wasn't that how Amati had put it? But what was a musician without an instrument?

So he had stolen from the luthier's workshop in Cremona one of the painted and gilded instruments intended for the French court of King Charles IX. Amati had been furious to learn of the theft and had immediately suspected him, rightly so. Perhaps if the blood thirst had not been so strong that night the master luthier would have lived. Ah well, all mortals must die. And the instrument bearing the coat of arms of a king of France became his.

"No," she said, "it was you. He told me that a music master is fortunate to have one such pupil in his lifetime."

Her voice cracked with emotion and a misty look passed over her blue eyes. With the back of her hand she wiped the tears that sprang anew.

"Here," he said. Reaching into his pocket, he withdrew what he thought was a handkerchief for her to dry her tears, but when he saw the alarming suddenness with which she flinched away, he realized his mistake. In his hand he held the bloodied neck cloth from his most recent feeding.

The crimson-stained fabric disappeared beneath his cloak in a movement too rapid for human eyes to detect. "Forgive me," he said. "I found a mongrel that had been struck by a speeding coach and used my neck cloth to staunch its bleeding. It was only a superficial wound. The ungrateful beast ran off without as much as a glance back."

The falsehood soothed her and even garnered for him a look of admiration from her beautiful eyes. "You are a lover of animals then?"

Well, yes, he thought sardonically, *when there is no human prey readily available, an animal will do*. "Most assuredly. I cannot turn away from a poor dumb creature in need. Is this better?"

He handed her a handkerchief decorated with lace at the ends.

She accepted it and dabbed at the tears that stained her cheeks. "You are very kind, sir."

"No, please," he objected, drawing his hand away, "you must call me Nicolae. And might I ask by what name I may call you?"

She lowered her gaze shyly, and then peered back up at him. "Prudence. But those who know me call me Pru."

"I should be honored to know you, Prudence." *In ways you cannot imagine*, he thought slyly. "Come now. I will escort you home."

An owl screeched from the gatehouse, and the murky scent of the river came drifting down the wind as they walked from the stone bridge toward her house in Folgate Street.

"Tedescu," she said presently, testing the name out loud. "I'm not familiar with the origin."

His muscles tensed beneath his cloak. "The name is Romanian."

"How long have you been in London?"

If he told her he'd been standing among the crowd on Tower Green and watched that insolent slut, Anne Boleyn, lose her head, what would she think? Or that more than a century later he was in the city when the plague took six thousand people in one week and the only sound that could be heard day or night was the tolling of bells. Or that the fire that broke out in Pudding Lane which destroyed nearly the entire city was caused when the king's baker, from whom he'd been feeding, knocked over a candle which, in turn, set the timbered building aflame. He had dwelled within London's medieval stone walls since fleeing his homeland and the gruesome rituals of the villagers who hunted his kind for reasons that ranged from fear to profit. He could have told her all these things, and she would have laughed in his face or, more likely, shrunk in horror. And then he would have had to kill her, and until he had satisfied his carnal lust, the killing would have to wait.

"I arrived two years ago," he lied.

"That's odd," she remarked. "Your speech bares only the slightest trace of an accent."

Oh, but she was a clever girl. He would have to be careful with this one. "I have done my share of world traveling," he said. "It is amazing what one loses along the way."

"Is your family with you?"

He answered flatly, "My family is dead." The presence of words left unsaid hung in the air between them. "And you?" he questioned. "You said you left for Paris when your mother died. Might I ask how she died?" One of his victims, perhaps? Now, wouldn't that be ironic?

She was silent for several moments, and then said quietly, "She drowned."

He felt a certain relief knowing that he'd had no part in it. It would make seducing her that much easier if there were no connection. "A swimming accident?"

"She threw herself off the bridge. They found her body when the tide fell, among the mud and shingle."

"She must have been very unhappy to resort to such a drastic measure."

She frowned. "I don't understand it. She was one of the happiest people in the world, always laughing and smiling. We were not wealthy, but we were a happy family. And then, darkness descended over her. Aunt Vivienne had just arrived from Paris for a visit, and not even she could chase the shadows from my mother's heart."

"Is that why you went to the bridge tonight?"

"I go there when I am distressed. I stare down into the water trying to imagine what it must have been like for her in those last moments." She looked at him then, blue eyes all shiny and vulnerable. "Do you think she was afraid?"

He knew what it was to take life, to watch the fear form in the eyes of his victims in those final moments. But what knowledge did he have of the kind of death of which she was speaking?

There were times when the loneliness had grown so unbearable that he had wished it were possible to take his own life, to put an end to the misery of immortality. But short of plunging a stake into his heart, or worse, letting a de Vere have the perverse satisfaction of doing it, his fate was sealed.

An impenetrable look darkened his eyes. "I cannot say with certainty, but I would think at times like that the greatest fear is in continuing to live."

"Sometimes I think she comes back to me. At night, in my dreams, through the veil of sleep, I see her face. She seems distressed. She looks so frightened and tired and pale."

An impulse of suspicion raced through his mind. A dream? Perhaps. Perhaps not.

***

Away from London's bustle, in a house situated in a secluded spot in Clapham, Simon Cavendish hunched over boiling crucibles in his shadowy laboratory, squeezing a bellows before a transformative flame.

He was a silent, solitary man who shunned personal relationships. So secretive was he that his comings and goings were relegated to a back staircase to avoid daily encounters with the housekeeper. The only social outlet he permitted himself was the monthly meeting of the Fellows of the Royal Society Club, but even the members there did not know much about the painfully shy and elusive man. Unlike other alchemists who put their talents to use in uncovering a technique to turn mere lead into gold, he was in pursuit of something much more life-altering that would affect mankind for all time, harboring a vainglorious desire to concoct an elixir that would prolong mankind's earthly span and unlock the elusive mysteries of life.

For more than thirty years he had pursued the elixir of life, a potion not just with the ability to prolong life but to actually create life. He began his experiments by dissolving simple sea salt in morning dew until a black powder formed, which was then calcined to become gray, and again dissolved in more dew and digested to whiteness. Virgin's milk, he called it. He was unsure of its powers until he tested it upon himself by ingesting a vial, whereupon he discovered that it enhanced his memory and the thinking power of his mind. More vials ingested opened the doors of his psychic perception into the spirit world, enabling him to hear and see things that could only be seen in the ultraviolet spectrum of light. And what he saw in the spectrum changed everything.

He turned his attention to leeches, the slimy creatures he collected from bogs that fed on human blood, and came to the realization that in blood lay the answer.

The Fellows of the Royal Society scoffed at the myths which went back thousands of years and occurred in almost every culture around the world of pagan creatures that come back to life to drink the blood of the living. At first, he too had scoffed. He was a scientist, not a member of the Roman Church which believed that incorrupt bodies were saints, or of the Orthodox Church that believed the creatures were vampires. And yet, as the folklore spread throughout the centuries, with more and more accounts of bodies swelling up like drums, corpses with ruddy complexions, dead cattle and sheep showing no outward sign of trauma, exhumed bodies with long hair and nails, he began to wonder.

He started collecting books and journals and first-hand accounts of undead creatures that drank the blood of their victims, turning his attention from the ones that dwelled in bogs and marshes like the leeches in his laboratory, to the ones that walked the earth on two legs as described in Eastern European folklore. The shelves of his library were crammed with dusty tomes. *Chronicles*, dating back to the twelfth century recording revenants in England. *The Malleus Maleficarium*, a witch hunter's bible of the fifteenth century which discussed how to hunt and destroy the undead. *Treatise on Vampires* by an Italian scientist in the sixteenth century who was burned at the stake for his views. *De Masticatione Mortuorum*, a German text of the seventeenth century.

Known by many names, *strigoi* in Romania, *bhuta* in India, *mullo* by the Slavic gypsies, he thought it strange that no such word for these creatures existed in the English language, when cases were documented of the undead preying on the living as far back as ancient Egypt. He had, in fact, come into possession of a German translation of a well documented incident in Serbia where an ex-soldier turned farmer who had allegedly been attacked by the undead years before, died while haying. After his death people began to die and it was widely believed that he had returned to prey on his neighbors. It was time to give the unwitting population of London a new word to add to their vocabulary, and the word was *vampire*.

But how could he test his theory when there was no tangible proof of the existence of nosferatu? Then, one night, as he sat alone in his parlor on a cabriole-legged sofa reading the *Evening Post* before the fire, his attention was drawn to a grisly story about a body that had been found by the wharf with no visible signs of bludgeoning or stabbing but completely drained of blood. A week later another such body was discovered in the East End. The victims were known criminals and their deaths aroused no particular interest from the populace of anything untoward.

Using his Fellowship in the Royal Society as an excuse to gain entrance to the morgue, he had examined each putrid body prior to burial. The first body exhibited two small puncture wounds on the neck at the site of the jugular. He had felt his own blood quicken. When the second body exhibited identical bite marks, he had raced back to his subterranean laboratory, convinced that nosferatu did indeed walk the streets of London.

Toward that end he devoted every waking hour to devising a scheme to trap the killer and unlock the secret of its immortality, roaming the dirty streets of London at night in search of telltale signs. This evening, the only thing he came across was a dead body in an alley in the East End. Too stinking to examine closely, he dismissed it as having been felled by disease.

***

It was Edmund de Vere's bloody luck to be the first born son of a first born son.

It began in a small town in the Loire valley where his ancestors had lived. There had been whispers racing throughout the villages that inquisitors of heretical depravity were torturing accused witches in the most diabolical ways to extract confessions, with innocence or guilt being trivial matters. No one was innocent, neither the milkmaid nor the *seigneur*. Edmund's ancestors were neither witches nor nobles, yet they were condemned by a special tribunal of pious Dominican friars and burned at the stake for heresy. Thus, in the small hours of the night nearly three hundred years ago a secret society known the Sanctum was born, an order that proposed a truth far more dangerous and grotesque than any the inquisitors had put forth. The truth was that many of the inquisitors were creatures without souls who drank the blood of the living in the depths of their dungeons and sent the bloodless bodies to the stake. From that day forward it was deemed that the first born son of the first born son of each family in the order would devote his energies, indeed his very life if need be, to the destruction of the blood drinkers.

From his father Edmund learned the tricks to lure a vampire out of hiding. A black horse might be used. Or a white one. Or a virgin astride a white horse. Sometimes the loathsome fiends could be tricked into revealing themselves by strewing poppy seeds on the path to the graveyard, for it was known among the sanctioned hunters that a vampire's fascination with counting would compel it to count the seeds one at a time, thereby revealing it for what it was.

There was one such creature Edmund swore an oath to eradicate, but which eluded him.

He knew not the creature's name, nor its beginning, but tales of its crimes were whispered among the Slavic people. He was a clever one, a prolific killer possessing a rare intelligence and an innate sense that seemed to warn him whenever a sanctioned hunter was in the vicinity.

He had first come to the attention of the Sanctum two hundred and fifty years ago when Philippe de Vere, Edmund's ancestor, had been found dead in his study, his body drained of blood by the *strigoi mort* he'd been hunting. Among Philippe's handwritten notes was the only clue to the fiend's identity—the brightest, most beautiful green eyes ever to exert control over a mortal mind.

To avenge the gruesome death of Philippe, the destruction of this particular *strigoi* became Edmund's goal to the point of obsession.

Edmund had tracked the green-eyed monster from Russia to Bulgaria, Serbia to Poland, and finally to London, where his penchant for feeding on thieves and murderers on the East End seemed to be his calling card. Several times Edmund stumbled across the victims only hours after they had been drained. He was close, so close to catching the creature that had thus far managed to stay one step ahead of the de Veres through the centuries.

By day, Edmund de Vere was a pewterer, fashioning sauce boats, chargers and candlesticks for the wealthy, stamping each piece with his own set of crowned initial marks, accumulating a respectable six thousand Pounds at his trade. By night, the amiable tradesman became a predator, as solitary and stealthy as the one he stalked.

Edmund stared down at his kit. Everything was in order. Stakes, mallet, crucifix, holy water, knives, rope, saw. As he donned his greatcoat and prepared to go hunting, he could not help but think that maybe this would be the night when he would catch the fiend and put an end to his centuries of bloodletting. But first, he would stop in Folgate Street to call upon Prudence. It was time he and his fiancée set a date for their marriage.

***

Lienore ran a tortoise-shell brush through her waist-length hair. It was pretty, but not as striking as her once henna-colored tresses that had been so appropriately like the color of blood. She heaved an involuntary sigh. If only she were able to view her former self in the cheval glass, but the image that used to peer back at her from glistening pools in days of old appeared not in the glass. In its place was the face and form of her current victim. All she had to recall her own startling beauty was an ancient memory of a strong, lovely face.

Some things, however, never changed, and for all the centuries that had elapsed since her making, she had lost neither her urgent desires nor the vanity that compelled her to choose only the fairest and loveliest hosts in which to dwell.

The present one suited her vanity quite nicely, with its heavy breasts, ample hips and face that turned masculine heads. Not at all like the last, which had been beautiful, but willful, and spiteful to the end, throwing herself from the bridge into the murky river to escape possession. This one was much more docile and so easily overtaken.

How many had there been since that fateful night when she'd been standing over the cauldron making earth magic, intoning the words of power, when the Druids dragged her away and sacrificed her blood in that awful ritual? Suddenly, she felt about a thousand years old. *Oh Goddess, Mother, why did you forsake me? Why did you not hear my cries that night as I writhed on the stone altar, begging for mercy? Would that I had died a mortal's death that night than to live as this...this thing that I am.*

Lienore's face flushed with anger. Her eyes glowed with an unearthly fire as hatred seared upon her heart, as it invariably did when confronted with her fate. Vengeance welled within, and as it did, she grew more ominous, more determined to wreck her menacing havoc on the living. And she would start with that old man. Damn him and his infernal music, and that deep, bellowing instrument that looked like an overripe milkmaid. Oh, how she despised not just his music, but all music for the unbearable memories it conjured of the night that sealed her fate. Until now she had merely toyed with this mortal who called himself the music master, but he was about to experience the full extent of her sinister power and the white-hot rage that propelled her through the ages.

Chapter 2

*P*ru waited in the receiving room of the house in Hanover Square.

Overhead a brass chandelier suspended from the high ceiling was lit by candles that threw a warm light over the lavish furnishings. Portraits hung about the dark wood walls lighted by candles from below. Ancestors, she supposed, although none bore any resemblance to man she met several nights ago on the bridge.

She recalled the smile that looked as if it could melt the coldest heart, and the bright green eyes that had caught and held her gaze more strongly than any man's ever had. She had sensed something strange emanating from him that night, a dark aura that made her shiver even now. She guessed him to be twenty-six or seven, or perhaps even a little older, and although he had seemed very mature, his face had borne the rosy flush of youth. Yet for all that, it was the sorrow she saw in his eyes that had softened her guard.

As she stood there fidgeting from foot to foot, unsure if she should stay or leave, the bittersweet strains of the violoncello began to stream throughout the house. Its anguished tones and sense of profound introspection infiltrated every corner, penetrating her thoughts and drawing her attention away from her unease. The soulful quality of the suite that was being played, full of light and shadow, sorrow and joy, emphasized the instrument's lower register, a resonant sound that she did not at first fully appreciate, until her ears became adjusted, and then, nothing else seemed important.

Like a siren's call, the rhapsody beckoned. It lured her out of the receiving room and through the doors of a smoking room.

As she moved across the carpet, she noticed a fine walnut card table with cabriole legs and acanthus carvings on the knees, atop which sat a flask and a half-filled glass of what looked to be dark claret. She followed the music to a sitting room whose open double doors revealed heavy fabric embellished with tassels and bows drawn tight over the tall windows even though the sun had not yet set.

The music led her up a narrow staircase to the garret floor set in the roof. Finding the door ajar, she tiptoed cautiously closer and peered inside.

As below stairs, the large windows were draped with heavy fabric, obliterating the burgeoning twilight. Big white candles cast a faint luminescence across the dusky room and threw flickering shadows over the walls. A soft golden light fell upon the dark locks spilling across the brow of the figure who sat behind the violoncello, head bent and eyes closed.

Pru felt like an eavesdropper, yet she could not will herself to move from the doorway where she stood listening uninvited to the most beautiful, mystical conversation she had ever heard. In his hands the instrument came alive, singing with a voice as clear and beautiful as any she had heard in a church choir.

She had no idea how long she stood there watching and listening from the shadows, for time seemed to have no meaning when wrapped in the rapture of his music. The prayerful, meditative concentration to the piece was perhaps the closest she would ever come to experiencing the soul of this man through his music.

Her father had been right. This man's talent was indeed special. With a pale hand he glided the bow across the strings for the final notes. And then, silence, as if the air inside the garret room had absorbed all the beauty it could hold until it could hold no more.

He put the bow aside, and with head lowered, eyes still closed, caressed the carved neck of the instrument with the tenderness of a man caressing his lover's neck. He rose fluidly, removed the endpin upon which the violoncello stood, and carefully placed the instrument in its velvet-lined case, all the while seemingly unaware of the woman who watched from the doorway.

With the music over, Pru was suddenly ashamed of her intrusion.

She stood there uncertainly, not knowing what to do. Should she slowly and silently back away and retreat unnoticed downstairs, or should she make her presence known to him and risk his ire? Her dilemma was solved in the next instant when, with his back turned to her, he spoke.

"Did you like the piece?" It was the same velvety smooth voice she recalled from the bridge, only softer, more melodious, like an instrument itself.

"I—I—" she stammered. "Yes. Very much."

How long had he known she was there? She prayed the flickering candlelight concealed the blush of embarrassment that flamed her cheeks. "It sounded much like the Prelude from Bach's Suite Number Five, but different."

He turned to her then and arched a dark brow, and asked, "You are familiar with the six suites for unaccompanied violoncello?"

Nervously, she explained, "I grew up to the music of Bach. I used to creep into my father's music room and listen to him play. I'm not familiar with the piece you were just playing, though. Is it Bach?"

"It's a piece I composed myself." He beckoned for her to come in.

As she came tentatively forward, she felt grit beneath her shoes. Glancing to the dark painted wood floor, she noticed a trail of dirt leading from the doorway across the room to the spot where he was standing.

He strode quickly forward with a panther-like movement and deflected her attention away from the path of soil with a diabolically sweet tone. "I must have tracked that in earlier when I came in from outside. I'll have my man sweep it up."

"Didn't he tell you I was here?" she asked.

"He knows not to disturb me when I am playing. To what do I owe the pleasure of this visit?"

"I brought something from my father." From beneath her cloak she withdrew a scroll. "It's a manuscript he has been working on for some time. His illness prevents him from finishing it. He said if anyone can do it justice, it is you. He would like you to have it, perhaps to finish it."

Those green eyes were staring with such ravenous intent that her hand trembled as she handed him the manuscript.

He took the parchment from her and unfurled it with his pale hands. "But this is brilliant," he exclaimed, as his eyes flew over the notes penned in black ink. "Your father does me a great honor."

She turned to leave, but the melodic rhythm of his voice stopped her. "Will you join me downstairs in the sitting room?"

She gave a guarded shake of the head. "I must go."

He moved between her and the doorway with a motion that seemed effortless, almost as if he were scarcely moving at all. "Is there nothing I can offer you in return for delivering this gift? Some brandy, perhaps?"

It must have been a trick of the flickering candlelight, Pru thought as she backed away. "No, thank you."

"I'm afraid I cannot offer you coffee. I've not quite acquired a taste for it, so I don't keep any in the house. Some tea, then? It's ruinously expensive, but much more tolerable. My former servant dried the used tea leaves and sold them, a practice he did not think I was aware of. It's illegal, of course, but…" He waved a pallid hand as if to dismiss the infraction.

The intensity of his stare was making Pru uncomfortable. She struggled to pull her gaze from his. "I must go," she repeated. "My fiancé and aunt are waiting for me in the carriage outside. We're on our way to Lincoln's Inn Fields Theatre."

Those handsome green eyes registered surprise. "The Beggar's Opera? I would not have thought you a fan of that sort of entertainment."

"My aunt has a taste for scandal. Have you seen it?"

"I have indeed. I'll admit it's a brilliant satire on life. I was amused to hear that your Sir Robert Walpole was not at all pleased by the depiction of himself and his mistress. Such is the hypocrisy of the esteemed Prime Minister. It's no secret that after Lady Walpole died he married his mistress, the woman with whom he's been seen openly in London society for years. She bore him an illegitimate daughter, did she not?"

Pru's cheeks colored. Was he purposely trying to provoke a reaction? Smiling shyly, ashamed to admit that it wasn't only Aunt Vivienne who was intrigued by the tale of the highwayman, the fence's daughter and the whores who betray him, she departed.

***

The theatre was illuminated by oil lamps that smoked terribly and smelled almost as bad as cheap tallow candles, but neither the audience nor the actors seemed to mind.

The auditorium seated more than fourteen hundred spectators and was lighted by six overhead chandeliers. The stage, with mirrors on each side, was larger than the one at Drury Lane. The audience this evening was lively, with an occasional riot breaking out in the footman's gallery.

Pru sat erect in her seat, her white gloved hands folded demurely in her lap while Edmund and Aunt Vivienne chatted before the curtain went up.

At one point, Edmund reached over and laid a hand atop hers. Ever so gently, she slid her hand from beneath his under the pretext of removing her gloves. Still smarting over the words they'd had several nights ago on the subject of their upcoming marriage, she was in no mood for his overtures.

Edmund was adamantly in favor of marriage by license to avoid the publicity of having the banns called in church. She, on the other hand, wished for the normal marriage of the Church of England in which banns were called on three occasions and the ceremony was held in open church.

Why he was so opposed to having his name announced in public was, to her consternation, beyond her guess. Furthermore, he had made it clear to her from the start that their evenings together would be infrequent, as he would be otherwise engaged at the working men's club where he and his fellow tradesmen spent their evenings relaxing, mixing with friends and playing parlor games. Parlor games, indeed.

When she complained to her papa about Edmund's apparent lack of interest, he dismissed her misgivings with a frown, advising her not to be impatient, that Edmund was merely taking his time in proceding down the marriage path.

And how was that? She wondered. By engaging in socializing when he should have been more intent on getting to know his future bride better? With papa ill, she dared not voice her qualms to him now and risk upsetting him.

That Edmund had consented to escort her and Aunt Vivienne to the theatre was only because of the displeasure she had expressed the other evening when he had called on her to discuss the wedding. An attempt to placate her, to be sure. But to what advantage? For since that night she had pondered long and hard over the wisdom of marriage to Edmund de Vere.

Having been brought up to believe that men like her father, and the one who would eventually be her husband, knew what was best for her, ordinarily, she made no demands, even suppressing her own will for the sake of others. But marriage was too important an undertaking to capitulate to someone else's will, and her pugnacious response that night had startled not only Edmund, but herself as well.

At the sound of Edmund's exasperated sigh when she withdrew her hand from beneath his, a little look of triumph crossed her face. She tried to think of all the ways in which her fiancé thrilled her, and was rather vexed to find that she was unable to name one. His kisses were mild at best, his touch failed to spark a quiver, and his attention always seemed to be focused elsewhere. A sensible marriage, that's what her papa called it, to a man with a sensible trade. But Pru was tired of being sensible. A lifetime of sensible left room for little else, least of all unrestrained gaiety or, dare she think it, passion. She knew her person was not attractive in the way that Aunt Vivienne was or Mama had been. With the exception of her blue eyes, she more strongly resembled Papa. Inasmuch as vanity was a trait she did not possess, she did not dwell overlong on her lack of physical beauty. But was a plain countenance enough reason to relegate herself to a sensible life for the rest of her days on earth?

There had been nothing sensible in the music she heard tonight in the house in Hanover Square. She had not thought it possible to be swept away on a wave of such unbridled emotion, to be held in sway by a pair of mesmerizing green eyes, to tremble to a voice that was so distinctly mellow, or to warm to a smile that looked as if it could melt the iciest heart. How was it possible to be drawn to a man she scarcely knew and yet through whose music she felt she knew more intimately than any other? She suspected something worldly and wicked about him, eliciting new and untapped emotions from within. So compelling was he that she could not chase the thought of him from her mind even as the curtain rose to riotous applause.

By the end of the first act Pru found herself on the edge of her seat, enthralled by the spectacle. The tall, enigmatic man and his music were all but forgotten. When the curtain came down, her cheeks were flushed and her eyes glittered with excitement. She turned to Edmund, but he was once again engaged in conversation with her aunt. Just then, something made her pause while still on the edge of her seat.

There was a sudden tension in the air, as if a wick had been lighted and sizzled close by. She thought she detected an uncommonly sweet scent, but when she lifted her head and sniffed the air, all she smelled was the oil lamps and a hint of greasepaint. She slid slowly back in her seat and glanced around, but saw nothing other than the happy faces that shared the box, and heard only the calamatous ring of voices inside the cavernous auditorium. Nevertheless, the hairs at the back of her neck were standing on end and her palms had grown inexplicably moist.

Behind the seats at the rear of the box, half hidden by the curtain, stood a tall figure unnoticed by the spectators, green eyes scanning the auditorium.

The small stage and two-tiered auditorium rivaled the King's Theatre in the Haymarket. Was it possible that thirty-five years had passed since he sat in this theatre for a performance of *Love for Love*? Or that nearly seventy years ago he had enjoyed a revival of Romeo and Juliet, with the original ending one night and an altenative happy ending the next? Ah, but what was the passage of years to one who had lived for so long?

His eyes misted over as a pang of longing gripped him, longing for a past that was so far beyond recall it was almost as if it had never happened. Had he really once been just a boy, with a boy's sense of devilish delight in tormenting his sisters? Had he really stood on the verge of manhood, aspiring to be a man like his father? Had he really grown into a young adult on the threshhold of marriage? Or had he dreamed it all, including the terrible night when it all came crashing down, when the man he had hoped to become had ceased to be, and in his place was this half man-half creature who was doomed to go through eternity nursing bitter memories and a thirst for blood?

He felt the rancor mounting inside of him as it invariably did whenever he struggled with the past.

Why had he come here? To satisfy some wicked whim, he supposed. Well, there she was, the object of his curiosity, seated with her hands folded primly in her lap. He sensed that beneath the demure lashes and shy smiles beat the heart of a demimonde and was equally certain that she herself was unaware of it. What perverse pleasure it would give him to unlock the door to her carnal nature.

But he also sensed the presence of a tenacious will, one that would not easily succumb to his preternatural charms. It would require something stronger than unholy charisma to seduce her.

And then it came to him. The music. He would win her trust with rhapsodies, her body with preludes, and her blood with the unfinished suite. He suppressed a devious chuckle. The music master would never know that in bestowing upon him the honor of finishing the suite, he had presented him with an even greater gift…his daughter.

He was about to turn away and leave, when a chill careened unexpectedly down his spine. Oh, how well he knew that feeling. Over the centuries he had trusted it countless times to alert him to danger. There was only one thing on this earth that he stood in dread of, and that was his own destruction, caused not by old age, nor disease, nor even the sunlight. The only thing that could destroy him was a hunter, but not just any hunter. He sensed that a member of the Sanctum was perilously close at hand.

His gaze moved stealthily about the box, searching the faces in the crowd, seeking out the destroyer. No, not that one. Nor that one. It could only be… Slowly, his scrutiny returned to the man seated beside the music master's daughter.

He froze like a wolf in the forest. His green eyes burned with a sulfurous glare, and his lips curled in an elegant snarl, revealing long pointed eyeteeth. One name seared through his brain like a red-hot poker…de Vere.

What opportunity for vengeance existed in this dark coincidence. It would make having the music master's daughter all the more sweeter. After she left him this evening he had toyed with the idea of allowing her to live for his own sexual amusement, but in choosing a de Vere to marry she had unwittingly signed her own death warrant. What she saw in the man was beyond him. What would she think if she knew that her betrothed was himself a killer and that he came from a long line of killers?

It mattered not. First, he would use her to sate his lust, and then he would use her to lure the destroyer into a trap. He would kill her while the destroyer watched. And then he would put an end to the de Vere line once and for all. He could not take the chance of these two mating and producing more first-born sons to hunt him through the ages. His mind was already at work on its evil plot as he transformed into an ethereal mist and disappeared with only the scarcest rustle of the curtain.

Chapter 3

*S*everal days passed before Pru summoned the courage to voice her misgivings about Edmund de Vere.

Storm clouds raced across the sky and streams of rain pelted the windows of the house in Folgate Street. Pru stood at the segmental-arched window watching figures hurry along the cobblestone street below, heads bent against the rain, leaning into the wind.

Just as the long case clock in the hallway struck the hour, a shapely figure in fluttering silk burst into the room.

"I cannot imagine why you chose this room as your bedroom when there are perfectly good rooms below," Vivienne complained, breathless from having climbed the winding stairs to the top floor.

James Hightower had been assigned the lease as a mortgage on the four-story weaver's house, chosen for its good light so that his wife could weave without breaking fragile threads and could properly match colors before the broad weaver's window on the upper floor. It was a typical weaver's house of simple utilitarian character, faced with stock brick and a narrow stone coping. Unlike the others, however, which were one room deep, this house had a receiving room, dining room and music room on the ground floor, a parlor and bedrooms above. The kitchen was set in the basement where Gladys, the Hightowers' cheerful, round-faced servant, cooked over an open hearth, sending flavorful aromas upwards throughout the house.

"Mama loved this room," Pru said softly as she watched the rain batter the street below. "Her loom was set up before this very window. She used to hum to herself as she was weaving."

"Weaving, yes," Vivienne remarked sourly. "Margaret did have a knack for it even as a child. I would have thought something more befitting a woman of her good looks, but I suppose having a trade came in handy when she chose to marry a man of such meager means."

With a pang Pru recalled how, as a child, she would lay for hours on the creaking floorboards beside her mother's loom, watching her graceful fingers weave the threads into the fabrics that she would later sell to the silkman and the linen-draper. She had been one of the finest silk weavers in Spitalfields. Pru would never forget the time Aunt Vivienne had come to London to visit and had remarked to her sister about the unseemliness of working to support her husband's paltry income, to which Margaret had responded that it was better to be known as the best at something than the best at nothing. Vivienne had flushed scarlet and stammered something in her own defense, but the truth was, if she did not have the generous settlement of a divorce from a well-to-do gentleman who'd been much addicted to drink, she herself might have been forced to take up weaving to support herself, for in the terms of her bed-to-board divorce there was no provision for remarriage.

For several moments neither Pru nor Vivienne spoke as Margaret's memory flooded the room like warm light despite the storm that raged outside.

Vivienne broke the static silence by announcing, "Brocaded satin, blue to match your eyes, trimmed with Mechlin lace. That would be my choice for your wedding dress. But with the satin at eighteen shillings a yard and the lace at thirteen, your father could never afford such a luxury. I spotted a blue gown at a little shop in Mayfair. It's not as formal as we would like, but lovely nevertheless. It has an open-fronted bodice that we could fill in with a stomacher, and bell-shaped sleeves caught up at the elbow to show the lace-trimmed sleeves of a shift beneath. It's not as fine as a gown made to order, of course, but it will have to do."

Pru had not failed to notice the distinct ring of dissatisfaction in her aunt's tone over her wardrobe of proper, somber-hued clothes.

"You're getting ahead of yourself, Aunt. No date has been set, and…" She paused, uncertain how to break the news. "I'm not sure there's going to be a wedding."

"Really, my dear," Vivienne said, now clearly annoyed. "I don't know why you would object to this marriage. I find your young man quite amiable."

Drawing a beleaguered sigh, Pru let the curtain slip from her finger and turned away from the window. "Yes, Aunt. Amiable."

"Child, now that your mother is gone, it is up to me to guide you. And I tell you this. Amiable may be as good as it gets. Men are, how shall I say it, primitive in their ways, if you take my meaning. They are such creatures of the flesh, wanting what they want, when they want it."

Pru's fair skin colored like a rose.

"Women are not thought to be the same as men, of course," Vivienne went on. "We simply require that we be treated with the deference and admiration which is clearly due us. You should consider yourself fortunate that you have found a young man who will treat you with respect and who, I might add, earns a good enough income to forego a dowry. For many men a dowry is the only way in which to set themselves up in business. You are fortunate that your young man is already well established in his trade. Although…" She paused here to ponder, a frown marring her lustrous features. "There is something a little disquieting about him. I cannot quite put my finger on it."

"So, you feel is, too," Pru exclaimed, blue eyes flashing.

Vivienne waved it off with a graceful gesture. "I'm sure it's nothing. He was most gracious the other evening at the theatre."

"To you, perhaps. He scarcely acknowledged my presence."

"Can you blame the poor man, after the row you had with him over your marriage?"

"I do not require ascending to a pedestal and demanding to be worshipped as some goddess," Pru asserted. "My mouth is too thin, my nose is too small and my figure is less than statuesque to warrant a man's adoration."

"Nonsense, child. Your eyes are quite lovely, and you have a splendid figure. Men make such fools of themselves over an ample bosom."

"It's kind of you to say that, Aunt, but the mirror does not lie and I do not delude myself into thinking that I am anything more than passing fair. But to press my point, I refuse to be dictated to about the most important event of my life. Have I no say in the matter?" She looked away, doubt troubling her features. "I'm not sure Edmund is the man for me."

"My dear, why are you being so obstinate about this?"

"Perhaps it is because I do not love him."

"Ah, love. So that is the problem. Trust me, child, it is far better that you do not love the man you marry."

Margaret had spoken about how, in their youth, Vivienne was always on the arm of an affluent new companion, while she'd had eyes only for a penniless music student. How different the sisters were. "Have you had many lovers, Aunt?" Pru ventured.

Vivienne's full lips parted in a smile to reveal flashing white teeth. "Oh yes. Many indeed. But I only truly loved two of them."

"And one of them ended in divorce."

"Yes, regrettably."

"And the other?"

"It began a long time ago, in the bracken."

Pru was not surprised that her aunt had lain with a boy in the woods. There had doubtless been many such boys in her life.

Vivienne turned away with a remote look in her eyes. "It was a very big mistake."

"Then you of all people should understand how I feel about marrying a man I do not love," Pru said.

"Honestly, Prudence, to hear you speak of things you cannot know about one would think you had your head in too many playbooks or novels."

"Aunt, may I confide in you?"

"Of course."

"I have met someone."

Vivienne's annoyance fled as she suppressed a gleeful giggle. "Do tell."

"He's handsome, if not a bit pale. I would not guess him to be older than thirty. His features are boyish and yet there is something about him that is very, I don't know, old. It's in his eyes. There is a sad, haunted quality about them, the kind of expression you see in the eyes of a man for whom the joy of living has disappeared."

"Nearing thirty, you say? And not yet married? Now, that could be a problem."

"How so?"

"When a man reaches a certain age and is still unwed, you have to wonder why."

"Perhaps he has not yet met the right woman."

"Yes, that could be. Hmm. Young and handsome and unwed."

"I can see where you are going with this, but I must tell you, I am not interested in him in that way."

"Then why go through such length to describe him to me?"

"Because it points out to me all the areas in which Edmund is lacking."

"What does this man do for a living?"

"I don't know much else about him, other than he is a pupil of Papa's."

"A musician? No, no, that will never do. The musicians I have known have all been penniless dreamers. I cautioned your poor mother not to marry James Hightower. Not that your father isn't a good man," she hastened to add when she saw Pru's frown of displeasure. "It's just that she could have done so much better for herself."

"Mama loved Papa very much," Pru said defensively.

"Love," her aunt chided. "Are we back to that again?"

"I shall not marry for any other reason," Pru said. "And when the time is right, I will tell Edmund that the engagement is off." A guilty look shadowed her features. "But first I must break the news to Papa."

"Your papa, yes, that reminds me. It's time for his tonic. I'll see to him."

Pru watched Vivienne sweep from the room, and gave a tremulous smile. When was it she first guessed that the gay, flirtatious woman who fled to Paris after her divorce had another side? She had witnessed none of it during the year she spent with her aunt in Paris after Margaret's death. It was soon after they arrived back in London that she discovered her aunt's spirit could change in an eye blink.

One moment she was giddy, her face unmarked by the passage of time. In the next, her eyes would grow dull, the youthful appearance would fade, and it seemed as if all joy drained out of her.

At times like those was she haunted by memories of lovers lost? Of a beloved sister's suicide? Was she pining for a companion to match her vigor? Or was the burden of caring for her sister's husband beginning to weigh upon her?

Despite Vivienne's contrary nature, however, Pru was grateful for her aunt's presence and assistance, for since her timely arrival, Papa had been growing weaker every day.

She turned her mind again toward marriage. Her father's meager income was no secret, so it must be viewed that Edmund's choice of her as his wife was based more on compatibility than on her father's long baggs.

With many London men opting for the financial benefits of bachelorhood, it was no wonder there was a surplus of females, and as she was fast approaching an age beyond which most girls were married, she supposed she was lucky to have Edmund.

Papa was in favor of Edmund for purely practical reasons, knowing that his trade would allow him to marry without the expense of marriage dragging him back down the economic ladder he so patiently climbed as a bachelor.

Aunt Vivienne was in favor of the marriage for purely emotional reasons. It was no secret that her gentleman husband had raised his hand to her when filled with too much drink, so to her mind to find a man who did not rule with his fist was fortunate indeed.

But both Papa and Aunt Vivienne failed to take into account one other reason for marrying—love.

Mama could have chosen any of the well-off suitors who came to call on the sisters, but she had chosen love. At times she would catch Mama and Papa looking at each other with a spark in their eyes that spoke of the passion they shared.

But what, exactly, was passion? Pru suspected that it went beyond love, to something physical. Never having experienced it, she could only imagine what it must be like, and she wanted it. God help her, she wanted it. There had been only once in her life when she had felt something that could remotely be defined as passion and that was when she had stood in a darkened doorway listening to the most sensual, moving music she'd ever heard.

Was it the music or the man who stirred such emotion inside of her? He was handsome in a rather unconventional way, with something almost hypnotizing about the green eyes that looked old beyond their years. She had sensed a danger about him and, if truth be told, found it a bit thrilling.

What would it be like to be kissed by him? She dared to wonder. Would his kiss be timid and respectful, or would it be fierce and irreverent, like the look in his eyes? Edmund's respectful kisses failed to stir any response in her. Fierce was something she had never experienced and secretly yearned for.

The feelings he ignited in her blood were unlike any she had experienced. Her pulse pounded at the thought of the kinds of pleasures such a man could teach her. She dared not let her thoughts go that way. Fortunately, the clock in the hallway struck the hour, relieving her of the unrealistic burden of her fantasies.

She was on her way downstairs to check on the chicken Gladys had roasting on the spit for the evening meal, when there came a rapping at the front door.

He was standing in the rain, hair tossed by the wind, several dark locks falling rakishly across his brow, his handsome face dotted with raindrops, looking like someone who had lost his way in the storm. Were it not for the startling green eyes, so bright and alert and potent, Pru might not have recognized him.

Even in his windblown state, he gave the appearance of a perfectly controlled energy, as if not at all affected by the discomfort of the storm. To look at him, one would never know it was raining.

"Mr. Tedescu, won't you please come in?"

"Thank you, Miss Hightower," he said with a slight bow.

As he moved past her into the house, she noticed that the cloak that swung from his shoulders was barely wet. He must have come by carriage, yet she had not heard the sound of carriage wheels on the cobblestones, and glancing up and down the street just before she shut the door, she saw no sign of a carriage anywhere.

"I thought that after the night on the bridge we could dispense with the formalities," he said, his mouth curving upwards at the corners. "You had agreed to call me Nicolae."

Pru blushed. "Yes, of course."

He looked into her eyes. It was, she knew instantly, the kind of look men used on women to induce them to fall into their arms. Not that she'd had much experience in such things.

At the age of twenty she'd been courted only once, by Edmund, although she suspected there was more to the courtship ritual than what he exhibited. Yet even she, as unpracticed as she was in the ways of courtship, recognized abject desire in a man's eyes when she saw it. She was at once flattered, frightened and perplexed by it.

She escorted him into the parlor. A coal fire was burning in the hearth and the red silk curtains were drawn over the windows. She took his cloak, again noticing that it was none the worse for wear from the frightful weather. "May I pour you a glass of port?"

"Thank you."

She went to the walnut cabinet and withdrew Papa's decanter of port and a single glass. Her hands shook treacherously as she poured. What was it about this man that set her nerves on edge?

She could see him so much more clearly here in the candlelight than she had that night on the bridge or in the dimly-lit garret room at his house. His fine, strong features were clearly not those of an Englishman, but indicative more of his Slavic ancestry. His well-featured face was full of haunting angles with eyelids as pale as harebells and delicate blue veins visible beneath the translucent skin. His clothes were well tailored, and though his bearing gave the impression of someone well bred, there was, nevertheless, an unrefined quality about him. He did not possess an imposing frame, yet even with his slender form and pallid complexion he managed to convey a solid, rock-like impression.

She returned with the glass of port. "This should warm you. It's frightful outside." The burning candles caught the golden highlights in her hair that cascaded past her shoulders reaching nearly to the waist of her simple dressing gown as she handed him the glass.

"You are not joining me?" he asked as he took a sip.

Pru gave a demure shake of the head. "I'm afraid it goes much too quickly to my head. We are about to take our evening meal. Would you care to join us?"

"That's very kind of you," he answered, "but I have recently fed."

"Won't you have a seat?" She gestured to the settee.

"I cannot stay," he said. "I came to thank you for delivering the sheet music. I took the liberty of adding my humble expression to your father's brilliance. I would be honored if you would allow me to play it for you."

"Certainly. You can play it in the music room."

"Not here. At my home." In answer to the uncertain look that flashed across her face, he swiftly added, "I am partial to my own instrument."

A part of Pru was relieved that he was not staying. "I would be pleased to hear you play it."

"Good. Then shall we say tomorrow evening at eight? I'll send a carriage for you." He swallowed down the rest of the port and handed the glass back to her. Swirling his cloak about his shoulders, he said, "I must admit, I am a bit shy about my music. Perhaps you would not mind to come alone."

Pru moistened her lips as she contemplated the invitation. Aunt Vivienne usually went out for the evening. Papa would be asleep, and Gladys would be here to look in on him. It was highly improper for her to be alone with a man in his house, but any objection she might have uttered was stilled upon her tongue when she looked into those intense green eyes and heard herself say, "Alone. Yes, of course."

She walked him to the door and did not see his malicious grin as he disappeared down the street and was swallowed up by the fog.

Chapter 4

"Will you ring for a cup of tea, my dear?" James Hightower asked in a thin voice that sounded like it belonged to a much older man.

"Of course, Papa."

Pru gave the bellpull a good tug. She went to the candle that had burned its beeswax nearly to its base and touched its wick to a fresh candle. In moments light sputtered into the bedroom.

Her father lay in his bed, his face looking ashen and lost against the feather pillow. Earlier in the day he had looked a little better, but this evening the tiredness had set in anew, washing the energy from his limbs and the color from his cheeks, giving him a pallid, death-like appearance and Pru fresh cause for concern.

She looked up when the maidservant came into the room. "Some tea please, Gladys."

During the time in which it took to draw the water and set it to boil, Pru jabbed a poker into the embers in the fireplace and threw in more coal she had brought up from the cellar. She tucked in the corners of the quilt and propped up the pillow behind Papa's head, all the while wondering how to tell him of her decision.

"Papa…" she began, but staunched her words when Gladys entered with the tray and set it down on the bedside table. Pru poured the tea and guided the cup to his hands.

His fingers were long and finely shaped, the pads of those on his left hand slightly roughened from years of pressing the strings of the violoncello.

There had always been a transcendent quality about him which her mother had called his musician's nature. And yet, he had shown amazing strength of character when he had given up performing in favor of teaching, which paid a better wage when he had a family to support and there were so many students eager to learn from the master.

Pru's attention was drawn to the gentle ticking of the chiming clock on the mantle. The carriage would be arriving within the hour. "Papa…" she began again.

"Where is your aunt?" he weakly uttered between sips of tea.

"Out for the evening. We must not fault her for wanting some amusement. She works so hard to take care of you, coming to your room as she does each evening before she goes out."

An expression of apprehension tugged at his tired face. "You must not let her come."

"She assures me it's no trouble at all." She offered a guilty little smile. "I know she talks quite a bit, but having her here has been a Godsend." But as it wasn't the subject of Aunt Vivienne she wanted to deal with, she said directly, "Papa, there is something I must discuss with you." She hesitated, chewing a corner of her lip. She had rehearsed the words over and over again, yet when faced with their delivery, she grew suddenly unsure of just what to say.

"What troubles you, my dear?" he asked of the cryptic look in her blue eyes.

"It's about Edmund."

He handed the teacup back to his daughter, signaling that she had his undivided attention.

She gathered herself and began slowly, choosing her words carefully. "I realize that your sanction of my marriage to Edmund is all important, and ordinarily I would never think to defy what you perceive as to be in my best interests. But Edmund is…oh, how shall I put it…perhaps not in my best interest."

"Has he dishonored the treaty of marriage?" her father questioned.

"No, Papa. His claims of character, fortune and expectations are as he stated them."

"Has he raised his hand to you?"

"No, Papa."

"Has he asked of you things meant only for the marriage bed?"

"No, Papa," she said, her cheeks coloring.

"Then why would he not be in your best interest?"

"Because I do not love him." Her hands fidgeted nervously in her lap. "Aunt Vivienne says it is neither necessary nor wise to love the one you marry, but I think if Mama were alive, she would say differently, and I suspect that in your heart you feel the same."

James Hightower's eyes misted at the mention of his beloved wife. "How did I fail her? I gave her the only thing I had to give, my love, and for the first twenty years of our marriage that seemed to be enough. But then everything changed. She became moody, striking out at me, claiming that my love was smothering her. The night I climbed the stairs to the upper room I found her loom smashed to pieces, silk threads scattered across the floorboards, your mother gone."

Pru's own eyes filled with tears. Her mother's body had been found two days later, broken from the fall. "Oh, Papa, I'm so sorry. I didn't mean to upset you."

Margaret's blue eyes stared back at him, yet it was Prudence who sat now on the edge of the bed. He touched her hand with his. "Ever since your mother…went away…," he said, voice brimming with sadness, "I have tried to do what I thought she would want. And in asking you, my sweet child, to marry a man you do not love, I have failed you, too."

"Oh no, Papa," Pru said tenderly. "You showed your love for me by wanting to secure my future. And for a while I, too, thought my future lay with Edmund. But I have come to feel differently. I can't explain it. It's something I feel in here." She placed a palm pointedly over her heart.

Her father nodded with gradual comprehension. "When will you tell him?"

She sank into warm relief and gave him a loving smile. "I will call at his shop tomorrow morning." The bed creaked when she rose.

"Pruddy."

He had called her that since she was a toddler unable to pronounce her own name. She paused at the door and looked back at him from over her shoulder.

"Your aunt," he said. "She must not come."

"Get some sleep, Papa. You'll feel better in the morning." But even as she said it, she despaired that it would not be.

In her bedroom, Pru perused her wardrobe, and sighed. Aunt Vivienne was right; it was much too somber, more befitting a matron.

She looked first at the coal-gray silk. With its bodice and full skirt cut from a single length of fabric, the skirt designed to part in front to reveal a contrasting underskirt, it might have been considered fashionable had it not been four years old and seen so much wear that the elbows were beginning to fray.

She then contemplated the black linsey-woolsey, its front fitted to the body by means of a tightly-laced underbodice, the back falling in loose box pleats.

Torn between the impulse to create a favorable impression on her host and the urge to appear austere so as not to foster an unfavorable impression, she stood before the cheval glass holding one dress up in front of her, then the other, back and forth, unable to decide. Somehow, neither seemed appropriate.

And then she remembered the Spitalfields silk dress with the dome-shaped skirt that her aunt had purchased for her, claiming it was wildly fashionable. Pru had taken one look at the heavy silk with lace patterns woven in beige and rust on a dark brown satin ground and shoved the scandalous thing to the back of her wardrobe. She reached for it now.

Her fingers worked quickly to undo the plait that held her waist-length hair. Brushing it, she re-braided it and wound it around her head. A quick glance at the mantle clock left no time to fuss with the strands that fell loose about her temples and the nape of her neck. From a velvet-lined case she withdrew the aigrette that had belonged to her mother and placed the spray of garnets foiled to resemble bright red rubies in her hair just over her ear.

When she finished dressing, Pru stood again before the mirror. Her cheeks flooded with color at how daringly low the neckline dipped. She was no slattern, but neither was she accustomed to showing off so much of her dewy flesh. At the walnut veneered chest she tugged on the brass handles of the top drawer and pulled out a lace kerchief and arranged it discreetly to fill in the low neckline, properly concealing the ample curve of her bosom.

For several moments all she could do was stare at her reflection in the mirror. She looked so much like her mother that the resemblance was chilling. Funny that she had never seen it quite so distinctly before this. Was it any wonder that Papa's eyes sometimes brimmed with tears when he looked at her? She had never thought of herself as beautiful, but the woman who looked back at her in the glass was quite pleasing.

As she came downstairs, throwing her cloak over her shoulders, a brisk knock came at the door. Having previously arranged with Gladys for her to look in on Papa, there was nothing left to do but answer it. A footman bowed to her and escorted her outside and helped her into the waiting carriage.

The carriage clattered its way through the noisy London streets, competing with the roll chaises and drays amidst the chimes from church towers, the hurdy-gurdies and tambourines of the mountebanks who hawked their quack medicines, past a bonfire of shavings that flared almost as high as the upper floors of the houses around which a circle of shouting beggar-boys, sailors and rogues assembled. And everywhere the stink of burning sea coal hung in the air.

As the carriage drew up before the house in Hanover Square, Pru struggled to keep her nervousness in check. Why was she so anxious about this visit, anyway? The man was merely going to play a piece of music, she reasoned. Yet recalling the effect his music had on her, not to mention the effect of the man himself, she was suddenly unprepared for what she had gotten herself into, to say nothing of her embarrassment for having dressed contrary to her own good judgment to impress a man who was not the least bit interested in her. This was all quite ridiculous, she thought, forcing a semblance of propriety into her being. She would listen to the piece, praise him appropriately for it, and then leave. And tomorrow she would resume her sensible ways, break the news to an unsuspecting Edmund, and resign herself to an uneventful life as an eccentric old maid.

Chapter 5

"Prudence, how delightful to see you." He caught her hand in his, lifted it briefly to his lips and brushed it with a kiss. "Do come in." He took her by the arm and escorted her inside. "I have taken the liberty of setting up my instrument in the drawing room. I did not think you would want to climb to the garret floor again."

Blushing, she said, "You must believe me when I say that I am not usually so…so…"

"Let us just say you are inquisitive. But you mustn't apologize for it. I find it a delightful trait." He went around her and helped her out of her cloak, his all consuming look sweeping over the back of her neck and shoulders, his tongue flicking across his lips as if he had just glimpsed a tasty treat.

He chucked deviously to himself. He only looked beautiful on the outside. Inwardly, his intensions were strictly dishonorable. Some might call him a nasty, evil creature. That was, after all, what he was, swooping down on unsuspecting mortals from out of the dark, grasping them in an unbreakable grip and sucking the life blood out of them. But he could also be charming and witty and utterly irresistible for the express purpose of seducing a mortal woman into having sex with him. Tonight, he would play the finished suite for her, and then the lion would lie down with the lamb.

"As I recall, you do not drink port," he said, "so I dare say brandy is also out of the question. Some tea, perhaps?"

"Yes, thank you." When she turned back to him, he could tell she was trying not to show her surprise at his attire.

He had eschewed the more luxurious velvets, satins and bright colored silks of the day in favor of a plain white cambric shirt with full sleeves gathered at the wrist and dropped at the shoulders and a high stock at the neck much like an undress shirt. In place of fashionable leather shoes fastened with buckles he wore high Hessian boots. His breeches were not hidden beneath a long waistcoat but were in full view, and unusually tight, revealing the shape of his legs. His dark hair was tied back at the nape of the neck with a black ribbon, a few careless locks falling across his brow and almost into his magnificent green eyes. He caught her staring, and smiled. "You must pardon my appearance, but I prefer to dress casually when in the comfort of my own home. The draper was good enough to import these trousers for me from my homeland where they are called *nadragi*. Have a seat."

He gestured to a carved walnut wing chair that stood opposite his instrument. "I have given my servant the evening off, so I'll brew the tea for us. I'll only be a moment."

He slipped from the room so noiselessly it was almost as if he hadn't been there at all. When he returned a short while later, he stood for a few wordless moments with the tray in his hands, smiling cynically, silently watching her as she was bent over examining his instrument.

There was nothing prim and proper about her tonight, dressed as she was in silk and satin. He had not failed to notice the decoration behind her ear with its garnets sparkling like fine burgundy in the candlelight. The scores of candles set about the room cast a radiant glow over her face and neck…yes, that neck, white, vulnerable and inviting. He placed the tray down and came forward. "It's quite old."

Pru straightened up at the sound of his voice. "I've never seen such a beautiful violoncello. The carvings are stunning."

"It was built in fifteen-thirty-eight, originally with only three strings, and later painted and gilded to serve as one of a set of stringed instruments for the French court of King Charles IX. Only a very few have survived. There, you see, the coat of arms of the King of France." He bent closer as he pointed to the emblem that graced the carved neck, his body almost touching hers. "And there, do you see? That is the mark of the maker, Andrea Amati, a master luthier."

"Yes, I know the name," she said, straightening up and smoothing her hands over her skirts. "But how did you come by such a splendid instrument?"

By killing him and drinking his blood, he was tempted to say. "The king's mother, Catherine de Medici, was somewhat neglected by her husband and found, shall I say, companionship, with one of my ancestors. This was her gift to him."

It was not a complete falsehood. The king's mother had indeed been neglected by her husband, a matter he himself had taken full and unadulterated advantage of in her bedchamber. She'd been quite an insatiable lover, for which he had benevolently let her live. But by then, he had already relieved Amati of the magnificent instrument.

He turned and strode back to the tray where he poured two cups of tea. Glancing slyly over his shoulder and seeing that she was still occupied with the violoncello, he slipped his hand into his pocket and withdrew a packet, the contents of which he swiftly emptied into their cups and swirled with a silver spoon until it was dissolved.

The ancient Romanian potion of black sandalwood and damiana, flavored with cinnamon, would cause her no irreparable harm. It would work within minutes to heighten her senses and create an aphrodisiac effect that she would be incapable of resisting, as well as increase his male stimulation. The potion, an unsuspecting virgin, and a few swallows from the decanter of blood he kept in the smoking room would be sufficient to arouse his phallus to mortal heights. Thankfully, by the time of full arousal he would be seated behind his violoncello and she would not notice the unmistakable press of anatomy against his trousers, until it was too late and it was firmly planted inside of her.

"Your tea," he said as he handed the cup to her. "I have taken the liberty of including some of these wonderful little berries. The children collect them and string them on pieces of straw and sell them in the market. They're quite good."

Pru sat down and accepted the cup from him. She sipped the tea and licked the savory flavor from her lips. "This is unusually good."

"It's a special blend I discovered at the market," he said from over the rim of his cup.

How quaint this is, he thought sardonically, *sipping tea as if we were at a social gathering and making small talk to pass the time.*

"So, tell me," he ventured, "how is your father?"

He was instantly sorry he asked when she placed the cup down, not having ingested nearly enough of the potion for it to do its trick.

"Not well, I'm afraid," she said broodingly. Her lower lip trembled, but she caught it in her teeth just shy of tears and looked down at her lap.

"That is too bad," he said, attempting a sympathetic tone that he did not truly feel. "Perhaps your spirits will rise when you hear the piece I am about to play for you."

Lifting her chin, she said, "There's to be a concert next month at Vauxhall Gardens. Papa was planning to play the piece himself. It has all been arranged. It's been awhile since he performed, and he was so looking forward to it, but now…" A sudden thought occurred to her, brightening her saucer eyes. "Will you perform in his place?"

Nicolae smiled with false modesty. "Why don't I play the piece for you and let you decide if it's worthy of a public audience?" His eyes darted to the teacup she lifted to her lips and he smiled inwardly as she drank.

He placed his own teacup on a side table and took his seat behind the violoncello, drawing the lower bout between his knees and the upper bout against his chest. Grasping the bow in his right hand, he drew it across the strings, beginning the Prelude.

The strong recurring theme of the arpeggiated notes of the chord played in rapid succession, followed by a scale-based cadenza movement that built to the final, powerful chords were as the music master had written them. But what came next was a difficult flowing eight-note movement. This part of the suite was written in much more free form than anything that preceded it, containing more cadenza-like movements and virtuosic passages. It was quite literally a symphony for the violoncello, evoking joy in every note and triumph in every chord. He had achieved a perfect balance between the formal approach of the music master and his own romantic, rhapsodic interpretation in a profoundly moving performance.

Moonlight radiance filtered into the room through a gap in the heavy drapery, catching his face in shadow and pearly light. The music curled like smoke from a distant fire, infiltrating every corner and crevice, hauntingly beautiful and serene one moment, fierce and anger-filled the next. It seemed to flow from a place somewhere inside of him that was untouched by awareness, a subconscious magic that stemmed from a wordless place.

A palpable silence settled over the room. Nicolae's head was bent, dark locks obscuring his eyes, his breathing challenged. The music stirred his emotions to such depths that he struggled to regain composure. When he opened his eyes, he saw that Pru was looking at him. There was a smile of admiration on her face. When most mortals looked upon him with revulsion and horror, there was only what could best be described as wonder in her blue eyes that were shiny with tears. It touched him unexpectedly with a new feeling, unfamiliar now for so long it was all but forgotten…happiness.

No, no, he must not lose sight of his objective. And besides, the brew he'd ingested was working much too effectively for him to turn back now.

He rose from his seat behind the violoncello, drawing her eyes to his and holding her gaze as he came toward her. The swelling in his breeches grew stronger with every step he took, but she did not notice, for like the hapless fly, she was already secured in his web, held fast by piercing emerald eyes that held sway over her.

He dropped to one knee before her. "Did you like it?"

"Oh yes," Pru breathed. "It was beautiful. Like a prayer."

All the heavenly prayers in the world will not save you now, he thought as he took her hand in his.

"You play with such…" She strained to find the words to describe the fluid splendor of his music. "…such depth of soul."

He dropped her hand as if it were a flaming hot poker and scrambled to his feet. "Do you mock me madam?"

The savage contempt in his voice was as sharp as a backhanded slap across the face. She opened her mouth to speak, to say something, anything, but no words emerged.

Nicolae towered over her, a mercilessly cruel look on his face that made him appear uncivilized, quite as if the music had been made by someone that bore no resemblance to the man who stood before her now.

Pressed against the back of the chair, she looked up at him, and said in a softly apologetic voice, "I don't understand."

She looked positively pathetic trying to hold back her tears. How could she know that he was a vile, soulless creature? His stance softened and the fury died from his eyes when he realized the extent of his overreaction. He reached again for her hand.

"Come with me," he whispered.

She drew back at what sounded at once like a request and a command.

He was prepared for her resistance, especially in light of his outburst. Those with strong wills always required more time to mesmerize. But as this was one sweet plum ripe for plucking, his gaze intensified, growing more heated and demanding until he sensed that she was sufficiently under his control. "Come," he coaxed in a deceptively gentle voice. "There is much I want to show you." Drawing her to her feet, his gaze never leaving hers, he led her out of the room, up the winding staircase and into the bedroom.

***

Pru looked past him at the large four-poster bed draped with yards of heavy fabric. In a far-away part of herself she felt a faint bolt of alarm. She knew she should turn and run, yet she could not. His eyes were so mystical and beautiful, the sound of his voice as sweet as a melody. His confounding behavior was all but forgotten. Her head was swimming with thoughts, none of which made any sense and all converging on a single revelation. Somehow she knew without knowing that all her questions were about to be answered, all her longings about to be fulfilled. And if she was fearful of the outcome, the fear only seemed to heighten the anticipation.

He caught her gaze once again with his. "How do you feel?"

"I...I don't know. I can scarcely breathe. It must be the music. Yes, the music."

He asked, "Do you wish to leave?"

"No," she answered truthfully.

"And if you stay, you know what is going to happen, do you not?"

"No. Yes."

He smiled that sweet diabolical smile of his, and said, "I am going to devour you." Giving her no time to respond or to react, he brought his face close and touched his lips to hers.

He tasted like strawberries and cinnamon as his tongue moved over her lips, his warm breath mingling with hers. Pru's whole body trembled with sheer joy.

His kiss was light and airy, yet filled with the promise of so much more that all modesty and every bit of virtue she had seemed to vanish into thin air when, in truth, she willingly let them go. Her mouth opened, inviting a kiss that was so ardent and powerful it sucked the breath right out of her lungs. Her pulse beat erratically in her ears. Her will was lost amidst this newly discovered amorous pleasure.

He forced her back up against the hard surface of the door, kissing her, holding her so close that she could feel the press of his hardened anatomy even through her voluminous skirts. A sound emerged from the back of her throat, a whimper that seemed to come from some far-off place as the last vestiges of salvation slipped away. She wanted this...craved this. Even though she had no tangible idea of what *this* really was.

Her hands were pressed against his chest as if to keep him at bay, yet her fingers moved toward his arms, wrapping around the taut muscles to draw him closer still. He responded with an animal growl, a sound so startlingly realistic that she gave pause, but before it could truly register upon her brain, he was tearing at her clothes, and God help her, she was letting him. Without knowing how, the dress of silk and satin was suddenly pooled around her ankles. The lace kerchief she had foolishly used to conceal her bosom fluttered to the carpet. The hoop of linen stiffened with cane was dispatched, followed by the linen stays as his hands hastily undid the front lacing, and finally the linen shift she wore next to her bare skin floated away like a feather on the air.

Pru shivered, not from the cold, for the fire that sputtered in the corner hearth threw enough heat into the room, but from the fact that she was now completely and utterly naked. Never before had a man looked upon her thus.

She felt a flood of embarrassment rise to her cheeks, tinting them with color. This could not be happening. Stop. Oh, please stop. Yet the words did not come.

He was running his hands all along her arms, caressing the curve of her shoulders, across her collarbone, pausing at the pulsing hollow of her throat as if it held some secret significance before moving downward to cup both breasts, their heaviness spilling over his palms, rubbing the hardened tips with his thumbs until they fairly ached with pleasure.

Mindless sensations raced through her being. He was kissing her again, his lips burning a trail from her mouth to her throat, pausing there again to run his tongue over the silky smooth flesh, the breath catching in his throat as he did, and then continuing downward, tugging at her swollen nipples with his teeth, first one, then the other, gently at first, then harder, making her wince with torturously sweet pain.

She was holding him tight to her, feeling the rasp of his garments against her naked flesh, reveling in the delicious sensations he was arousing in her, and oh so mindful of the hard bite of his phallus against her, telling her there was yet more of this erotic pleasure to discover.

She had no idea what the true nature of it was, until he took a half-step back and trailed his forefinger across her belly to her most intimate place, where it lingered at the dark curls for a moment before slipping between her secret folds.

She gasped, part shock, part libidinous reaction, when his fingers entered her. His exploration was shocking and lascivious and spread white hot pleasure through her.

Her body trembled, wrenching soft cries from her when he pushed harder. Withdrawing his fingers, he worked swiftly to unbutton his trousers, pushing them down past his boots. When his engorged member was freed of the confines of his trousers, he reached up and placed his palms on either side of her face. They were both breathing deeply.

In a voice that was smooth and commanding and filled with centuries of experience, he told her, "Look into my eyes."

All her life Pru had obeyed men. Her father. Edmund. And now this immoral man. Slowly, she lifted her gaze to his.

"There is something you must do for me. If I ask it, will you do it?"

She shuddered with apprehension, yet when his gaze was fixed so strongly upon hers, she was incapable of refusing any wish or command he might make. She gave a tremulous nod of her head.

He took her hand and guided it toward his swollen phallus. "Don't be afraid."

"I've never—"

"I will guide you. Place you hand thus."

Her hand shook as he placed it upon himself, wrapping her fingers around its thickness. Pru sucked in her breath. This part of him was all heat and dark fire, at once compelling and dangerous.

"You hold great power in your hand," he whispered against her flesh. "You can bring me to my knees with such power."

"What would you have me do?" she asked in a voice that seemed not to be her own.

"I would have you move your hand smoothly up and down, like so." He taught her the movements and then let go of her hand. "That's it," he rasped, his breath coming now in short, rapid bursts.

She was an avid pupil, but there was still so much more to learn. Her body was on fire, too enflamed to notice the coldness of his touch as he placed his hands on her shoulders and exerted downward pressure. She looked at him questioningly.

"I would have you on your knees," he said.

She could not know the reason for this strange request until she was kneeling before him and his hand at the back of her head guided her face closer and the tip of his phallus brushed her cheek, and then the objective was all too apparent. She turned her head to the side. "I cannot."

"You can. You must."

"No, please."

"Prudence, look at me."

She was too afraid to refuse the almost cruel command in his tone and looked upwards with pleading eyes and dilated pupils.

His green gaze burned fiercely into hers. "You will do this," he said thickly. "You will do whatever I ask."

She swallowed hard. What was happening to her? Why was she no longer in control of her own will? Why was it that the only will that mattered was his?

With malicious authority, he said, "Consider this my gift to you. And you will take great pleasure in receiving it."

Her lips moved to that part of him that held no secrets and opened to receive his gift.

He was a wicked man to ask such an unholy thing of her. Yet the taste of him was not all together unpleasant, and hearing his guttural moans and feeling the spasms wracking his body made her feel strong and powerful in ways she'd never felt before.

When he could stand no more of her maddening kisses, he lifted her back up and clasped her against him. His hands moved to the soft flesh of her buttocks. Grasping her there, he lifted her into the air before him, held her there for a moment and brought her down with force, impaling her on his hardened member.

Her cry of pain attested to the fact that she was, indeed, a virgin, uninitiated in the ritual of lovemaking. She was moist and hot and so sublimely tight that it took every ounce of willpower he possessed to keep himself from coming too fast.

The force of his penetration, the tearing of the hidden shield that guarded her virtue, made her flinch with pain. She struggled, but only half-heartedly. Even if she had not been seduced by his mesmerizing eyes, even if she had fought him in earnest, she would have been no match for his strength.

The hurt was drowned out by the almost primitive desire that drove him. His penetration burned so deeply inside of her that she could no longer tell if it was truly pain or pleasure. She lifted her arms around his neck and clung to him, wrapping her slender legs around him, drawing him in deeper and feeling the contraction of the muscles of his buttocks against her calves as he thrust into her. He moaned, lifting her with each stroke and pulling her back down upon him, thrusting harder and faster...faster...using his immortal strength to withhold the moment of his own release until he was sure she was on the brink.

Pain and pleasure, fear and euphoria enveloped her. Something was happening, something almost other-worldly. She gulped in the air, unable to draw enough of it into her lungs to satisfy their need. Every muscle in her body tensed in anticipation of something coming. Every nerve ending screamed for sweet release. When it came, her body wracked with involuntary convulsions and she cried out with joy over what she had just discovered and sorrow over the innocence she had just lost.

Nicolae felt the tension drain from her body just as he poured his profane seed into her, shuddering over and over again with such force, his moans sounding like those of a wounded beast in torment. He gave one final bursting shudder, the summation of everything that was lustful and corrupt, an unearthly growl rising from deep within his chest.

Between shaking breaths he lifted her off of himself, held the swaying woman upright while he pulled his downed trousers back up over his boots, and carried her limp body to the bed where he placed her down. Come morning she would recall little of what had occurred here tonight.

He stood for several moments looking down at her as she lay exhausted on the linens. Somewhere in the frenzy of their coupling her hair had tumbled loose from the braid and now fanned over the pillow in disarray. Her face was flushed, her saucer eyes were closed, dark lashes wet with tears. Immortal though he might be, he was still capable of being aroused by a sensual woman, and this one, with her imperfect features and plump breasts, was a sensual feast.

She was a fool, however, for thinking that one such as he possessed a soul. Anger and frustration tore at him. Oh, that it were so. Well, he had shown her the true nature of what he was. He had meant to use her, and use her he had. But what he had not counted on was this blasted feeling of…what? Regret? Hardly. Pity? Not likely. What, then? Salvation? Now, there was a novel thought. The deed was done. Why, then, wasn't he feeling like the triumphant warrior? He turned away with disgust.

It was then he felt the wet sticky blood that had come from her and which now stained the tip of his member crimson. His green eyes brightened. A taste. Just a taste. With the tip of his finger he wiped a glistening red drop away and brought it to his mouth. He smoothed the blood over his lips. Sweet. Like honey. He ran his tongue over his lips and felt his pulse begin to pound, not as before with carnal desire, but from the age-old curse that made him what he was.

Her blood was sweeter than any he had tasted over the centuries. Was it because of this insane physical desire he had for her that made him imagine it to be different? Were his preternatural senses playing tricks on him? The cause of it did not matter. What mattered was now that he had tasted it, he knew he could not go through the rest of eternity without ever tasting it again.

He pondered his choices. He could drain her and make her into a creature like himself, but once done, there would be no more of her sugared blood from which to partake. Or, he could mesmerize her like he had done tonight until she eventually rebelled and exerted the strong will she herself was unaware she possessed.

The answer lay in the way she had responded to him, with neither fear nor virtuous denials, but with a wanton abandonment that had surprised him, yes, even him, who had seen so much of the world that very little shocked him. She was as lustful for life as he was for taking it. He would make her dependent upon him for her pleasure. She would never bleed her virgin blood again, but once under his spell, a little nick here and there, just to taste, would be enough to satisfy him. And then, when he was ready, he would use her again, as bait to lure that accursed de Vere to his doom.

Chapter 6

In the small windowless room at the rear of the shop Edmund de Vere sat hunched over his business records, spectacles perched on his nose, scrutinizing the inventory of his stock and itemizing the sales and loans of pewter ware to his customers.

He began his trade in sadware for the middling class, casting the metal in flat pieces, rolling it into sheets and hammering it into shape. For a while his business in trenchers, platters and large flat ware enabled him to pay his quit to the landlord.

As Edmund's aspiration exceeded beyond his station, and having taken into his employ a journeyman and an apprentice whose wages he was obliged to pay, he had expanded his production to hollowware, casting the pewter into molds and fashioning it with hand tools into the mugs, pitchers, basins and porringers for the tables of the wealthier classes. For export to the American colonies he made pear-shaped teapots, creamers and sugar bowls. These days he had more customers than he could want and business was thriving. For those who could least afford his wares he used black metal, a nearly even division of tin and lead, to cheapen the pewter.

It was through his use of lead that he came into contact with Simon Cavendish, an alchemist in Clapham, a solitary, squirrelly little man for whom he made pewter bottles of exact measures of drams, quarts and pints, each carefully stamped with his touchmark.

Cavendish had recently requisitioned a large number of bottles, to what purpose Edmund had not the slightest clue. When questioned, the man had become quite agitated until, running out of evasions, he had run right out of the shop.

Well, that was all right, Edmund supposed, giving it as his view that everyone was entitled to their little secrets. God knew he had a secret of his own, a secret born out of a bloodbath of terror and which dwelt amidst the murky shadows of the unthinkable.

What would sweet Prudence think if she knew of his nocturnal pursuits? Prudence. Ah, now there was a dilemma. She came with no wealth or power or anything that might enhance his position in the world. Nevertheless, he'd been fortunate enough to find a young woman whose meekness posed no questions and whose mild manners demanded no answers. She was so utterly malleable to suit his purposes in a wife to perfection, except for the display of appallingly bad manners she exhibited on the subject of their wedding. He had not known her to be quite so, well, outspoken, and hoped it was not a sign of things to come.

There was nothing but ill to be gained from announcing the banns. If the evil monster he was hunting was indeed prowling the streets of London, any public announcement of the de Vere name would surely drive him away, so he took care not to needlessly divulge his identity. Not even the sign above the door to his shop bore his name. *Pewterer* was sufficient to draw clientele. Nor did he use his full name as a mark, but rather a three-touch mark common amongst pewterers consisting of the city to indicate the place of origin, his initials E de V, and the symbol of an angel or a crowned rose, depending upon the quality of the piece.

For seven years he served as apprentice to a master pewterer, devoting daytimes to erstwhile occupation and nighttimes to hunting the undead. Before he was allowed to strike his own touch mark, he'd been presented to the court of the Pewterer's Company to show an example of his work. After providing proof that he had sufficient capital to start a business of his own, he was permitted to strike his mark. Once he had hung the wooden sign above the door of his shop, he was free to pursue his vendetta against the undead, and in particular, the green-eyed demon his family had been tracking for the past two hundred and fifty years which he had reason to believe was now walking the streets of London.

This was a dangerous secret he could not share with anyone, certainly not with the woman who was to become his wife. The alchemist, perhaps, at a future time, if the need arose. But not Prudence. Never Prudence.

He looked up from his ledgers when his apprentice entered the room.

"Beggin' yer pardon, sir, but this 'ere piece is full o' chatter marks."

Removing the wire-rimmed spectacles from his nose, Edmund appraised the young man standing before him. He was a good lad, hard working and honest despite the brutish life from which he'd been plucked. And though he showed potential in the trade, he was still too inexperienced to work the lathe on his own, as evidenced by the coarse lines extending outward from the center on the bottom of the tankard he held in his hand. Skimmed on a lathe with wooden bearings, it would take time for the lad to become accustomed to the vibrations of the skimming tool.

Edmund heaved a sigh of displeasure and rose from behind the desk. His intolerance for anything that did not suit him was evident in his tone.

"We'll have to include this piece among those we export next month and hope the American colonists will not notice the defect."

The tankard bearing the chatter marks was placed with other pieces of cheap black metal.

He dismissed the apprentice with an impatient wave of the hand, for he was suddenly reminded that he was running low on lead. It was time to pay a visit to the Simon Cavendish with whom he had arranged a neat barter to obtain the alchemist's unused lead in return for finished bottles and flagons. He gathered up the gill bottles he had made, grabbed his tricorn off a peg and had just slapped it on his head when the door opened again.

"Good morning, Edmund," Pru said as she entered.

The black silk bonnet she wore framed her face like a shadow. The only color that radiated from beneath its stiffened brim was the blue of her eyes which, this morning, were looking very solemn.

She made a great effort not to wrinkle her nose at the smell of garlic that hung in the air. Edmund did have a propensity for the pungent bulb, hanging it in wreaths above all his doors.

Early in their courtship, when she had questioned him about the need to surround himself with the strong, unpleasant odor, he had explained it was family tradition whose roots went back to sixteenth century France, although more than that he would not say.

She removed her short cloak and placed it neatly over a ladder back chair, revealing a dress of sober gray which hung freely from her shoulders front and back, its only adornment the poufed trim of the same hue running from the robbing to the waist. The tucker of white lace at the neckline concealed her cleavage and threw the tiniest bit of light upwards to her face which did not bear its usual deferential smile.

"Why, Prudence, I'm delighted to see you this morning," he said

From the dour look upon his face, she judged that less truthful words had never been spoken. "I did not mean to disturb you."

"Nonsense, my dear," he said in that fatherly tone that made her feel like less of an equal. "What brings you here?"

"I was out walking and…" she began. No, no, those were not the words she had rehearsed. *Courage*, she told herself, but it failed to bolster her composure. She had hoped to find a polite way to avoid an unpleasant scene, but her resolve rapidly faded when his eyes were set so firmly upon her face in an expression of expectation. She managed a half-smile. "There has been a development." Her words sounded completely witless to her ears. "Well, not a development exactly. I realize I have no right to ask this of you. There is the contract, after all."

He arched a dark brow at that. "Have you done something?"

Good God, yes, she wanted to scream. Last night. The music. The power. I didn't mean for it to happen. It somehow just did.

She was not entirely sure of the events of last evening, only that she had returned home, undressed and gone directly to bed, only to be awakened before dawn by the ache in every muscle in her body. A glance in the mirror had revealed the most shocking marks, long red scratches along her back, livid traces along her arms of having been grasped in too strong a grip, discolorations on her buttocks, of all places, and most mysterious of all, what appeared to be bite marks on her neck, although the flesh showed no sign of having been broken. A quick examination of her clothing revealed similar trauma, rent seams, broken cane and tattered lace.

Oh, if only she could recall fully what had happened. But even for someone with such limited knowledge of seduction, there could be no doubt that she had been utterly and irrevocably ravished. Her first impulse had been revulsion, then fury so intense it turned her mortified cheeks scarlet, and then hatred. What a sinister man he was to have betrayed her in such a fashion by taking undue advantage of her. She had stalked about her room in a rage, fists balled at her sides, venting her anger and frustration on her green-eyed seducer. But then something happened. The first faint traces of dawn broke over the treetops, bringing with it a sense of something more than betrayal. Her head began to swim with other thoughts, these more distinct although no less rational.

She remembered the music and the sensations it aroused in her. The beauty of it had been so terrible it had reduced her to tears. She had a vague recollection of something stirring deep within, something that went past her mind and her heart, to her loins.

The pulsing. Yes, she remembered the pulsing and the flush of warmth and wetness that came from the private spot between her legs, how at first it had startled her and then grew to a tumultuous pitch as the music had soared to a deafening crescendo, as if she and the music were one.

Through the distant and murky memories that washed over her she heard a voice, soft, smooth, hypnotic, asking if she wanted to leave. It was answered by another voice, familiar and yet not familiar. It was her own tremulous voice uttering one word and one word alone. "No."

With the memory of that single utterance she had known in a heartbeat what had happened last night. She was no longer chaste.

Even if she had not determined to call off her betrothal to Edmund de Vere on the grounds that she did not love him, she could not, in all conscience, offer herself to him now when he would not be getting a virtuous wife. She felt ashamed and yet not ashamed. As her bedroom had filled with light, a new revelation burst upon her. She was aware of herself in a way she had heretofore never known. Her body may have been bruised, but it felt alive for the first time in her life. Her memory of last night may have been muddled, but she clung to this new awareness as if it were a lifeline to her innermost self.

She had picked up from the floor the gown purchased at the Mayfair shop and shoved it to the very back of her wardrobe, hiding all outward evidence of last night's events. This was her very own secret, one not to be shared with anyone, not even with Aunt Vivienne.

As for Nicolae Tedescu, she was not at all certain what her feelings for him were. She could hardly be thankful for the way he had used her for his own devilish pleasure, but neither could she completely hate him for it. Surely, it was not his doing that she had only hazy recollections of last night's events. And he had, after all, given her the opportunity leave, hadn't he?

She hardly fancied herself in love with the wicked man, yet she could not help but make mental comparisons of the two men. Edmund's hands were fleshy, the fingers thick. Nicolae's were elegant and finely shaped. Edmund was certainly not what one would call a handsome man. His eyes were close-set and a dull gray, strikingly similar to the sadware he produced. His nose was too large for his face, and his mouth was fixed in what seemed to be a perpetual state of displeasure, with lips thinly pursed as though he were harboring some secret determination, although what that could be, she could not fathom. Neither was Nicolae a handsome man in the strictest sense of the word. Still, there was something about his features that caught the gaze and held it, an almost ethereal quality that transcended true beauty. His mouth, upon which she must have only imagined a cruel smile, was full and expressive, his nose perfectly aquiline, and his eyes, those magnificent eyes, seemed to possess a will of their own. Edmund hid his natural hair beneath a wig of white, tightly curled about the face, and never went anywhere without his tricorn. Nicolae, on the other hand, flaunted convention by not wearing a wig or bothering to push back the dark locks that fell across his brow. Edmund's stature was that of a mild man very much of the modern time. Nicolae, although slender, imparted an impression of strength and power, steadfast qualities that seemed to come from a bygone era.

She looked up from her dark thoughts to find Edmund's expectant gaze upon her. "No, I have not done something," she lied.

"You mentioned a favor."

From his tone she could tell he was annoyed by her evasion. He had a tendency toward impatience when matters did not go his way.

Is that what his lovemaking would be like? She dared to wonder. No matter. It was something she would never find out.

Pru moistened her lips. It seemed outrageously unfair to lie to him, but she could not give him a true explanation when she was not certain of it herself.

She hung her head, speaking now to the floor. "I would ask you to relieve me of our marriage contract."

She did not have to see his face to know his shock was genuine. She heard it in the awful, deafening silence that filled the room.

"I know this must come as a surprise to you, Edmund, but I have given it much thought and have come to the conclusion that a marriage between us would be most ill advised."

For him, she thought wretchedly, who would be getting damaged goods, and for herself, for relegating herself to a life with a man she did not love.

She lifted her head, and after a long agonizing pause, said, "Oh, Edmund, please do say something."

He locked his fists behind his back, much like a teacher about to deliver a stern lecture to a recalcitrant pupil. "I daresay you have considered the consequences. You are not well endowed financially. And you are—how can I put it tactfully—beyond marriageable age."

His meaning was clear. She would be hard pressed to find a man to marry her.

Pru's back stiffened. "Cruelty does not become you, Edmund."

"Nor does prevarication become you," he said sourly.

She could have told him that he was a humorless person, an overbearing and pompous man, and pointed out all the other flaws in his character. But as it was not in her nature to be cruel, she said instead, "Edmund, you cannot profess to love me."

"Of course, I do," he exclaimed. "Would I have proposed marriage otherwise?"

She shot him a sidelong glance. "Now, who is the prevaricator?"

"Love is vastly overrated," he said. "I hold you in the highest esteem and have the greatest affection for you. In time love will come. That's the way of things."

Esteem. Affection. The words rattled like sabers in Pru's brain.

"Fine words," she said sullenly, "except when used in place of the only word that matters…love." She drew in a deep, supportive breath, and said, "No, Edmund, I cannot settle for anything less."

"Is there someone else?"

Maybe. Possibly. It was still too soon to tell. But no, wait; what foolish notion was she entertaining? After the way she'd been treated by Nicolae, if she thought that he was that someone else, she was ready for Bedlam. With all the confidence she could muster, she looked him in the eyes and said, "There is no one else."

In a tightly controlled voice, he asked, "Your father is aware of your decision?"

"Yes. Papa has given me his blessing to do what I must."

"Then I shall call upon him and relieve him of your obligation to marry me."

A profound silence fell over the room like a heavy woolen cloak as the unfolding events sank into his brain. The floorboard creaked as he shifted from foot to foot. "I can think of a score of reasons why you should not do this," he muttered at length. "But I would be bloody hell wasting my breath on a crazy woman who thinks she can find God-knows-what elsewhere."

Pru drew in her breath. "Only God knows what fate He has in mind for me," she hissed, a blazing flush rising to her face and a ferocious look in her eyes that he had never seen before. "Until it is made known to me, I must follow my own conscience." *And my heart*, she thought defiantly. "Perhaps it is all for the best, now that your true colors have been revealed to me."

Tossing her chin up, she snatched her cloak from the back of the chair and threw it over her shoulders. "Good day, Edmund. I'll tell Papa you will be calling on him."

She stormed to the door and reached for the handle. Shooting a glance back at him, she said, "And do remove that ridiculous hat from your head."

So furious was she that she did not hear the bell atop the shop door jingle, nor was she even aware of the strange-looking little man who entered past her as she left the shop.

She sucked the cool spring air into her lungs, taking deep gulps in an attempt to calm her wildly beating heart. Hugging her cloak tighter about herself, she proceeded down the street, heedless of the shouting hackney-coachmen and the jostling chairmen and the insolent footmen who thrust their way through, making a hideous noise on the cobblestones and splattering mud on the hem of her dress.

As she hurried on past the shops of crumbling bricks and knotty timbers of the cobblers, broom-men and pointers, she was oblivious to the bells of the postmen, the cries of the merchants who sold hot and cold viands on street corners, and to the whole noisy, smelly metropolis that was London. Upon passing the botcher's shop, she was unceremoniously reminded of the torn gown and made a note to bring it in for repair.

At the Spitalfields market the women were still arriving with basket-loads of soft fruit perched upon their heads. She entered beneath the canopy to make her daily purchase of fruits and meats, vegetables being much too costly to afford but a few. She chose half a pound of cheese, a loaf of bread, some eggs, three fat mutton chops, a jar of preserved peaches, and although fish was dearer than anything else, a piece of salt-cod for Papa. She finished with some roots and herbs, salt, vinegar, mustard and pickles.

"At'll be a bob and sixpence, miss." The merchant, a hatchet-faced man, extended his hand, palm up, for payment while keeping an eye out for filchers. "Aye, ya hafta watch for em buggers, ya do. Ain't as bad as Field Lane where ya can have yer handkerchief dipped at one end and buy it back at the other, but ya can't take no chances."

Pru offered a commiserating smile as she delved into her pocket for the coins to pay for her purchases. It was then she spotted the basket of strawberries, and froze.

An unsettling sensation overwhelmed her. As she stared at the ripe, red fruit, she could almost taste the sweetness upon her tongue. Odd indeed, considering that she had never tasted a strawberry until…last night. And then she remembered the tea of the most unusual flavor, and strawberries so succulent that her mouth fairly watered to taste them again. She reached out to scoop a handful, but though better of it, trying hard to convince herself that the cost was too steep for her pocket, when she knew the truth was of a far more intimate nature than that.

"C'mon now, miss," came the merchant's impatient voice. "I got more customers 'ere."

Pru turned away from the strawberries and the memories that converged upon her with the force of a steam engine, memories so tawdry and thrilling she thought she might swoon.

She emerged shaking from beneath the tent to a sky that was overcast and gray, reliving what little she recalled of those passionate moments when she had become initiated into the art of lovemaking. She had a vague recollection of his hands on her body, teasingly soft, then harsh, a touch so intimate it could only have been a dream, of writhing against him, of opening her eyes to his covert smile that seemed at once both sweet and cruel. Her heart quickened at the thought of the disgraceful things he had done to her.

Through it all, one question begged for an answer. Why her? She knew she was not beautiful. She'd been courted only once, by Edmund de Vere, who had made it brutally clear today that it had not been for her good looks. From whence, then, had come Nicolae's lust? Had he, too, been moved past irrationality by the music? Had he been overcome by some ferocious itch that needed scratching? Had he been so long without a woman that any female body would do? Although it was difficult to imagine that a man as compelling as he was would not have his choice of women and all the sexual pleasure he could possibly want.

She tried not to think about it, for if she did, she might still hear the sound of her own ragged breath at the moment of explosion, still feel the pain and the pleasure mingling until one was indistinguishable from the other, still experience the shame with which she had responded to his demanding caresses. Had he guessed how badly she had wanted it? How his ravenous kisses had kindled her own dark hunger? But try as she might, she could not turn her thoughts away from last night.

Her shoes clattered on the cobblestones as she hurried down the street. Something, she knew not what, compelled her to look up. There, on the far side of the street was a figure she had come to recognize only too well.

He stood there watching her, his amazing green eyes shining like beacons out of the perpetual mist, the barest hint of a smile turning up the corners of his mouth.

Pru struggled for composure. Her throat felt so arid she thought she would choke. She remained rooted to her spot, unable to move, until she saw him take a step in her direction, and then she backed away slowly. She could not face him, not after last night. Tearing her gaze from his, she turned and started to run, straight into the path of an oncoming coach.

The coachman yelled for her to get the bloody hell out of the way. The grating rattle of wheels against the cobblestones loomed in her ears. The hot breath of the horses was upon her, the smell of the froth on their coats overbearing as they bore down on her.

It all happened so fast. One moment she was standing in the middle of the street, looking back over her shoulder at Nicolae. In the next instant her basket of produce and meats was airborne as she was tackled to the ground with an unceremonious jolt that sent her senses reeling. The coachman cussed as he careened on past. There was a concerted gasp from the onlookers. She felt herself being lifted to her feet and righted on wobbly legs. When her eyes finally stopped rolling around in her head and her vision cleared, she found herself looking into Nicolae's handsome face.

"W—what?" Her head whirled around to the place where he'd been standing only moments ago, then back to where he was now, within mere inches, his hands firmly clasped about her waist. "How did you…?" Bewilderment brightened her eyes. It simply wasn't possible for him to have reached her so fast. Why, she hadn't even seen him move. She shook her head to clear the confusion. "You were just…there." She pointed a trembling finger to where he'd been. "And now you're…here." And holding her much too tightly, of that she was suddenly acutely aware. With a quaking breath, she squirmed away from him.

Nicolae took a step back. "Are you all right?"

"Yes, quite," she replied as she patted the dust from her cloak and ran her palms over her dress to smooth the wrinkles. "I suppose I should thank you. If you hadn't been so…so…quick, I shudder to think what would have become of me."

He bowed courteously. "It was my pleasure."

Pleasure. The word conjured up all sorts of memories that Pru wanted desperately to forget. She drew back, frowning. "Do not mistake my thanks for friendship," she told him. "Not after the liberties you took with me last night. Or perhaps you think I have forgotten your ungentlemanly behavior."

His smile froze and faded from his face, his mouth now forming a savage little line. "I never claimed to be a gentleman." He chuckled, a flash of mockery in his tone. "On the contrary, I fully admit to being a very bad man."

Pru's mortification was complete. And to think, she had actually entertained the preposterous notion that she was attracted to this rake. Whatever charm she imagined he possessed was lost in the narrowed eyes and the shadowed mouth and the awful truth that she'd been used by a clever debaucher.

"It appears I have been mistaken about you," she announced.

"How so?" he asked, although the lazy lifting of his brows seemed to indicate his utter disinterest in her reply.

"You are not the person whose soul I thought I glimpsed through your music. Why, you, sir, have no soul at all."

His look turned hard, almost vicious, for a moment, causing her to shrink in fear of retribution. Then he laughed, so hard that his shoulders shook beneath his cloak, but the frigid sound left little doubt that he was not amused.

"So, you have discovered that about me, have you? And shall I tell you what I have discovered about you?"

"I've no wish to hear it."

She cast a look around for her basket and gave out with a little cry of distress to find its contents strewn about the street, the eggs broken and their runny contents spreading over the cobblestones. She gathered her purchases and placed them in the battered basket, all the while muttering under her breath. When she was done, she straightened up, whirled around to face him, and exclaimed, "You are a detestable man."

"You seemed not to mind last night."

She sucked in her breath. "I...I was not myself last night."

"Well, whoever you were," he said mockingly, "was most accommodating. And may I add, not the least bit shy about it. You were made for it, you know."

"Oh!" Her shoes clacked furiously against the cobblestones as she stormed off.

His boot heels made no sound at all when he fell into place beside her. "I meant that as a compliment. Some women spend their entire lives learning the skills with which to please a man. You seem to come by them quite naturally."

Pru ground her eyes shut at the possibility that there was more to last night's escapades than what she was able to recall. "Oh, do shut up." Frustration made her sound uncharacteristically harsh.

"That's just one of the things I discovered about you," he went on in a teasing and dangerous voice. "Another is that you pretend to be modest, but beneath your unassuming manner of dress and your almost-convincing meekness beats a heart that burns for passion. I wonder if your fiancé knows what a little Messalina you are."

Having been educated in the liberal arts at Mrs. Draper's School for Girls, she had learned Latin, Italian, geography and enough Roman history to know that Messalina, the wife of the emperor Claudius, was a woman of uncommonly loose morals. The comparison was dreadful enough, but what was even more shocking was the apparent ease with which he had looked past her veneer to her secret longings. How was it possible for him to know this thing about her innermost self that was only just awakening within her? A lucky guess, although she would never admit it to the likes of him. "I no longer have a fiancé," she said. "I broke it off today, not that it's any of your business."

"I see. Is there anything I can do to take your mind off your broken betrothal?"

Astonished, she said, "Certainly not."

With sugary sweetness, he ventured, "Not even if I were to play a piece I composed especially for you?"

"I doubt anything you do is for anyone but yourself."

"I take that to mean you do not want to hear it? Very well. But it may interest you to know that I have decided to take you up on your offer to play the suite I finished for your father at the concert next month. I was on my way to make the arrangements when you were so very nearly flattened by the coach. And how is your father? Has his condition improved?"

She detested that condescending tone and note of false concern and was sorry she had asked him to play the piece at Vauxhall Gardens. But his inquiry into Papa's health thrust her misgivings aside. When she left Papa last night, his face had looked so pale and drawn that whatever wild hope had invaded her heart for his recovery had been all but dashed. She heaved a beleaguered sigh, and admitted, "Not well."

"Would you care to walk with me to the quay?"

Pru looked at him, mystified by the change. How could he be so malicious one moment and so beguiling the next? So heartless and then so caring?

What cruel sport was this? And why, despite every reason she had to mistrust and hate him, did she feel herself softening beneath his beautiful green gaze?

Struggling to wipe her feelings from her face, she stiffened her resolve, and asked, "For what purpose?"

He answered, "I go there sometimes at night to watch the ships when I feel lonely. The sight of their dark sails coming and going fills me with a sense of…I don't know…meaning, I suppose."

He's lying, flashed through her mind. But the expression on his face, so downfallen, so heartfelt, gave her pause.

A paralyzed silence fell over them during which Pru floundered for words to say.

Just then, the clouds parted a little to reveal a rare blue sky with the sun peeking through. At the first faint ray that slanted across his path, Nicolae thrust his head downward.

"Perhaps another time," he said quickly. "I must go." But before he took his leave, he brought his face close to hers and whispered diabolically, "The day will come when you will seek me out for your pleasure, and I will be waiting."

With that, he was gone, disappearing through the throng as quickly as he had appeared a short while ago, leaving her standing in the middle of the crowded street, her mouth agape at the scandalous prophecy, her sensibilities reeling, and a thrill unlike any she'd ever known careening through her blood.

***

Nicolae hurried down the street to escape the invading sunlight, but as the clouds closed in again, his footsteps slowed and his thoughts turned back to the woman.

She was right when she said that anything he did was for himself. Ah, how well she was beginning to know him. He'd been up all night working on the piece for her, or more precisely, for himself with which to woo her. With the crowing of the cock and the breaking of the dawn he had put the last finishing notes to paper and retired to his bed.

No entombment in a casket for him, thank you, although where that preposterous notion arose from, he had no idea. He much preferred the comfort of his four-poster beneath whose linens was spread a thin layer of his native soil upon which he was obliged to rest.

So, she had broken her engagement to de Vere. He made a mental note to be especially careful now that de Vere had been soundly rejected. Men scorned tended to take their vengeance out in one way or another, and the last thing he needed was a stake through his heart, not at any time of course, but particularly now that he'd met this precious little pretender, for he was not finished with her just yet.

With all the confounded protection de Vere availed himself of—the crucifix suspended about his neck, the holy water he no doubt doused himself with each morning, and that God-awful garlic he hung everywhere—he'd never be able to approach him unawares. A crucifix posed no danger to one as strong as he, and all garlic did was render the wearer odorous. But if de Vere had gotten hold of the consecrated host, now that was a different matter all together, for of all the weapons at a hunter's disposal, the Holy Eucharist was the most powerful. Since de Vere was not likely to come to Prudence's rescue now that she was no longer his darling, his plan to trap the hunter needed altering. Well, no matter, he would think of some wonderfully sinister way in which to finish him off.

What was more important to him at the moment was Prudence. The crestfallen look on her face at the mention of her father had touched him unexpectedly. Perhaps it was because of the hopelessness it evoked, an emotion he knew only too well.

He'd lost count of the years upon endless years of wishing for that which cannot be and the despair that came from knowing that nothing would ever change it. He knew what it was like to be drunk with sorrow, to yearn for peace. For him, the only peace to be found lay in the darkness that waited at the end of each day. For her, it would be in the recovery of the music master, a dark gift that was within his power to give and for which she would truly hate him. But if she lost her father, she would have no one.

Oh, yes, he recalled, the aunt. The stunningly beautiful woman he glimpsed at the theatre.

Outwardly, she displayed the qualities of a frivolous, scatterbrained woman, but his astute senses perceived something controlling and calculating lurking beneath the surface.

It was better to belong to no one, he thought. Like himself. Did he belong to anything? To anyone? Did he belong to God, who had cruelly abandoned him? He felt suddenly glum, bereft of a single, solitary friend in the whole, wide world, save Prudence Hightower, the timid little mouse of a woman who had actually thought she'd seen a soul in him.

Chapter 7

A voice drifted out of the mists of slumber.

I know that voice, she thought. *How beautiful it is. How sad. How cruel.*

"You must come to me," it said.

No. No, I cannot. I will not.

Hot breath against her cheek, fanning the ends of her hair that was spread over the pillow. She struggled to move, but couldn't.

"A kiss is all I ask."

She felt an icy hand caress her face and trace a line down to her neck where it paused, a fingertip lingering at the warm pulsing hollow of her throat.

Terrified, she bunched her fists and arched her back, but blackness came down over her, and with an elegant hiss he wrapped his cloak about them both, drawing her up into his embrace and pressing himself against her. A cool touch slid up her thigh to the heated place that trembled and ached. An involuntary moan escaped her lips as ice struck fire.

I know who you are. You are a devil. A seducer. Oh, when you touch me like that. Her fingers opened to grasp his head from behind, tangling themselves in the silken locks, pulling his face closer to her own. *I hate you.* Receiving his kiss, the tongue that probed the warm, wet recesses of her mouth, the mellifluous breath that flowed into her.

"I want to taste you," he whispered against her mouth. His body pushed against hers with urgency, flooding her with his lust.

She whimpered helplessly. *No. You cannot.*

Yet her hands molded themselves to his back, fingers pressing against the taut muscles that flexed beneath her touch.

"Don't be afraid."

What do you mean to do?

"It will hurt only a little."

Why are you doing this?

As if he could read her terrified thoughts, he answered smoothly, devilishly, "Because it is my pleasure to do so."

How I hate you. You are a detestable beast.

"I am a man," he coldly replied. "With a man's hungers that you cannot deny me."

I'll never let you touch me again. Yet even as the oath formed in her unconscious mind, she was reaching for him, pulling him closer and wrapping her slender legs around him, desperate for the shocking intimacy of his hard, driving body.

The hardness of him entered her, filled her up, pierced so far inside that it took all of her breath away, forcing her head up against the headboard with every savage thrust.

Yes. Oh, yes!

With her legs locked about him, her hands clawing at his back, weeping miserably, she let him take her to that place again, that place of humiliation and dark longing, to the very center of the fire from which there was no escape and which scorched her with pulsing pleasure down to her soul.

Pru opened her eyes and squinted against the darkness. What a dark and terrible dream she'd had. So unsettling was it that she forcibly pushed it from her mind. Yet though the thought of it was banished, the physical excitement of it lingered. Reaching beneath the covers, she stifled a gasp at the wetness against her inner thighs. A sudden rush of embarrassment flamed her cheeks in the dark.

How was it possible for a dream to feel so real, its effects so powerful? She was afraid to turn over and fall back to sleep, lest the shameful dream reappear, so she lay there, her breathing staggered from the nightmare. At length, weariness overtook her and she slept again, this time with no dream to haunt her slumber.

Something, she knew not what at first, awakened her, not with a start, but gradually, like the dawn that tints the eastern sky with pinks and purples as it breaks over the treetops. Her eyelids fluttered open, but instead of finding daylight piercing her bedroom through the heavy drapes and hearing the chirping of birds outside her window, the room was dark and still. The long case clock in the hallway struck the midnight hour. Daybreak was still hours away. That was odd. She could have sworn she heard...

Music.

The vibrant strains of the violoncello lured her fully awake. But how? Who? It could only be Papa. A wild surge of hope filled her heart as she threw the covers aside, lit a candle and went to the door.

Cupping the candle's flame, in her bare feet she followed the sound to the music room where the soft glow of firelight seeped from beneath the door.

She stood outside for several minutes, listening. She recognized the piece Papa had begun composing, the very one he had entrusted to Nicolae. The music filled her with hope. Oh, could it be that Papa was beginning to get well? Tears hazed her eyes, summoned by the joy of hearing Papa playing his beloved instrument again, and by the sheer rhapsody of the piece.

She leaned her head against the door and closed her eyes as the music filled her like a cup that spilled over with love. But just when she expected it to stop at the point where he had finished composing, it went on, building in emotion, until she felt the aching in her soul and realized that what she was listening to was not Papa's creation, but Nicolae's.

How this was possible, she did not know, but in Papa's delicate condition, it wasn't wise for him to exert the kind of energy the piece demanded. Grasping the handle, she opened the door.

"Papa," she began warningly.

Her mouth fell open and a thousand thoughts careened through her brain when she saw Nicolae seated behind the instrument, Papa reclined in a wing chair before the fireplace, a blanket thrown over his legs.

The flames leapt up to greet her as she came in, orange, blue and blood-red dancing in the soft breeze that followed her through the door. Sudden clarity chased all doubt from her mind. It wasn't Papa she'd heard playing at all. It was Nicolae.

She glanced quickly at her father who sat with his eyes closed, his head swaying up and down ever so slightly in time to the music. And then to Nicolae, who looked up from the instrument with a faintly insolent smile on his lips.

How dare he come to this house, and at this hour? She wanted to scream at him to get out. But glancing back at Papa her anger ebbed away like the tide. By the light of the fire his face did not look worn and weary, but serene and untroubled for the first time in long weeks. The music had done for him what no apothecary's elixirs had done. Were the days without joy, or hope of joy, finally over? Laughter rose in her throat, but she choked it down, not wishing to mar the moment for him, no matter how angry she may have been at Nicolae.

Without a sound she went to stand before the fire, feeling its warmth on her skin as the heat of the music filled her within just as it had that night when she had surrendered to it and to a clever seduction. The memory of it filled her with shame and longing.

The music tossed her to and fro, like a ship on a sea of emotion. The notes hit a crescendo, and the air suddenly filled with expectancy as the bow slid across the strings for the final notes. A hush fell over the room.

After several moments Papa's eyes opened, and Pru's heart sank to see the same weary look in them. The blush that had tinted his face only moments ago fled, leaving in its wake the colorless hue of someone whose life was slowly, irrevocably slipping away.

"Papa," Pru cried softly.

"Ah, Pruddy," he said, his voice tired and thin, "I didn't hear you come in."

"You shouldn't be out of bed."

"Did you hear it, my dear? Did you hear what this young man has done to my composition?"

Pru forced back the tears to toss an unappreciative look at Nicolae. "Yes, Papa, I heard."

"I knew it," he said. "I knew my composition would be safe in his hands."

Your composition, yes, but not your daughter, she thought belligerently.

Nicolae rose from behind the instrument and came forward, inclining his head. "Miss Hightower."

How proper he was. Why, if she didn't know any better, she might have mistaken him for a gentleman, although by his own admission that was something he was not. "Mr. Tedescu," she said rigidly. "I didn't hear you come in."

"No, you would not have. You were fast asleep."

Pru was taken aback. How would he have known that? She was about to ask, but was silenced by his gaze that swept over her in an all-consuming rush. Suddenly, she was aware of the sight she must have presented in her nightgown and bare feet, her hair suggestively loose as if she'd only just awakened, which, of course, she had. His stare unnerved her. Standing before the fire, she was painfully conscious now that her silhouette must surely show through the thin white linen. She moved nervously to stand behind her father's chair.

So mired had she been in that terrible dream, like quicksand pulling her down into its treacherous depths, that she hadn't even heard the rapping at the front door. With Aunt Vivienne out as usual for the evening, poor ailing Papa had been forced to come down himself to answer it. Another reason to dislike the insufferable man, as if the unshakable effects of the dream weren't enough. "Are you in the habit of calling on people at this hour?" she questioned.

"Pruddy." Papa's tone was mildly chastising. "It's not at all unusual for Nicolae to call at this hour. As a matter of fact, all of our lessons were conducted in the evening owing to his business obligations."

"Oh? And may I ask what business that would be?"

With a frozen little smile, Nicolae replied, "My daytime hours are devoted to personal matters. My father was a prince in my homeland and presided over a large family residence and extensive land holdings of which I am heir to. Maintaining the accounts takes up a considerable amount of my time."

James put up his hand. "There's no need to explain."

Pru cast a contrite look down at her bare toes, recalling that he had told her his family was dead. That night as they had walked from the bridge she had seen the impulse of distress that passed over his face and had sensed that the mention of it had unlocked something deep inside of him, a pain of the heart that mere words could never express. She wondered if she would ever know the truth behind his sorrow. Of course there would be matters to attend to, especially if, as he said, his father had been a prince.

It was all very intriguing and only added to the air of dark mystery surrounding him. Not that it absolved him from the liberties he had taken nor diminished the lecherous gleam in his eyes.

"I put the finishing touches on the piece only this evening," he went on. "I was anxious for your father to hear it. It was not my intention to cause any inconvenience. I saw a light coming from within and reasoned that it would be all right for me to knock."

To Pru's discerning ears there wasn't anything about the piece that sounded different or altered from the other evening, but she could not say that without revealing to Papa that she had already heard it played to perfection. He would not be at all pleased to learn she had been Nicolae's guest that evening without a chaperone. Though these were enlightened times where intelligence and reason reigned and women were no longer looked upon as fragile flowers, Papa was, nevertheless, still painfully old-fashioned about such things.

She felt the weight of Nicolae's eyes and lifted her gaze to find him watching her intently. Was it her imagination, or was there a triumphant gleam in those bright green jewels? In the glow of firelight his features seemed even more refined, and she struggled to ignore the strange, almost savage, beauty of the man. She cast about for a fitting reply, but Papa spoke up to break the tension that sizzled in the air.

Turning to Nicolae, and said, "Hearing the way you play, my boy, I am more than convinced that you should play in my place at Vauxhall Gardens. Do say you will."

Nicolae bowed from the waist. "It would be my honor."

"Before I took ill I had in mind to play my composition which you have so brilliantly completed, as well as Bach's Suite Number One. You played it quite well during our lessons. With a little more practice of the thumb position you should be able to reach those demanding chords with ease."

"But Papa, you aren't well enough to conduct lessons."

"No, no, my dear, you are quite right. That is why I want you to work with Nicolae to ensure that the piece is all it can be."

Pru was mortified. "Me? But how? I'm not the music master."

"Indeed you are not, but you have heard me play the Bach suite a hundred times and I dare say you know it note by note."

Hoping to put an end to her father's preposterous notion that she should help the insolent man, she said, "If Nicolae is going to play the piece at the concert, shouldn't he play it in his own way?"

"Of course, my dear, and so he shall, but you have an excellent ear for rhythmic timing." To Nicolae, he said proudly, "She composed her own little baroque ricercare when she was just a child and is quite adept at pinpointing the differences between Gabrielli and Antonii. No, no," he said to his daughter, "I insist that you work together on this." He rose from the chair with difficulty. "Now, if you will excuse me, I am tired."

Pru was immediately at his side, her hand at his elbow. "I'll help you to your room."

"No, my dear. You stay and offer our guest something to drink. I know how difficult that piece is to play. I'm sure he is in need of sustenance. But first..." He paused to bring his face close to hers, and whispered, "Perhaps you should run upstairs and put on something more appropriate." He patted her hand and disengaged himself to shuffle off. At the door he turned briefly to cast a loving glance over his shoulder, neither at his daughter nor his pupil, but at his instrument that stood on its endpin. A look of sorrow passed over his eyes, as if he were saying goodbye to a dear old friend.

When he was gone, the room filled with a silence so palpable it could be cut with a knife. "I...I will be right back," Pru stammered, grudgingly adding as she picked up a candle and hastened to the door, "Make yourself comfortable."

In her bedroom, she threw on a loose-fitting serge dressing gown of dark blue. Her hands fumbled nervously with the surplice front closure. When it was secure, she headed back for the door, but not before pausing at the mirror to smooth her hair in the dim light.

Minutes later she returned to the music room to find Nicolae seated in Papa's favorite wing chair, one leg crossed casually over the other as if he belonged there. She went immediately to the violoncello and proceeded to remove it from its endpin, saying as she did, "If you're hungry, I could go down to the kitchen and make a plate for you. We should have some boiled venison left from dinner." She was just following Papa's orders, although privately she did not care if the man starved. It would have served him right.

He watched her with an amused smile on his face. "No, thank you. I'll feed on my way home."

"That's an odd way of putting it. Oh well, some port, then? Papa likes to sip his port after playing a particularly difficult piece."

"Only if you were to join me. But since it goes much too quickly to your head, I'll pass." He saw her look of surprise. "You didn't think I remembered? There's much about you that I remember."

"A gentleman would not have reminded me of something I wish to forget," she said with a huff.

"I'm no gentleman," he reminded her.

Pru felt her temper beginning to rise. "You, sir, are a most disagreeable man."

"And I suppose your uncharitable behavior toward me this evening is any better?" He smiled grimly. "Your pretense is almost as transparent as the shift beneath your dressing gown. And while I'm on the subject, I do wish you would discard those sober colors for ones more suited to your personality. You know, the personality you try so hard to disguise. The dress you wore to my home was much more fitting."

The dress she had dropped off at the botcher's shop for repairing only this morning, she was reminded with an inner groan. "My clothing is none of your concern," she snapped.

"You're right. What difference does it make to me what colors you choose for your clothes when you look so much more fetching out of them."

"You are being impertinent. I think you should leave." If she could have willed the wretched man to go, she would have done so.

He rose gracefully and reached for his cloak. "Very well," he complied. "But do try to be a little more amiable if we are to work together on the musical piece. Shall we start tomorrow evening?"

Pru's mouth fell open. "It was inappropriate for you to come here tonight and overtax my father in this manner. I told you he isn't well. Now you have seen it for yourself." She could not keep the caustic tone out of her voice even as her heart ached with every word.

Throwing the cloak over his shoulders, he started for the door, but stopped. Perhaps it was the anguish in her blue eyes, or the sigh he heard behind him, like the moaning of the wind, or just an uncommon moment of benevolence, that made him turn back to her.

"If I were to tell you that I could help your father regain his health…" It was neither a statement nor a question, but rather the workings of his mind spoken aloud.

"How could you do what the doctors have been unable to do?" she asked. There was no suspicion in her voice, not even disbelief, just the weary uncertainty of one who was afraid to trust in the miracle she had prayed for.

He shrugged. "Let's just say it's a skill I acquired a very long time ago in my native land."

With nothing but heartache behind and sorrow ahead, Pru gazed into his beautiful green eyes, searching for a trick, but finding only an earnest expression.

"You would do this for me?"

"Yes." At the hope that sprang into her eyes, he lowered his tone, adding, "But there is something you must do for me in return."

Ah, there it was. He meant to strike a bargain with her. *Do not fall into his trap,* Pru cautioned herself. She felt her hope rapidly dwindling once again, as always it did whenever she thought there might be a cure for her father's illness only to find out there was not. And yet it was that very hope which she clung to now as she looked at him, searching his expression for signs of entrapment.

He reached down and took her hand in his. It was cold, she thought numbly. Why was his touch always so cold when there were fires burning in his eyes? With the tip of his thumb he traced a pattern across her palm, a design of no particular import of itself were it not for the suggestive look in his eyes. Bringing her hand to his lips, he kissed her open palm while she watched in mute silence, her thoughts all jumbled and incapable of reaching her voice.

He brought his face close to hers and whispered in her ear. "I would have you come to me of your own free will."

Pru pulled her hand back and broke free of him. Her eyes were huge and luminous, her face flushed with anger. Through the thoughts that careened inside her mind, one word broke free when she finally found her voice.

"Never!"

She glared back at an expression she had not seen before, black and scowling, eyes sulfurous, the smile momentarily malicious before disappearing behind a faint insolent smirk.

"Never is a very long time," he said. "And from what I have seen tonight, your father does not have the luxury of time. That is the reality of the situation, Prudence."

"How do I know this is not a trick of yours to take advantage of me again?"

"Oh, I fully intend to take advantage of you."

"That's not what I meant. If I were to agree to this…this…bargain of yours, how do I know you will keep your end of it?"

Flatly, he replied, "You don't."

She shook her head. "I can't."

"Can't or won't?" he demanded.

She stood her ground before him despite the shaking of her knees beneath her dressing gown. "It is the same thing."

"Suit yourself. Perhaps you can always dream a cure for your father." He turned toward the door, adding with a flash of mockery in the candlelight, "Dreams can seem very real, after all."

She could hear his softly derisive laughter as he let himself out, followed by a curt, "Good evening to you, madam," as he hurried down the steps toward his waiting carriage.

"Prudence, who was that man who just addressed me?" Vivienne demanded as she swept into the house, her garments fluttering around her like leaves on an autumn night.

"That was Papa's pupil," she answered. "I am to coach him in his lessons in Papa's place. Although I'd rather be committed to Bedlam," she added with uncharacteristic defiance that made her aunt look at her.

Vivienne withdrew her hands from the long, narrow muff of marten and tossed it onto the entry table. "I do not like him" she said as she undid the clasp at the neck of her cloak. "Not one bit."

Her cheeks were rosy, whether from the chilly night air or from the rendezvous from which she had just returned, it was hard to tell, but Pru was in no position to judge her aunt's nocturnal activities, not with the shameful secret she herself was harboring. "Yes," she said, "he is a very disagreeable man."

"It's more than that. There is something, I don't know, different about him. The way he looked at me just now sent shivers down my spine. I won't have him in my house."

"*Your* house?"

"I only meant—"

"With all due respect aunt, there can be only one mistress of this house, and I am perfectly capable of filling that role."

Though she tried to sound authoritative, Pru's heart beat wildly. Where had she summoned the courage to confront her aunt on this issue? Perhaps Vivienne's tryst had not gone as planned tonight, but that was no reason for her to assume that she was anything more than a guest in this house. Pru had all she could stand of impertinence for one night.

"Besides," she added, "it is Papa's wish that he come here for his lessons."

The look in Vivienne's eyes turned dark. "Nonsense," she said in a chilling tone. "I will talk to your father about this." She moved toward the stairs.

Pru's voice rose behind her. "Don't disturb him."

Vivienne paused on the first step and turned to her niece, her eyes widening at what sounded distinctly like a command.

"He's sleeping," Pru said in answer to the fury forming in her aunt's eyes.

"Very well," Vivienne stiffly replied. "It can wait until morning."

"If Nicolae's presence displeases you so much, perhaps you should arrange not to be here when he calls. I'm sure you have plans for your evenings, anyway."

Vivienne cast a slow measured look over her niece. "Why Prudence, it seems you have developed some gumption. Be careful, my dear, that you do not overuse it. Men do not like women with whom they are forced to compete on any level."

"Yes, aunt, I'll keep that in mind."

Vivienne tossed her head and the menace that had vibrated in her voice only moments before was gone. "Prudence, my dear," she crooned, her voice now conciliatory, motherly, "you are so young and inexperienced. When you have been initiated into the ways of men, then perhaps you will be able to discern which ones are sincere and which ones are not. And that one most certainly is not. I say this only to protect you." She glanced away and clutched at her heart. "You cannot know the evil men can do, nor the wretched existence they can force upon you."

Her aunt made no secret that she preferred the virility of young lovers. Had one of them scorned her? Teased her about her age in spite of her beauty?

When viewed by the half light of a fire or candle's glow her skin had the rosy blush of youth, her eyes the gleam of innocence. At other times, however, like just now on the staircase, or under the harsher light of day, she looked older than her years. Perhaps that was why she ventured out only at night to meet her lovers, when the rare starlight that peeked through the London fog and the radiance of oil lamps masked her true age.

Pru watched her aunt ascend the stairs and felt suddenly sorry for her. It could not be easy being a woman alone in a world dominated by men. Now that she had called off her betrothal to Edmund, it seemed that this was to be her plight, as well.

She heaved a sigh and went back into the music room. For many long minutes she stood there contemplating her father's violoncello.

Compared to the decorative one in Hanover Square this one was plainly made with a spruce top and maple for the back, sides and neck. There were scratches along the narrow C-bouts of its body and a slight chip in the bridge hole just below the middle. Decades of playing and the weather had taken their toll on the instrument, and were it not for the purfing which prevented cracks from forming, all the dropping and bumping it had suffered over the years might have rendered it useless.

All in all, it was not a handsome instrument. Nevertheless, the sounds that emerged from it were the closest thing she'd ever heard to the human voice. The sweet whisperings of love. The gaiety of laughter. The mournfulness of despair. The bellows of rage. The screams of outrage. The moans of longing. It was the voice that dwelled inside the instrument, coming to life at the hands of a master musician like Papa…or Nicolae.

Having grown up with this instrument, Pru looked upon it endearingly as a member of the family. And yet, for as long as she could remember, she had never felt the connection to it that she felt right now. She and the instrument were alike, from the plain, unassuming countenance they shared to the depth of emotions swirling within. Unlike the instrument, however, she had always kept her sentiments to herself, locked up so tight inside that she herself had failed to recognize them.

Until that night in Hanover Square, when she had listened to the most powerful emotion coming from an instrument and had realized that those emotions dwelled also within her. As she had listened from the shadows to Nicolae playing the violoncello, something had taken place inside of her, a transformation so subtle at first she'd been scarcely aware of it, until tonight when she looked into her aunt's furious gaze and had not backed down, surprising even herself.

No external influence could cleave through the heart quite like music, but not just any music. She'd been listening to Papa's music all her life and had never felt so emboldened. It was Nicolae's music that had done this to her, just as it was his savage passion that had initiated her into the ways of men, as her aunt had so stylishly phrased it. Yes, he was arrogant and filled with his own self-importance, and in the brief time she had known him, she had found him to be cunning and cruel, and yet...

There was also an elegance about him, a sharp intelligence and a quick wit. He could not play as beautifully as he did had he not possessed a sensitivity that was rare in the common man.

And never had she seen a man more beautiful than he, not in the traditional sense, but in a way that went beyond classic beauty to something that had nothing to do with his physical features. It was the way in which he had gazed out over the water that night on the bridge, with an expression of hidden melancholy that had tugged at her heart. It was the sorrow she glimpsed on his face when he thought she was not looking. The wince in his eyes as if he were remembering past hurts. The terrible secret he must be harboring that turned the corners of his mouth downward before it disappeared behind a sad smile. The sound of loneliness echoing in his voice when he spoke about going to the quay at night to watch the ships.

No, she would not allow his sensitive nature to sway her. He was, after all, still very much the rake. Although, she could not help but wonder if he was really capable of curing Papa, or if that was just one of his tricks to get her alone again.

Don't be a fool, she cautioned herself. *He cannot cure Papa.* Oh, what a vile man he was to taunt her with the only thing she had left...hope. Come to him of her free will? Ha! That would be the day.

Drawing in a long shuddering breath, she went to the violoncello, picked it up and placed it in its case, just as Papa would have done, her heart breaking to think that he would never play this instrument again.

The next morning Pru opened the door to her father's bedroom and went inside, balancing the breakfast tray on her palm. Her footsteps creaked on the floorboards as she carried the tray to the bedside table and set it down. The linen of her skirt made a soft whooshing sound as she went to the tall window and drew the curtains aside. A thin ray of morning light rushed into the room.

From the bed came the rustling of covers and a protracted yawn.

"Good morning," Pru said, trying to sound cheerful.

"Pruddy, what a delight it is to see your pretty face first thing upon waking."

"Oh, Papa, I'm not pretty," she said. She went to his side to fluff the pillow beneath his head.

He lifted himself up with great effort. "Has no one ever told you so?"

The edge of the bed sagged when she sat down on it. "Only you," she said quietly.

His gaze caressed her face "You have your mother's eyes."

In a small wistful voice, she said, "And if I had more of her features I might not be facing a future as a spinster."

"Ah," he said, nodding. "Is that what has put that sad look in your eyes?" He lifted his hand to touch her face. "Some day you will meet the man who will see in you beauty beyond compare."

Unprepared for such a prophecy, Pru shifted uneasily and smoothed a wrinkle on her skirt with her palms, muttering, "I do hope he hurries."

"All in good time, my dear," her father said. "You can't hurry fate."

"No, indeed." She rose and went to the tray. "Gladys has fixed you a delicious breakfast."

He waved away the bowl of oatmeal with sweet cream. "I'm not hungry."

She reached for another plate. "Some fried kippers, then. You know how much you love them."

He shook his head.

Holding back a tidal wave of feeling, Pru implored, "Please, Papa, you have to eat to keep up your strength. I've brought you a glass of beer, but if you'd prefer I can run downstairs and get you a drink of chocolate."

"I have no appetite for food," he said weakly. "There is but one thing that would strengthen me, if not my ravaged body, then my spirit."

The plate of kippers nearly fell from Pru's hand. "What is it, Papa? If it's within my power, I'll do it."

He smiled kindly. "I'm afraid it's within no one's power to grant me this one wish." He turned his face away, but not before she saw the tears forming in his eyes. "Did you hear it last night? The way he played? Was it not the most sublime thing you have ever heard?"

"Yes. No. I mean, please tell me what it is you wish for, Papa."

"Oh, daughter," he whispered, "to play my instrument again. To feel it come alive in my hands the way it did last night for our young friend. That would be my wish." He lay there gazing off into the air, his eyes dark and meditative and his face awash in sorrow.

Pru felt suddenly close to tears herself. Her poor father had lost the two things he cherished above all others, his wife and his music. How he must be suffering. Her heart wept. She left him like that, staring into space, clinging to a worn and weary hope of something that would never be.

Beyond the window of her bedroom white wisps of clouds and a sky tinted pink and blue were visible through the haze of sea coal that blanketed the city. Morning light came sifting through the fog. The air was filled with the cries of the gulls as they winged their way toward the ever-hungry maw of the wharf to steal from the salt cod boats and filch oysters from the fishermen's baskets before they could be hoisted up to the wheelbarrowmen. Downstairs the kitchen door below street level was opened to the everyday goods peddled by merchants who made the rounds of the Spitalfields houses. The stands and stalls that lined the crowded streets were coming alive with hawkers and peddlers selling buns and mackerel, newspapers and tinware.

Pru paced the floor of her bedroom in her bare feet, lost to herself. Back and forth. Back and forth. Poor Papa. How he must be suffering.

She wondered if it pained him to look upon her, to see his beloved wife in his daughter's eyes and to feel the crush of memories. She stopped pacing before the scrolled frame mirror that had belonged to her mother, and turned to contemplate her reflection. Her father thought her pretty, but wasn't that what all fathers told their daughters? She had never deluded herself into thinking she was anything more than prepossessing, with a resourceful mind and a pleasing nature. But pretty? She heaved a beleaguered sigh as Edmund's uncharitable words came back to haunt her. He had said that she was beyond the age at which most girls marry, and it was true. But it was what he had left unsaid that hurt the most. Pretty? No, not she. In fact, the only time in her life that she had ever imagined herself as even remotely beautiful was when she'd been wrapped in Nicolae's arms, and then, it had been only an illusion, created by his lust.

She could still hear his ragged whispers at her ear, feel the warm breath against her throat, telling her she was beautiful. Lies, of course. But for that moment in time she had actually imagined it to be true, and though she longed to feel that way again, she would have given up all hope of it if only there were something she could do to help her papa.

And then the words came back to her. "If I were to tell you that I could help your father regain his health…"

Could he really do it? No, of course he could not. It was a joke, to be sure, a vindictive jest to exact revenge against her spiteful opinion of him. She had no reason to trust him. No reason at all, save the sliver of hope to which she clung, the tiniest ember that continued to smolder, like the last faint piece of coal in a cold hearth.

The realization came to her on a wave of despair and a surge of ruthless anticipation. *Oh God,* she thought wretchedly. *Is this what it has come to?*

Was she such a servant to the unbridled pleasure he had aroused in her that she would knowingly place herself at his disposal again? For Papa, she told herself. Yes. Papa. She would sacrifice her pride, indeed, her very life, to grant his wish. And if she were to derive some wanton pleasure from it, who was to say it was wrong to want a little bit of something for herself?

For several minutes she stared at her reflection in the mirror, trying to fathom the person who looked back at her, whose features were so familiar and yet who harbored the inner longings and selfish motives of a stranger. Where had this woman come from? A sudden clarity pierced her consciousness like a ray a rare sunshine through the perpetual fog. This woman had been here all along, hidden beneath somber grays and browns, veiled in propriety and decorum. Aunt Vivienne had called it gumption, but it was more than that. So much more.

She turned from the mirror in anguish. She knew what she had to do.

Chapter 8

"*P*rudence, how good of you to come."

He was not at all surprised when he answered the knock at his door and found her standing there, silhouetted against the night. The hood of her cloak was drawn up over her head, the striking blue of her eyes the only color radiating from her pale face. For a fleeting instant he thought of Edmund de Vere. There was little doubt that all de Vere saw was her prim façade. Had he ever suspected that beneath that proper veneer beat the heart of a beautiful and passionate woman? No, it was not likely, or he never would have let this little gem slip through his fingers. It took one such as him, possessor of extraordinary senses, to recognize her true beauty. Hers was not the kind of beauty that slammed into a man with the power of a runaway coach. It was subtle, working its way insidiously into the senses. He would have sold his soul to have her, not just for his sexual amusement, but for a partner with whom he could share eternity. If she were willing, which was highly improbable, and if he possessed a soul, which he did not.

Yellow candlelight glowed from the interior of the house, creating a luminescent halo all about him, imparting the disconcerting impression of a saintly figure. But the irreverent look in his green eyes and the sardonic smile dancing across his lips dispelled any notion of piety. Stepping aside, he made a deep, formal bow that contrasted sharply to his casual attire, and with an exaggerated sweep with his hand, bid her enter.

"So, you have decided to take me up on my offer."

"I have come to hear more about your ability to help my father regain his health," she said tartly. "When I have heard it, then I will decide if there is to be a bargain between us."

He went around behind her to help her off with her cloak. The hood fell back, releasing a torrent of fragrance from her hair, catching him unaware.

"I came by this afternoon," she said.

"Did you now?"

He purposely laid the garment over the seat of a carved and tufted wing chair, leaving only the silk upholstered settee upon which to sit.

"Your manservant said you were not to be disturbed."

In an even tone, he said, "I was resting."

It was not precisely a lie, but far removed from the truth. When he had awakened from his unearthly slumber at dusk and been informed that she had called, he knew she would be back tonight, and he wanted to be ready. Although he had fed as recently as last night, a quick trip to the East End and an infusion of fresh blood and the transmutation into physical energy insured his potency and promised an unrestrained coupling. That she had come to him of her own free will would only intensify the sensual pleasure that waited.

And here she was, almost like the workings of a clock, so predictable, so timely. That she had gone out of her way to look as austere as possible, with her hair of tarnished gold done up in a braid and wearing an intolerably drab dress of gray silk, did not deceive him in the least, not when he caught the scent of the blood that pumped through her veins, as sweet as a sugary confection and peppered with anticipation.

She may indeed have come here tonight for the purpose of finding a cure for her ailing father, but there was no mistaking the urgency that simmered just beneath her calm surface, infusing her face with color, her eyes with brilliance and her lovely, voluptuous body with lustful longing.

No, she did not fool him one bit. She had a dual purpose in coming, not the least of which was her own simmering passion. She was as much a slave to her sensual nature as he was to his blood thirst. The only difference was that he had known for centuries what he was while she was only just discovering her true nature.

His face bore no trace of his thoughts as he gestured to the settee, and said, "Have a seat while I pour myself some wine. I haven't forgotten what it does to you. I've given my manservant the night off, but I'd be happy to go to the kitchen and brew some tea for you."

Pru moistened her lips. "Wine would be fine."

So, this was going to be easier than he thought. No need for an aphrodisiac-laced tea. Not even for his mesmerizing powers, he thought triumphantly. The crystal decanter clinked against the glasses when he poured. The blood-red wine swilled in the glasses as he carried them to the settee. He sat down beside her, not touching close, but near enough to throw her off her guard, which was what he wanted.

She took a sip of the fortifying wine. "So, perhaps you will tell me about this skill you acquired in your homeland."

He just smiled at her. "All in good time."

"But you said…"

"I did not say I would tell you about it." Christ, no. If he did that, she would despise him and then he'd never get what he was after, namely, her soft, willing body in which to spill his lust. "What I said," he went on evasively, "was that I could help your father regain his health. The method is of no importance. But I do recall that we had an agreement." His green eyes glistened and the silky curve of his mouth was shadowed in the flickering candlelight. He caught her gaze with his and held it tight for many wordless moments before setting it free.

He took a deep swallow of wine, then got up and walked to the window where the heavy drapes were pulled aside instead of drawn as was customary in most households at night. For several minutes he stood at the window, a dark angel gazing out at the night, a glittering figure in a ray of opalescent moonlight.

"Do you feel it? The loneliness of the night?" He spoke against the pane, softly, but with a strange melancholy.

"The nights are always difficult," Pru whispered from across the room.

He turned his face toward her with a look that seemed to say, *so you understand*.

"But things always look better come dawn," she said.

Dawn. A signal for his retreat to the dark confines of his bed. The death sleep during which he was at his most vulnerable. Dawn. That cursed time of day when any notion he harbored about being remotely human was squashed under the thumb of daylight. Her mother's death and her father's illness may have given her an understanding of what it was to feel lonely at night, but she knew nothing of the torment he experienced day after wretched day with the crowing of the cock.

"I'm sorry if something I said has upset you," she said.

Her voice brought him back from his beleaguered thoughts. He turned from the window and went to stand before the fireplace. "Memories," he said, "have a way of coming back to haunt you at the most inopportune moments."

The orange flames caught his face in profile, shadow and light playing across his features, mouth drawn downward into an inexpressible frown, a wince in his eyes beneath the thick dark lashes. There was nothing cruel-looking about him now, but rather a helpless vulnerability and an expression of unfathomable sorrow.

"Is there anything I can help you with?"

He hesitated, unsure of how to answer.

"Perhaps we could work on the suite tonight," she said. "The Bach prelude has always had the power to lift my spirits."

Why was she being nice to him? Didn't she know that he wanted to ravage her, and worse, to turn her into a creature like himself so that he would have a partner to combat the loneliness? Even now, just thinking about it, he could feel his eye teeth straining and called upon every ounce of willpower he possessed to keep them at bay and her smooth white neck intact. He placed his glass down on the mantle and strode to where she sat and knelt before her on one knee.

"Do you know why you're here?" he demanded.

Pru drew back at the sudden shift in his bearing. "I…I…my father…"

"Oh Prudence, for God's sake, cut the pretense. Yes, your father. But why are you *really* here? Shall I tell you?"

She started to rise in protest, but his hand clamped over her shoulder, forcing her back down. "You are here because you cannot deny what you feel. Just as I cannot deny what I am."

The way he said it made her look at him intently. She remained strangely composed under the grip of his fingers. "What you are? I don't understand."

He laughed bitterly. "The world is a much crueler place than you can imagine. All you need to understand is this." He ran his palms under her dress and up her stockinged calves, the worsted wool soft beneath his touch, past the garters that held them in place, to the bare skin of her thighs. With nothing to obstruct him, his hand cupped her downy mound.

Pru made no move to stop him, convincing herself that she was paralyzed with outrage when, in truth, she hungered for the mortifying pleasure she knew he could give her. She shivered at his touch, cold, so cold against the heat he aroused in her, and gasped for breath when his fingers slid between her folds and entered her, in and out, in and out, softly probing at first, then deeper and faster, drawing her into a maelstrom of desire from which she could not escape even if she had wanted to.

With his thumb he teased the hardened nub, bringing forth a desperate groan as she writhed to the maddening sensations. And then his hands were again on her thighs, forcing them apart as he moved into the space between her legs and brought his head down to that spot that ached with want and need and reckless desire.

Her head fell back against the settee and she closed her eyes with a helpless moan. It was happening so fast. Sitting still and alert one moment, flooded with dark hunger the next. She pressed her balled fist against her mouth to keep her cries from escaping as sensations as sharp as knives shot through her. Her body convulsed with shame and excitement at the way he was kissing her, exploring her most intimate place with his lips and his tongue, making her feel like a wanton trollop and not caring. Her back arched and her legs fell open of their own accord.

She reached for his head, fingers grasping his long, tangled hair, and held him there, his face pressed against her, thrilling to the searing intimacy of his feather-light kisses and gently suckling lips, the hardened tip of his tongue demanding a response, and receiving it. Her hands slid forward to cup his face. The skin over his cheekbones was as smooth as a child's. Yet this was no child's work. This was the shocking seduction of a potent and powerful lover who possessed the ability to reduce her to a quivering mass.

Just when she thought she would die of breathlessness, he lifted his head and rose to his feet. He stood there looking down at her, smiling wickedly. What a sight she must have presented with her skirt and shift pushed past her thighs, her legs open wide, making no attempt whatsoever to cover herself, her desire-narrowed eyes transfixed on the telltale sign of his arousal.

His fingers tore at the pewter buttons of his trousers, sending one of them arcing across the room. With a cry of impatience he pushed them down below his knees, freeing his engorged phallus.

Pru drew in her breath sharply. His body was beautiful, so perfectly made with its narrow waist, slim hips and lean well-muscled thighs. She had never before so boldly looked upon a fully naked man, except perhaps the statue of Michelangelo's David that she and the other girls at Mrs. Draper's had seen in a book, whose nudity had reddened their faces, though none had looked away. Her gaze took in all of him, and she bit her lip, partly in fear, partly in wonder, at the hardness and virility of him.

He bent forward and moved his body into the space that beckoned between her legs, his stiffened member brushing the inside of her thigh as he forced his weight onto her and brought his mouth toward hers. For a few moments it lingered there, brushing her lips with his warm, wine-scented breath.

In a distant corner of her mind she wondered fleetingly how it was possible to be so overcome with lustful, almost painful, passion one moment and in the ensuing moment filled with such tender feelings as his gently nuzzling lips induced. This man was capable of stripping all modesty from her, eradicating her virtue, leaving her defenseless against her own desperate longings and a slave to his. He has done this before to other women, drifted through her thoughts, but she didn't care.

His tongue moved over her mouth as if she were a piece of honey-coated fruit to be savored slowly. When he took her lower lip between his teeth to gently nibble at its fullness, she briefly suppressed a giggle of joy before her mouth opened to receive his tongue.

He tasted salty and sweet, and she realized with a start that it was the taste of herself that lingered on his mouth. The effect was as heady as too much wine.

His kiss was tender, almost too tender, like a dream, enveloping her in a misty security that was shattered in the next instant when he pushed her back onto the settee and settled his body atop hers. His male hardness slid up her thigh and entered her.

Her body yielded with a will of its own, accepting his penetration as if it were an eagerly awaited guest whose arrival was long overdue. She stirred her hips, tilting them upward to meet him. A muffled groan emerged from his throat as he pushed forward, filling her with his heavy, aching manhood. She moaned and twisted beneath him, gasping his name into the heated air as she grasped his bare buttocks and instinctively wrapped her legs around him, pulling him in deeper.

His breathing rose and fell in great labored pants as he thrust into her, then withdrew to the point of agonizing anxiousness, the moistened tip of his phallus hovering just at her entrance.

And so began a rhythmic assault, thrusting and withdrawing, thrusting and withdrawing, again and again, flooding her with fierce sensations until she was unable to silence the guttural sounds in her throat.

She could not breathe. God help her. She was going to die. Her body jerked with ecstatic convulsions, wave upon wave of unbridled, undisciplined pleasure breaking over her, converging into one final explosion that caused her whole being to shudder. And still he thrust, harder and faster, with rough, frantic motions that brought them both to the brink of ecstasy.

"Oh, God!"

A cry such as she had never heard spilled from his lips. It was animal and human all at once and muffled against her neck as he clutched her tighter, pulling her so close she could scarcely breathe in an embrace that seemed far too powerful for a man to exert.

She opened her eyes and looked at him, and what she saw frightened her. His face was contorted, lips curled back over flashing pointed teeth, the shadow of his dark lashes sweeping his cheeks before lifting to reveal eyes not green, but yellow-gold, the eyes of a wolf.

She shut her eyes tightly against the fearsome spectacle. *It's the wine*, she thought wildly. It had to be the effect of the wine that caused the terrifying hallucination.

"Oh God!" he cried again. His body gave one last great shuddering tremor, and then went rigid as he collapsed against her. "Save me." These last words spoken as a tormented plea, but to whom? To God? To her?

She found the courage to open her eyes and look at him again. His face bore none of the hideous features she imagined she had seen. His eyes were closed and his lips were moving as if in silent prayer. Sucking in the air, he relaxed his hold on her and buried his face in the crook of her neck. She could feel the warm bursts of breath gradually easing and heard what she thought was a whimper, a sound barely audible over the roar of her own emotions. She clung to him, to this man-child of passion and sorrow, who had awakened her slumbering soul to the dark glory of lovemaking.

After several long minutes he raised himself onto his elbow and looked down into her face. With the tip of his finger he traced the fire's glow that shimmered along her temple, her cheekbones, and the corners of her prim little mouth. His voice was husky with the heaviness of satisfied desire. "That's what you came here for, isn't it?"

The question should have seemed impudent and taunting, but the tone in which it was asked was sincerely inquisitive.

Pru gazed into his beautiful face, the hard jaw, the full, strong mouth, the blinding emerald of his eyes, and answered honestly, "For too long I have denied this part of myself. I feel…" She looked past him, as if the words she was searching for were to be found floating in the air. "I never dreamed it could be so frightening and yet so…so…wonderful." She turned her face away, embarrassed.

With his thumb beneath her chin he guided her eyes back to his. "There's nothing to be ashamed of. It's quite natural, you know." He lifted his weight off of her and rose from the settee, drawing her gaze along.

Pru bit her lip and dared to ask, "Is it always so…big?"

Nicolae glanced at his still-swollen phallus and suppressed a chuckle at her refreshing innocence. Although she was technically no longer chaste, she was still very much a virgin in the ways of the world. Oddly, he had never really cared much for virgins. They were too much trouble, with their feeble protests of no, no, when they really meant yes, yes. He much preferred an experienced lover, one who made no pretense about what she wanted.

Other than this delectable flower, the only other virgin with whom he'd been involved was the one he almost wed. But that was a very long time ago, when he was still a mortal man and the world did not look as old and tired as it did to him now. Why this one? He wondered. What was it about her that drew him like a hapless moth to the hungry flame? Now that de Vere was no longer in the equation, he was at a loss to comprehend the pull she exerted on his senses. Well, some things, he supposed, were to remain forever a mystery. Like the reason Fate had doomed him to wander this wasteland that was his life, brutally compelling him to despise himself for all eternity.

He shoved the painful memory with its awful secret to the back of his mind. What could he say? That for ordinary mortal men it was common for the phallus to return to a flaccid state after the sex act, but that as he was no ordinary man, it was possible for him to retain a robust erection long after the act had been completed? Being the creature he was did have its advantages after all, the most obvious one a prolonged and insatiable appetite for sex.

"Only when it sees nourishment it craves," he said. Reaching down, he took her hand in his and drew her to her feet. "Let's go upstairs to my bed. I desire to see you fully naked and to teach you things, very wicked things."

"There's more?"

"Oh, yes," he breathed. "So much more." He scooped her up into his arms and carried from the parlor, taking the stairs two at a time, his feet scarcely touching ground as if in flight.

Within minutes their clothing lay in a jumbled heap on the floor. Standing beside the bed, he held her at arm's length to look at her. Her body was fuller and richer than he had dared to hope, her heavy breasts like ripened fruit, their delicate rose-pink tips hardened with anticipation. Her hair had already come partially loose from the pins that held it. All it took was his deft touch to bring it spilling across her shoulders and down her back, a rich mass of dark burnished gold that shimmered in the candlelight. Reaching down, he cupped her mound, slipping his fingers into her. She was moist from his previous leavings, moist and hot and ready for him again. She could hide behind the meaning of her name, but there was nothing prudent about the way her body responded to his touch.

He grasped his hardened member in his hand and rubbed it over her belly, sliding it downward to sketch circles in the jet-black curls.

This time, when he placed his hand on her shoulder, she dropped willingly to her knees. With its glistening tip he traced the line of her jaw, her cheek, and then her lips which parted willingly.

His dusky lashes closed over his eyes and a husky groan came from his throat as her lips closed around him. She was the kind of woman who all her life had given willingly to others of her time, her attention, even her love. But never pleasure. Until now, using her lovely mouth and tongue like a seasoned courtesan, bringing forth his moans and whimpers and making him shudder all over. When he could stand no more of her maddening magic, he drew her back up to face him, and gave one of his heartless little smiles. "What a little tart you are," he whispered.

He turned her around and bent her over so that her hands were splayed atop the down mattress, and positioned himself behind her, running his hands over the smooth white skin of her bottom. Pushing her legs apart with his knees, he mounted her, slipping inside her warm wetness and rejoicing in the tightness that closed around him like a glove. Leaning over her, he brought his face close to her ear, nipping at her lobe with his teeth and whispering in an animal-like growl, "This is how the wolves do it."

He pressed kisses to her shoulders and back and brought his mouth to her neck where his tongue flicked the fevered flesh. And then he bit her. Not hard enough to draw blood, just enough to taste the promise of it. She gave a little yelp and sucked in her breath, and for a moment tried to pull away. But he held on to her, his member sliding in and out of her silky wetness, the rhythmic motions gentling her.

At last he pushed into her with one violent thrust, causing her to cry out. But he would not come. Not yet. He reached between her legs to her pleasure spot and rubbed and caressed until her sweet body strained and knew she was on the brink.

Withdrawing, he pushed her down onto the mattress and rolled her over onto her back. Straddling her, he cupped her breasts in his hands and brought each one in turn to his mouth, suckling the engorged tips, biting none too gently with his teeth, making her writhe in exquisite torture. Smoky lashes cast a shadow over his cheeks when he lifted his head and gazed down at her.

"Nicolae," she gasped, her breath coming hot and fast as she curled her fingers around his arms.

The sound of his name startled him, spilling from her lips as naturally as it did. He lifted her breasts in his hands and brought them close together. Slipping his heated maleness between them, he said breathlessly, "Is this what you want?" But he knew it wasn't.

"Yes. No."

"Tell me," he demanded in a gruff whisper as he pumped his hips.

"I want you inside me. Please. Oh, please. Now."

All pretext of tenderness fled as he slid his eager maleness toward her entrance and came into her with a violent acquiescence. He took her with all the viciousness that was in him, sating his lust and pouring all of his terrible anger and sorrow and pain into her.

They clung to each other, two writing, panting bodies in the throes of passion so fierce and desperate, with emotions in disarray and in an all-consuming fire of lust and longing.

***

Nicolae lay there trying not to think, feeling spent and anxious as little by little reality began to intrude on his senses. How long could this go on, luring her here at night, partaking of her beautiful flesh and letting her think it was a normal mortal coupling? What would she think if she knew the truth, and why should he care? He had never been remotely tempted to reveal his true nature to any of his lovers, and there had been many of them over the centuries. Some he had killed afterwards, but only because they were harlots with unsavory habits—he was no killer of innocents. Others he had let live, leaving them with the memory of the most fantastic, explosive sexual experience of their lives. The little tricks each one had taught him along the way on how to pleasure a woman to complete distraction had made him a quick learner and an utterly unforgettable lover.

Why this one? The question repeated in his mind. And why, for all that was holy, was it suddenly, inexplicably necessary for him to tell her everything?

He felt her stir in his arms, and turned his face toward her. Her eyes were closed but he knew she was awake. "What say you to that, Prudence?" he asked devilishly.

Pru's hand sought the spot on her neck where he had bitten her. The skin was not broken, but there were two tiny distinct indentations. Rolling onto her side, she propped herself up on her elbow. "I say we try it again."

He disentangled himself from her and sat up. "Another night, perhaps. You've quite worn me out."

Her mouth formed a pretty little pout, but she did not object. "Are you ill?"

He looked at her questioningly. "Why would you ask that?"

"Because you are always so cold to the touch. I thought perhaps…"

His whole body jerked away from her. "No," he said flatly. "I'm not ill." He rose from the bed, his nakedness shadowed by the candles that had nearly burnt themselves out. The prolific erection that had drawn her attention was now gone, the unexpectedness of her observation rendering it as limp as a wet dishrag. Frowning severely, he went in search of his clothes. "Get dressed," he said.

She swung her legs around to the side of the bed and got up. "Papa always told me not to pry into other people's lives," she ventured as she dressed, "but I know so little about you."

He pulled his cambric shirt over his head and reached for his trousers. "There's nothing to know." His fingers fumbled nervously with the buttons. "I told you. I am from Romania. My family is dead. There really isn't anything more to tell than that." He flopped onto the bed and pulled on his boots. "Now, finish dressing. There's something I want you to hear." He went to the candle stand and touched the wick of a nearly spent candle to a big fat one. Immediately, the tallow began to burn, throwing light into the room and onto his face that bore an expression of displeasure.

When she was dressed, she gathered up her hairpins that were scattered about the floor, wound her hair into a braid and fastened it atop her head as she followed him from the bedroom.

He led the way up the darkened stairs to the garret floor, the candle throwing softly shifting shadows across the narrow walls, to the room where she had first listened to his magnificent music.

He gestured to a side chair with cabriole legs, and said, "Sit there."

She noted that the chair had not been in the room previously. Had he been expecting company? If there was any doubt as to whom he'd been expecting, it was quashed when she saw his violoncello standing on its endpin, not tucked inside its velvet-lined case, but waiting quietly for his fingers to give it voice.

Her being flooded with something akin to shame when she realized that he'd been expecting her all along. Was she that predictable and so easily manipulated that he could control her comings and goings with only a few vague words about a skill he had acquired in his homeland?

She sat down and waited patiently for him to take his seat behind the instrument.

With the hands of a master musician he enticed the notes and chords from the instrument, at times with the tenderness of a lover, at times with the raw ferocity with which he had coaxed her basest emotions out of her very soul.

He played a piece she did not recognize but which she knew she would never forget. In it she heard the deep, mournful longing that could only come from his innermost being and the heartrending sorrow she'd seen on his face earlier in the evening as he stood by the fire.

She closed her eyes and drew in a ragged breath, feeling taken again, this time by the music. The same fingers that had brought her such incredible pleasure glided the bow across the strings with equal fervor, caressing, teasing, demanding, bringing the instrument to the peak of ecstasy, the piece culminating in a crescendo of emotion that filled the small garret room with fire and ice and all the words that were beyond uttering, to a bursting finale that was as powerful as the one she had experienced in his bed.

A profound silence fell over the room.

His head was bent, his hair falling recklessly into his eyes, chest rising and falling with unspoken emotions. For a long time neither of them spoke. Then, he lifted his face. In the half-light of the candle she saw again the sorrow that haunted him.

"I can think of a thousand reasons why you should hate me," he said softly.

From the darkened corner her voice answered in scarcely a whisper. "How could I hate you?" There was resignation in her tone. "No," she said, "try as she might, I cannot hate you. Not because you initiated me into scandalous pleasure. Not because of your claim that you can help my papa. Not because you are beautiful. But because of this, the music. How could I hate someone whose music touches my very soul? That was beautiful."

"Like you."

She lowered her lashes. "I'm not beautiful. I'm plain and ordinary, with nothing unusual to recommend me."

"You are more beautiful than you can know." His green eyes radiated out of the dimness, the angles of his face caught in shadow and candlelight. "I composed that piece for you. I call it A Bridge of Light."

"For the bridge where we met," she said shyly.

"And for the light you bring into my dark and dreary life."

"Nicolae." She rose from her chair and came forward, her shoes making a soft sound against the floorboards. "What is it that troubles you?"

His voice came from a hollow place inside of him. "I can't tell you."

She reached forward and cradled his face in her hands. He found it strange that she had touched his most intimate places, yet the feel of her hands on his face felt like the most intimate touch of all.

"Tell me."

He looked at her for a long agonizing moment as he battled for the words to say. He shook his head, slowly, then adamantly. "You would never understand."

"There are many things I don't understand," she said gently. "Like why I came here tonight. Why I long for the comfort of your music. Why a man with such a beautiful soul can look so wounded, so bereft of hope. What I said to you that day on the street, that you have no soul, I was wrong to say that."

"Unkind, perhaps. But not wrong. On the contrary, if only you knew how right you were."

"What are you saying? That you have no soul?"

He offered a straightforward look in reply.

"Oh, come now," she said with a little laugh. But something in his voice gave her pause.

She aimed a sidelong glance at him. "I do not believe it. There is nothing you could have done for which you would have lost your soul."

"Not lost," he said hoarsely. "Taken."

Her hands dropped from his face and she stared at him incredulously.

He laid his head against the violoncello and closed his eyes. "I am tired," he said, his voice scarcely a whisper. "So very tired. A lifetime of dashed hopes and shattered dreams weigh on me. My body aches with despair. At times every breath I take is a laborious effort to forget the terrible truth of what I am and what I will never be." He fell silent for many minutes, willing himself not to feel, but the expression on his face said he was failing.

"I long to place my faith in you," he said at last. "To confide my deepest, darkest secrets, and in doing so, free myself of the dreadful burden I have carried alone for so long. If only I could share my torment with another being, one who would not turn from me in horror and revulsion, but who would look upon me with pity and understanding." His gaze burned into hers. "Are you that being, Prudence?" The fire in his eyes faded as he turned his face away.

"If not me, then who?"

"You have no idea what my life is like."

His gaze came slowly, tentatively, back to hers. There was no sign of fear in her blue eyes, no tremble of trepidation in her voice when she gently urged, "Tell me."

"You would never believe it."

Her whisper floated into the air, drowning out all doubt. "Trust me."

Rising, he enveloped her warm fingers in his chilly grasp and led her toward the doorway. In a weak, uncertain voice that seemed to come from far, far away, he said, "Come with me to the parlor. I have an incredible tale to tell."

Chapter 9

"*H*ere," he said dispassionately, "drink this. I fear you are going to need it." Into her hand he thrust a glass of sherry.

Pru looked at him dubiously, hesitating.

"No tricks," he said, his expression somber and uncharacteristically fearful. "Not this time."

She lifted the glass to her lips and took a sip.

"No. All of it. Quickly. Trust me, it will fortify you against what you are about to hear."

She drank it down. In moments it sent a flush to her cheeks.

Nicolae returned to the decanter, and with a nervous hand poured a glass for himself in haste, spilling some of the golden Oloroso on the mahogany table. With unceremonious speed he downed the drink. From across the room he stared at her with a perplexed expression on his face, searching her eyes for a sign to turn back before it was too late.

He drew in a shuddering breath, and said, "You do know what I am, do you not?"

"I don't know what you mean."

"Tell me what you see when you look at me."

"I see a man who seems very mature. At times much older than his years. At the same time there is a youthful quality about you. I see a brooding, temperamental man given to outbursts of temper and bad humor. But are not all musicians sensitive by nature and eccentric in character?"

He leveled a hard stare at her as if to say, *no, no, that's not what I mean.* "Go on," he prompted.

Pru's gaze swept over him. "Your complexion is unusually pale. Your smile can be both tender and cruel. I've noticed that the corners of your lips rise when you are angry, much like a snarl, I'm sorry to say. Your movements are smooth and…Do not be offended if I say they are very cat-like. Your voice can be like the soft coo of a bird, yet there is a rumbling of malice in it that I can only assume is caused by some secret from your past. And your eyes…" She paused and looked away, and in an embarrassed little voice, said "…are quite simply the most beautiful eyes I have ever seen. But I see such sadness in them. Sadness that I don't understand and perhaps never will." Her gaze returned to his. "I have tried to understand you, to see past that fearsome façade of yours to your heart, but my efforts are invariably blocked by some invisible shield of hostility with which you protect yourself from the rest of the world. Only tonight, right now, do I see the tiniest crack in that shield, a gentle crumbling of the walls that surround you. You seem to feel the need to express yourself to me, for what purpose I cannot guess."

"Only to be known," he said quietly, "for what I am."

"Don't you know who you are?"

"Not who. What."

He could see the confusion tearing at her, doubt creasing her brow and clouding her eyes, turning them dark blue in the dusky light. "Surely, you must have guessed, or at the very least, suspected."

Her voice issued from a place far within, scarcely audible." Tell me what you are."

He inhaled deeply, steeling himself against the fear and revulsion that were sure to follow when the dreaded words were uttered.

"I am a vampire."

He searched her face for a sign of horror, but saw only a blank stare. "Oh, that's right," he said, remembering. "I don't believe the word has found its way into your language yet. Ah, well, soon enough. Do you know what a revenant is, then?"

She answered cautiously. "A person who returns to life. A ghostly spirit."

"Well, imagine that a person has died and returned to life, not as spirit or mist or some ridiculous apparition, but as flesh and bone. He walks. He talks. He breathes. He is just not, how shall I put it, alive, in the truest sense of the word."

"You mean, sort of like…" She looked around helplessly, and for want of a better word, said, "…undead?"

"I prefer immortal. It has a much nobler sound to it, does it not? But yes, undead will suffice."

Despite the urgent look in his eyes, she said dismissively, "How can such a thing be possible?"

"You're asking me? I haven't the slightest clue. But here I am, standing before you, proof that such a thing is entirely possible. What say you to that, sweet Prudence?"

"I say blessed is God who restores life to the dead."

He looked at her, appalled. "Is that what you think this is?" he said, explosively. "A gift from God?" There was fury in his eyes that glistened now like shards of broken glass. "More like Satan's curse, if you ask me."

Pru shrank back from his vehemence. "I only meant…"

"You meant to cruelly mock me."

"Perhaps it is you who mocks me," she said indignantly, "with such a ridiculous claim. Dead, indeed. And just how am I supposed to believe such a thing?"

Of all the possible reactions—fear, horror, revulsion—the one he never expected was ruthless disbelief. He was seized by the impulse to grip her by the shoulders and shake her hard and shout *look at me, damn you. Look at me!* But now that he had begun this sordid tale, there was no turning back, and throwing fear into her with physical force would only lose her forever. He rushed to the settee and sank down beside her. Taking her hand in his, squeezing with his fingers, he said urgently, "What do you feel?"

He knew he was hurting her with his terrible grip and when she tried to pull free, he held on fast. Slowly, with intense purpose, repeating each word as if it were a solemn prayer, he said again, "What do you feel?"

Her hand trembled in his. "Cold."

"Yes, cold. You've said it yourself, how cold I am to the touch. Do you know why that is?"

She shook her head. "I don't want to know."

"It's because I am dead. Look at me," he commanded. "Really look at me."

A tense silence settled over the room. The air seemed abruptly thick and difficult to inhale. The fire ceased its friendly crackle. The orange flames that licked the hearth grew unearthly still.

Pru's gaze swept his face. Tiny blue veins appeared beneath his pale, translucent skin. Upon closer scrutiny, his full lips bore a faint bluish tint. His face was handsome…and bloodless. Like a heavy rock dropped into the darkest depths of the river, the full extent of what he was saying sank into her brain. Her hand suddenly splayed open and the glass fell to the floor, shattering on impact, the myriad shards glistening in the light cast by the fire. From a distant place her voice drifted into the waiting stillness. "How can this be?"

"That is a story unto itself. I've never told it to anyone, but I'll tell it to you if you wish to hear it. If you don't, tell me now."

For a long while she did not answer.

A transient plea rushed through his mind. *Oh God, don't let her say no, not now, not when it is so desperately important for me to tell my story.* For so long he had carried this secret around like a beast of burden, sagging under the weight of it. He yearned to share it with another human being, one who would understand and take pity on him, and in doing so, lighten his unbearable load.

"Well?" he asked.

The fire faded from his eyes, leaving them sad and hollow.

She nodded her head, just the barest inclination.

He released her hand and slumped back against the tufted silk of the settee, his head resting on the carved mahogany border. A great sigh of relief spilled from his lips as he squeezed his eyes shut. Liberation lay at hand. Salvation. Deliverance from the deadly secret that held him in its spiteful grip, tearing at his nerves and ripping at his heart. For many wordless minutes he remained thus, gathering his thoughts and his strength about him. At length, he opened his eyes and sat forward. Lowering his head, he held it in his hands. He began carefully, testing each word, concentrating so hard he thought his mind would burst.

"I was born in the year fourteen-fifty." He heard her muffled gasp, but did not...could not...stop. "My father was a prince of Transylvania. My mother was from a long line of Magyars from the Kingdom of Hungary. I lived with my parents and two younger sisters, Izabella and Gizella, in a village at the foot of the Carpathians, the land of the ancients. The house and surrounding lands had been a gift to my grandfather by the Hungarian king as a reward for his military deeds and for his discretion in not betraying the king's love affair with the young wife of the prince of Walachia."

She remained so silent it was as if she were not there. He stopped and lifted his head. She was still sitting beside him, a small motionless figure etched against the growing darkness. Running a hand through his hair, he swept the dark locks from his eyes, and went on.

"When the prince's son, Vlad Tepes, came to the throne, he gave a feast for his boyars and their families to celebrate Easter. He was well aware that many of those same nobles had been part of the conspiracy that led to his father's assassination and the burying alive of his elder brother. My grandfather was a member of the Order of the Dragon. He trained Prince Vlad in the skills of knighthood when the prince was a boy. But on that day the prince had scores to settle. The boyars were executed for their conspiracy, my grandfather for his loyalty to the Hungarian king. Shall I tell you how?"

The bitterness built in his voice as the dreadful memories emerged like demons from the shadowed past. "A sharpened stake was gradually forced into his body through his groin until it emerged from his mouth. Death by impalement is slow and painful and was Prince Vlad's preferred method of execution. Victims can linger for hours. In my grandfather's case, it was days. I was but six years old, but I was brought by the prince to view my grandfather's body as it decayed on a stake along the roadway. You could smell the rotting corpse from half a kilometer away. It was picked apart by crows and his bones were bleached by the sun as a chilling example of the fate that awaited traitors."

The flames from the fire had all but died out. He stopped again and turned toward her. Her face was as pale as moonlight through the shadows.

"We did not hear from the prince for twenty years. He was busy waging his war against the Turks. But he never forgot us. I was twenty-six that year of fourteen-seventy-six, about to marry a girl from the village, the granddaughter of one of the boyars who had been executed on Easter Sunday. One night, as my family was seated for dinner, there came a rapping at our door. My mother sensed danger and cautioned my father not to answer, but Gizella, whose pure heart would not allow even a mongrel to remain outside on such a cold night, invited the caller inside. It was to be our undoing."

There was a wild look in his eyes as the memory of that night returned like a festering wound, infecting his being with a sickness for which there was no cure. He shut his eyes tight, but he could not block out the sight that was forever imprinted on his clouded vision. It all came rushing back to him—the moonlit snow, the crackling fire, the table set with a platter of seasoned sausages, his sisters' laughter—gone, all gone in one maddening swoop.

Chapter 10

*I*t had snowed heavily all day, the pewter clouds dropping a new layer over the heavily whitened landscape. As dusk fell, the snow-covered foothills took on an opalescent glow in the moonlight. Behind them rose the Carpathians, their passes and broad valleys laden with freshly fallen snow. All was silent amidst the moonlit snowfields.

A warm yellow light shone through the windows of the ochre-colored house in the Citadel Square, near the Clock Tower. Surrounded by the houses of Saxon and Magyar merchants and the townhouses of the nobility, it was an unassuming house with storks dwelling on the chimney top and nothing noble about it to suggest that it was the residence of a prince.

As the sun was setting a horse cart rumbled down the pitted road and stopped before the house. Two figures alighted, slung fresh pelts over their shoulders and went on inside.

"Gabriel, Ambrus, what a mess you have brought into the house with your wet boots."

Gabriel Tedescu gave his son a sardonic look, and said, "When you marry that girl of yours, if she speaks to you like that, you must beat her soundly."

Ambrus laughed and shook the snow from his dark hair. "I'll take the pelts to the cellar, mother. After we eat I'll dress them and bring them to the furrier in the morning. He should get some dolmans and a winter coat out of them."

"And we should get a few *leus* for our pocket," said Marta, "so I can go to the market."

"Oh, Mama, can we buy some *gogosi*?" ten year old Gizella pleaded. "My mouth waters for sweet fry bread filled with apples."

"No, some *placintas*, please," implored Izabella who, at fifteen, fancied herself quite the connoisseur of the tortes.

"Izabella, pour your father and brother some *tuica* to warm them."

Ambrus downed the plum brandy in two strong gulps and headed toward the steps that led to the cellar, the wolf pelts over his shoulder leaving droplets of blood on the slate floor, drawing the wary attention of the family dog.

"I don't think anyone will be going anywhere tomorrow," said Gabriel as he shrugged out of his sheepskin coat. "There's more snow on the wind."

"Only November and already it's so bad," Marta complained. "There's enough firewood in the cellar to last at least through January, but our stores of beef are almost gone. Ah, well, then it's cabbage and potatoes tomorrow night."

"Not again," Gizella moaned.

"With your father and brother gone for three days hunting wolves, I have not had a chance to get to the market. You'll eat what I put on the table."

Ambrus stomped back upstairs in his heavy leather boots. "I don't care what you put on the table. I'm as hungry as a wolf myself."

He was a handsome young man, with dark brown hair that sparkled like gold in the firelight, fine, strong features, a tall, thin frame, and his mother's green eyes. In his white shirt and black woolen pants, with a wide leather belt worn over the shirt and a vest of leather embroidered with traditional motifs of their region, he was a striking specimen.

Marta wiped her hands on her embroidered apron, and said, "Is that all you can think about? Come everyone and sit down. Gizella, leave that stupid dog alone and come to dinner, or I'll throw him outside."

The smell of vegetable soup and seasoned sausages filled the room.

"Tell us about your hunt, Papa," Izabella said. "Are the pelts you brought back from the wolves that were preying on the livestock?"

"I can't be sure," Gabriel replied. "But they were fat enough for this time of year, so it's possible."

"We saw tracks of *lupari*," Ambrus said as he stuffed a piece of sausage into his mouth.

"The wolvers take too many," Gabriel grunted. "They are more interested in the bounty offered for each wolf than in protecting their own livestock."

To his father, Ambrus said, "Tell them about the wolf we saw."

Gabriel spooned his soup and did not answer, but something in his expression caused his wife to look at him closely. "Gabriel?"

"He was big," he said, and then fell uncharacteristically silent.

"That's it? He was big?" Izabella questioned.

"Bigger than any wolf I've ever seen," Ambrus said. "And unafraid. He watched us from the frozen underbrush and did not run as we approached. His eyes were large and yellow and…" He paused to ponder the bit of sausage on his fork. "There seemed to be an almost human intelligence about him. I can't explain it. I didn't think it was possible to be any colder than I already was, but when that wolf looked at me, it felt like hands of ice touching my spine. It was as if he could read the thoughts inside my mind and knew that I was afraid."

"You?" Gizella said with a laugh. "Afraid? You're so big and strong, I didn't think you were afraid of anything. Except maybe your bride-to-be."

Gizella and Izabella dissolved into silly laughter at their brother's expense.

"You would have been afraid, too, little sister," he said.

"So, what did you do?" Izabella asked. "Is that one of the pelts you brought home?"

Ambrus glanced at his father, but Gabriel was staring down into his bowl of soup without saying a word or offering his son any support in this.

"No, we didn't catch him. When we went to the place where we had seen him, he was gone."

"And the big wolf hunter didn't follow his tracks?" his little sister scoffed.

"That's just it. There were no tracks. Not of a wolf, anyway. The only tracks we saw were—"

"Enough!" Gabriel said. "How many times have I told you not to scare your sisters?" He exchanged a tense look with his son, bringing an abrupt end to the subject.

Ambrus looked down at his plate and continued eating in silence. His father was right. What was the sense in scaring the girls with the truth of what they'd seen? Yet in his mind he carried a vivid picture of the hard-crusted snow marred by prints, not of a wolf, but of a man. *Lupari*, he told himself then and now. The wolf hunters. But try as he might, he could not make himself believe it. "I'll go dress those pelts." He got up and disappeared down the stairs.

The girls fell into chatting about boys and the dresses they would wear to their brother's wedding while Marta tried to ignore the veil of tension that had settled over her husband.

Soon there came a rapping at the door. Marta cast a fearful look at her husband. "Do not answer."

"Gabriel Tedescu," called a voice from beyond the door. "May I enter?"

The spoon fell from Gabriel's hand, clattering into his bowl. "Who calls at my door?"

"Gabriel Tedescu," the hoarse voice called again. "May I enter?"

A question twice asked.

Under her breath Marta whispered, "It is not wise to answer until someone has called your name three times. A question twice asked can only mean—"

"Oh, Mama, it's so cold out tonight," Gizella said as she jumped from her chair and rushed to the door. "We would not deny shelter to a shivering dog, would we? It can only be a traveling merchant."

"Gizella! No!" The words exploded from Marta's lips. "Don't invite him in!" But it was too late. The door was opened.

He stood there in the cold, misty wind, the snow swirling in wild gusts all around him.

He was not a very tall man, but stocky and strong, with a cruel and terrible appearance, distended nostrils, wide green eyes framed by bushy black eyebrows, a thin reddish face shaven except for a moustache. Swollen temples increased the bulk of his head. A bull's neck supported his head from which black curly locks fell to his wide shoulders.

He had come, the dark, ancient threat, the evil that the pious priests tried to exorcise, the demon that even the sorcerers dared not evoke, the curse that haunted the imagination and blighted the sleep. He had come, this woe to mankind, shouting his name without even speaking. *I am the one—I am he—I am shouting my name—yes, you hear me.* Over and over he repeated it in the minds of his terrified hosts. *I am strigoii. I am moroii. Dead. Alive. I am everything you fear and more.*

He came forward as if on a dark wind, his boots scarcely brushing the slate floor, wielding his horrible power over them and paralyzing them with unspeakable fear. Before their transfixed eyes his visage transformed from that of a man to something grotesque. With taloned hands he reached for the nearest figure.

Gizella's scream was cut short when those fingers wrapped around her neck and pulled her close. In a movement that was too quick to subvert he threw her up against the wall with a force so shocking and great that her neck snapped like a dried twig and she crumbled to the floor, silent and broken.

Gabriel grabbed a knife from the table and lunged. The creature lifted the able-bodied man high into the air by the throat in one gruesomely strong hand and held him there kicking and writhing until all that emerged was an awful little gurgle and one last spasm as the life was choked out of him.

Izabella's back was pinned to the wall in abject horror, her voice choked into silence. Those eyes turned toward her, riveting and glowing like red-hot coals. In the next instant the flesh of her neck was ripped away as if by a rabid wolf.

Marta flew at him in a frenzied rage. At the sight of the crucifix suspended from a leather thong about her neck he hissed, drawing back his lips to reveal the razor-sharp, blood-smeared fangs of an animal. In seconds she was torn apart with the power of a hundred strong men.

The carnage was complete in mere moments. The figure turned half around and spotted the dog cowering in the corner. It took a step toward it, and stopped.

There, in the doorway to the cellar stood Ambrus, his green eyes widened with shock at the death and destruction scattered about the room. No. No. It could not be. This was not happening. This was a dream. *Wake up*!

A movement from the corners of his eyes caught his attention and he turned numbly toward it.

He stood frozen to his spot as the man came toward him and he recognized him. It was the same vengeful face that had brought him to see his impaled grandfather twenty years earlier, but this face bore no sign of aging. It was as youthful and as hateful as it had been that terrible day. How could this be? Oh God, how could this be?

The man approached him, so close he could smell his breath. He turned his face away, nearly choking on the hideous odor which brought to mind the charnel house, the only place they'd been permitted to commit his grandfather's rotting body after his father had climbed up to remove it from the stake. With its absence of Christian symbols, the foul-smelling, filthy breeding ground for disease had been his family's final degradation. Until now, when past sins, real or imagined, against the prince were to be reckoned for.

A preternatural fire burned in the eyes that scrutinized him. Somewhere in the distant hills he heard a wolf howling. His heart pounded wildly in his chest. What a pitiful sight he was, a full-grown man cringing like a babe. He expected to meet a fate no less gruesome as that which had befallen his family. But the rending of his limbs did not come.

"What is your name?" the man...the thing...demanded in a voice that did not rise above a whisper and yet resounded in the blood-soaked air.

From somewhere he found the strength to reply. "Ambrus."

Laughter, the sound of devilish delight. "Yes, I remember it now. Young Ambrus, how you have grown."

"Wh...what...happened here?" He was crying.

"Unfinished business," came the chilling reply.

"My sisters..." His voice choked. "My sisters were innocents."

"Nits turn into lice." This spoken with a negligent, uncaring shrug.

Ambrus felt his will to live leak from his being. "Kill me, too." Challenge. Plea. Resignation. All resonated in his voice.

"Oh, no, not you," the monster hissed. "You are destined for a different fate, one befitting your name." The face drew closer, pale lids closing over bloodless eyes as the mouth opened.

Frightful-looking teeth, projecting like those of a wild animal, hideously, glaringly white and fang-like, sank into his neck.

Unbearable pain. Exquisite pain. The world receded into mist and muck, swallowing him up like a bog that consumes the unwary creatures of the night. Sucking him down further into its murky depths. Sucking. Harder. Stronger. Sucking from him all life. Draining from him all hope. Banishing him into the darkness where nothing existed, not God's glorious light nor the world created by God. He crumbled to the ground. And then he felt...nothing.

He awoke with a start to an incredible thirst. For a long time he lay there unable to move, or think, or feel. Gradually, his thoughts returned. His head pounded and his whole body ached. The first thing he saw when he opened his eyes and turned his head was the dog. Still lying on his back, he stretched out his hand, but the dog drew back, bearing its teeth as it backed away. Somehow, he found the strength to push himself up onto his elbows. The room was dark and still. His nose wrinkled at a pungent odor in the air. With difficulty he got to his feet and stood swaying while he gathered himself.

He found one of his mother's candles and touched the wick to the fire's last ember just as it burnt itself out.

In the flickering candlelight a grisly sight greeted him. The bodies of his mother, his father and his two sisters were sprawled in disarray across the floor, like earthenware that had been hurled against the wall by a savage hand, broken into a thousand pieces that could never be put back together again. A horrific sickness welled up from his stomach and lurched into his mouth, spilling from his lips in a violent upheaval. He staggered across the room toward the open door and stumbled out into the snow, retching and crying, the bile stinging his mouth, the tears burning his eyes. Oblivious to the cold that swirled all around him, he collapsed in a heap on the frozen ground.

He had no idea how long he laid there, his mind numbed by all he had seen, all he had lost. His cheek lay against the wet snow. His shirt and pants were soaked through, yet he felt no cold other than that which came from within. He tried to shut out the sound of the wind that whirled down from the mountains and the sickening reality it brought with it.

Hoisting himself up from the wetness, he turned back toward the house. For several long, agonizing moments he stood staring listlessly at the darkened bulk of the house where so much joy and promise had once dwelled and where now only death and unspeakable emptiness remained. He shivered uncontrollably, not from the cold but from the awful finality of it all. Chewing his knuckles, breathing deeply, he entered the house.

The smell hit him the instant he went inside. It was thick and putrid and at the same time sweet and pungent. Something stirred inside of him. His throat was dry. What was this thirst that had suddenly taken hold of him, not for water or *tuica*, but for…what? Oh God! But suddenly, even the silent entreaty seemed meaningless, hopeless. God had forsaken him, slipped from his consciousness, vanished from his being as if He'd never been there at all. In His place was a new god, a new religion shrouded in darkness and evil. And in his throat a new thirst.

And then he saw it, the dark liquid pooling on the slates, the slick splatters on the walls, the table, and the chairs. It was everywhere he looked, glistening in the misty moonlight that slanted in through the window. It filled his being with a hunger unlike any he'd ever known. An abrupt realization sank into him, staggering him, and in that moment he knew what the smell was and what it was he thirsted for.

Blood.

Chapter 11

When he looked at her, she was huddled against the back of the settee, her head bowed, not looking at him. *Oh God*, he thought wretchedly, *she despises me. What have I done? Must I now kill her?*

"Prudence?"

She lifted her head and stared at nothing.

He made himself stand up. He had dropped his terrible secret into her lap, expecting... what? That she would understand?

"I died that night," he said suddenly. "I can't explain it. I'm dead. And yet...I walk around, I talk, I feel. Do you hear me, Prudence, I *feel*. How can that be, you must be asking yourself." He heaved a black sigh. "I don't know. God help me, I just don't know."

He began to speak faster, the words rushing from his mouth. "I'm not here and yet I am. I'm an aberration. Human and yet not human. I've done things I'm not proud of, but only to survive. I've become the thing that made me, the hateful monster that drew the blood from my body, taking my life and all that I might have been."

"Did you love her?"

Her voice, small and timid, spliced through the cacophony of his jumbled thoughts.

"What?"

"Did you love her? The girl from the village."

He paused to consider the question, thinking it odd that after all she had just heard, and with all the questions she must have, this was what she wanted to know.

"Yes, I suppose I did. But I no longer know for sure. It's been such a long time and I don't remember the feeling. That, too, has been erased from my being. Love." A bitter laugh split the tension in the room. "Who even knows what that is? Not me, I can assure you. Besides, what would be the point?"

He exhaled resolutely and went to the fire. Picking up the poker he stoked the fire, watching listlessly as the flames sputtered to life. The silence stretched so long that for a few moments he forgot that she was even in the room. When next he spoke, his voice hinged on anguish.

"He spared me the fate of my family, for what reason I don't know. Instead, he dealt me a different kind of death, the kind that does not end with the passing of the body but condemns you to an eternal state from which there is no end." *Save a pointed stake to the heart*, he thought miserably, *or the manner in which my maker was destroyed*.

He turned back toward her then. "I can see it in your eyes. You are questioning how a man can accomplish such a thing. Ah, but there, you see, is the answer. A man cannot. Only the undead can create the undead. The man that brought me to look at my grandfather's rotting corpse on the stake was mortal, of that I am sure. But somewhere along the way he was transformed into the demon that slaughtered my family and made me what you see before you. Some years after the Easter massacre the Turks forced him to flee to the mountains of Transylvania. Perhaps it was there that it happened. The villagers tell of a prince who was bitten by a wolf and drained of blood, who became a predator so terrible that no one dared speak his name." He shook his head and exclaimed with disgust, "They call him simply Draculea. It means son of the Dragon."

With slow, dawning awareness, she said, "Your name. What does it mean?"

"Ambrus?" He snorted derisively. "In my mother's language it means immortal. Now, there's irony for you. Do you think when my parents bestowed that name on me they knew they were condemning me to this fate? I prefer to be called Nicolae. I live in this wretched state. I need nothing further to remind me of it, least of all my name."

"What happened to him?"

So, the questions begin, he thought wearily. And why not? After the chilling tale he just told, it was understandable.

"He was slain in battle against the Turks near the town of Bucharest the following month, surrounded by the bodies of his loyal Moldavian bodyguards. His body was decapitated by the Turks and his head sent to Constantinople where the sultan had it displayed on a stake as proof that the horrible Impaler was finally dead. Fitting, don't you agree?"

"How can you kill someone who is already dead?" she questioned, doubt rifling her tone.

He answered matter-of-factly, "You cannot kill the undead, but you can destroy them. Decapitation will do the trick, as was the case for him. And, of course, there's always the stake through the heart."

"You have a heart?"

He looked at her, aghast, and replied angrily, "Of course I have a heart. And a mind, and feelings. The only thing I do not possess is a soul."

Pru stifled a gasp and echoed in a shocked whisper, "No soul?"

"It's one of the curses of the undead, my sweet. We get to wield all kinds of evil and never find redemption. How can you redeem that which you do not have?"

He slanted a look at her from the corners of his eyes to test her reaction and saw her body convulse with a shudder. For an awful moment he thought he'd gone too far, revealed too much.

She drew in a shaky breath "How can that be?"

Her questions were beginning to irk him, for they were questions he had asked himself a thousand times, never finding the answers. "How the hell should I know? Go ask a bloody alchemist. They're into all that supernatural rubbish, aren't they?"

Pru shuddered. Something about the way he had told his lurid tale, with fear in his voice and tears in his eyes, made a compelling argument for the truth. She bit her lip, hesitating. "What is life like for you?"

"Worse than you can imagine. At night I am obliged to rest upon a layer of hallowed ground from my homeland. Without my native soil I would not be able to travel more than a hundred kilometers from the place where I was born."

"The trail of soil I saw on the floor in the garret room," she said, half to herself.

"Although the sunlight will not destroy me, it hurts my eyes and if very strong will burn my skin. That is why I have taken up residence in London. The fog shields me from it."

"Yes," she said, "I remember. That day on the street, when you pushed me out of the way of the speeding coach, the look on your face when the sun peeked through the fog and the haste with which you departed."

"I am a creature of the night," he said. "Lurking in shadows. Rising at dusk. Feeding in the dark."

She nodded, as a gradual understanding took shape. "Music lessons in the evening. Resting this afternoon when I called. It all makes sense, and yet none of it makes sense. Maybe you're just trying to frighten me, or trick me."

"Or maybe you think it's all the figment of a demented mind," he said, sarcasm dripping from his tone. He came back to stand before her. She looked so lost and confused, and unbelieving. "You do believe everything I've told you, don't you?"

"I...I...don't know." Her blue eyes were clouded with doubt, her face shadowed with suspicion and, for the first time, fear.

"I see my word is not enough for you. You require more proof of what I am? Very well. Come with me." Without waiting for her to respond, he reached down and grasped her hand in his. Yanking her to her feet, he pulled her along, her shoes clicking against the wooden floor as he hustled her out of the parlor.

He brought her into the hallway and stopped before a tiny alcove beneath the staircase. Planting his hands on her shoulders, he turned her around to face a drawn curtain. With an angry gesture he shoved the heavy brocade fabric aside to reveal an intricately carved and scrolled mirror.

"What do you see?" he demanded.

She answered obviously, "Myself."

He came to stand beside her. "Now what do you see?"

Pru blinked hard against the shifting light that flickered from a corner candle stand. The man standing beside her cast no reflection. The only face she saw in the glass was her own. She swallowed hard and tried to speak, but could not.

His voice was a soft hiss beside her. "Since vampires have lost their souls, they cast no reflection. Now do you believe me?"

Her legs went weak and threatened to crumble.

He let the curtain slip back over the mirror and placing an arm about her waist to steady her, led her back into the parlor.

"Sit down," he said. "You look like you're going to pass out."

For a long time Pru remained silent, too afraid to speak and not knowing what she would say even if she could.

"Here."

When she looked up, she saw the glass of sherry he was holding out to her. This time she took it and drank it down without ceremony. There was a pinched little look on her face, indicating that all doubt had been eradicated from her mind. The sherry warmed her blood and sent an immediate flush to her cheeks. After several minutes she regained her voice.

"It must be terrible for you."

"At the beginning, it was. But think of all the things I have seen and been a part of. All the inventions and strides and achievements of mankind yet to come that I will see. Shall I tell you a secret? No, no," he hastened to add in answer to the fresh wave of horror that blanched her face, "not terrible like the first. Actually, I am rather proud of this one."

He sauntered to the decanter, poured himself a glass and drank it down. "In fifteen-oh-one I found myself in Florence, drawn there after the fall of Savonarola, the Dominican priest who ruled the republic with his narrow-minded hatred of all things artistic. I had not yet discovered my true calling, music, and as I fancied myself a rather good artist, I gained an apprenticeship with a young sculptor who was commissioned to complete a colossal statue portraying David as the symbol of Florentine freedom. I persuaded him to portray this David not as the victor standing over the slain Goliath, but rather in the moment immediately prior."

The glass slowly lowered in Pru's hand as she listened.

"It was I who suggested that in order to save both time and money he use a marble block from the quarries at Carrera that had been abandoned decades earlier by another sculptor. For weeks he searched for an appropriate model to portray the young shepherd, until he glimpsed me rising naked from the pool in the grotto behind his studio and entreated me to pose for the statue that was finished four years later and placed in the *Piazza della Signoria*."

She stared at him, mouth agape. "*You* were the model for the statue of David?"

"The proportions are not quite true to form," he admitted. "The head and hands are larger than normal. My hands, as you can see, are much more refined and elegant. Can you imagine playing the violoncello with hands such as those? The rest of the statue is, how shall I put it, quite true to form. If you've ever seen the statue of David, I'm sure you, of all people, can attest to that."

Oh, yes, she thought with a rush of embarrassment and excitement. She could very well confirm that he had been the model for Michelangelo's statue. The image of the picture she'd seen in the book on Italian Renaissance art at Mrs. Draper's came suddenly to mind. The muscled thighs. The taut abdomen. The power and tense energy. The vigorously fit specimen whose body echoed that of the man standing here now, two hundred and twenty-six years after its completion.

"There are other stories I could tell you," he said, his voice winding its way through her thoughts. "Of places I have seen, experiences I have had. Perhaps some other time. For now, it is important to know that you believe me. That you understand what I am."

In a distant part of her mind Pru knew she ought to be afraid for her safety, but she was not. "You must be very lonely."

He sighed deeply. "At times the loneliness has been as heavy upon my shoulders as that block of Carrera marble. I am almost ashamed to admit that I have often taken comfort in the arms of whores."

At her gasp of disapproval, he said, "The pleasure I derived with them helped me forget, for the moment at least, the vague, worthless sadness of my life and the isolation it imposes on me. My immortality makes it difficult for me to form permanent attachments. Except for others of my kind."

"There are others?" she exclaimed.

"More than you can know. But as I was saying, except for others of my kind, the mortals I have known have all grown old and died. It makes for a terrible loneliness. At times it has been so acute that I thought I would die, not literally, of course. But you learn to adjust. You have to. Eternity is such a very long time."

Into Pru's mind sprang the words the priest had spoken at her mother's funeral and his description of eternity.

"Imagine," he'd said, "that a bird flies to a beach somewhere in the world and picks up a single grain of sand and flies off. One year later a bird takes another grain of sand, and it is repeated year after year until that beach is bare of sand. Then a bird flies to another beach somewhere else in the world, each year taking away a single grain of sand. And so it goes, again and again and again, until all the beaches and shores in the world are bare of sand. And that would be only one minute of eternity."

"Immortality is not new to my kind," he said. "Mankind built the ancient pyramids in an attempt to gain immortality. For me it comes naturally."

"Nevertheless," she said, "it must be a burden."

"Aside from the obvious, the only thing I am burdened with is the ridiculous folklore that has come down through the ages. Contrary to the stories illiterate peasants tell their children, not all of us sleep in coffins or disintegrate into dust in the sunlight. And let's not forget about garlic."

She looked at him, puzzled. "What does garlic have to do with anything?"

"Nothing. That's the point. All those fools get from wearing garlands of garlic around their necks is a nasty odor. About the only thing the folklore got right is the blood thing. Regrettably, we must feed on blood in order to survive."

"You kill people?" Pru's shock resonated in her voice.

"Never the innocent," he said defensively. "Only the scum of the earth. And if there doesn't happen to be any such filth available, rats will do. Don't look so horrified. What you look upon as unthinkable becomes entirely possible when no other option for survival exists."

She swallowed hard. "Do they all become like you?"

"My victims? No, they just die. *Mort. Guasto. Muerto. Tot. Dood.* In any language, dead. To make another I must not only drink from them but they must drink from me, and I'm quite selective about whom I share my own blood with."

Pru twisted her fingers nervously in her lap. "Why have you chosen me to tell this to?"

He shrugged elegantly beneath his cambric shirt and gave her a silken smile. "Why did you choose me as the man to whom you would surrender your virtue?"

Her cheeks burned scarlet. "You tricked me into acting like a wanton. Now that I know what you are, I'm just beginning to realize the power you exerted over me."

He reached down and ran a finger across her cheek. She flinched. Cold. So cold.

"You give me too much credit for your own carnal desires. Do you really think it is possible for me to trick you into fulfilling your true nature? Yes, I have the power to mesmerize, but not without the surrender of the victim's will, such as you surrendered your will to me for the price of passion."

She turned her cheek away. "You're disgusting."

He withdrew his hand and emitted a bored sigh. "Are we back to that again?" He sat down beside her. "Shall I tell you about my other powers?"

"I don't want to hear."

"I can take away a person's voice, a man's strength, a woman's beauty. I have only to catch the gaze of my intended victim to exert my control. I hold sway over nocturnal creatures, the wolf, the bat, the rat. My powers of perception are higher than any mortals. I can transform into mist before your very eyes. And I'm fast, so fast, it's almost like flying. But I believe you discovered that the day I prevented you from being flattened by a coach. I am a pagan creature, unmoved by the fear I see now in your eyes. Oh, yes, you are disgusted, but you're also intrigued by all you are hearing. And that, my dear Prudence, is why I chose you."

In a quivering voice, she asked, "What is it you want from me?"

His own voice dropped to a caressing whisper. "Let me drink from your heart. There will be no pain, I promise."

The blood left her face. "*What!* You would turn me into this…this…thing that you are?"

"Think of it Prudence," he urged. "The things we would see. The places we would go. To remain forever young. To ease this terrible, crushing loneliness of mine."

Shock thundered through Pru's brain and from the look on her face, it was as if his words were poison. "I could never love *you.*"

Her words were as sharp as a dagger, swift and deadly, the last one uttered with such contempt that it made his preternatural flesh crawl.

Masking his wounded pride with a sneer of disdain, showing a glimpse of pointed teeth in the firelight, he laughed harshly. "Who said anything about love? I must say, my dear, your carnal talents are so delightful, love would only get in the way."

He seized her face in one cruel hand. "Tell me you don't want me, not in spite of what I am, but *because* of what I am."

"No!" She struggled to be free.

His fingers moved to caress the silken hollow of her throat and downward to cup her breast beneath the fabric of her dress. He buried his free hand in her hair and drew her head back for a kiss.

She quickened like lightning at his touch. Her fingers trembled to touch the smooth skin beneath his linen shirt. His strong scent, flavored with lust and sherry, rose to meet her. A shudder of yearning and dread coursed through her.

"Nicolae." Part cry, part moan.

She was in his arms, locked to him, feeling his heart beating savagely against her own, his stiffened member pressing against her, throbbing, pulsing with unchained desire.

"You are mine," he breathed against her skin. His strong arms went under and around her, lifting her effortlessly and carrying her from the room and up the stairs.

He placed her on the soft down mattress. Overhead the billowy hangings of his bed rustled. He lifted her skirts and worked hastily to undo his buttons to free his aching member from the captivity of his trousers for the salvation that beckoned between her legs. He moved easily into her. She was wet and ready for him. With no need for preliminaries his slim hips thrust harder and faster, matching his movements to the sounds of her throaty moans. His lust exploded and his eye teeth lengthened. Just when the moment of savage release was upon him, he brought his mouth to her neck and pierced her tender skin with his sanguinary kiss. At the first taste of her hot, sweet blood upon his tongue indescribable pleasure flooded his being.

Afterwards, the crimson and gold threads of the hangings sparkled in the great shafts of evening light that bathed the room. He lay beside her, tracing patterns across her heavy breasts. Lifting his hand to her face he felt a tear tumble down her cheek.

"You're crying."

Pru turned her face away from him, and said, "You bit me."

"Never fear," he said thickly. "You're still quite mortal."

She rolled away from him.

"Is there more on your mind?"

With her back to him, she asked, "Are you able to...to father children?"

"Well, actually, yes, but it would be ill advised. Any offspring you and I might produce would likely be short-lived and prone to destroying its parents."

"Then we must not meet like this again," she said, sitting up. "I cannot take the chance of, well, you know."

"Of bearing the spawn of the devil?" he said bitterly.

"That's not what I said."

"No, but it's what you meant."

"Nicolae, I have done my best to understand all that you have confided in me. Please try to understand it from my point of view. We cannot meet like this again, and that's final."

"May I remind you that you are to work with me on the music?"

"Of course. At my home. Where there will be no temptation to—"

"Devour your lovely flesh."

"Oh, do be serious, would you? What would happen to me if I were to bear a child out of wedlock?"

"I never thought of myself as the marrying kind, but I suppose I could make the supreme sacrifice."

"Your humor leaves much to be desired," she said dryly.

He spread his hands innocently. "It was not intended as a jest."

"Be that as it may, if it were ever discovered that I had married a...a...what did you call yourself?"

"A vampire."

"...a vampire and bore his child, I'd be locked away in Bedlam. I much prefer my home in Folgate Street than Finsbury Square, thank you."

"You could do worse," he said indignantly. "May I remind you of your former fiancé?"

"There's one more thing," she said.

Nicolae rolled his eyes. "More demands?"

"No. A question."

"I can hardly wait to hear it."

She ignored the sarcasm dripping from his voice. "We had a bargain. If I came to you of my own free will, you were going to help my father. By what means would you do so?"

He smiled—that familiar cruel smile she'd come to know so well. "By what means do you think?"

Pru bit her lip. "You would turn him into a…" She was almost afraid to utter the word. "…vampire?"

He replied simply, "There is no other way."

Her fingers touched the place on her neck where his sharp teeth had pricked the skin. "Would there be any pain?"

"Some, but only at first."

"Would he have to kill to survive?"

"Not necessarily. He could drain a victim just enough to get the sustenance he needed."

"But you kill."

In the pale moonlight that came in through the window she saw the sulfurous glare in his eyes. "To avenge the despicable act that was perpetrated on my family," he said vehemently. "To punish the world for the vile place it is. To remind myself of the sickening thing that I am."

To punish the world or to punish himself? Pru wondered as she turned away from him. After everything she had learned about him tonight, she wondered also if she would she ever really understand him. She shook her head. "If I were to agree to such a thing, would it be wise to tell him?"

"I cannot make that decision for you. If you tell him and he declines, he will die."

She shivered at the biting reality in his tone. "You said there are others like you. Are they all as callous and cold as you are?"

"Some are worse. Some do not feed on blood at all. There's one in particular who carries an ancient hatred in her heart."

"Was she made in the same way you were made?"

"No, it was very different. For the Celts of ancient Ireland, Beltain marked the time when the Sun God returned to Mother Earth. Basically, it was the beginning of the summer season, when the herds of livestock were driven out to the pastoral pastures. It was three days of feasting and celebrating his union with the Mother Goddess, marked by young girls dancing with abandon at the feast and laying down beside the fires with men they did not know."

Ignoring the blush of embarassment that rose to her cheeks, he went on. "Lienore, that was her name, was caught laying in the bracken with a lover during Beltain, but her lover was not a young man. It was another woman. The Druids accused her of being a witch, which of course she was, and sacrified her in a blood ritual."

"How gruesome," Pru remarked.

"Not nearly as gruesome as the hatred she has perpetrated through the ages. If you think I am an aberration of nature, she is worse, much, much worse. She exudes the innocence of a child, but she harbors a ruthless guile that has brought destruction to countless unsuspecting mortals."

"If she is so evil, why hasn't anyone destroyed her? Lopped off her head or run a stake through her heart?"

"Because she is spirit. To form flesh and bone she must inhabit the body of a living human being. She flits from one host to another, always choosing the most comely, from what I am told, such a vain little thing she is. It's generally not known that she has even been there until it's too late. She drains her victims of their life force and then discards the host like a petulant child, leaving the victim and the host as dead as can be. I would love nothing more than to lop off her pretty head, as you so elegantly put it, but I have no idea what she looks like."

Pru looked at his strange, unearthly beauty in the swaying light, and shivered. "I want to go home now."

He got up from the bed and straightened his trousers. "I'll take you."

She looked at him dubiously. "Are we going to fly, or something?"

It was not meant as a joke and she was surprised by his sudden burst of laughter.

"Flying would arouse too much attention, don't you agree? I think it's best if I hail a carriage."

Chapter 12

"*H*ow are the lessons going, Pruddy?"

She raised her eyes from the book in her lap at the sound of her father's pet name for her, so unlike Nicolae's formal pronunciation. Laying the book aside she got up and went to him. "Quite well," she said as she straightened the covers around him. "It's hard to imagine that he can get any better than he already is."

"Our young friend's talent is reminiscent of my own." He turned his head away and stared pensively at the window across the room.

"Would like me to ring for some tea, Papa?" she asked, hoping to draw him out of his quiet remembering.

"Tea? No."

"Would you like—?"

"What I would like," he said suddenly, struggling to rise to his elbows, "is to get out of this bed. Look at it out there, Pruddy. Spring is upon us, and here I lay, unable to do anything. What I would like is to walk in the garden. To resume lessons with my students. To play my instrument again." This last part uttered with an exertion that took his breath away. He slumped back against his pillow, weakened further by his effort. "If only there was a way. If only…"

Pru turned from her papa's tortured expression and went to stand before the window. Spring was indeed in the air. The trees were sporting new growth, the leaves sparkling like bright shiny emeralds in the rare and scattered sunlight, reminding her of a certain pair of mesmerizing green eyes.

The mornings and evenings were still cool, like the touch of his hand across her flesh. But the afternoon breeze carried the promise of warmth, like that which flooded her being at the thought of him.

Was there no path her thoughts could take that did not lead to Nicolae? Her heart ached with doubt and confusion. More than her own selfish pleasures, the thought never left her mind that he could take away her papa's illness and make him whole again. That he could wipe the pallor from his face and restore strength to his weakened limbs. That he could give her papa the thing he wanted most, to play his beloved violoncello once again.

Gazing out the window at the burgeoning spring, she ventured, "Papa, if you could live forever, would you choose to do so?"

From the bed came a deep inhalation and a slow, weak exhale of breath. "What have you been reading to put such a thought in your mind?"

"Only Robinson Crusoe by Daniel Defoe," she answered, returning to his bedside. "No, Papa, I mean it. If immortality were offered to you, as a gift, say, would you take it?"

He lifted his head a bit. "If immortality were offered to me, it would come as a gift from Satan, and I shudder to think at what price. Although…" He paused for a moment, and confessed, "I must admit, the temptation would be great indeed to accept."

She had hoped for something a trifle more definitive which would have enabled her to make a decision on what to do. "What if it were to come from me," she said, "and it could make you well again?"

"Only God can make me well, and it appears to be in His plan that my mortal soul should soon join Him. But, Pruddy," he said, smiling kindly, "you're a good girl to wish such a thing for your poor ailing papa."

No, Papa, she wanted to cry, *I'm not good. I've done things with a man, scandalous things that would break your heart if only you knew. And I do hold in my hand the power to give you your life back, but to do that it would mean taking your life. Oh, Papa, I don't fully understand it, but I do know that one word from me and it would be done.*

"What is it, my dear girl? What troubles you so?" He laid his hand over hers and gave it a fatherly pat.

On his first visit after revealing his shocking tale, Nicolae had sworn her to secrecy and she had obliged him with her solemn oath that she would not breathe a word of what he had told her to anyone. How could she tell Papa what was wrong without betraying a confidence? Besides, he would never believe it. Who knew? Maybe she was a fool herself for believing it. She was wicked and weak, a prisoner of her own desires. Was she to add gullible to her list of shortcomings, as well?

Each passing day she moved further away from the person she had been until she scarcely recognized herself. Even the reflection she saw of herself in the mirror looked somehow different. The features were the same, and yet they bore a maturity that hadn't been there just a few short weeks ago. The eyes that stared back at her were just as round and just as blue, yet there seemed to be a perception in their depths, a knowingness that she had never noticed before. Upon close examination her body appeared to be the same, but a flush rose easily to her skin and her breasts fairly tingled with excitement, straining at the bodice of her dress for the caress of a familiar cold hand. She wished she could go back in time and reverse all that had happened since the night she had heard Nicolae playing in the garret room and a series of events had been set in motion that would change her life forever. Yet if she could, she would never have known the shameful pleasures he had unleashed in her. In all probability, she would have consigned herself to a joyless, passionless future as Mrs. Edmund de Vere.

"Will he be ready for Vauxhall Gardens?"

Papa's tired voice drew Pru away from her perilous thoughts. "He's ready now, if you ask me. But what do you think? I know you can hear him playing from here. You cannot pretend to be asleep and not hear it."

"If I pretend to be asleep, it's only so that your aunt will not trouble me with her meddlesome presence."

"Well, you needn't worry about Aunt Vivienne. She has taken a distinct dislike to Nicolae and manages to absent herself when she knows he will be here."

"Where is she now?"

Pru shrugged. "In her room, I suspect. I heard her come in last night just as the clock was chiming the midnight hour. She's probably still asleep."

"Is he coming tonight?"

"Yes," she replied with a note of despair as she headed for the door. "While I'm getting the music room ready, why don't you try to get some sleep? If you're feeling up to it, perhaps you can join us tonight."

He nodded listlessly and closed his eyes.

Downstairs, Pru tidied the music room, placing the sheet music on the stand before the chair, just to the side the way Nicolae preferred it. He was already well prepared for the concert in one week's time, and she suspected that his visits now were about more than just the music. Although nothing further had been mentioned about her joining him in immortality, the way his eyes sought hers and the urgent expectation mirrored in their green depths told her it was still very much in his mind. Good God, what must he have been thinking to ask such a thing? Oh, she supposed if she was totally besotted with him, she might have actually given it a second thought. But the dismal fact remained, she was not in love with him.

What she felt for him was more difficult to explain. She craved his touch, his body inside of hers, the dizzying heights to which he brought her. She was swept away by the music he created, even more so now that she understood from whence came the despair she heard in the sorrowful notes. That she was attracted to him was undeniable. What woman would not be drawn to those boyish features and magnificent eyes?

Given the transitory nature of human life, she was forced to admit that the idea of living forever did have a certain appeal. Creatures such as he cheated death, albeit at the dreadful price of subsisting on blood. The very thought of that sent chills down her spine. But it was, she supposed, an ironic victory compared to the slow, lingering deaths awaiting some mortals, like Papa she thought with anguish. Nevertheless, it would be sheer folly to think she might have a future with such a man. She would grow old and infirm and he would remain as he was now, young, robust and beautiful. In time he would come to resent her, not just as the young sometimes do of the old, but because she represented what he was not and never would be, mortal, and possessed something he did not have, a soul.

She could not fathom how it was possible to have no soul. If he was truly dead, as he described it to her, would not his soul have lingered?

A line from scriptures came to her mind. *"Then shall the dust return to the earth as it was and the spirit shall return unto God who gave it."*

Were the spirit and the soul one and the same? Was not the soul the life force which ended in death and was restored in the resurrection?

Papa would know of such things, but she could not very well ask him without arousing his astute suspicion. And besides, he was far too ill to trouble with her foolish wonderings.

She doubted Aunt Vivienne had given it any thought at all.

Perhaps the Anglican priest who had given the sermon at her mother's funeral could explain it to her. But there was more at stake here than just a lost soul, and she dared not reveal as much to a priest and risk excommunication. To be excluded from the communion of the faithful, to be unable to participate in church activities or to receive the sacraments would be akin to the damnation to which Nicolae was eternally committed.

And then she remembered something he had said the night he revealed to her that he had no soul and she had asked with incredulity how such a thing could be.

His angry words came back to her now. *How the hell should I know? Go ask an alchemist.*

Yes, an alchemist. That was it.

With this thought in mind she removed her papa's violoncello from its case, positioned the end pin at the bottom and set it on its stand, then withdrew the bow and laid it across the seat of the hardbacked chair, all the while her mind working feverishly to plot her course of action. Where was she going to find an alchemist?

It dawned on her that Edmund had mentioned he often bartered lead for finished flagons with an alchemist. Her pulse began to race. More than the answer to Nicolae's dilemma of a lost soul was the possibility she had never considered that an alchemist might provide an elixir for poor Papa.

She searched her brain, trying hard to recall if Edmund had ever mentioned the alchemist's name or where he lived. No, she was sure he had not. Her pulse raced with uncertainty. She had neither seen nor heard from Edmund since the day she had gone to his shop to tell him that she was calling off their bethrothal.

If he had any regret over it, he might have shown up at her house and asked her to reconsider, but he hadn't, leading Pru to conclude that, despite the anger and bad manners he had displayed that afternoon, he was no longer troubled by it. Was he approachable now? There was only one way to find out. She grabbed her cloak and rushed from the house.

***

"No, miss, he ain't in today," the young apprentice answered when Pru arrived at the shop and asked to see Edmund.

"I see." It was just as well. If the need arose, she would have used Papa as an excuse for asking about the alchemist, but she had no wish to see Edmund, after all.

She hesitated, and peered up at him from beneath the brim of her bonnet. "May I ask, do you know of the alchemist with whom he barters?"

"That queer chap over in Clapham? Oh sure. Name's Cavendish. That bloke gives me the creeps, with those beady little eyes and pinched face, always lookin' like he's been suckin' on a lemon."

Pru had seen that face, here, in this very shop. He'd been on his way in as she'd been on her way out. "Thank you, sir, you've been very kind."

"Aye, miss. I'll tell the master you was here."

"Oh no, please don't. I'd rather keep this just between us." She offered her sweetest smile but no further explanation.

The boy looked into her bright blue eyes and his freckled face broke into a smile. "Oh, don't worry none, miss, I won't tell him."

At the house in Clapham Pru gave several raps with the pewter knocker, recognizing the mark on the underside as Edmund's. A severe-looking housekeeper answered the door and spoke not a word to her as she showed her inside and pointed a boney finger toward a door that led to a back staircase.

The heavy oak door creaked eerily on its hinges when Pru grasped the knob and pulled it slowly open. Before her was a great dark empty space.

A sliver of light fell upon the top step and she realized that rather than going up, she was meant to descend to the depths of the house. She swallowed down the lump of apprehension in her throat and slowly proceeded down the narrow, winding stairs. With no light to guide her, she braced her hands against the walls on either side and felt her way along, stepping carefully as she wound her way downward.

Gradually there appeared a faint bluish light tinting the narrow staircase. As she descended the last curve it grew brighter, bathing the walls in an unearthly light. When she reached the bottom of the staircase, she found herself standing in a small dark antechamber. At its far end was another door that stood partly ajar. From its scant opening spilled the strange blue light.

Pru approached cautiously, eyes sweeping the darkness for any sign of treachery. Licking the dryness from her lips she placed her fingers ever so lightly on the door and pushed it open, just enough for her to pass through.

At first, it appeared that she was standing in a dungeon. It filled her with dread and the impulse to run. Choking back her fear, she looked around. The walls were built with shelves from the floor to the low-hung, rough-beamed ceiling, each shelf crammed with books, more books than she'd seen at the lending library. Vats of pulsating liquid bubbled and boiled in the corner. On a table before the bookshelves strange glowing vials stood erect in a receptacle. Others lay carelessly about. The smell of sulfur hung in the air, stinging her nostrils. Beneath it, like an undercurrent of hope, the sweet smell of holy water.

Into her mind sprang the vision of a wizened, white-haired wizard, cackling over the bubbling pots, chanting secret formulas, a demented, obsessed charlatan. She began to back away slowly, regretting the foolish impulse that had brought her here, when a voice from the shadows froze her in mid-step.

"Some men conceive of wisdom only when it comes in the form of a clergyman delivering a sermon in a church pulpit. To others, if a man does not conform to the laws of society, he cannot be taken seriously."

A figure emerged from a shadowy corner. "I, on the other hand, subscribe to neither precept. I am free from the solemnity to which men of religion and philosophy are burdened."

He approached her and gestured around them.

"What you see here is the product of my free thinking. I have long suspected that human life may have a duration longer than ordinarily attributed to it. It is the negative activity placed upon our nerves and the acid of our fears that consume the body. If we were able to rise above our emotions, suppress the anger, control the fear, we might be capable of living far longer than we do. Of course, it's all just a theory, but if I were able to stop the workings of the human clock during sleep, I could prevent the wasting of the energy it takes for our hearts to beat and our lungs to breathe and thus prolong life. Do you see that?" He pointed to a jar in which was suspended in liquid the head of a rat.

Pru's stomach heaved.

"I was able to stretch that creature's life tenfold. It died a ripe old age. I have preserved its brain in a salt and vinegar solution for further study." He looked away from the bodyless rat to scrutinize Pru. "But you did not call on me to learn about prolonging life. Or did you?"

Her first rational thought was that anyone contemplating a life in alchemy instead of a steady trade had only to glance at Simon Cavendish to be disuaded from the notion. "Mr. Cavendish," she began, her voice scratchy with fear. "My name is Prudence Hightower. My father is the music master in Folgate Street. I did not mean to disturb your...work...here."

His face registered neither interest nor disinterest. The only thing that moved was his mouth that puckered, as if he were indeed sucking on a lemon.

"My father is quite ill. The doctors are all mystified by what ails him. Each day he grows weaker for no apparent reason. I thought—"

"You thought," he interjected, "that I might whip up a magic elixir that would restore your father to good health."

"I don't believe in magic," she said.

"You're rather young to be so cynical."

"What you call cynicism I call reality. It's not magic that will cure my father. As I started to say, I thought you might know of something, a remedy perhaps, that the doctors are unaware of."

In the phosphorous blue light his face looked swollen, his eyes like small round objects.

"To the doctors, anything not learned in university is black magic," he said. "Perhaps they would not be entirely wrong." He gave a little chuckle, but when she failed to respond in kind, he shrugged, and said, "Yes, well, without knowing precisely what ails your father I am at a loss, you understand, to offer you anything of importance, but I suppose I could concoct something." He crooked his finger, beckoning her closer to the table.

She approached cautiously, careful to stand out of reach, in case he meant to bludgeon her to death, dismember her and preserve her brain in a salt and vinegar solution.

From a cauldron that sat beneath a plume of glassy smoke, he carefully decanted some liquid into a vial, then extracted several vials of glowing liquid from their slots in the receptacle and poured a drop of this and a drop of that into it. "This should do it" He pressed it into her hands. "Give him two drops a day, one in the morning, one at bedtime, no more than that, and see what happens."

She realized that she ought to be reasonably afraid for herself, but instead, her fear was beginning to recede. He was nothing more than an eccentric old man, she realized, somewhere between a scientist and a mystic, and perhaps a little bit of both. The liquid in the vial gleamed dully in the smoky light. She slipped it into her pocket. "Thank you," she said. She glanced around, trying to hide her nervousness.

He tilted his head at her. "Was there something else you wanted?"

"Well, yes, I...that is..." She had no idea how to begin. "I was wondering..." She ran her tongue nervously over her lips. "If you could tell me...about the soul."

"The soul?" he repeated in slow surprise. Very carefully he replaced the vials in the receptable, saying, "Theology would suggest that the soul is the part of a person that remains after the body dies. Clever of the theologians, don't you agree, to invent such a thing rather than face the possibility that nothing exists after death? But you did not have to come to me for a definition of the soul. You could have gone to any priest."

"That is true, but I don't think a priest could give me the information I seek. I was thinking more along the line of reclaiming the soul."

His puckered mouth stretched into a grin. "Now, that is much more interesting, isn't it? And whose soul would you like to reclaim? Not your own, I would hope."

"No, my soul is perfectly intact," she said. "Let us just say, hypothetically, of course, that a person thought himself to be evil…and was…dead." She bit her lip and waited for his reaction.

Those marble-shaped eyes scrutinized her with intense interest. "Well, let me see. I seem to recall something about that." He went to the bookshelf and ran his finger down the line of age-old tomes. "This one, I believe." He pulled one from the shelf, blew off the dust and flipped through the pages. "It's the account of a Russian prince known as *Upir Lichy* dating back to the eleventh century. It says the soul of the undead can be reclaimed through a Reclamation Chant. There is a minor passage here somewhere containing the chant. Ah, yes, here it is." He looked up at her. "But, of course, this chant must be spoken in a combination of Gypsy-Romani Romanian and you would need a witch for that. Unfortunately, my area of study does not include witchcraft."

"What is your opinion?" Pru asked. "Do you think it is possible to relcaim the soul?"

He tapped his fingers against the book's worn leather, and conjectured, "What is the soul? It is the principle of life, feeling and thought, is it not? It is the essential element of a human being, the emotional part. It is assumed to be a distinct spiritual entity separate from the physical body. But is it? I have done some thinking on this subject and have concluded that the soul consists of one's intellect and personality. I do not consider it to be a separate, ghostly occupant of the body. Is it possible to lose the soul through wickedness? Oh my, yes. But I do not believe that it is ever truly and irrevocably lost. It dwells within, sometimes so deeply that it is only presumed to be lost. Misplaced, you might say."

"So, it is possible," she said.

He looked at her askance, his beady eyes narrowing, and said carefully, "Perhaps. If the evil-doer were to repent. We are talking hypothetically, are we not?"

"Of course."

"Because you will note that the passage I read refers to the *undead*. If such a being were to actually exist—"

"No, no," she said, affecting what she hoped was a convincing air. "I was discussing folklore with a pupil of my father's who is of Slavic descent. He was telling me that in his country there are legends about the dead coming back to life. I found it intriguing and thought to learn more about it."

"For what purpose?" he asked.

"I am writing a novel. I hadn't meant to tell anyone about it until it was completed and I could present it to a publisher, but I feel I can trust you with my little secret." It had never been in her nature to lie, but then, she had become adept at many things that had heretofore been out of character to her. She could tell by his expression that he believed her and felt a pang of guilt in the knowledge that she had perfected the act of dishonesty.

"And what, may I ask, is your novel about?"

"It's a love story about a mortal woman and an immortal man. It's a bit unusual, I will admit, and highly improbable, but owing to the popularity of Mr. Defoe's *The Fortunes and Misfortunes of the Famous Moll Flanders*, I thought to try my hand at being a novelist."

She had indeed read the scandalous book, squinting against the candlelight after Papa and Aunt Vivienne had gone to bed. Although she took frequent offense at the heroine's escapades, she found herself regarding the unfortunate girl with compassion even when taking advantage of the kindness of others. Was committing an immoral deed out of necessity really immoral at all? Surely, such behavior could be excused by dire circumstances. Just as circumstance might excuse Nicolae's behavior, as well as the lie she told the alchemist.

"I see," he said in a measured tone. "Well, if you are in need of research materials, I would be happy to put my library at your disposal." He swept his hand toward the leather-bound books lining the shelves. "You will find a wealth of information in these."

None of which are quite so informative as a first-hand account, Pru thought wryly.

"If I may ask, what does the character of your novel look like?"

She answered hesitantly, "His hair is dark and his eyes are shockingly green. And I imagine him to have very pale skin."

"I cannot speak to the hair and eyes," he said, "but the pale skin aptly describes it. There is a word for the creature you are referring to. It is *vampire*."

Pru felt the breath smack at the back of her throat. That's what Nicolae had called himself.

"The vampire myth goes back thousands of years and occurs in virtually every culture around the world, but it has yet to appear in any current writings. Perhaps you will be the first to introduce it into the English language in your novel. The superstitions of the Slavic countries, Romania in particular, are unusually vivid."

"Then the stories my friend told me are accurate?"

"More than accurate, my dear."

"But the soul," she prompted. "Do you think it is possible to only *think* you have lost your soul?"

"Quite possible, I should think. Eastern Orthodox Christianity has very specific teachings about the relationship of the soul to the body after death and its connection to the physical body. It could be that the religion is so deeply ingrained that one would truly believe himself to be soulless."

"Thank you so much for your time," Pru said. "The information you have provided will make my novel so much more real."

He walked her to the door. "If it is reality you want, consider that the creature you write about is, indeed, very real. The undead preys upon the living, severing the juguar and draining the blood from its victims, leaving the cold, lifeless corpses to rot. It is a nasty, vile creature, but one I would give anything to meet."

Pru struggled to banish from her mind the gruesome vision of Nicolae severing jugulars and draining blood. "What would you do if you could meet such a..." She could not bring herself to utter the word *creature*. "...person?"

His face brightened and his eyes widened into round orbs. "Oh, the questions I would ask."

"You would ask questions of him? That's all?"

"If you mean would his head wind up in a jar of salt and vinegar, no, no, not at all. The information such a creature could provide would unlock the mystery of immortality. It would serve me no purpose at all to kill the thing."

For one perilous instant Pru was tempted to take him to task. Nicolae was no *thing*. He was flesh and bone, and if not alive in the truest sense of the word, he was more emotionally alive than any man she had ever met. But she quashed the impulse. She wished to be polite despite the anger simmering just beneath her calm façade.

Favoring him with a smile, she said, "Thank you for your time."

"You are quite welcome, Miss…?"

"Hightower," she prompted.

"Ah, yes. You must forgive me. I am not very good when it comes to remembering names."

Outside, Pru squinted against the daylight, shook herself and filled her lungs with the spring air. She was not offended that he didn't remember her name, just relieved to be away from that terrible, smelly dungeon and that peculiar man. The rein she'd held on her emotions deserted her as she hurried from down the street. She could not wait to tell Nicolae the news that his soul was not lost.

Chapter 13

"Not coming back?" Pru's voice sounded hollow and unbelieving.

"Yes, dear. His manservant brought this note by this morning."

Disappointment radiated throughout Pru's being as she read Nicolae's note.

The handwriting penned on the ivory parchment was neat and impersonal, with nary a curlicue or flourish to indicate it was written by the same hand that played the violoncello with such emotion. The words were spare and to the point and offered no explanation of why he was not returning.

She'd been hoping to tell him what she learned from the alchemist when he came for his final music lesson. She looked at her father with a bleak expression. "I don't understand." He was the one brilliant spot in her dreary, otherwise uneventful life, she wanted to say.

"It's likely he feels there is nothing more to be gained from his lessons," her papa said weakly. "And he would be right."

A frown marred Pru's features. That was the logical reason, but she could not help but wonder if she was the cause of it.

Did Nicolae regret confiding his dreadful secret to her? Was he angry that she rejected his offer of immortality? Or maybe, she thought with a start, he'd met someone else, a woman more experienced. It made awful sense. After all, she had scarcely known what to do. He'd had to guide her every step of the way.

She straightened indignantly. What did he expect? He knew she was unpracticed in the art of lovemaking. It must have pleased him immensely to know she was a virgin. And now that he'd taken from her the only thing of value she possessed, was he done with her?

She balled up the note and hurled it across the room. It bounced off the fireplace grate and landed on the carpet. "I'm not going to the concert," she announced.

"Pruddy, you must."

"How can I, Papa?" she said in horror. "After everything we have done for him, this is how he repays us? With a note and no explanation?"

"I suppose," he uttered reluctantly. "But perhaps you are too quick to judge him."

"I wouldn't be the first. Aunt Vivienne absolutely abhors the man."

"Your aunt has not heard him play. You have, and so you know there is more to him than what his note conveys." He lifted his head a little higher on the pillow and looked at his daughter. "Are you in love with our young friend, Pruddy?"

"Certainly not!"

"Then has he done anything that would cause this uncharacteristic display of irritation?" His gaze strayed tellingly to the crumpled note on the floor.

Pru closed here eyes, trying hard to block out all the ways in which Nicolae had tricked her. Had it been all a ruse just to take Papa's place at the concert? Was the story he told her even true, any of it? She had believed it, but was that because she wanted to or because he wanted her to? What a fool she was for trusting him, for believing everything he said, even the part about her being beautiful.

He was a lying dog. Son of a prince, indeed! Undead. What utter nonsense. But then she recalled his face the night he'd told his fantastic story. The anguished look in his eyes and the tremble in his silky voice had been too real to be concocted. And the alchemist had confirmed that creatures such as he really do exist. Pru's head swam with uncertainty. The strength seeped from her legs. She reached out her hand and felt behind her for the chair and sank into it.

"No, Papa," she said, choking back the lie.

"Then it's settled. You will attend the concert."

"Very well," she said with a sigh of resignation. "I'll ask Aunt Vivienne not to go out that evening so she can stay with you."

"Take your aunt with you. Gladys has agreed to stay with me until you return. Oh come now, Pruddy. Why the long face? I do so long to hear him play, but as I cannot, you must act as my ears."

The candle on the bedside table flickered from the exasperated breath she expelled. She would attend the concert, but only for Papa's sake, certainly not for that scoundrel's.

Who did he think he was, treating her like a common trollop, then pretending to care what she thought of him? He was a scoundrel for the callous way he had used her. Wasn't he afraid that she would reveal his secret to the world? Or was he so arrogantly confident that no one would believe her? Simon Cavendish would believe her. She was of a mind to march over to Clapham in the morning and tell him where he could find his vampire.

Pru's whole body shook with humiliation. He must have thought her an easy mark for the way she succumbed so shamelessly to his prurient pursuit. Had she been nothing more than a gullible virgin to him? Never in her life had she felt so completely stupid. Not even Edmund's uncharitable assessment had affected her like this. Edmund. Her mood soured even further when she thought of him. What would Edmund think if he knew how she had debased herself for the sake of passion? No doubt, he would laugh in her face.

***

Edmund de Vere was not laughing. In the pale moonlight bathing the wharf he stared at the corpse that lay crumbled on the muddy ground. He knelt on one knee and touched the pale, dead flesh. It retained a glimmer of warmth. This was a fresh kill, no more than an hour old. Turning the head to one side, he noticed a streak of red on the neck, and smudging it away with his thumb, saw two deep puncture wounds, like two hideously gaping little mouths, the calling card of the living dead. The creature that loved the darkness was once again only steps ahead of him. He'd been too late to prevent this killing. Too late to hear the dying cries of this latest victim. Too late to catch the beast gulping down his sanguinary meal.

Edmund's patience was wearing dangerously thin. Thoughts gathered around his head like moths. Where was the creature hiding? Was he watching from the shadows? Brooding behind his mortal-looking façade? Laughing at him? Instinctively, Edmund's fingers touched the crucifix suspended by a leather thong about his neck and then slid to his breast pocket which held the thin wafer he had stolen from the tabernacle. With this protection he was safe from the monster, but the rest of humanity was not. Something had to be done. He had thought long and hard about this, and had come to the conclusion that there was only one person he could think of who could help him catch the fiend. His thin face was tense with purpose as he snatched the bag that held the killing tools and stalked off toward Clapham.

***

Simon Cavendish studied the pewterer. The full moon that struggled to break through the fog threw a misty blue light into the room and over the tight curls of the man's white wig that peeked from beneath the tricorn hat that sat askew on his head as though it had been slapped on in a hurry.

The alchemist's gaze moved to the black bag clutched in his hand, much like a physician's bag, only larger and heavier, and then settled on his face that was a mass of tension, with lips stretched thin and nostrils slightly flared.

"I must ask you to keep what I am about to tell you in the strictest confidence," Edmund said.

Cavendish ceased tapping his fingers on the arm of the cabriole-legged sofa upon which he sat, and replied, "You have my word that I shall not breathe a word of it to anyone."

Licking his lips anxiously, Edmund said, "The memory I carry has been handed down to me from my ancestors."

"Memories are such fragile, fleeting things," Cavendish said, "and not altogether reliable. Yet they also possess the power to sustain us. It would appear from the look on your face that your memory has sustained you to the exclusion of everything else. Do go on. You have piqued my curiosity with this memory of yours."

Edmund swallowed down the lump in his throat. "Most families carry treasured memories of their ancestors' smiling, happy faces. The images I carry are of my ancestors being burned at the stake for heresy. But there is one in particular, of Philippe de Vere, slumped over his desk in his study, eyes staring vacant, a bloodless corpse. That was two hundred and fifty years ago."

"Bloodless, you say?" Cavendish leaned forward urgently.

"Puncture wounds on his neck. Here." Edmund jabbed two fingers toward the spot on his own neck. "His body had been drained of every drop of blood." There was a deep pause as Edmund turned his face to the wall. "You may well ask what kind of creature…thing…would cause such a gruesome death."

Into the hushed stillness one scratchy word issued from the back of the alchemist's throat. "*Vampire.*"

Edmund whirled to face him.

"I know all about vampires," Cavendish said.

A look of wild relief washed over Edmund's features. His breath came in rapid bursts. "Then you know how dangerous they are."

"Oh yes. It's quite well documented. Not so much here in England, of course, but when a myth appears in virtually every culture around the world, you have to wonder if it is really myth."

Edmund's face flushed. "I am greatly relieved to know that someone other than myself here in London knows of the creatures' existence. Will you help me, then?"

"To do what, my dear man?"

"A vampire is roaming these streets."

"I know. I have been reading accounts of some very curious murders and had my suspicions."

"No one is safe from the fiend. Just tonight I discovered another of his kills, a bloodless body on the wharf. He must be destroyed."

"Or captured."

"*What?*"

"Think of what we could learn from him."

"You cannot catch the thing," Edmund said, aghast. "It would destroy you before you could learn a damn thing from it."

Cavendish raised a finger to the air. "Not necessarily. If I were to concoct a potion to render it immobile and subdue it and lock it up without any means of escape, I could perform some experiments that could very well unlock the mystery of immortality."

"You're mad," Edmund exclaimed. "There are no chains that could hold it, no bars that could imprison it. It has the strength of a hundred men and would break loose and snap your neck like a twig."

"But that is what you are here for, isn't it? A potion to render it immobile so that you can slay it?"

Edmund drew a little closer and dropped his voice to a conspiratorial whisper. "I have in mind a poisonous mixture to be ingested by some derelict, and when the creature drinks the tainted blood, it will be rendered immobile long enough for me to destroy it. But the potion must be undetectable to even the most acute sense of smell and leave no trace in the dead body."

"Capital idea," Cavendish said. "I will strike a bargain with you. First, we will capture the thing and subdue it. Yes, yes, I know how strong it is. We will figure out a way to imprison it. And when I am finished conducting my experiments and have obtained from it the secret to immortality, then you can do whatever you want with it. No doubt you carry an arsenal of methods by which to destroy the creature."

He rose from the sofa and took a step toward the black bag. "May I?"

Edmund held back, drawing the bag closer to his body, but reluctantly relented, handing it over to Cavendish as if he were handing over his own first-born son.

Cavendish opened the bag and squealed with delight when he saw its contents. "Hawthorn stake. Sword. Mirror. All blessed, no doubt. Very well stocked, indeed. Have you given any thought as to how you would actually destroy the creature once it had ingested the tainted blood?"

"I thought to place it in the sunlight."

"Sunlight will not kill it. You have been swayed by the folklore."

"Then I will inject it with holy water."

"If the thing were to regain its strength, you would not want to be near it. That would also rule out extracting the heart. Aside from the fact that it would be very messy, you would then have to boil it in oil, or wine would do. You could behead the thing, but you would want to avoid splattering the blood. Fire has the power to purge evil. Just as fire was used to save villages from the Black Death, it can be a most effective method to destroy the undead."

Edmund eyed him suspiciously. "How is it you're so knowledgeable about these creatures?"

"Immortality is at the root of my studies. I have made it my business to know."

"And you do not fear them?"

"I assure you, I wholeheartedly fear them. But I take precautions. Look around you. This room is filled with candles. An abundance of light deters them, and these candles have been blessed." He snickered. "I may be intolerant of religious rites, but I'm no fool. I also keep this on my person." He slipped his hand into his pocket and withdrew a vial of dark liquid. "Appeasement with blood is rarely useful, but it can stall for time until dawn arrives. The rooms of this house are adorned with holly, and you may have detected the aroma of incense, the Eastern variety. I am well protected."

"I'm impressed," Edmund said. "You know your subject."

"Not as well as you do, perhaps. But you have not told me why you are searching for this thing."

"My ancestor."

"Ah yes, Philippe de Vere," Cavendish said in a skeptical tone. "You are avenging the death of an ancestor who died more than two hundred years ago? With all due respect, I think it is more than that."

Recalling the oath he took as first born son of a first born son to keep the mission of the Sanctum secret, Edmund said simply, "I am not at liberty to say."

"I see. And I suppose the contents of your bag are not the tools of a sanctioned vampire slayer? Don't worry, your secret is safe with me. But remember, the strength of the cross you wear around your neck rests not in its substance but in the power it emanates, magnified by the faith of the wielder. Without a firm belief in the triumph of good over evil, it is effective only against the weakest of the undead."

"You doubt my belief in what I am doing?" Edmund questioned with sharp annoyance.

"Not at all. I merely question whether it is for the purpose of thwarting evil or for a personal vendetta. Tell me this, is it all vampires you seek to destroy, or just this particular one?"

"I have destroyed others, but this one is killing people on these very streets. It must be stopped."

Cavendish shrugged. "From what I have observed, it appears our immortal friend kills only the, how shall I put it, dregs of society. He does not drink the blood of the innocent. I suspect he has retained a naiveté despite centuries of killing and feasting."

"My ancestor was an innocent," Edmund said flatly.

"Perhaps not as innocent as you think. The passage of centuries does tend to muddy the picture."

"So?" Edmund said impatiently. "Do we have a bargain?"

"Yes. I will prepare a potion. But remember, I get him first. Then you can do whatever you want with him. Although I must say, your plan for the creature is far more realistic than the young woman's."

"What young woman?"

"The one who came to see me. She plans to write a novel, a romantic tale about a mortal woman who falls in love with a vampire, if you can imagine such a thing."

"A vampire? That's what she called it?"

"Well no, but the protagonist she described certainly fits the description of the undead."

"What did she want from you?"

"She had questions about the soul, or rather, the loss of the soul and if it can be reclaimed. I told her that as far as I know it depends on the circumstance and what you believe."

"How did she know that a vampire has no soul?"

"She said a pupil of her father's told her about the folklore of his native land. In any event, my explanation seemed to satisfy her."

"Did she say who this pupil was?"

Cavendish shook his head. "A musician I should think, since her father is the music master."

Edmund's insides turned cold.

"She asked for an elixir for her father who is ill. I gave her something to appease her, but I doubt it will work."

The slow churning in Edmund's stomach grew to a furious roil. "What was her name?"

"Her name, now, let me see. I'm so bad at that sort of thing. But I do recall seeing her before, coming out of your shop, as a matter of fact."

The blood left Edmund's face. "Prudence?"

"Yes, that's it, Prudence. I don't recall the surname."

"Prudence was asking about vampires?"

"Yes, for her novel, I told you."

"Did she say what the vampire of her novel looks like?"

"Well, let me see. I seem to recall she said he has very pale skin. No stretch of the imagination there. And dark hair. And his eyes were, oh yes, I believe she described them as shockingly green."

The owls called from their perches in the eaves of the house, but the sound was lost on Edmund who struggled to hold back the tide of his furious thoughts. It was intolerable to think that Prudence actually knew that fiend. But how? Good Lord, was that the reason she had called off their engagement? Questions dive bombed at him like a flock of furious birds. The sense of humiliation that swarmed over him was unbearable. Humiliation and disbelief and red hot rage. He realized that he had begun to breathe too fast, but he could not control the frantic rise and fall of his chest as the dead weight of realization sank into his being. His vision clouded and turned black. All noise around him ceased. For several precarious moments he felt as though he had been rendered unconscious, yet by some miracle he remained upright.

He emerged out of the dark swoon and gradually regained his senses. The light in the room weaved and bobbed, throwing thick shadows across the walls. A floorboard creaked close by. He flinched when a hand touched his shoulder, reminding him that he was not alone.

"My dear man, are you all right? You are as white as milk."

Edmund blinked and gave a short nod of the head.

"You gave me quite a start there," Cavendish said. "Can I get you something to drink?"

Edmund tested his voice. "How soon can you have the potion ready?" It was level enough to disguise the fury he was feeling.

"It will take me a few days, a week perhaps, to come up with the right combination of ingredients. I will call at your shop when I have something for you. But there is one thing I am not clear about which perhaps you can clarify. How can you be certain the creature will feed from the derelict you infuse?"

Edmund turned and strode to the door. "Leave that detail to me."

Outside, he drew the thick, sea-coal scented air into his lungs and smiled with sly relish at the ugly coincidences of life.

A music student, of course. An entry in Philippe de Vere's journal had attested to the beauty of the creature's music, in hideous contrast to its evil nature. And throughout the course of his pursuit he had heard stories about its music. He just never thought it would fall into place like this. It was all too convenient. And Prudence knew the creature for what it was. Why else would she have gone to the alchemist seeking answers about the soul? That she would prefer that thing to him was an insult beyond imagining. And to think he had almost made her his wife, vile slut that she was.

His plan to infuse several worthless vagrants with the alchemist's deadly potion in the hope that one of them would catch the attention of the monster had suddenly changed. Why take the chance that the insidious thing would bypass one of the infected bodies when there was one body in particular it was not likely to ignore? Edmund chuckled deviously as a new plan emerged. He would use Prudence as bait to lure the creature to its doom.

Chapter 14

"*E*dmund! This is a surprise. What brings you here?"

He removed his three-cornered hat, and said, "I came to inquire about your father."

"Do come in."

He followed her into the candlelit parlor. "How is he?"

Pru could not help but notice his sorry rigging. His wig was mussed, like that of someone who has rushed down the street. The long line of narrowly spaced buttons on his coat was undone. His shirt of Holland linen was rumpled, his breeches and stockings had dark stains at the knees, and there was mud caked on his buckled shoes. She was tempted to ask him where on earth he had been, but realized that she didn't really care.

"Not well," she answered.

"I'm so sorry," he said. "Is there anything I can do?"

Something in his tone did not ring true. Pru lifted her gaze and looked at him forthrightly. "There is nothing anyone can do."

"You are looking tired, Prudence," he observed. "Are you all right?"

"The thrust of Papa's care has fallen on my shoulders since he has taken a curious objection to Aunt Vivienne's help."

"She does have a knack for trying the patience of the heartiest of souls," he said.

Aside from the unpleasant remark he had uttered that day at his shop, Pru had never known him to be unduly mean-spirited and was quite frankly surprised by his uncharitable, if not accurate, assessment of Aunt Vivienne.

Ignoring the sarcasm, she said, "You need not worry about me, Edmund. I'm quite all right."

"You know, Prudence," he began, "we parted in the most unfortunate way. Since that day you came to see me some weeks ago, I have been tossing on a sea of regret."

Pru's stomach lurched. Was he here to make amends? She hoped for his sake that he was not.

"My foolish pride spoke too harshly."

"We both said things we should not have said," she conceded.

"Do you think—?"

"I think it would be unwise to say any more," she interrupted. "It's better that we part as friends than…whatever the alternative might be."

"Of course, you're right. And I'm greatly relieved that you harbor no ill will toward me. We might even see each other socially on occasion. Perhaps you would join me for coffee at Mrs. Rochford's Saturday afternoon? As friends," he hastened to add.

Was it her imagination, or did he seem just a trifle too eager to renew their companionship? Something about it troubled her, but she could not put her finger on it.

"I'm attending a concert at Vauxhall Gardens Saturday evening." Pru was relieved that the truth spared her from a lie. "There are things I must tend to during the day."

"I see," he said stiffly. "Is that the concert at which your father was going to perform before he took ill?"

"Yes. One of his pupils will be taking his place. He will be performing a rhapsody co-written with Papa. But then, you've never been much interested in music, have you?"

His mouth tightened. "No, I haven't."

"That's a pity," she said. "He's quite remarkable."

"I shall have to meet him some time."

Pru's pulse quickened. "That's not possible," she said, a little too quickly. "He's very private, and busy, and impossibly shy around strangers." It was not a complete lie, she reasoned, but far from the truth.

An uncomfortable silence settled over the room.

"I believe we have a mutual friend," Edmund said at last, breaking the static tension in the air.

"Oh? Who would that be?"

"Simon Cavendish."

Pru's lips compressed into a thin line as her calm deserted her. Had Edmund's apprentice betrayed her confidence? His stare unnerved her. Why was he looking at her like that?

"I take it the elixir he gave you has not worked."

Inwardly, Pru blanched. So, he had learned of it from the alchemist himself. What else did he know? She took a deep breath. "Papa's fate is in God's hands now."

She watched his face carefully, searching for a sign that he knew her secret, noting the little quivers of tension that flitted across his features. She stood straight despite her wariness and hoped her thoughts did not show.

Her boned stays were feeling impossibly tight, restricting her breath. In an attempt to keep her voice as level as possible, she asked, "Did he mention anything else?"

"No. What else would there be?"

"Nothing. Nothing at all. I was upset that day, about Papa, you understand."

"Of course I understand. And I would like nothing more than to help you, if you will permit me. Getting out will do you some good. Do say you will join me, if not Saturday then another day soon. Trust me, Prudence. I have only your best interests in mind."

Pru's formerly stalwart sensibilities had taken on a feral quality, like those of a forest creature that senses a danger it cannot see. And then it came to her, the thing about him that she'd been unable to define. He was lying. She saw it in the way he grasped his earlobe as he spoke to her and how his hands, ordinarily so animated, had gone suddenly still. Her skin grew clammy beneath her smock and a small voice at the back of her mind cautioned her to be wary.

"You're very kind, Edmund, but I don't think that will be necessary."

He lifted an iridescent glass inkwell from the desk, ran his fingers over the brass inlay and placed it back down. "Then it appears we have nothing further to say to each other."

It was only after she had walked him to the door and closed it behind him that Pru let the air trapped in her lungs out in one long, low whoosh of relief.

"I do hope you had the good sense to reconcile with that young man."

Pru rolled her eyes at the sound of her aunt's voice. She was in no mood for reproaches. Turning, she saw her aunt gliding down the narrow staircase in a swish of Spitalfields silk. In a deep blue mantua with a closed petticoat and open-fronted bodice she managed to look wellborn despite their middling class. The rouge she had daubed on her cheeks made a pleasing contrast to her pale, powdered face. She paused at the mirror at the base of the stairs to admire herself.

"Fashion must be obeyed," Vivienne said, patting the complicated style into which she had arranged her hair. "I allow myself the hot tongs and white powder, but I draw the line at having my hair larded. I prefer to catch the attention of men, not hungry mice."

"Going out, Aunt?" Pru ventured.

"Of course. I've met the most delightful gentleman. We are dining out and then we are going to his house. He plays a marvelous game of dominoes."

Dominoes, indeed! Pru was tempted to say, but held her tongue.

The lace at her elbows fluttered when Vivienne flicked open her paper fan and waved it before her face. "So? Have you?"

"Have I what?"

"Reconciled with him?"

"I have not."

"Prudence—"

"Aunt, please. You rule your life. I rule mine."

Vivienne frowned. "Very well," she said tersely, "but if you will not commit yourself to a proper marriage, then do not consign yourself to a life void of love."

Pru's temper flared. "You call it love? Falling into the beds of men you hardly know?"

"Love. Pleasure. It's all the same thing. If you are waiting for one true love, I'm afraid you are going to be much disappointed."

Pru met her aunt's gaze without flinching. "I wish you joy with whomever you choose to couple with. I will know my one true love when he comes."

With a dismissive laugh, Vivienne said, "How can you know the one when you have not tested others? By what will you compare him to? Men place a high premium on virginity, but I assure you, it is much overrated. Men will even overlook the absence of it when properly pleased."

Pru face suffused with anger. "We are made of different stuff, you and me."

"You refuse to take that which is rightfully yours?" Vivienne demanded, her eyes flashing with fire. "To go the way of all womankind?"

It's not true, Pru wanted to cry. She knew about the pleasures of the flesh. She'd been taught by a master. She bit her lip to keep from shouting the truth and looked questioningly at her aunt. "All womankind? You sound like something from the dark ages." She could not keep the caustic tone out of her voice.

"You think that much as changed since then?" Vivienne laughed harshly. "Men like to think of themselves as the superior sex, but let me tell you, Prudence, since the time when the earth was young it has always been women who ruled."

Pru stood transfixed. More and more these days her aunt's changeable moods were becoming erratic. Her eyes were sweet and loving one moment, wild with undisguised vehemence the next. "Despite the sheer numbers of your lovers, it is obvious that you are not happy here. Perhaps it is time for you to return to Paris. Excuse me. I must see to Papa. Enjoy your evening."

"Oh, I shall. And Prudence, you mustn't mind me. Women go through, what shall I call it, changes, when they reach a certain age. It's nothing more than that, I assure you. Good night, dear."

Despite the coo in her aunt's voice, Pru noticed that the fury had not dimmed from her eyes and was glad when the door closed behind her.

***

A figure lurked in the shadows, eyes glowing with an unearthly fire.

Goddess, Mother, how long must I endure this suffering? Why am I judged by the morals of mortals? When will you free me from this worthless shell and restore me to myself?

The rain that had been coming down in fits and starts all day was now coming down in earnest, running over her face and soaking her to her flesh.

The slow, plodding hoof beats of time carried her back, far, far back to a place almost beyond memory, to another rain-soaked night, to the smell of sputtering torches and the wet fur of the howling dogs that chased her through the woods. The wagons and drays that made such a hideous sound on London's cobbled streets could not drown out the sound of her own screams tearing from her throat and the cries of "Death to the witch," that still rattled in her brain.

She had inherited her mother's skill of enchantment and for that she'd been branded a witch. But it was for taking her pleasure with a girl that she had been sacrificed that terrible night so long ago. Worse than the blood ritual with its offerings of herbs, mead and cakes was the music. The *ollamh re ceol*, the master musician, playing his harp to lure her toward the forest where the others waited. And then the same notes played over and over again as she writhed on the stone altar, the keening, the death song, resounding in her brain even now, a thousand lifetimes later. Gods above, how she hated music, all music.

Her fiery eyes strayed to the candlelit windows of the house in Folgate Street. At least the old man was not still making his infernal music. She'd seen to that. But she was not finished with him yet. She would make him pay with his mortal life for the life that had been stolen from her. A life for a life. She could have taken him in the blink of an eye, but that would have been too easy, and certainly no fun. Like a cat she toyed with her victims, slapping them between her paws until there was no more life left in them. The old music master was merely the latest in a long line of playthings to meet their doom at the hands of her wicked vengeance.

Through a thousand lifetimes of regret and despair she wrecked havoc on all who crossed her path, leaving a swath of destruction in her wake. When she was finished with the old man, she would move on to another. Who knew? Perhaps that simpering daughter of his would be next. With that thought in mind, a savage sense of triumph swept through Lienore as she hurried off into the rain-soaked night.

Chapter 15

"You go on, dear. I see an old friend I want to say hello to."

Pru glanced in the direction her aunt was gazing. Across the crowded walk a man was smiling back. He was tall, handsomely dressed, and impossibly young. Another of her aunt's many lovers, she supposed, as she watched Vivienne glide away. It was not likely she would see her aunt for the rest of the evening, but that was all right. She had brought Vivienne along only because Papa had insisted on it, but knowing her dislike of music in general and of Nicolae in particular, it was just as well that she amused herself with her young lover.

At the gate Pru delved into her pocket, paid the one guinea admission to the tea garden and entered an enchanted world laid out into avenues and covered walkways where crowds of people strolled up and down. The walks were lined with tents in which wine and snuff and almost anything else was sold at very dear prices. Fountains splashed, colored lights glittered in the twilight, and ladies walked unaccompanied dressed in their finest gowns with gold watches hung around their necks.

Before her was a grove from whose treetops sang a choir of birds, and spreads of flowers gave the place a wild, untouched look, their magical fragrance in the air all but obliterating the smell of the oil lamps. Passing through a triumphal arch she came upon a statue of Handel. Beyond it, illuminated with the luster of crystal glass, stood the orchestra.

Pru's heart gave a thump in her chest, not only for the elegance of its decoration, but for the thought that in a short time Nicolae's music would stream forth into the garden and fill the spring air with its unparalleled beauty.

She found a seat in the second row where she would have ample view of the musicians. But there was really only one musician she wanted to see and hear. Flicking open her fan, she fluttered it before her face while she waited.

Members of the orchestra walked on stage and took their seats. As if on cue, hundreds of candles enclosed in crystal glasses were lit. The air was still and sweetly scented with the fragrance of the gardens' flowers.

A little breeze fanned the leaves as the orchestra began to play one of Handel's cantatas. Pru smiled. She could just hear Papa complaining that Handel adapted his style to satisfy the public because, although he ran his own company in London, he constantly struggled to turn a profit.

From there, the music progressed to an oratorio and finally to a moving concerto for viola and orchestra. It was a quiet, graceful piece, and after the viola's last trill, the work drifted off into peaceful nothingness.

The musicians stood and bowed to an appreciating audience, and then took their seats again.

The crowd settled down and the musicians grew quiet in their places. Pru's pulse began to race with expectation. Her eyes grew bright and dazzled, her head giddy when a tall, slender figure stepped onto the stage and seated himself behind his beautiful gilded instrument.

The concerto opened with a dramatic flourish, the solos alternating between the violoncello and the viola, the main theme passing back and forth between the two instruments, the viola presenting a light-hearted, lyrical section followed by the noble and stately undertones of the violoncello.

In Nicolae's hands the instrument virtually sang, sweet and nostalgic one moment, dark and menacing the next. How like the man himself, Pru could not help but think.

The piece closed to thunderous applauds.

This time Nicolae stood up with the rest of the orchestra and bowed deeply from the waist.

His gaze pierced the candlelit dusk as it searched the faces in the audience. Pru sucked in her breath when those penetrating green eyes found her in the crowd and lingered on her face for a moment. He smiled, a simple uplifting of the corners of his lips, as if some secret existed between them, and then turned away to take his seat again. It was brief, an instant really, but it filled her with a pleasure that was both sweet and fierce, a heartrending reminder of the intimacies they had shared flooding her face with color. The fan fluttered rapidly now.

She tried not to dwell on those memories, of the bruising pleasure he had given her, of his warm, wine-scented whisper against her mouth, of his voice silky soft and smooth telling her she was beautiful, of the cold press of his palm against her hot flesh. When she recognized the opening notes of Bach's Suite Number One for unaccompanied violoncello, she struggled to push the unsettling thoughts aside and concentrate solely on the music.

This was the piece her papa had instructed her to work with Nicolae on, not that Nicolae needed any guidance from her when it came to music, unlike she who had needed guidance from him when it came to lovemaking. Was there no way her thoughts could turn that did not lead back to that flood of dark hunger he had unleashed in her? That little smile on his lips when he spotted her in the audience seemed to suggest that he could read her thoughts. Was that one of his powers? Did he know how much she wanted to tell him about the true nature of the soul and hope for its reclamation? Could he guess at all the questions she had that begged to be answered, like why he had not shown up for his final lesson, and if it was because of anything she had done? But as she sat beneath the flickering light of a thousand candles, the questions fled from her mind as the music took control.

And then, the moment arrived for which she had been waiting. The tempo of the Bach Suite slowed until it became almost stagnant. A faint rustle of whisperings and uncertainty sifted through the crowd. The audience was confused by what they were hearing. Until he sounded the first note of her papa's composition, and then an expectant silence passed over the crowd. Even the birds in the treetops ceased chirping, as if they, too, felt that something magical was about to happen.

Pru quickened like lightning as the first notes filled the air. It felt as if she were hearing the piece for the first time. She closed her eyes to its rhapsodic beauty as its passion and yearning infiltrated her blood and spread through her being like a forceful seduction from which there is no escape except to yield. With its blistering energy and anguished tones, the piece moved like an ocean tide. To her papa's prayerful, meditative notes, Nicolae added his own broad, expansive tempos and introspection in a work of technical brilliance and impeccable communication, leaving her breathless. The intimacy of the piece made it feel as if they were alone in the world, just the two of them, secreted in the garret room of his house in Hanover Square, and that he was playing it only for her. She closed her eyes, drinking in the music, every nerve swaying in time to the tempo. Like a dark lover it carried her far from this place of fragrant flowers and lustrous candlelight to a bed draped in billowing hangings of silk and lace.

He played with his eyes closed, hugging the instrument against the long line of his body, the sunset playing across the dark hair that fell onto his brow. His features were harshly etched in the angled light that fell across his face. Anguish and despair radiated from him like a beacon of light warning ships to stay far out to sea lest they venture too close and crash against the perilous, jagged shoreline that was his life.

Up, up, the music lifted her, like a feather borne aloft by the wind to heights scarcely imaginable, where she tossed and tumbled and floated on the glorious currents that streamed from the violoncello. Caught up in the rapture, she was unaware that the bow had slid across the strings for the final heartrending note, until she heard the audience erupt into deafening applauds.

She opened her eyes, and through her tears she saw Nicolae rise from behind his instrument and walk to the edge of the stage.

Dark locks tumbled into his eyes as he bowed deeply. In the lingering light he removed his violoncello from its endpin and placed it in its velvet-lined case. With nary a glance back at the audience, he strode from the stage and disappeared behind its curtain.

As the orchestra began another piece, Pru jumped up from her seat and hurried from the row.

***

Tree by tree, the twilight gave way to night, until the moon glimmered through the tangled branches and the lights in the glasses twinkled like stars spread across the sky.

Nicolae handed the case off to his manservant.

"Take it home," he brusquely ordered. "Put it in the garret room."

For the first time in his monstrously long life, he could not wait to get the instrument out of his sight. Those fools had no real idea of what they were hearing or from whence came the tortured emotion behind the piece.

My God, he thought, *if only they knew for whom...or for what...they were applauding, they would stampede out of here so fast they would trample themselves to death in the process. And what a bloodbath that would be*, he grimly mused.

He hadn't played for them. He played for himself, for the sense of triumph he would feel over the mortal world. Or so he thought. Now that it was finished, however, there was no victory in what he felt, only emptiness and confusion.

Buried in the back of his mind was the staggering thought that it had not been for himself at all. It had been for her. He had been playing for her, damn it. For her pleasure. For the wondrous look he would see in her luminous blue eyes.

His body shook with anger. Why should he care what she thought? Why should he care anything at all about her? And yet, he cared enough to realize that she was in danger, not from Edmund de Vere or her own foolish innocence, but from himself.

He regretted having told her what he is, not because she did not believe him—because she did, every last sorry word of it—but because she did not truly comprehend the magnitude of it and the extent to which he could hurt her. Satisfying his physical lust for her was one thing, but sating the blood lust was something even he, with all the powers he possessed, could not control.

It was only a matter of time before her beautiful white neck and the red blood that coursed through her veins became her undoing. Yes, even someone who imagined she had seen a soul in him was not immune to his particular form of depravity.

He wanted to get away as fast as possible, from the crowds and from her. Were there not so many mortals milling about, he would have transformed himself into a bat and flown off, a feat well within his powers but which his vanity permitted him to avail himself of under only the most dire of circumstances. Bats were such ugly little creatures, after all.

He hurried down a winding path. A female of doubtful morals dressed as finely as a lady of quality beckoned to him with her flirtatious eyes and a suggestive offer as he went by. At another time, another place, he might have stopped to partake of her wares and rounded out the adventure by drinking from her delectable neck. But tonight he had no appetite for whores or blood. He wanted only to escape this place. Behind him the orchestra was playing. All around him he breathed in the suffocating sweetness of wild flowers and the cloying fragrance of lavender and rose water. Before him stood the gate to the entrance. He moved toward it now with a singular purpose.

"Nicolae!"

The sound of his name called by a familiar voice from behind froze him in mid-step. *Christ*, he thought vehemently, as he turned slowly around.

She was standing in the middle of the path, her chest heaving from having run all the way after him, her bright eyes looking all the brighter in the illumination of the oil lamps.

A transient wish flittered through his mind, that he could take her into the shrubs, drink from her heart and then tear the skin at his wrist and give her his own dark blood to drink, and then she would be like him, and they could fly away from this place together.

But he had already offered the gift to her and she had not only refused it, but had been repelled by it. In the face of that sobering reality, all he could do was watch with cool disdain as she came toward him.

Her face was clouded with questions. "Where are you going?" she asked.

As far away from you as I can get. "Home," he said.

"But—"

"Did it please you?"

"Very much. But—"

"But what?" In answer to her puzzled gaze he gave an elegantly forced shrug. "We accomplished what we set out to do. The concert is over. What else is there?"

"How can you be so cold, so indifferent? Have you forgotten our…our…" She cast about for a fitting description of what they had shared, and swallowing hard, ventured, "…friendship?"

"Have you forgotten what I am?" came his chilling reply.

She shook her head, rustling the tendrils that framed her face and glowed like tarnished gold in the lamplight.

"Then you should know why it is best if you forget our *friendship*." The strain was visible on his face as he spoke. A scowl sifted over his features like a shadow. His voice was flat. "Go back to your safe little life, Prudence, and forget that you ever knew me." His green eyes rested for a moment on her mouth, then looked quickly away.

"Forget?" she echoed, her voice brimming with incomprehension. "Better to ask me to forget how to breathe."

"You place too much stock in something that can never be," he told her. "Besides, you said it yourself, you're not in love with me. Nor I with you," he added, forcing a cruelty into his tone when what he really wanted was to take her hands in his and bring them to his lips. "I am a soulless creature. I can bring you nothing but heartache and doom."

She looked at him with blue eyes wide and solemn. "But that's just it. That's what I was going to tell you when you came for your last lesson." Her voice hardened a bit, the remnant of her wounded pride. "But you sent a note instead. If you had come, you would have learned that you are not soulless. You only think your soul has been lost. But it hasn't been. It has only been misplaced."

A dark threat blossomed in his eyes. "Be careful what you say," he warned. "Mockery brings out the worst in me, and trust me, Prudence, the worst in me is something you never want to see."

"I mock you not," she exclaimed. "It's true. I went to see the alchemist. He told me about the soul."

He tilted his head and scrutinized her. "What made you think an alchemist would know anything about it?"

"It was you who put the thought in my mind," she replied. "You said an alchemist would know about such things."

"Well?" He shrugged. "What did he tell you?"

"That the soul can be reclaimed through a witch's chant."

He laughed, but it was a harsh, contemptuous sound from deep in his throat. "There is only one witch I know of powerful enough to reclaim a lost soul. Lienore. I told you about her." His laughter dissolved into a fatalistic sigh. "But even if I did know how or where to find her, it's not likely she would help me. Our history is, shall we say, less than amiable."

He looked away as the memory flooded back. "The year was, oh, let me see, sixteen fifty-five, as I recall, at the court of Louis XIV. She was inhabiting the body of a voluptuous young creature who I happened to bed and bite. She didn't like that one bit, no indeed. Just as I was drinking the last drop, she hopped into another host, a pretty little courtier, although not as striking as the other, and proceeded to hurl the most vile insults at me, claiming I had robbed her of the most magnificent body she had ever stolen. Our little body thief disappeared, leaving me holding her beautiful but dead host in my arms. No," he said, shaking his head and staring into the night with a peculiar tightness about his mouth, "she's not likely to favor me with one of her chants."

He turned to her then, and said impassively, "Go home, Prudence. Tell your father I will send my man by in a few days to return the completed manuscript to him."

"Why are you doing this?" she asked, her voice sounding small and pleading.

"You can pride yourself in knowing that I am not always this benevolent to mortals. Go. Now. Before I change my mind and turn you into something very much like me for which you will be eternally sorry."

Pru's body went rigid, her face suffusing with anger. "I'll not go. Not until you explain why you are being so horrid to me. And after I went to the alchemist on your behalf and told him—"

An alarm sounded in his mind. "Good God, Prudence," he cut in. "Did you tell him about me? About what I am?"

"No, of course not. I would never do that. I lied and told him I was writing a novel about an immortal man and a mortal woman."

"And he believed you?"

"Yes. He was very much intrigued and said he wished he could meet someone like you."

"A novel. How, well, novel," he scoffed. "And where, may I ask, did you find him?"

"In Clapham. Edmund does business with him."

At the thought of that accursed slayer his lips curled in a snarl. "Be gone, Prudence. If you were a dog, I would throw stones at you to chase you away. Do not force me to be crueler to you than is necessary."

Her ire perished in the wake of his caustic remark, and she gazed back at him with an expression that told him she was suffering a thousand sorrows—the grief of losing her mother, the fear of losing her father, the betrayal of his nasty turn-about, the fury she felt at herself for succumbing to his lies and seduction.

He was seized by an impulse to reach forward and grasp her by the shoulders and shake her hard enough to snap her neck with the ugly truth of what he was. Instead, he just stood there with a malicious grin on his face.

"You are a vile creature," she said hotly as she fought back the tears. "Beyond vile."

It was better to hurt her now, he reasoned, this way, with harsh words and cruel lies than to take from her the only thing she possessed that was of any value—her life.

It wasn't that he did not know how to be magnanimous. After centuries of killing and feasting on the blood of mortals, he had merely forgotten. Is that what made him push her away now? Magnanimity? Oh God, he made himself sick.

"We had a bargain."

Her voice, small, spiteful, and yet unafraid, infiltrated the dark place where his self-loathing resided.

"Ah yes," he said, snapping back to the moment. "Our bargain. Are you certain you want your father to become a vile creature such as myself?"

"He could never be like you. He is good and noble, and something else that you will never be. He is loved. Nobody loves you. Except perhaps for yourself, for some mistaken notion you have of your own importance. I do believe your story, every word of it, and I should feel sorry for you, but I don't. I despise you."

So, the little chit knew how to gouge and slash as fatally as an Ottoman's *kilij*, the single-edged curving blade of her sharp tongue cutting as deeply as any saber. But he had suffered worse than this.

"I fully intend to keep my end of the bargain," he said, "but it will be at a time of my choosing, and only if you do not reveal to anyone what you know about me," he added warningly.

"Fear not," she said. "Your sordid secret is safe with me. I may be a lot of things—gullible, naïve, unworldly. But I am no betrayer of confidences. Besides," she added flippantly, "who would believe me? Only I know that you only look beautiful on the outside but that your intentions are strictly dishonest. That you are ruthless and tyrannical and bent on domination. That you are—"

"Enough!" he cried.

Heads turned in their direction.

"For God's sake, Prudence," he hissed under his breath, "shut up and get control of yourself. You're acting like a spurned lover."

The fan fell from her hand unnoticed. There was a deep pause during which her angry blue gaze struck his threatening green one like steel striking steel.

He bowed stiffly, turned around and walked away, leaving her standing in the moonlight.

Pru did not feel the flagstones beneath her feet as she staggered back. She was not accustomed to being cruel, and only now did the words she had flung at him return to haunt her. Nevertheless, that did not absolve him for his hateful behavior. The man...the creature...whatever he was...was loathsome. She literally ached with fury. She did not know him at all. The man who played music with such sensitivity and emotion had never really existed. The being whose life had been ripped from him on a snowy night in Transylvania was no longer the tortured romantic hero she had imaged him to be. But the worst part of it was, he had never pretended to be anything other than what he was, a callous, clever seducer. This was a betrayal of the most devious kind, for it came not from him, but from herself. She had betrayed herself into believing the fantasy.

"I hate him", she fumed. But it was not hatred she felt as she stood in the middle of the lamp-lit path, with people moving like blurred images all around her. It was despair, leaving inside of her a hole so deep and hollow that nothing could fill it.

Looking into his fierce eyes just now had been like looking into the eyes of a stranger, and Pru realized with a start that the man she had thought him to be was merely the man she had wished him to be.

She ran her tongue over her lips and tasted salt, and became suddenly conscious of the tears that snaked down her cheeks. People passed by looking at her queerly. If there were anything in the world she could have wished for at the moment, it would have been for the earth to open and swallow her up.

For a haunting instant she thought she had seen a wince in his eyes as she had flung her terrible insults at him. She did not think she had the power to wound him, and a rush of empathy unnerved her. She was not used to such purposeful maliciousness, although, if the truth be known, it served him right and was no more than the scoundrel deserved.

Her hands fell to her sides, and only then did she realize that they were balled into fists. What a sight she must present to the passers-by, she thought dismally. Nicolae's last words scorched her pride. A spurned lover. Is that what she was? How dreadful. How mortifying. How utterly common.

Aunt Vivienne had told her that lying down with a man would bring a joy such as she had never known, but she had failed to mention the pain that would come with it. Joy and pain, woven together on a shattered loom, such as the one that had lay strewn in broken pieces across the floor of her mother's room.

Oh Mama, where are you when I have need of you most? Would you have counseled me to run headlong into the arms of a man I do not love to experience a physical joy to be found nowhere else? Or would you have cautioned me to keep my distance at the expense of my pride? But even as she thought it, Pru knew what the answer would be. Love, and only love, was worth the pain she suffered now. Yet she would be lying to herself if she said she was in love with Nicolae. His music, his aura, his power, thrilled her in ways she had not thought possible. His cold touch on her heated flesh drove her to irrational passion. But love? How could she say it was that when she did not even know what love was? Oh yes, she loved her papa and her poor dead mama, and even Vivienne when her aunt was not provoking her. But the love a woman has for a man that binds two hearts together as one, no, that was something that seemed destined to elude her.

As she turned away and lifted her eyes from the flagstones, her dismal thoughts fled when she saw a familiar figure watching her.

He came toward her.

"Edmund, how long were you standing there?"

"Long enough."

Waves of shame coursed through her. "It's not what you think."

"Who was that man, Prudence?"

"That was my father's pupil, the one I told you about. Did you hear him play?"

"No. I arrived only a short while ago. Why were you arguing with him?"

"It was a misunderstanding. Nothing more."

"You look positively ashen," he remarked. "Did he say something to insult you?"

"No," she said. "It was I who said the insulting things." A lie and not a lie.

"There was a time when I would not have believed that of you," he said, "but you seem to have changed, Prudence. You have become, I don't know, harder, somehow."

Harder perhaps, but only because she was wiser now about the ways of men and the lies they tell. Even Edmund, standing there with a solicitous look on his face, as if her feelings were the only things that mattered, when she knew he had only his own self-serving interests at heart.

"If he treated you with disrespect, I will hold him accountable for it. But I did not get a good enough look at him. If I am to seek him out, you must tell me where he lives."

An inner voice cautioned Pru to hold back. Maybe it was the way he was looking at her, with expectation written in his eyes, or the sound of his voice, a little too eager. It seemed he was after something, but what that could be, she had no clue.

"Thank you, Edmund, but there's no need for you to do that," she said dismissively. "I'm sure he feels as badly about the misunderstanding as I do."

"Nevertheless," he said, "you appear to be quite upset. Come, I'll take you home."

"My aunt—" she began.

"I saw her leave with a man young enough to be her...oh well, none of that. Come now. I have a carriage waiting just outside the gate." He reached for her hand. "Why, Prudence, you're trembling. Never mind. I have just the thing for you. A little tonic that should calm your nerves and make you forget all about this nasty incident."

The footman jumped down from his perch to lower the steps for them to enter the enclosed cab of the carriage. Edmund offered his hand to help her and climbed in behind her.

"You know, Prudence," he said, "I came to the gardens tonight looking for you." As he spoke, he pulled the ring on the isinglass curtain beside him and lowered it.

Pru stared straight ahead, feeling numbed by her disturbing encounter with Nicolae. "Really?" she mumbled.

"Yes." He reached past her to pull down the curtain beside her.

"What are you doing, Edmund?" she asked.

"I want to talk to you without any distractions," he answered.

There was a queer note in his tone that made her look at him. "It sounds serious."

He licked his lips nervously. "It is. But first..." He reached into his coat pocket and withdrew a closed palm. "I have something for you. It will calm your nerves."

"My nerves don't need calming, Edmund," she said, growing a little suspicious.

"Oh, but they will when I tell you what I have learned about your father's illness."

Pru sat up straight against the tufted back of the coach seat. "Papa? What have you learned? Is it bad news? Oh Edmund."

He patted her hand. "There, there. Here, drink this. It will help." He opened his palm to reveal a small vial.

She drew back. "What is it?"

"Just an herbal remedy. Trust me, Prudence. It will help with what I am about to tell you."

Trust was something she no longer equated with the male gender except, of course, for her papa. Bad news? She felt the blood drain from her face. "Tell me, Edmund," she said. "You must tell me."

"Drink this first."

"I don't want to drink it. I can bear whatever you have to say."

He sat back in the seat, shaking his head. "Prudence, I'm afraid I must insist, or I can go no further with what I have to tell you."

She glanced at the vial in his open palm. It looked familiar to her, yet she could not immediately place where she had seen it, or one like it, before. For several seconds she wavered as panic clutched her. "Oh, give me the thing," she said at last.

He pulled the stopper from the vial and handed it to her. She held it to her lips, and hesitated, looking from the vial and up to Edmund's eager gaze and back again. And then she drank.

"There," she said, thrusting the vial back to him. "Now, would you please stop torturing me and tell me what you have learned about Papa's illness."

The vial disappeared back into his coat pocket.

"Why are you looking at me like that, Edmund? As if—" As if, what? She floundered for the words, but they vanished from her mind. "Oh dear. My head." Her fingers went up to her temples which had suddenly begun to throb violently. She shut her eyes tightly against the onrush of pain. When she opened them again, the whole world seemed to be spinning out of control. She tried desperately to focus on Edmund, but his face looked distorted.

"Wh—what...have...you...done?" she said between gasping breaths.

"No more than you deserve," he harshly replied.

"Why...?"

"What better way to kill a blood-drinking fiend than to bait him with the vile slut he has been fornicating with?" came his seething answer. "How could you?" he said with disgust. "You knew what he was and still you went to him." His lips curled into a detestable sneer. "I knew the instant I saw him tonight that he is the one I've been hunting. Do you know how I knew it was him?" he taunted. "His eyes. Those fiendish eyes. The eyes of a killer."

Edmund's hateful diatribe pierced Pru's consciousness like a hot iron. "No," she protested feebly. "He's not...he's not..." But her words trailed off into nothingness and darkness swooped down like a bird of prey to snatch her up in its terrible talons and carry her away.

Chapter 16

There were some good things about being immortal, but at the moment, Nicolae could not think of one of them. He was not even sure when to begin counting his life as having begun, the day he was born or the night he was made. But what difference did it make to one who had lived as long as he had, although living was not exactly how he would have characterized it. Existing was more like it.

His was a horrible, hungering existence, the pain of which only blood could appease. It was a harsh and lonely thing, bereft of friendships, deprived of the glorious light of day, robbed of the hope of ever having a wife and family. There was no woman to share his bed, only centuries of lifeless corpses from which he had fed. Cold, inanimate bodies with faces as pale as frost and crimson droplets staining their precious necks. If he possessed a sliver of guilt over what he had done to them, it was assuaged by a cavalier notion that they had experienced with him the most fantastic sexual experience of their lives. But killing the whores he bedded did little to calm the growing hunger in his heart, not for blood, nor lust, but for something whose identity eluded him.

Those who sought to destroy him—Edmund de Vere came disgustingly to mind—were after, of all things, his heart. The great seat of life from which blood issued, giving strength and vitality to the body. The destruction of his heart had been the singular goal of the de Veres for centuries, whether through staking, piercing or simply being ripped from his body with merciless, righteous force.

But what those damnable de Veres did not know was that his heart had already suffered a fatal blow, and it had been delivered not by a de Vere, but by his own cruel hand.

Loathing himself for what he could not help being was one thing, but the cruelty he had exhibited last night at the gardens was too much even for him. Prudence was right when she said he was beyond vile. Yes, yes, that's what he was. Vile and contemptuous and evil to the core. And yet, there lingered somewhere within his wretched self a conscience so deeply buried that he had long ago given it up for dead. The shame he felt for the way he had treated her was surely a symptom of conscience. Wasn't it? What else could it be?

The more he contemplated his behavior toward Prudence Hightower, the more baffled he became. He paced the wide-planked floor of the garret room, trying hard to understand why he should feel any twinge of conscience at all. He'd done the noble thing by casting her away, yet the thought of never seeing her again pierced his heart as surely as any hawthorn stake ever could.

What he felt for her went beyond the desperate need to appease his insatiable lust. It was more than the sexual gratification he derived from her warm and willing body. He was perplexed by it. After all, there had been countless warm, willing bodies through the centuries. When had she transformed from an object of sexual desire to something more? What was this feeling that was so profound he could not attach a name to it and which overwhelmed him with warmth and desire and a sweet benevolence that was too-long absent from his being?

His feeling for her went beyond amorousness, past silly romanticism and God-awful sentimentality, to a thirst that surpassed the blood thirst to which he was forever doomed. This was no mere infatuation, no casual dalliance, no fanciful longing. This was a raw and naked hunger that spread its heat into every part of his being, infusing his limbs with vibrant energy, his loins with passion like never before and his heart with a desperate, almost physical, ache. Having never experienced this before, it took a while for the realization to fully form in his mind and for his world-weary heart to recognize it for what it was. He stopped pacing abruptly and sucked in his breath.

Love.

The awareness stunned him. The thing he had been searching for since that cold, snowy night in the Carpathians and which had eluded him for centuries was now thrust upon him with such violent force that it was almost unbearable. If he could have retched it out of himself, he would have done so, just to be rid of it, so long had he dwelled in a state of malicious uncaring.

Love was for foolish mortals, not for the undead.

How had this happened to him? He had no wish to be prey to his feelings. How dare she do this vile thing to him? He hated her for it, for invoking in him a semblance of the humanity that had been wrenched from him and for which he had longed so desperately without success that he had long ago given up any hope of it. He had become accustomed to living without love. He shuddered to think where it would lead. Love led to tolerance, tolerance to understanding, understanding to kindness. And if there was anything he was not, it was kind. He was no knight in shining armor, not he. More like a tarnished angel, fallen from grace, void of human emotion, plagued by the evil that made him, driven by a hunger that defied all logic.

Whatever memories he had of a mortal life were so far distant to be all but forgotten. Now, all he had to remember it by was the miserable failings of the mortals he saw all around him. How he loathed them, with their beating hearts and sanctimonious souls. He had no wish to be like them, to experience their petty beliefs, to partake in their feeble enjoyments, to grow old and wither and die. He was far superior to them, physically stronger, with youth everlasting and powers they would never comprehend. And yet, here he was, beset by the one emotion that made him a mirror image of the mortals he detested.

He loathed this new feeling that overwhelmed him. He stormed around the garret room, his body pulsing with feral grace, cursing and reviling it. Yet try as he might, he could not banish it from his consciousness. The harder he fought it, the more deeply entrenched it became until, at last, weary from fighting, wracked with despair, a slow recognition seeped into his mind. It began like the dawn, hazy and translucent at first, then bursting over the tops of the trees with radiant sunlight such as he had not seen in hundreds of years, bringing forth a new understanding with its blinding light.

It was his heart's immortal hunger to be completely known, and in knowing, forgiven.

He hated Prudence Hightower for exposing this weakness in him. Hated her. But wait. Hatred was not the emotion that haunted him. There was a great roaring in his head. A white hot rage gripped him, piercing his flesh down to the bone. A howl of despair tore from his throat, a lonely, protracted, wolf-like sound that echoed off the walls of the garret room. He did not know how to be human, and yet the most elemental of all human emotions raged within his heart.

He loved her. God help him. He loved her.

But why her? Why that little mouse of a woman when there were so many others more beautiful and worldly whose cunning temperaments matched his? Why did it have to be Prudence Hightower, so naive in the art of lovemaking that he'd had to mesmerize her that first night, so good and kind, yes kind, despite the harsh words she flung at him at the gardens?

If only it had been one of his own kind, someone with whom he could go on his nocturnal hunts and who craved the blood feast as much as he did. But all the 'if only's' in the world meant nothing in the face of what was. And the 'why' of it was simple enough to comprehend. In all these long, lonely years of wandering the earth, of hunting and being hunted, of being called the most vile names and accused of the most foul deeds, only she cared enough to see past the hideous façade to the man beneath who suffered for his sins every day of his life. Christ, she even claimed to have seen a soul in him. And he sent her away, the only true and good thing that had ever happened to him. Gone by his harsh words and for her own good.

He glanced at the instrument that had brought them together. Its centuries-old paint and gilt glittered in the twilight that whispered through the open window. *Damn you*, he fumed. *If it had not been for you, she never would have come into my life and I would not be here now torn between need and despair.* He picked up the nearest thing, a candle stand, and hurled it against the wooden wall with such force that it splintered into a thousand pieces. Next, the chair upon which he sat when he played the instrument, and flung it into the air so high it slammed against the rafters and crashed to the floor. He moved menacingly toward the violoncello and reached for it, but stopped. He could not do it. He could not destroy the last vestige of his sanity, the only thing left that mattered.

Slowly the room returned to its previous calm. When all was still and his breathing had resumed a normal pitch, he became aware of a banging on the front door. He lifted his head and sniffed the air, but his acute sense of smell detected no hint of who was calling. Was it Prudence? He rushed from the room, his feet not even touching the winding stairs as he flew down them, a sight that would have curdled the blood of any mortal who witnessed it.

He reached the front door in less than a heartbeat and pulled it open. "Prudence!"

But it was not her. Standing there in the illumination of a street lamp was a woman whose face he did not recognize.

"Beggin' your pardon, sir," she said.

"Yes?" he growled with harsh impatience. "Who are you?"

"I'm Gladys, sir. The Hightowers' maid. My master sent me with this here note."

Master, not mistress, he noted with disappointment. "Very well, give it to me."

She thrust the note at him and hurried off into the rising fog.

Expelling a disillusioned sigh, Nicolae closed the door and carried the note to the parlor where a fire was dying in the hearth. His first impulse was to toss it into the embers, wanting nothing more to do with the music master or his daughter. He tapped the note against his palm as he contemplated what to do with it. In the end, curiosity got the better of him.

Imperative that you come at once.

Nicolae stared at the note that was signed simply JH. What was so imperative? he wondered. And why was it the music master who was summoning him and not Prudence? Was he going to be chastised for the callous way he had treated her? The sense of urgency the note conveyed hinted of more than a father's concern for his daughter's wounded pride and made the hairs at the back of his neck stand on end.

For several moments his level stare fixed on the coals, eyes glowing like green stones. He gave a desperate laugh. Did they think he was a pawn to be moved from square to square at their whim? Somewhere high in the eaves an owl hooted, and far beyond the house his sharp ears picked up the sounds rats scurrying around the wharf. A pawn, he thought dismally, as he snatched his cloak off the back of a chair and swirled it around his shoulders.

Outside, he paid no heed to the scent of blood on the wind and the age-old hunger gnawing at his belly as his boots struck hard against the cobblestones. A sense of urgency overtook him. Vanity be damned. Spreading his arms wide, he closed his eyes, and with a violent force of will called upon the terrible power of transformation.

Suddenly, his face began to take on hideous proportions, bulging and contracting and settling into a short conical muzzle. His nose flattened and points sprouted at his ears, and a grayish-brown fur spread over his body that became smaller and smaller until it was no bigger than a man's fist. In a series of rapid movements, his steps turned into short hops and his cloak took on the rough shape of wings, nasty-looking boney membranes that lifted him aloft and billowed and changed shape with every stroke he took. The moon was rising and the stars were its cold companions as the lord of the night sky winged his way toward the house in Folgate Street.

He did not expect the maidservant to answer his knock; her slow, cumbersome human body was no doubt still on its way home. But when no one else came to the door, Nicolae grew suspicious. Casting a sly look around him and seeing no one about, he moved toward the front façade of the house. Hand over hand, fingers spread and claw-like, as nimble as a spider, he scaled the brick to the second floor.

The window was thrown open, the sheer linen drapery billowed inward by the night breeze. A single candle flickered on the table beside the bed, throwing scant light into the room and the tall eerie shadow of a human form across the wall.

The music master was seated in a chair beside the bed, his head hanging, chin nearly touching his chest as though asleep. *Should I do it?* Nicolae thought. *Should I grant Prudence's wish and turn the old man into the undead?*

It would have been so easy to bite into the crinkled skin of his neck, and then drip his own immortal blood into the shocked, gaping mouth. He could feel his eye teeth pressing at his gums, not the little needle-sharp teeth of the bat, but the big, pointy fangs of the wolf, the kind with the strength to rip through skin and muscle. He hadn't fed yet tonight and imagined the music master's blood would taste like fine barrel-aged port.

"You sent for me?"

At the sound of the deep voice that issued from the shadows, James Hightower's head snapped up.

"I didn't hear you come in."

Nicolae moved smoothly toward him. "No one answered, so I let myself in."

The music master glanced toward the fluttering curtains.

"I can shut the window if the breeze bothers you."

"No," the old man said with a beleaguered sigh.

"Your note said it was imperative."

A worried expression darted across the old man's face. "Where is Prudence?"

Nicolae shrugged. "In her bedroom, I would imagine."

"Her bed has not been slept in," the music master said, urgency creeping into his voice. "She did not come home last night."

"Are you certain of this?"

"Quite."

"Perhaps she spent the evening with a friend," Nicolae suggested, but the thought that the friend may have been another man sent a bolt of jealousy ripping through him.

"My daughter would never do that." He struggled to rise. "The bed," he said. "Help me to the bed."

Nicolae came forward. He placed his hands around the old man's shoulders to assist him and was shocked at just how frail he was beneath his bedclothes.

The music master shivered. "Your hands are so cold."

With a roll of his eyes, Nicolae replied, "It is the result of an unfortunate incident when I was a boy." When the man was settled beneath his covers, he said, "Now, tell me about Prudence. Did you question her aunt?"

"Yes, of course. Vivienne knows nothing. She says they were separated early in the evening. My sister-in-law is not the most reliable sort, but in this I believe her. Did you see my daughter last night?"

Nicolae thought back to his confrontation with Prudence and a tremor of guilt passed through him. Was he to blame for her disappearance? Had she run off to nurse her wounds? "Well, yes, I did. After the concert."

"How did her behavior seem to you?"

"I'm not the best judge of that," Nicolae admitted. "Your daughter has always been a bit short-tempered with me. You have seen it yourself."

"That's because she does not know what to make of you," James explained. "But if she knew you, really knew you, I am sure her opinion of you would change."

Oh, but she does know me, Nicolae thought. *Better than anyone else on this earth. And still she hates me. Especially after last night.*

"I'm afraid I may have been the cause of your daughter's uncharacteristic behavior. After the concert, some unpleasant words passed between us. She was quite angry with me."

"What did you do or say that would cause her to lose her temper?"

I bedded her and then cast her away.

"She seemed to suggest that she wanted something more than just a tutor and pupil arrangement with me," he replied innocently.

"What's that you say? First you complain that she is short-tempered with you, and now you claim that she wants to…to… My dear boy, have you no understanding of women? If the circumstances were different, I would demand to know what your intentions are."

Dishonorable. Strictly dishonorable.

"But I did not call you here tonight to inquire into your relationship with my daughter. Prudence is missing and I need your help in finding her. So you argued. What couple does not? Please, you must think. Has she ever said anything to you about where she may have gone? The two of you have spent some time together."

More than you can know.

"She must have mentioned *something*."

Nicolae shook his head, rustling the dark curls. Inwardly, however, his anxiety was rising like steam from a boiling kettle. "I must go," he said quickly. "If I remember anything, I will be sure to let you know." He strode to the door.

"Nicolae."

The music master's frail voice made him pause to look back over his shoulder. "When my daughter suggested a…different kind of arrangement…" he said, lifting his head and picking his words carefully, "how did you respond?"

"I told her it was not possible." Even now, the truth tasted like bitter bile upon his tongue.

The music master emitted a sigh of disappointment. "I see," he muttered, and slumped back against the pillow.

On his way out, Nicolae passed the Hightowers' maidservant who was just now arriving home. He could read the question in her wide eyes when she saw him. How had he gotten here so fast? How indeed. He offered a perfunctory nod as he rushed past her.

He had not wanted to alarm the music master with his own growing concern, but now that he was alone, he could no longer conceal it. The pitch of his breathing increased to a full pant until he felt his heart hammering in his chest. Where was Prudence, damn it? By all that was holy or, in his case, unholy, he would find her. But where would he even begin to look? Suddenly, a thought slammed into his brain like a hard-driven nail. Of course! Why hadn't he thought of it before?

Once again, he closed his eyes and willed himself to transform, this time into a creature whose heightened sense of smell and superior night vision would lead him to the prey he was seeking. His boot heels clicking against the cobblestones fell silent to a soft padding sound and a light, loose, loping gait. The top hairs of his grayish grizzled coat caught the moonlight. Large ears captured the sounds of the night, sending him into the safety of dark corners when humans approached. His eyes shone like golden-yellow lanterns through the darkness. Trotting through puddles of mud, the tracks left behind on the cobblestones were of four pad prints, dog-like to anyone who did not know the true nature of the beast that passed within their midst.

Chapter 17

Simon Cavendish returned to his laboratory some time past midnight after another futile search for the creature that held the key to the great mystery of eternal life. The perpetual mist plagued the ache in his joints, and he wanted nothing more than to sit for a while and sip some sherry before retiring for the night.

He took off his coat and bent to light a candle, but at the flame's first flicker, a chilling sensation crept over his flesh. Something sinister hung in the air, accompanied by a strangely sweet aroma. He turned around, eyes sweeping the room. And then he saw the creature sitting in a chair in the corner of the room, one leg crossed casually over the other as if he had come to chat about the new Walpole Ministry.

Green eyes, hypnotic, riveting, glowed like simmering coals through the darkness. "I believe you have been looking for me." A voice as warm and smooth as decanted sherry issued from the impossibly handsome face.

Despite the heat emanating beneath the creature's preternatural flesh, an ice-cold chill careened down the alchemist's spine. He staggered backwards, upsetting the small table that stood beside the sofa, sending the candle to the carpet spread atop the floorboards.

Nicolae nodded toward it. "Hadn't you better put that out before you burn your house down?"

But the alchemist, frozen with fear, was unable to move.

With a sigh, Nicolae got up and came forward in a gliding movement to douse the flame beneath his boot. "Light another," he said. "Now!"

The force of the command snapped Cavendish out of his petrified stupor. He withdrew another candle from a drawer in the overturned table and lit it with shaking hands.

"That's better," Nicolae said. "I spend enough time in the dark."

He turned and walked back to the chair, his tall figure thrown up in relief against the wall. Sitting down, he fixed his eyes on the man's pale face.

"Fear not, alchemist. If I had wanted to kill you, you would already be dead."

"Wh—why are you here?" Cavendish asked, his voice a painful scratch at the back of his throat.

"I have come seeking information that I believe only you can give me."

"I? What could I possibly know that would be of interest to…to someone like you?"

"Go on," Nicolae taunted. "Say it. Say what I am, or what you think I am."

Cavendish hesitated. "Is this a trick?"

"Not at all. I merely want to know if you are fully aware of what *someone like me* is."

"You are a… He drew in a deep breath. "…vampire."

"Why do you whisper it?" Nicolae chided. "Are you afraid to say it out loud? Shall I do it for you? I am a vampire." His voice rose to a frightening pitch. "A vampire!" The thunderous declaration bounced off the walls and made the alchemist tremble.

When the room quieted down and the walls stopped shaking, Nicolae said, "There, that's better, isn't it? Now there is no need to hide behind false identities or pretenses."

He placed his elbows on the armrests and laced his finely-shaped fingers across his midsection. "So, as I was saying, I have come seeking information. A friend of mine has disappeared and I have reason to think you may know something about it."

Cavendish licked his lips, regarding him carefully. "Why would you think that?"

"Because my friend mentioned you to me recently."

"I see. And how is it you think I can help you?"

"Information," Nicolae prompted.

"Ah, yes. But what would be my incentive for helping you?"

In a blinding fast movement, Nicolae was standing before the frightened alchemist, his frame growing in stature until it towered over the other man. His hand reached out to catch him by the throat and lift him off the floor. Those green eyes settled tersely on the alchemist's face. "I could snap your neck in two," he said viciously. "Would letting you live be incentive enough for you?"

The alchemist's eyes bulged. His feet wiggled, toes pointing in a panicked search for solid ground. A gurgling sound issued from his constricted throat. He managed a desperate nod of the head.

Nicolae released his grip and the alchemist fell to the floor.

"If you kill me," Cavendish said, gasping for breath, "you will never get the information you seek."

Nicolae looked down at him and smiled. The expression accentuated his handsomeness, masking the underlying threat. "You are a clever one, aren't you? Very well, I will strike a bargain with you." He sauntered back to the chair and sat down.

Cavendish staggered to his feet, his hands protectively at his throat. "A bargain with a vampire? Why should I trust you?"

"Because I have something you want."

"And what would that be?"

"Don't pretend nonchalance. We both know what it is you want. The elixir." Nicolae's smile turned sly. "The very thought of it excites you. I can hear the excitement racing through your veins. I can smell it seeping from your pores. The others waste their time experimenting with lead and the morning dew, but you know that the answer lies elsewhere, don't you?"

"I have long suspected." His pounding pulse was audible clear across the room.

"I can give you what you want," Nicolae said. "Make you so famous your name will be heralded throughout the ages as the man who unlocked the mystery of life."

"And all for a bit of information?"

"Yes. Now let's stop playing games and get to the point, shall we? There is someone I must find and I believe you know where to look."

"Do you mean that with all your powers, you cannot find—"

"I'm not a mentalist," Nicolae cut in, annoyed.

"No, no, of course not. I did not mean to imply that you were. I just thought—"

"What you thought is of no consequence to me, alchemist. I have something you want and you have something I want. Will you help me find her?"

Cavendish's eyes narrowed. "A woman? Now I begin to understand your urgency. And is this woman...er...like you?"

"No. She is very much a mortal."

"She must mean a great deal to you to be making bargains with me."

More than you can know. "My bargain with you is this. In return for your help in finding her, I will give you what you seek."

"There would be experiments involved," Cavendish said. "They could be very dangerous for you. Are you willing to risk your own destruction?"

"There are no experiments in alchemy that could destroy me, you stupid man." There was contempt in the cold green eyes. "But yes, since you ask, I am willing to risk my own destruction."

Cavendish bristled, but pressed his advantage. "Very well then, I will tell you what I know. What is her name?"

"Prudence Hightower."

"I have heard that name before. Where was it? Let me think for a moment."

The silence stretched. "You are trying my patience, alchemist," Nicolae growled. "Would it jog your memory if I told you that she was the woman who came to you with questions about the soul?" He could tell by the spark of recognition in the man's eyes that the memory had returned.

"Of course," Cavendish said. "A lovely young woman, but odd."

"How so?" Nicolae demanded.

Cavendish looked at him as if the answer were obvious. "The soul?"

Nicolae replied with a negligent shrug, "She thought she was doing me a favor."

"She said she was writing a novel. I had no idea she was speaking from personal experience. I told her—"

"I know what you told her," Nicolae cut in sharply. "I'm not here to reclaim my lost soul. Oh, that's right, it's not lost, is it?" he said, his voice dripping with sarcasm. "It is merely misplaced. Now, get to the point. Where is she?"

Cavendish shrank back from the menace he heard in the vampire's tone. "I don't know."

"But you must know *some*thing. Think, man. Think! Did her visit give you any reason to suspect where she might have gone?"

"*Her* visit? Well, no." He hesitated. "But the other one's visit, perhaps."

"What other one? Do not talk to me in riddles or I will kill you as you stand there."

Trembling from the devilish passion he saw in the vampire's eyes, Cavendish said quickly, "The pewterer came to see me. He was quite surprised when I told him about your Prudence."

A cold dread seep into Nicolae's being as he looked away. "de Vere," he hissed.

"Yes, that's him. He hates you, you know. Something about one of his ancestors."

Nicolae's features were grim and dark, the alchemist's words shuttered from his vengeful thoughts as the silence lengthened. Sweeping the midnight hair from his eyes, he half turned and glared at the alchemist. "Tell me everything about the pewterer's visit."

As he listened, he felt the bloodlust rising, accompanied by the frenzy that comes with the urge to kill, not out of hunger but out of unadulterated hatred. In keeping one step ahead of the de Veres he had made a fatal blunder. With sudden clarity he realized that he had exposed his one weakness, namely, Prudence. He'd been a damned fool for thinking that her only danger arose from him. He should have known that were his relationship with her ever discovered by de Vere, he would not hesitate to take full advantage of it. And what grisly trap had Edmund de Vere set for him now using sweet Prudence as bait?

The light from the single candle gave his face a sudden cast of viciousness. "Where has he taken her?"

"I don't know," Cavendish said emphatically. "Truly, I don't. Although..."

Those green eyes turned on him like rabid dogs.

"If I were you, I would be on the alert for a fire."

Nicolae grimaced with disgust. "Was that your idea?"

Cavendish shrugged. "Fire has the ability to purge evil. My guess is, he intends to lure you to a burning building where you will find your beloved and the two of you will perish in the flames."

Having heard all he needed to hear, Nicolae turned and strode to the door.

"Wait!" Cavendish cried. "We had a bargain. Will you return for my experiments?"

Nicolae turned back to the room. "So, you want to know the secret to immortality. Very well. But experiments are really so unnecessary."

As he spoke, the candlelight flickered upon his face. The alchemist fell back in horror.

The handsome face was bloodless, the eyes like polished glass, the lips drawn back over the fang-like teeth of a wild animal, hideously long and glaringly white.

Chapter 18

*T*he click of measured footsteps against the cobblestones broke the ominous calm. From out of the strangling fog a figure emerged.

The dreary night found Nicolae wandering the length and breadth of the city, from the ever-hungry maw of the port, to the houses in Coney Street that harbored thieves and vagabonds, to the rookeries, and now here, to the narrow, unlit passageways and stinking alleys of the East End. It was a dangerous place to be. Pick-pockets, emboldened by the darkness, were not beyond bludgeoning unsuspecting pedestrians. Thieves and footpads roamed at large, no match for the few decrepit old watchmen with their antiquated lanthorns. Packs of scavenger dogs gathered at the pools of refuse thrown out from upper story windows, ready to defend their rancid meals with bared teeth beneath the glimmer of oil-dripping lamps.

With each step he sniffed the air, trying to detect the sweet scent of her, but the air was choked with cinder smoke, the rank odor of decaying garbage and the stench that came from the river.

Where was she? The longer she eluded him, the more frantic he became. The anger welled inside of him like some terrible force of nature, threatening to explode in violence that he swore would send every Londoner running for their lives. His temper rose with each futile step. A thousand fears jangled through his brain. What had de Vere done with her? Was she even still alive? The hatred bubbled and boiled until its heat was almost too much to bear, even for him, who had borne so much for so long.

Suddenly, a thief darted out of the shadows and came at him, knife in hand. Without breaking strike Nicolae thrust out his hand and strong armed him to the chest, propelling him into the air with the brute force of a hundred men, shattering his bones and snapping his neck.

He continued on without so much as a glance back, reproaching himself sharply for the way he had treated Prudence the night of the concert, the cruel, callous things he had said to her, the lies he had told just to keep her safe. But in an attempt to protect her from himself he had exposed her to an even more deadly harm. It was time to put an end to this game of cat and mouse he and the de Vere's had been playing for more than two centuries. Time to deal the fatal blow to Edmund de Vere. Senses sharpened by hatred, he prowled the sordid streets, sniffing the air that was thick with clouds of black smoke belched by coal-burning hearths.

Soon there came from deep within a familiar, dreaded sensation, faint at first, but growing stronger with every step he took. He sought to push it from his mind, but it was a determined little beast, seeping into his thoughts like water, the steady drip, drip turning into a rush of madness that threatened to drown him. The thirst. Oh God, the thirst. Reminding him of what he was and what he never would be. It grew upon him until he could no longer banish it from his thoughts, until it was all he could think about, until it devoured him much like the madness that devoured the pitiful souls at Bedlam.

Blood. He needed it. He craved it. At this moment it was all that mattered. His throat felt parched, his veins empty. Among his kind he was not old enough to feast on mortals merely to savor the taste, nor was his spirit strong enough that he did not require the fortification of the blood feast. Some day perhaps, centuries from now, but at this moment he had a desperate urge to feed.

"Hey, luv, lookin' for a little fun?"

A woman clothed in tatters approached him from out of the doorway of a ramshackle building. A crooked smile revealed a mouth of missing teeth.

"Fer a tuppence, I'll make yer wildest dreams come true. Want a sample, luv?"

With one hand she slipped the shoulder of her dress down to reveal a plump naked breast while her other hand reached between his legs to fondle him.

With scarcely a glance, he favored her with a sly smile. Putting his arm around her, he drew her close.

The solemn tones of the cathedral clock drowned out the muffled laughter coming from the dank East End alley. The doxie who offered sordid delights for a tuppence was in for more than she bargained for. For that price he could have bought himself enough gin to render himself drunk. A whore like this one that wasn't disease-ridden was a rare find indeed. He would have screwed her good, stuffed the damn tuppence down her bodice between her overstuffed breasts and been on his way. But the hunger gnawed at his belly like a wharf rat, its ever-sharp teeth driving him beyond the need for sexual gratification to something far more primal.

With one arm wound tightly about her waist supporting her weight, he bent her over backwards, exposing the column of her throat. His mouth went first to her exposed breast, to the engorged nipple that strained up at him.

"That's right, luv," she crooned. "Ya do that so good. The best I ever had. Oh!" she exclaimed when his teeth nipped her too hard. "Yer a hungry little devil, ain't ya?"

"More than you can know," came his deep-throated response.

His mouth moved slowly from her breast, licking the salty flesh that led to her throat and pausing to linger at the pulsing on the side of her neck. He could feel the blood coursing through the artery that pumped just beneath his lips, hear the rhythm of it, smell the sweet scent of it beneath the repugnant odor of her unwashed body. He was deaf to her fabricated moans of pleasure. All that mattered was the hunger, so bad now that it was a palpable pain.

The smile she gave him when she thought she'd found her mark froze upon her face. Her eyes flared wide and disbelieving when his mouth clamped on her throat and the animal fangs pierced the skin. Her body writhed and her legs shook violently, but he would not release his iron hold. He had to drink, not just to satisfy the terrible age-old hunger, but to convince himself that he was indeed as vile a creature as Prudence Hightower asserted him to be and that he'd been right to cast her away to save her from the evil that was himself. Most often, he drank like a man wandering too long in the desert, in great, breathtaking gulps, as if the means to his salvation lay in the very last drop of blood. But tonight he hesitated, and in that moment of hesitation, he was lost.

He lifted his head to take a breath and chanced to look into the whore's eyes. He froze. By the light of a random moonbeam he could see that her eyes were blue. Another pair of blue eyes loomed into his consciousness, staggering him with the memory. Visions of Prudence came back to him, each one as sharp as a knife, the burnished gold of her hair, her smiling eyes, the somber grays and browns of her dresses, the flush of embarrassment that turned her cheeks rose-red. Suddenly, he was no longer thirsting for blood. The few drops he had taken from the whore sat now like wet poison upon his tongue.

The woman was in a deep swoon, hanging like lead across his arms. He dropped her to the ground where the low-lying fog swallowed her up. Wiping the blood from his lips with the back of his hand, he stepped over her prostrate body and stumbled out of the alley.

What was happening to him? He'd never before left a victim alive. It wasn't that he was concerned that she would tell others what had happened to her—who would be crazy enough to believe it? At best, it would be assumed she'd been the target of a vicious footpad. At worst, she would be dismissed as a madwoman.

The fresh infusion of blood that he needed to strengthen him would have to wait. His face grew paler as he made his way through the streets. A shriek of laughter from a darkened corner spilled into the night. His thoughts turned back to Edmund de Vere. Where was he hiding? From the music master he had learned the location of the pewterer's shop and living quarters. When he'd gone there, a sign on the front door read "Closed", with no further explanation, and the rooms de Vere leased above the shop had been vacant, the bed unslept in. The odor of garlic hung heavy in the air. What a fool the pewterer was to think a garland of garlic was protection against a force as powerful as him.

The alchemist had said to be on the alert for fire, but the night air carried no such scent to his nostrils. In a few hours it would be dawn. Frustration tore at him. A great, mournful howl pierced the night. Windows were thrown open and frightened residents poked their heads out. But there was no sign of a wolf anywhere on the street below, only the solitary figure of a man in a dark cloak hurrying through the fog.

He arrived home and took the stone steps two at a time. He was about to enter, but stopped. Tacked to the front door was a note, its edges fluttering in a faint breeze.

What you seek can be found at the distillery.

Nicolae leaned closer and sniffed the paper upon which the note was written. His nose wrinkled in distaste and his lips curled into a snarl at the scent of lead, the kind used in pewter ware.

He swiped the note from the door with a savage gesture. With untamed grace and speed he headed in the direction of the distillery.

***

Prudence crawled painfully awake out of unconsciousness.

She tried to lift her hands to massage the pounding at her temples with her fingers, but found she could not. Opening her eyes to darkness all around her, she gasped to find rope binding her wrists to the sides of the cot upon which she lay. Her fingers clenched and her wrists curled in a futile attempt to loosen the bonds.

Her head felt like lead when she lifted it and peered down the length of her body. Through the darkness the outline of her legs showed beneath the musty woolen blanket that covered her. The air she breathed was dry and dusty at the back of her throat, and when she opened her mouth to speak only the barest semblance of a moan emerged. What was happening to her? Where was she? Why did the air all around her reek of juniper berries and the pungent smell of grain spirit?

She tried to focus her thoughts on the last thing she remembered, but her mind was clouded. It was like trying to maneuver through the London fog, with each footstep not knowing what the next would bring, like a blind person feeling her way through the darkness. And then, as if emerging from the shroud of fog, Nicolae's handsome face came to her troubled mind, green eyes blazing at her through patches of moonlight. With an onrush of pain, the cold, callous words that had issued from his sensual mouth came back to her. Her friendship meant nothing to him. Tears welled and spilled from the corners of her eyes. Oh, how she hated him.

Another intrusive memory jarred her consciousness. It was of standing alone on the slate footpath feeling utterly humiliated. And then what? There seemed to be something more, but she could not visualize it. Something hovered on the periphery of her consciousness, hidden in shadow. Someone was speaking to her, but who?

"I see you're awake."

Yes, that was the voice she'd heard. She opened her eyes and turned her head toward the voice that spoke now, and blinked.

Edmund. Oh God.

The sight of him brought on a tidal wave of distressful flashes of something she dared not remember.

By the light of the single candle he carried he looked distant and shadowy. She blinked harder to clear her vision of the cobwebs that prevented her from focusing on him. Was that a smile on his face? No, it was not a smile at all, but a sneer, a contemptuous, scornful uplifting of his lips that looked even more hideous above the dancing flame. Her face turned bone white.

In an excruciating rush it all came back to her—his odd behavior in the carriage, the vial of liquid that he insisted she drink, the bitter taste of it upon her tongue, the sudden collapse into unconsciousness. And then, nothing, until a few moments ago.

Her head spun, and her voice, husky and weak, sounded like a stranger's to her ears. "Wh—what have you done to me?"

"Only what was necessary," came his emotionless reply.

"Necessary? For what?" She tried to rise, but her bound wrists forced her back down onto the moth-eaten cot. "Why am I tied like this?" Her stomach seized and she thought she would be sick, but with each breath she took her strength grew and her temper rose. "Answer me, Edmund!"

He approached and looked down at her. "What better way to trap a rat than to bait the trap?"

Realization shot through her. He was referring to Nicolae.

"What has he done to you that you hate him so?" she questioned.

"To me? Nothing personally. To my ancestor who had the blood drained from his body, now, that's a different story."

Pru stared at him, dumbfounded. "Then you know what he is?"

"A vampire? Oh, yes. My family has known for centuries about the creatures. We have sworn to destroy them wherever we find them. This particular sadistic creature has been a thorn in my side. I've been hunting him for a long time. But I grow weary of this hunt. It's time to put an end to it when he gets here."

Pru sank back onto the cot. "We parted under very bad terms. He won't come."

"Perhaps not. In which case, I'm sorry to say, dear Prudence, you will be just another unfortunate woman to disappear off the streets of London without any trace."

A chill careened down her spine. "You would kill me?"

He gave a negligent shrug. "A small price to pay for ridding the world of evil."

"Now who is the sadistic creature?"

"I have an oath to fulfill," he said. "I do what I must."

"Even if it means killing innocents?"

"Do you think he differentiates?"

"He has no choice," she argued. "He cannot help what he is. But you, Edmund, you do have a choice. You can control your actions. You're not a killer."

"Ah, there's the rub. You're right. I'm not a killer. Not of humans, anyway. But you chose a killer over me, didn't you?"

"Is that what this is all about? Your pride is wounded? I have not chosen anyone. I choose merely to be free."

"You have changed," he charged. "You were not so argumentative before you met that fiend. You were quite content to be my wife."

"No!" she exclaimed. "You're wrong. I was never content to be your wife. I only thought I would be. He did nothing to me that was not already in my nature yet which I had suppressed for far too long. If you are angry with anyone for the failure of our relationship, Edmund, be angry with me."

"Oh, I am," he replied smoothly. "Which is why, after tonight, you will be but a memory to me. A mistake, if you will. As far as that creature goes, if he does not show up, it doesn't matter, for I know where he lives."

Pru was afraid, not only for herself, but also for Nicolae, the hunter who was now the hunted. In a voice choked with fear, she asked, "Who told you?"

"Your aunt. I was surprised that she was not out with one of her young lovers when I called at your home the night after the concert. When I mentioned your father's pupil, the one with the green eyes, she became quite agitated. At first I attributed her behavior to your disappearance, but then I realized it had more to do with that fiend than with you. She positively abhors him, for what reason, I cannot imagine, for she cannot know his true nature, unless, of course, you told her, and I sincerely doubt you did."

"Of course I didn't tell her," Pru replied without masking her disgust.

"On the surface he certainly fits the mold of one of her preferred playthings," Edmund ventured.

"My aunt is selective in the men she chooses," Pru said, coming to Vivienne's defense. "Perhaps she is not attracted to him despite his handsomeness."

"Oh, come now, Prudence. All of London knows about your aunt's penchant for young lovers. Why, she is the main topic of conversation at the working men's club. Although, from what I hear, her extracurricular activities are not limited to men, if you take my meaning."

"Edmund!"

"I am only repeating the whisperings of others," he replied innocently.

"I don't believe it. The worst thing she can be faulted with is not being the best judge of human nature. After all, she likes you well enough."

He studied his fingernails for a moment, ignoring the barb. "It would be so much more convenient if he were to show up. Two birds with one stone, so to speak."

"I told you, he won't come. Not after the way he and I parted."

"Then I shall have to come up with another plan. And now, if you will excuse me, I have to prepare a large shipment of hollow-ware for the colonies." He turned and walked away, taking the scant light with him.

"Where are you going?" she called after him. She could not keep her growing sense of panic from infiltrating her voice.

"Good-bye, sweet Prudence."

"If you kill me, it will be on your soul for all time!"

But her words flung into the darkness brought no reply.

A door closed, solid, heavy, irrevocable, plunging her into a pit of terror. Was Edmund coming back to kill her? Did he mean to leave her here to wither away and die? Her thoughts spun out of control, hazy and disjointed one moment, sharpened by fear the next. Rage flood through her. Why had she not seen him for the monster he was? It all made sense now, why he claimed he would not be around much in the evening after they were wed. He would be out hunting vampires instead. And now that he knew where Nicolae lived, he would be laying in wait. If only there was some way she could warn Nicolae of the danger that stalked him. Oh, but why should she care? He was a heartless rogue for the way he had treated her, tossing her friendship away like a piece of rancid meat. Would he even give her death a second thought?

In the whole world, there was only one person who would grieve for her, and that was her papa. At the thought of him hot tears leaked from the corners of her eyes. Poor papa, who had borne so much sorrow and was now more than likely drowning in worry over her disappearance. What would become of him if she were not there to care for him? Aunt Vivienne was growing tired of being a caretaker and would probably return to Paris, and he would die alone in his bed, just as Pru was certain she was destined to die alone on a moth-eaten cot in the darkness.

Breathe, she ordered herself. Slow, ragged breaths of air filled with that strange juniper smell entered her lungs. Now, think. There must be a way out of here. There *has* to be.

She struggled against the ties that bound her, wincing at the pain of tender flesh rubbed to rawness. There was a chill against her skin, much like when the air strikes moist flesh, and she realized with a start that she was bleeding from her struggles. Blood seeped from the raw wounds at her wrists to stain the cot.

The thought of her own blood turned to tortured thoughts of Nicolae. With every breath she took she prayed he would come, but the part of her mind that retained a semblance of rationality knew he would not. Hope was in vain. Prayers were useless. Hot, desperate tears slipped silently from her eyes and trickled down her face, flooding her mouth with salt. She made a little whimper, but the sound was lost amidst the terrified jumble of her thoughts. Staring up into the darkness, tears stinging her eyes, she wished silently to die.

The scurry of little feet threw a new terror into her. Rats were all around her, scuttling here and there in the darkness, dragging their skinny tails along the floor in their search for food. How long before the scent of her blood showed them the way to a tasty meal? How long before they began to gnaw on her flesh? And when she was finally discovered—if indeed she ever was—what would be left but an unrecognizable corpse with bones picked clean of flesh. A tremble such as she had never known went through her, shattering her sanity. She made a strange noise, a lament from a bleak and lonely place that echoed off the walls and bounced back at her. With a great shuddering breath, crying now for herself, she lay there in the sweltering darkness, too battered to care any more what happened to her.

She didn't notice at first that the scurrying had ceased and the rats surrounding her had all come to a dead halt in their tracks, until a deathly silence infiltrated her numbed mind. Opening her eyes, she strained against the darkness to hear better, but all was silent and still. Had the rats deserted her? A wave a wild relief washed over her.

And then, as if on cue, there was a frantic dashing of little rodent feet this way and that. Running in all directions at once, squeaking in terror, the rats fled. For an instant she was almost sorry to hear them go, for now she was truly and utterly alone.

Or was she?

Through the stillness came a soft padding sound. She shut her eyes tight and trained her senses toward it. Had Edmund returned? No, that was not the tap of boots on the floor. What, then? The footsteps came nearer, then stopped. Into her nostrils came the smell of fur, like that of a wet dog. A bolt of terror shot through her. Had one of the feral dogs that roamed the city found its way in? It sniffed the air, and from its chest issued a deep, rumbling growl. It was then that she began to scream.

"Prudence! Prudence!"

Not even the sound of her name shouted desperately could staunch her shrieks and cries.

Hands were grabbing at her. The coarse rope snapped like thread and her wrists were freed. With irrational fear clutching at her, she sprang up and tried to run, but those hands held tight, refusing to let go.

"No! No!" she cried.

Balling her fists she pounded at him, pummeling him with all the fury and fear and desperation that were in her, but still he would not relinquish his hold.

He held her tight against him, calling her name, softly now, like a mournful chant, over and over again, until it registered upon a remote part of her brain, and then her struggles began to subside. But it was not until she felt his stroking touch at her cheek, cold and familiar, that the realization sank into her, and she collapsed against him, sobbing.

Chapter 19

*H*e hugged her to his chest, rocking her until her trembling body grew calmer, stiller, in his embrace. Gradually, the smell of fear receded until only a scent that was unmistakably female drifted into his nostrils, accompanied by the familiar perfume of her blood.

She whimpered a little, and spoke in a soft, almost childlike voice against the rough fabric of his shirt. "I was sure you wouldn't come," she whispered. "I thought I was going to die."

"I'm here," he said reassuringly, "and you aren't going to die."

He lifted her hand and pressed a blood-moistened wrist to his lips. The ambrosia infiltrated his senses like a sugary confection. He could have taken full advantage of the circumstances and satisfied his dark hunger with the sweetest blood he had ever tasted, but a nobler impulse prevailed. He kissed the sanguinary wound and merely licked the blood from his lips.

"Edmund," she uttered, part dread, part disbelief.

"I know all about Edmund de Vere," he said, unable to disguise the vehemence that accompanied that name.

"Nicolae, he wants to kill you."

"His family has been hunting me for centuries. They are members of a secret society called the Sanctum. They fancy themselves purveyors of Christianity and are devoted to destroying all that which does not fit their definition of righteous. Within each family the first born son of a first born son is a dedicated vampire hunter. Your Edmund has become quite skilled at it."

She pushed herself away from him with a shudder. "He is not *my* Edmund," she said. "He is a detestable monster. He drugged me and brought me here to use as bait to get to you. He left me here to die and said he would seek you out and destroy you. Nicolae, you must be careful."

He smiled at her refreshing innocence. "It is he who must be careful, my sweet Prudence. He has been hunting vampires for what, twenty years at most? I have been eluding vampire hunters for centuries. I will deal with Edmund de Vere. But right now, I must get you out of here."

"What is this place?" she asked, her eyes searching the darkness.

"We are in the cellar of the distillery."

"That smell."

"Juniper barriers. Used to brew the gin."

"How did you find me?"

His thoughts flew back to the note tacked to his front door and to the impending doom awaiting Edmund de Vere. "I'll explain everything later."

"The rats," she said, her voice scarcely a breath.

"They're gone now," he assured her.

"Something chased them away. A dog, I think."

He turned his head away. "Yes," he said, losing a beat in his response and praying she did not notice. "It must have been a dog. Come, let's go."

Pru held back. "I told him you would not come. Why did you? After the things you said to me I thought you wanted nothing more to do with me."

"Prudence," he uttered, though in truth he did not know where to begin or how to explain.

He hated himself for the terrible things he had said to her. If he were a drinking man, he would have drunk himself senseless to numb the consuming guilt he felt over it. He had told her what he is and how he was made, but how could he explain what dwelled beneath the surface, the centuries of slaughter and death and bloodlust that were so much a part of him?

The only thing that mattered was the music, and even that seemed to have lost much of its meaning since the night of the concert.

There had been no joy for him in playing for an audience of pompous, self-righteous mortals. He realized that night with a start that the only person he played for was the only one who imagined him capable of possessing a soul.

Often, he thought about his life, the eternal wanderings in search of sustenance, the trail of bloodless bodies, the failed hope of ever being loved for what he was, the dashed illusion of ever being mortal.

He dared not even admit it to himself as a conscious thought, but in the deep, dark recesses of his being lay a relentless wish that some day, somewhere, a hunter would catch up with him and put through his heart the stake that would end this eternal misery.

He lived and yet he was not alive. The truth was he died that snowy night in the Carpathians and had been gone for centuries. Not even sweet Prudence, who offered a taste of salvation to a man starving for it, could save him from himself. If there was any semblance left of the man he had once been, it resided in the sense of right she had awakened in his long slumbering conscience.

He needed desperately to know that she saw in him the one thing that gave him the illusion of mortality, a soul. But the only way to keep the fantasy alive was to keep her safe and to do that he had to protect her from himself. It was a conundrum he had not previously thought possible. The music in him now was a rhapsody of blood.

"Nicolae, you're hurting me."

At first, her voice did not register, lost as it was amidst the ghastly memories and disillusionments that plagued him. He made a sound, a deep, guttural moan from somewhere so far inside that its source eluded him.

"You're hurting me."

This time her voice was louder, more forceful. But it was the undercurrent of fear in her tone that penetrated his murky thoughts of past and present. He realized that he was holding her tightly against him, crushing her to him as if clinging to life itself. He felt suddenly foolish and let her go.

He reached for her hand but she pulled her fingers from the cold confines of his.

"You haven't answered my question," she said. "Why did you come to rescue me?"

He answered as truthfully as he knew how. "You don't know me, Prudence. If you did, you would have wished for another rescuer."

"Oh, I think I know you," she said.

"You know only what I have told you," he flatly replied.

"The story you told me, of that terrible night so long ago, is only part of who you are. The other parts of you I have come to know from observing and from what I have experienced when I am with you."

He remained quiet and scarcely breathing, waiting for her to put into words the searing definition of what he thought of himself.

"You are a scoundrel, of that I am certain. You care only for yourself and nothing for others. The harm you inflict can reach deep down into one's soul. Those of us who have souls, that is."

He cast his gaze downward at her biting sarcasm so that she could not witness the wince in his eyes.

"You are immoral and a liar," she went on in a slow, measured tone. "You have lived so long hiding in shadows and darkness that you would not recognize true friendship if it bit you on the nose."

She was right. God help him. How well she knew him.

"You are beautiful on the outside, which I can attest works to your advantage quite well. One can only imagine the sheer numbers of women you have lured to your bed over the centuries, ones who did not require the tutelage that someone as inexperienced and unworldly as myself had need of. Not that I am ungrateful for the benefit of your teachings. You have taught me things and awakened in me a passion I thought existed only in novels." She drew in a deep breath. "Don't misunderstand. I am not trying to be purposely cruel," she said, adding matter-of-factly, "That is your specialty, not mine."

"So much for the other parts of me," he said with a characteristically cynical note.

"I'm coming to that," she said. "Don't rush me. I wanted to make sure you know what a truly reprehensible man you are."

He gave a short laugh. "There is no doubt."

"Yes, well, despite all your shortcomings…"

"Which are legion."

"…you do have some redeeming qualities, although I suspect that even you are unaware of what they are."

"Let me see if I understand what you are saying. I am a lying, reprehensible, immoral, self-centered scoundrel with redeeming qualities. Do go on."

"You have a talent that quite simply takes one's breath away."

"Ah, we're back to the bedroom again."

She gave out with an impatient huff. "I'm talking about your music. The way you play can only come from a place of goodness and courage. There is no malice in it. No cruelty except for the wrenching of emotions of those who hear it. Although I would like to think of you as truly evil, I am obliged to admit that listening to your music is like opening a portal through which angels pass. There is something magical, almost heavenly, about it. I know what you told me about losing your soul, but I do not believe it. The alchemist said—"

"To hell with what the alchemist said!"

Angels. Heaven. He'd heard enough. He jumped to his feet and began to pace the floor.

"You don't know what you're talking about." He ran a hand through his hair, pushing the midnight locks from his face. "There is no soul. Don't you understand?"

"But the music—"

"Is just that. Music. Nothing more. I have a gift for coaxing sounds from my instrument. Do not imagine it as some gift from God. Why would God give me *any*thing when He took from me *every*thing?"

"He did not take your talent," she countered. "He did not take your mind. He did not take your beauty. And he did not take your redemption. 'In Him we have redemption through His blood, the forgiveness of our trespasses.'"

"You quote Sriptures to me?" he exclaimed. "Here is one. 'For they have shed the blood of your saints and prophets, and thou hast given them blood to drink.' If you believe that in God there is redemption, then you must also believe that He made me a blood drinker, and in doing so, has taken from me all vestiges of humanity, including my damned soul."

"You cannot adapt Scriptures to suit your meaning," she objected.

"And if I do, who is to judge me? Will God deprive me of the kingdom of heaven for it?" He laughed, a sharp, mirthless sound. "He could have shown mercy and let me die with the rest of my family, but instead, he damned me to eternal hell. For what reason? Because I killed the wolves that were taking our livestock? Because I failed to say evening prayers with Izabella and Gizella? It may have been Draculea whose bite turned me into this creature who stands before you, but it was God who forged my destiny."

His bootheels made scarcely a sound as he paced back and forth over the earthen floor that was soaked with gin. "You ask why I came to your rescue. All right, I'll tell you. It is because I love you. Despite the things I said to you, I love you. Do you hear me, Prudence? I love you. And that is another cruel joke God has played on me, that I should love a woman who will never love me back."

He cast a quick glance at her and through the darkness saw the stunned look upon her face. "I'm surprised you hadn't guessed it by now. Ah, but you're much too guileless to see through my façade, aren't you? But it's all been for you. The finished manuscript. The concert. Even the cruel things I said."

"Nicolae, I—"

"Don't say anything," he cut in. "I'm feeling foolish enough as it is." His pacing ceased and he stood there, a tall, slender figure etched against the darkness, shoulders slumped in resignation. "You don't love me," he muttered. "The truth is, you'd be a fool if you did."

"But I do care for you," she said.

"Spare me the friendship speech, Prudence. Don't get me wrong, a person such as myself can use all the friends he can get. I was just hoping for…" He stopped, then went on with the bitter taste of bile on his tongue. "What does it matter what I was hoping for? There's not a thing about my life that is how I would wish it. It is what it is and no amount of hoping will change that." An expression of silent pain passed across his handsome face like a shadow.

"If I interpret Scriptures to suit my own miserable existence," he went on, "it is only because all belief has been bred out of me. What you see before you is an empty shell where once a man existed."

"And yet you love." Her voice drifted like a chill wind into the dank space between them, sending a shiver across his preternatural flesh.

"In vain," he replied.

"But the feeling exists, filling up the empty space inside."

To the point where I can think of little else except you, he thought miserably.

But he had already risked too much by revealing his feelings. What would be the point of destroying what little pride he had left by admitting that his love for her had become a dark hunger as essential to him as the bloodlust?

"The empty space grows even deeper because of it," he said, his voice torn between need and despair.

"Would you rather I lie and tell you that I love you?" she asked. "I can do that. We can both pretend it is so."

Nicolae smiled grimly and turned away.

"Lies are like strangers who knock at your door. Once you let them in, they never leave. For a while they provide comfort, even if it is only within the confines of your own mind. Sooner or later they awaken, yawn, stretch their slimy limbs and proceed to devour you. For all that I am, and all I am not, I choose truth over lies any time. Never will I see the rapt love in your eyes or hear you whisper lovingly in my ear, and nothing can alter that meloncholy fact."

Something touched his arm. Soft, tentative, turning him back toward her.

She moved into his arms that opened to receive her and laid her head against his breast.

Oh God, yes, he thought, *let us pretend, just for tonight.*

He bent his head and brougt his lips close to hers and was about to capitulate to the lie when something froze him within a hair's breadth of kissing her. His body went rigid.

"What is it?" she questioned.

He cocked his head to the side. "Did you hear that?"

"No," she whispered. "I heard nothing." Her hand was smooth and warm against his cheek as she turned his face back toward hers.

He felt his emotions stir, his willpower weaken as he touched his lips to hers, tentatively at first, then stronger, more forceful as the feeling overpowered him.

Her lips parted to allow his eager tongue entry to the warm, moist hollow of her mouth. He felt her shudder and heard the small sound that caught at the back of her throat.

He drew one hand through her hair and down her back, across the torn and soiled fabric of her dress to cup her buttocks and pull her hips hard against his. He was breathing deeply, his ebony lashes sweeping downward to conceal his eyes as he moved in rhythmic thrusts against her. It didn't matter if she did not love him. She loved what he could do to her, and for now, it was enough.

Her breasts pressed provocatively against his chest. The tantalizing female scent of her was almost too much to bear. His breathing quickened and his shoulders trembled. He clutched her tighter, pressing himself against her as if clinging to a life raft that tossed on a turbulent sea of emotion and desire.

"Oh God," he moaned against her mouth, an anguished sound from deep in his throat. "Oh God." But not even God could save him from this madness.

He knew his kiss was hurting her and that the superhuman strength in his fingers was biting into her flesh, but the hot need welled up within and nothing could stop him now. Nothing except...

A faint odor drifted from somewhere beyond his consciousness to nag at his senses. Little by little it pierced the irrationality that clouded his reasoning and forced a vestige of reality into his being. The smell of blood wafted to him. It was old blood, soaked into the hard-packed earth of the floor. Why hadn't he noticed that before? But it was more than that which set the hairs at the back of his neck on end.

All of his senses came alert at once. Panting, he thrust her away from him, so hard that she lost her footing and almost toppled over backwards.

He silenced her gasp with a forceful command. "Be quiet."

"Nicolae, what—?"

"Shut up, damn it."

His eyes spliced the darkness with a fierce green fire, then narrowed to mere slits as he focused his attention on the sounds of crackling and spitting that were discernible only to one whose senses were as acute as his. Lifting his head, he sniffed the air and snarled in pure reaction. He would know that smell anywhere.

The rats knew it, too, for there suddenly converged upon the static stillness a frantic scurrying of little rat feet and squeals of terror.

Fire!

Chapter 20

*T*hrough the darkness Pru saw something in Nicolae's eyes that she had never seen before, turning their beautiful green glow into something dark, dangerous and scornful.

Why did he look like that? Mere moments ago he'd been like a fervent lover, ready to take her right then and there on the gin-soaked floor, and she would have let him. Indeed, she craved the dizzying heights to which he took her. But now there was a wild, panic-stricken look in his eyes, like that of an animal caught in a trap from which there was no escape. His lips were curled back in a snarl, his face knotted in a look of terror that distorted his handsome features. The sight of it drove a bolt of alarm through her.

She drew in an unsteady breath, but before she could utter a sound, there came to her nostrils the smell of smoke, shaking her with a violent tremble.

A hush as still as death descended over them. For several tense moments they just stood there, frozen like the marble statues in Vauxhall Gardens. And then, a sudden, crashing sound split the stillness.

"Let's go!" Nicolae grabbed Pru's hand and yanked her toward the exit.

The great wooden door that rolled on iron tracks was bolted from the outside.

"Stand back," he ordered.

He took several steps back. Gathering his incalculable strength about him he lunged at the door with his shoulder. It did not budge. Hissing and swearing under his breath, he tried kicking the door in, but again his strength failed him. His face twisted with emotion, he said through gritted teeth, "I haven't fed tonight. My strength is weakened."

Pru knew he was referring to the liquid meal that was so crucial to his existence. Horrified, she cried, "What will we do?"

"Blood. I need blood." He searched the dark corners of the cellar for a sign of the rats from which to feed, but they had all scurried into their holes.

Without heeding the consequences, Pru rushed forward. Pulling at the collar of her dress, she exposed the white skin of her neck. "Here is the blood you need."

"Are you mad?" Nicolae exclaimed.

Her face was very pale. "It's the only way."

He gave her a look that burned with indecision. His hesitation stretched into maddening delay. "Yes," he said finally, his voice a low drone. "The only way." He reached for her and drew her close. "I'll take only what I need, not a drop more. I swear it."

She went rigid at his touch.

"I won't make you into something like me."

Her voice shook treacherously. "Will it hurt?"

"Only a little. Only a little."

His arm felt like an iron bar at her back as he pressed her to his chest. Pru was too frightened to even shut her eyes, but stared wide-eyed at the unnaturally pale face that hovered so close to hers. Dark lashes swept down to conceal his beautiful eyes. His mouth opened. She saw the fangs.

She recoiled and was seized by an impulse to scream. *No, no, I've changed my mind!* But the words hovered like cowards at the back of her throat.

At the first prick of her skin from the knife-sharp fangs, white-hot panic surged through her being. It hurt, and she let out a cry. His thumb was at her throat, pressing against the jugular, forcing the blood to the surface and into his waiting mouth. That's when she felt the sucking begin, soft lips drawing the precious fluid from her heart, a little bit at first, then more, stronger, faster, keeping rhythm with the awful sucking sounds.

She struggled in his locked embrace as terrifying thoughts began to swirl in her mind, caught like so much flotsam in a whirlpool. What had she done? Was it better to be scorched alive in a burning building than to have the blood drained from her body in such a gruesome manner as this? Would he stop drinking in time? Did it matter?

Then, ever so gradually, like dawn breaking over the treetops after a night of terrorizing nightmares, something strange began to happen. She became aware of a shocking sensation that accompanied the sucking. It was not unlike her first experience of passion when he had entered her with a thrust of pain that coalesced into indescribable pleasure. Now, as then, the pain subsided into a promiscuous rush of excitement, a shameless titillation that spread a warm, wet feeling throughout her entire being. Through it all she felt the strength increasing in his arms that crushed her to him so tightly she could scarcely draw breath. Despite everything that was going on around them and the desperate immediacy of their situation, she felt a surge of unrestrained satisfaction knowing that it was her blood that was providing the strength he needed to save them from certain doom.

It was over in seconds. She was standing upright before him, his arm around her steadying her on her feet.

Panting heavily, Nicolae took a step back. "That's enough," he said between breaths. "Are you all right?"

Pru nodded. Her fingers sought the puncture wounds at her neck, and the pleasurable spell she'd been under vanished at the hideous reality of what had just occurred. A small gargle of shock rose in her throat.

"Don't worry," he told her, "the wounds will heal. Now stand back while I give it another try."

He drew in his breath and charged the door. This time it gave way, splintering beneath the force of his superhuman strength fortified by her blood.

An explosion of scorching heat slapped them in their faces. Pru screamed and shrank back. Nicolae issued a harsh epithet through gritted teeth.

Beyond the remains of the oak door an old wooden staircase wound its way upwards.

"Come on!" Nicolae yelled.

Pru's eyes were wide and terrified, and she dug in her heels at the sounds of the fire that was in full rage on the upper floor. Its lurid light could be seen dancing over the wooden walls of the staircase.

"The building's on fire!" she screamed. "We can't go up into it."

"We have to. It's our only chance!"

"No! No! I can't! I won't!"

He grabbed her as she tried to run back into the cellar and spun her sharply around. "Damn it, Prudence, we'll be burned alive if we stay here."

"No! Let me go!" She fought him harder than she had ever fought anything in her life, struggling desperately to wrest herself free of his powerful grip.

His eyes went wide with rage as he brought his hand up and struck her sharply across the face. She stumbled to the side and would have fallen to the ground had he not scooped her up in his arms and carried her kicking and screaming toward the staircase and the fire that raged above.

Mindless of the thick clouds of smoke that billowed at the top of the staircase, Nicolae ascended to the demon fire with uncontrollable fury. No sooner did he reach the top of the stairs than the old wooden staircase collapsed behind them, leaving them no way to go except toward the seething mass of flame, and not a moment too soon. With a crash heard above the din of the flames, the cellar ceiling fell in.

Inside the burning building the old timbers creaked and groaned as they succumbed to the ravenous flames. An explosion on the upper floor blew off the distillery roof, shattering windows and throwing large embers into the street. The heavy gray smoke was so thick Pru couldn't even see Nicolae's face as he carried her in his arms. It was the kind of smoke that stuck to everything, skin, clothing, hair, even their eyelashes. Up, up the burning walls he climbed toward the gaping hole that used to be the roof.

Pru buried her face in Nicolae's neck, her cries muffled by the roar of the flames. The scorching heat was painful against her skin. Every breath she took was like swallowing boiling water. Showers of burning splinters fell on her arms, singeing her flesh. Through the abject fear that enveloped her one persistent thought reverberated through her brain.

We're going to die.
We're going to die.

***

At the end of the street, away from the blinding glare of ignited spirits, Edmund de Vere watched the spectacle.

Masses of glowing wood blown hither and yon by the wind set nearby shops ablaze. Sparks and burning flakes fell onto the roofs of rickety wooden tenements which proved good kindling for the hungry flames. The fire swallowed everything in its path and threw massive pitches of flame into the sky, illuminating the night with a blaze brighter than the light of day.

Beyond the smoldering walls of the distillery, gushes and eddies of wind blew this way and that, wrapping the street in fire until the whole district looked like an erupting volcano.

Crowds of onlookers gathered in the overcrowded warren of narrow, cobbled streets to watch the terrible spectacle.

With a furious clatter of horses' hooves on the cobblestones, a pumper arrived. Men with hooks and axes could do nothing but stand by and watch helplessly. Others formed a brigade of leather buckets that continuously supplied the engine's tub, while a hand-operated piston pump forced the water out through a nozzle onto the raging fire, with little effect.

The fire was given ferocious life when an engine commandeered by unwitting spectators began pumping through its hose not water but gin from the stills that were in a portion of the cellar miraculously untouched by the flames and whose crumbling walls provided easy access.

Some of the onlookers, seizing the opportunity to get something for nothing, raced into the raging building and came back out choking, faces blackened, eyes bloodshot, carrying untapped casks of gin.

The heat below ground became so intense that the stills burst and overflowed and the gin gushed up into the streets where it ran in warm currents in the gutter and over the cobbles.

Men and women knelt down and dipped their faces into the river
of fiery gin, gulping down as much as they could before their throats
were burned raw. Downing the gin in its raw state, they writhed in
the street, screaming in pain, their faces blue, tongues swollen from
the poisonous liquid. Some who had run down the stone steps and
into the gaping holes in the cellar wall were trapped by the flames.
Overcome by fumes, they were scorched to death.

Edmund was unaffected by the sounds of death and dying that
rose into the night, a cacophony matched only by the hideous roar of
the flames. From his father he had been taught that at times it was
necessary to sacrifice a few innocents for the betterment of all
humanity. Nobody could have survived the inferno. Confident that
the beast that had drained his ancestor and eluded every first born
son of a first born son since that time was, at last, destroyed, a slow,
sinister smile spread across his lips. His work here was finished. He
bent to pick up his black bag. Casting one last long look over his
shoulder at the blazing distillery, he walked off into the night.

Chapter 21

*E*dmund de Vere stood at the window of his shop looking up at a gray sky that covered the city like a shroud. Even now, days later, the stench of burnt timbers, mortar and bodies could be smelled throughout London. His head ached from the amount of sherry he had consumed since that night to help dull the guilt. Killing the undead was one thing, but sacrificing innocents always left a bad taste in his mouth. Alas, he'd done what had to be done. There was no sense brooding over it. The only thing he remotely regretted was Prudence.

It was too bad, really, that she had to die. Perhaps in time she could have been made to see the error of her ways. But it mattered naught. As he watched the flow of carriages and pedestrians pass his shop, his face screwed up against the hurt she had inflicted in choosing that evil demon over him. She had caused him great pain and paid for it.

In the days following the fire, as he settled back into his work preparing a shipment of hollow ware for the colonies, he was able to lose himself in the business of accounts and customers—although it did seem odd to him that Simon Cavendish had not called to pick up his latest order—and it was only when he stopped for a few moments to contemplate what he had done that a small measure of guilt infiltrated his conscience. He turned from the window, forcing his morbid thoughts aside, and returned to his desk and his ledgers.

Presently, a knock at the door brought his head up.

The apprentice poked his head in. "There's a gentleman waitin' ter see yer. Do yer want me ter tell 'im yer not in?"

"Do I look like I'm not in?" Edmund snapped.

"Right then. Right. I'll send 'im in."

"Is it Simon Cavendish?" Edmund shuffled through some papers, searching for the alchemist's latest order.

"No sir, it's some bloke I ain't never seen before."

"A new customer?"

"Don't 'ave the look of a new customer ter me."

Something in the lad's voice made Edmund pause. "What does he look like?"

"Tall. Right. Well dressed. Has a scar on 'is boat race." He pointed to his cheek. "Sort of like 'e was burned. Maybe 'e was one of them that got too close ter the fire."

Edmund frowned uneasily. The reminder of the distillery fire made his head ache even worse. "Send him away."

"Yo' doesn't look like yer feelin' too fine. Ah can helter-skelter an' git th' docko fo' yo'."

"I don't need the bloody doctor. What I need is to be left alone."

"Right then, as enny fool kin plainly see. I'll git back t'mah wawk. Th' shipment's almost ready."

Edmund closed his eyes and rubbed his temples in a vain attempt to ease the pressure. When he heard the click of the closing door, he shoved himself away from the desk and rose. Taking the back staircase up to his living quarters, he flopped down onto his bed with a cloth of camphor across his eyes, and fell asleep.

When he awoke and removed the cloth from his eyes, it was dark in the room. Tatters of pale moonlight hovered just beyond the window that was swung wide open on its hinges. That was odd. He could have sworn he had closed that window.

A scent permeated the air, not the strong, aromatic aroma of camphor but of corruption and decay. His headache had dissipated, but the scent that invaded his nostrils made his stomach lurch. He hoisted himself onto his elbows and drew in a deep breath that caught in his throat when he heard the sound of breathing close by. A rustle of movement of something coming nearer, and then a touch, as cold as ice, upon his shoulder, paralyzed him with fear.

"You and I have a score to settle."

The voice that spoke at his ear was smooth, mellifluous, almost like a song. A dizzying contrast to the odor that spilled from the speaking mouth. He knew instantly what it was and shrank back in horror. Something—fear or survival, he was too frightened to know which—made him reach for his pants pocket and fumble for the cross inside. With fingers shaking and eyes ground shut, he drew it out and thrust it forward.

Laughter, scornful and mocking, followed the action. "The cross is effective only against the weakest of us. Now, if you had the sense to brandish a cross bearing the form of the crucified Christ, that would be different. Or a consecrated host. But as a member of the Sanctum, you already know that, don't you?"

The hand tightened on Edmund's shoulder. He winched at the fingers that grew long and taut and the sharp claws that bit into his flesh through his shirt.

"You have grown lazy, pewterer. Or are you overly confident?"

The cruel hand withdrew and Edmund heard the click of boot heels retreat across the wide-planked floor. Somehow, he found the courage to open his eyes and turn his head. The creature stood now gazing out the window, his back to the room, a tall, lean figure silhouetted against the pale moonlight, a gentle midnight breeze rustling the ends of his dark hair.

That beautiful voice spoke again against the glass pane. "You thought you had destroyed me, didn't you? You know there is only one thing that can destroy me. Well, two things, really." He ran his finger along the mullion as he spoke. "But you are too cowardly to get close enough to me to drive a stake through my heart, so you chose fire." He sighed. "I could almost forgive you for what you tried to do to me. But not for what you did to Prudence."

Edmund sat up. "Is she—?"

"Is she what? Burnt to a crisp for choosing me over you?"

"No!" Edmund cried. "I never meant to harm her. You must believe me."

"Must I?"

"Prudence is—"

The figure at the window whirled suddenly to face the darkness that blanketed the room. "You will not speak her name," he demanded, his voice sounding now like a half-strangled groan. "You will never again speak her name."

The palpable silence that followed the outburst was broken by the ticking of a clock and by Edmund's erratic breathing.

"You will notice I did not say that you are to never speak her name again or I will kill you. But that does not mean I don't intend to kill you anyway."

Edmund cringed at the soft, toying quality of that voice. Making no attempt to mask his hatred, he said, "The way you killed my ancestor?"

"Philippe de Vere deserved to die."

"What's that you say?"

"He was a traitor, giving up innocents to the Dominican friars in return for a portion of the wealth they stole from those they burned at the stake. How else do you think your family acquired its wealth?"

Edmund sprang to his feet. "You lie!"

"I have no reason to lie. I was there. I witnessed it. I confronted him with his treachery and he did not bother to deny it. The only thing that prevented me from killing him that night was the crucifix he waved at me. I wasn't as strong then as I am now, and it forced me to flee. But I returned." The voice hardened like rock. "And he paid for his treachery with his blood."

Edmund's heart beat wildly in his chest. His eyes scanned the darkness and spotted his black bag on the floor across the room. He had to find a way to divert the fiend's attention and get to the bag.

"I cannot see you in the darkness."

"Ah, but I can see you, pewterer. I have spent countless lifetimes shut away from the light. My eyes have acquired the ability to see quite clearly in the dark. I can also hear the beating of your heart and smell your fear."

"I would see the face of my killer," Edmund said.

"Why, of course. Light a candle, if you wish."

Rooted to his spot, Edmund made no move.

"Oh, very well, I'll do it for you. Where do you keep your candles?"

Edmund nodded toward the dresser. The creature moved toward it in a flash of movement so swift it scarcely registered.

A single candle sputtered to life, illuminating the walls and draperies of the room.

"Is that better?" He turned back to Edmund, the candlelight falling upon his face.

Edmund could not answer, shocked by what he saw.

Why, it was a man. Just a man.

Where was the terrifying demon that had saturated the room with its foul countenance? He could have passed him on the street and never guessed the evil that lay beneath the all-too-human-looking face with its finely sculpted features and beautiful green eyes. His fingers flexed at his sides as his gaze strayed to the ominous black bag. Within it lay the hawthorn stake that would accomplish what the fire had failed to do and put an end to the creature once and for all.

"How did you gain entry to my room?" Edmund asked, stalling for time. "I always latch the door."

A lazy smile spread across the lips of that impossibly handsome face. "Through the window. But you already know that."

"There are no stairs outside leading to my window."

"I am as nimble as a spider."

Edmund inched closer to the bag. "Can you fly?"

"Do you see wings?"

"Can you control the elements?"

"You give me too much credit if you think so."

"Do you have the strength of ten men?"

"More like a hundred."

"Can you transform into vapor?"

"Now, that is true, and particularly useful when there are no windows."

The bag was so close to Edmund's foot now he could almost touch it with the toe of his boot. "Before you kill me, I would like to know your name."

"Ambrus Nicolae Tedescu at your service." He bowed from the waist in a gesture that was both grand and mocking at the same time. "Is there anything else you would like to know about me?"

Edmund licked his lips. "Yes. Out of curiosity, would you mind telling me if any of the Sanctum's methods of destroying your kind are accurate?"

"Such as?"

"The use of Sabbaratarians."

"Only if they wear their clothing in a particular fashion, and therefore hardly worth the effort."

"Stealing a left sock?"

"Oh, come now. I would expect something like that from a child, not from a seasoned vampire slayer."

"Drenching the gravesite in holy water?"

"That might work, but huge amounts would have to be hauled to the gravesite to assure a clean kill. And please don't ask me about garlic. I'm so tired of putting that old tale to rest."

"What about sunlight?"

"Weaker vampires might succumb to it, but for one as strong as me, a mild burning is all that would result and would heal in a matter of minutes."

"Was that you who called at my shop earlier today?"

"Yes. That illiterate fellow who apprentices for you told me you were not in. I didn't believe it, of course, so I bided my time. I'm very good at that."

"He said you had a burn on your face, yet I don't see any."

"My kind has a miraculous ability to heal quickly. What that crude fellow saw was the remnants of the scars left by the fire. I will admit the burns I sustained would have sent women and children screaming had they seen me. I was forced to rest for several days to heal. But as you can see, I'm quite recovered, and growing weary of this idle banter. There are more pressing matters to discuss."

It was Edmund's turn to question, "Such as?"

"The manner of your death, de Vere. I could do it quickly, humanely, so to speak, with a mere twist of your neck. Or, I could prolong your suffering, make you cringe in fear the way poor Prudence cringed, or cry out in horror as she cried out."

"Allow me a drink of water at least, to fortify myself against whatever manner of death you have planned for me."

Nicolae heaved an impatient sigh. "All right, have your last glass of water. But don't choke on it. That would deprive me of the satisfaction of choking you myself.

Edmund held out his hands that were visibly shaking. "I cannot pour it myself. Would you do it for me? It's over there in the pitcher."

Those green eyes rolled and an irritated breath spilled from Nicolae's lips. "You really are the most annoying man." He looked about the room and spotted the pitcher on a bedside table.

Edmund held his breath. When the vampire's back was turned, he reached down, and without making a sound, opened the bag.

A swift glance revealed the hawthorn stake sitting atop the other instruments of death. With as much stealth as he could muster, he drew the stake from the bag and straightened, holding it surreptitiously behind his back.

Nicolae returned with a glass half filled with water and thrust it at him. "Drink. And be quick about," he warned in a low animal growl. "I have already wasted enough time on you."

Edmund's grip tightened around the stake. One blow. One solid blow to the chest was all he needed. Mentally, he prepared himself for the harrowing shriek that was sure to come, followed by copious amounts of blood. He had to get it right the first time. There would not be a second chance. He took a sip of water.

"Is there anything else?" Nicolae asked impatiently.

"Just this."

In one swift move, he flung the glass of water at Nicolae.

Nicolae let out a howl and stumbled backwards. Holy water! Burning like acid through the sleeve of his coat down to his skin.

It was all the distraction Edmund needed. In a lightning quick move, he drew the stake from behind his back and lunged with a terrible cry. Without the use of a mallet to pound the stake home, he threw all of his weight and fury into the motion.

The sharpened point plunged towards Nicolae's breast. With vampiric speed a cold hand flew out to capture Edmund's wrist, stopping the stake within a hair's breath of puncturing its beating target.

With physical strength untethered to the natural world, he crushed the bones in Edmund's wrist, wrenching from him a cry like that of a wounded animal. The splintered stake was forced loose from the mangled hand and flung across the room.

This time, when the candlelight fell across the vampire, his eyes glowed like red-hot coals from a bloodless face gnarled with hatred. One clawed hand reached for Edmund's neck and raised him off the floor. Higher. Higher. Until his legs dangled like a puppet's and a gurgling sound emerged from the constricted throat. He was lowered back down with torturous slowness, his neck still locked in the death grip.

"This is for Prudence." A seething voice showered malignant breath on the struggling man.

The mouth opened. Razor-sharp fangs dripping with saliva sank into Edmund's neck, ripping the flesh like a hungry predator rips the belly of its prey.

He lifted his head and looked into the eyes of the mortal hunter. "That sound you hear is your heartbeat growing weaker and weaker. That smell is of your own death."

Edmund tried to scream, but all that emerged from his mouth was a bubble of blood. His fading vision cleared momentarily, long enough to see those hellish eyes and the thin stream that trickled down the blood-drenched mouth.

The vampire spit the blood to the floor as if it were poison. From some faraway place his voice taunted, cruel, and inevitable.

"I would not drink your blood if it were the only meal left for me on this earth."

And then, something strange occurred. Edmund blinked hard. Was it a trick of his wilting vision, or one last dream to remember in a life rapidly failing? The face that looked down at him was the most beautiful he had ever seen, with eyes that sparkled like emeralds, the expression in them like that of an angel's. The only thing amiss was the smile. It was broad and cruel, reeking with sinister satisfaction and dripping with blood.

Chapter 22

"*N*icolae, the most dreadful thing has happened!"

He stopped playing when she burst into the garret room. Her bonnet was hanging down her back from its tie around her neck, the burnished-gold hair wind-tossed, and her cheeks were ruddy as if she had run all the way from Folgate Street.

"It's Edmund," she said, a shaky break in her voice. "He's dead. His apprentice found him in his room. His neck had been broken."

Nicolae's dark hair spilled over his brow as he bent his head and drew the bow across the strings, coaxing a long, protracted note.

"Nicolae, did you hear what I said?"

"Yes, Prudence, I heard you."

She pulled off her gloves and approached him. "I didn't expect you to weep at the news, but— Why do you look like that?"

"Like what, Prudence?"

"My God," she said with a sharp intake of breath, "You knew."

His eyes caught the lingering light of day that murmured through the garret room windows. "One evil deed deserves another," he said flatly.

Pru closed her eyes in anguish at the realization that Edmund died at Nicolae's hand. "When you told me to say nothing to anyone about Edmund's role in the distillery fire and the lives lost, that you would take care of it yourself, I assumed that meant you would inform the authorities, not that you would kill him."

He stood up and spun his instrument on its endpin. "Don't tell me you have feelings for him."

"What I feel for him is pity," she asserted.

"Pity? After what he tried to do to us? After the lives lost in that fire? I am what I am, Prudence, but I am not a killer of innocents. And Edmund de Vere was no innocent. I did it for you. To avenge you, Prudence."

She drew in a breath at the disquieting truth. "When I think of that night, the fire, the fear…Oh, Nicolae, I thought I was going to die." She began to tremble as the memories of that terrifying experience converged on her, as they had every night since, turning what should have been peaceful dreams into nightmares. The rats scurrying in the darkness. The feral dog, or whatever it was, that scared them away. The choking smoke that constricted her throat and made the mere act of breathing impossible. The burning flames that grabbed at her arms, her legs, and her dress. The unspeakable fear that had threatened to drive her insane.

"Poor Papa," she said, looking down at her hands. "If I had perished that night, he would never have known what became of me."

"He was happy to see you, no doubt."

"Oh yes. He wept uncontrollably."

"What did you tell him?"

"That I was out all night with Aunt Vivienne. I hated lying to him and begged his forgiveness, but he believed me."

"He didn't question your appearance?"

She rolled her eyes at him. "I had the good sense to discard my burned clothes and bathe before I went in to see him."

"And your aunt?"

"I told her I was with a man. She seemed pleased by the news and was quite happy to let herself be used as my so-called excuse for having stayed out all night."

"And your father's health has improved?" he ventured.

"No. It grows worse. There is only one thing that can save him now. I know I said I didn't want it, but I cannot bear to see him suffer so."

Nicolae swallowed hard. "What you ask is…difficult. I must feed from him and then open my vein for him to drink from me."

She made a small sound of dismay. "But surely you have done it before."

He hesitated, admitting, "On occasion. The last fellow drank so much it nearly killed me. It took me days to recuperate."

She looked at him through the growing darkness. His strange immortal beauty had drawn her from the start, compelling her to act beyond her nature, and in doing so, to discover herself capable of things she had not thought possible. She did not know whether to thank him for it or revile him.

Her feelings for him were conflicted. He had saved her from certain death at terrible peril to himself, having used his body to shield her from the flames, sustaining injuries meant for her. Through the haze of terror that had enveloped her, she had gotten a glimpse of him when he deposited her safely back at her home that night. He had looked scorched, his beautiful, translucent skin red and raw, his glowing green eyes dulled with pain. She had tried to say something to him, to express with words that would not come the gratitude she felt deep in her heart for his heroic deed. But he had thrown his arm up before his face, turning away from her so that she could not see the awful damage done by the fire.

"Your face," she said, coming closer for a better look, "It's all healed. Thank God."

"God," he said in a dull voice as he turned away, "had nothing to do with it."

She watched him closely as he ran his hand over the violoncello. "You never did tell me how you knew where I was."

"The alchemist was right," he said. "He told me to be on the alert for fire."

Surprised, Pru questioned, "You went to see Simon Cavendish?"

"Yes. I made a bargain with him. If he told me where Edmund had taken you, I would help him unlock the secret to eternal life. He mentioned something about experimenting on me, if you can imagine such a thing. In any case, he claimed he didn't know where Edmund had taken you, and I believed him. I went out looking for you and returned to find a note tacked to my door. *What you seek can be found at the distillery.*" The words dripped like poison from his tongue. "Edmund planned the whole thing. Right down to the fire. Damn his soul to hell."

He had killed for her, and though a part of her was aghast at the thought of it, another, deeper part of her was secretly pleased. She owed him an unfathomable debt of gratitude and could think of only one way to repay it.

"Nicolae." Her voice was soft and seductive. "You asked me once if I would join you in eternity."

His brows knit in a questioning expression.

"I want to give you what you want," she whispered.

He looked askance at her. "Are you toying with me?"

She shook her head and came toward him, close enough to place a palm on his chest and feel his heart thump hard under her touch.

"Why would you do that?" he asked.

"Because I care for you," she answered.

"But you do not love me. That much we have determined."

"I am offering to give myself to you for all time. Isn't that enough?"

His green eyes narrowed upon her face. "You would sacrifice yourself to be with me?"

"It's the least I can do for the way you were willing to sacrifice yourself for me."

Sudden understanding flared in his eyes and he pulled away from her. "Gratitude?" he exclaimed. "You would give yourself to me for all eternity out of *gratitude*? Forget it, Prudence. There is no need to thank me. I was trapped in the fire too, remember? It was to my advantage to get us out of there."

"But your bargain with Simon Cavendish," she reminded him.

He laughed sharply. "It was never my intention to allow him to experiment on me. I'm not a laboratory rat, for God's sake. I told him I would give him what he wanted. I never suggested it would be me."

"Then what—?"

"Let's just say the streets of London are a little less safe these nights."

Pru could not contain her shock. "You turned him into—"

"The undead, as you would so inelegantly call it."

"Nicolae, how could you?"

"The man said he wanted to know the secret to eternal life. How else was I to do it? I'm not a magician, you know."

"If you would do it to him, then do it to me."

"No."

"But—"

"No buts, Prudence. You say you are grateful for what I did, but you cannot know what you are asking. No, that is something I will not do."

"You have suddenly become so noble that I hardly recognize you," she said, sarcasm dripping from her tone.

"Not noble," he corrected. "Just selfish. If I turned you into something like myself, you would only hate me for it. Ask anything else of me. Would you like me to make love to you, right here and right now? That I can do. Just lift your skirts and spread your pretty legs and I will devour you in a different way."

The thought of those pale, beautiful hands touching her, of him entering her and carrying her to unimaginable heights, sent a warm rush of excitement through her. But Pru wanted more than that. She wanted to feel the rapture that only his music could bring.

"There is something," she said in a breathless whisper. "Play for me. Play only for me. I want to feel the power of your music. Fill me with it, Nicolae. Fill me up with it until it spills from every nerve."

"As you wish." He gestured to a chair. When she was seated, he took his place behind his instrument, took bow in hand and drew it across the strings.

She recognized instantly the Prelude from Bach's Suite No. 5. In Nicolae's hands it was a transcendent balance between romance and rapture, pure sweet love and unbridled lust. She swayed in time to the music with her eyes closed. The heat of the fire was slight compared to that which coursed through her now. It spread through her body, setting every nerve on end, evolving from something deeply emotional to something desperately physical. The heat coursed from her mouth that ached to taste him, to her breasts that yearned to be cupped in his pale, cold hands, to her belly that was filled with a mad fluttering of butterfly wings, to that place between her thighs that was already moist and hot and ready for him.

Pru continued to sway, unaware that the music had stopped and that the only sound in the room now was that of the rapid rise and fall of her breath.

He came forward in a silent movement, reached down and pulled her up into his arms and hard against his chest, fingers closing with intentional force in her hair.

Pru's eyes snapped open at the grip that tilted her face upwards towards his. The eyes that looked down at her were fiery bright, almost scornful it seemed. She opened her mouth for a breath of air to gird herself against the onslaught she knew was coming, and craved, but his mouth came down over hers, depriving her of the fortification, leaving her weakened against his powerful lust. She closed her eyes, ashamed of the weakness but unable to stop herself from wanting him.

She could taste the anger in his kiss, but she did not fight it. Her breasts were pressed against his chest, their shape crushed against the pressure. It made no difference what he was, only that when she was in his arms like this nothing else mattered except the bruising pleasure he and he alone could bring.

She splayed her hands across his shoulders, pulling him closer, her fingers moving upwards to his neck and twining in the dark hair that spilled like silk over his collar. She heard him groan deep in his throat when her tongue slid past his lips to explore his wine-flavored mouth.

His muscles were powerful, whether because of his inhuman strength or otherwise made no difference. What mattered was only that when captured in their potency she felt herself weak and incapable of resisting. Those muscles flexed as he forced her to the floor and covered her body with his.

With his mouth still pressed to hers, he pulled her skirts up, forced the stiff hoop aside and tore at the linen shift with rough, frantic hands.

The cool air slid across her naked belly and hips and her thighs that fell open of their own accord. A soft whimper trickled from her lips when his mouth moved to her throat to spread feverish kisses over her heated flesh.

Lowering his head, he sought the tip of one breast through the Indian cotton of her dress and drew it against his teeth as she arched her back with a gasping moan. She heard the snap of her whalebone stays and the rending of the laces. Her head fell back against the hardwood floor when he pulled her stays away to expose her breasts and drew one swollen nipple into his mouth, then the other, tugging at each one in turn, sucking with his lips and nipping with his teeth, pleasure and pain all at once.

He cupped the downy mound below her belly and slipped two fingers into her, pushing in and out of her sweet wetness, deeper, faster, until she was writhing beneath him. Her hips curved upwards, wanting more of the maddening caresses.

Lifting his head from her breast, he gazed down into her desire-narrowed eyes, a dangerously teasing smile on his lips. "Is this what you want, my little strumpet?"

Oh, he was so cruel to call her that, but she didn't care. It was true. She was a wanton, worse even than the women of the East End who sold their bodies for a tuppence, for unlike them, she had a choice. Unlike them, she loved every maddening moment of it.

She gave a faintly acquiescing sigh.

"And what shall I do next?" he asked, his own voice a ragged whisper as he slid his fingers in and out of her. "Shall I taste you?"

"Yes. Oh yes."

She heard him chuckle deviously as he slid slowly down the length of her body, settling himself into the space between her open legs. He ran his tongue in lazy patterns across the smooth flesh of her inner thighs.

"You smell like perfume," he murmured. "Sweet, intoxicating perfume." He kissed and caressed and teased, tickling her skin with anticipation.

She sucked in her breath when his tongue moved to the source of her most powerful sensations. "Nicolae," she gasped. She reached for his head, tangling her fingers in his hair as his hands moved beneath her to cup her buttocks and force her harder against his mouth and teasing tongue.

She tried to smother the great, gasping sounds that came from her throat, but it was no use, her breathless cries and moans filled the garret room, bouncing off the walls and echoing back at her. He took her to the point of explosion, and then stopped, drawing his face back up to hers and kissing her savagely with lips that were wet and sweetly pungent with the taste of her upon them.

His silky laughter brought a flame to her cheeks. "You think it funny that you can reduce me to this?"

"Only when I think of the long way you have come," he smoothly replied. "I told you once you were made for this, and it appears I was right."

"Oh, you are a devil," she said breathlessly. "But one evil deed deserves another, does it not?"

His green eyes brightened at having his words echoed back at him. "What did you have in mind?"

Forcing him off her and onto his back, she said, "You shall soon see."

She ran her palm across his chest and past his taut stomach, to the swelling that strained at his trousers. One by one she popped each button open, slowly, maddeningly, until his erection was exposed. She gave him a sly look and then wrapped her fingers around him.

His breathing quickened. He was not quite so arrogant or amusing now. He was completely and utterly under her command. With strong, smooth strokes she massaged him, and it gave her a different kind of pleasure to know that she could reduce the fierce and powerful vampire to a quivering mass.

"What shall I do next?" she teased. "Shall I taste you?"

He answered raggedly, "If you don't, I shall have to force you."

She lowered her head, her hair brushing the wiry down at his pelvis, and heard him suck in his breath sharply when she touched her lips to him. Her mouth opened and closed around him, drawing him in. She could feel his urgency in the way his body strained and in the deep, guttural moans that infiltrated the darkening garret room.

"Oh, Prudence," he rasped, "you are a demon, after all. A she-devil after my own heart. Don't stop, my love. Harder. Harder."

She knew by the gathering storm within him and from the glistening drops she tasted at the tip of his member that he was at full arousal and close, so close to the moment of explosion. It was then she slid her lips from him and raised her head. Pushing her voluminous skirts out of the way, she straddled his hips and used her hand to guide him into her.

Thrilling to the feel of him inside of her, filling her up, she began to move, up and down, up and down, rocking back and forth with motions that began like a slow prelude and built to a pounding crescendo. His hands squeezed the plump breasts that bounced with each movement. Tugging them forward, he buried his face in them, his cries of ecstasy muffled in the warm cleavage. She felt his body shudder and would have ridden him to climax had he not grasped her by the shoulders and flung her onto her back.

He rolled on top of her, crushing her against the hardwood floor. The stiff swell of his body brushed her thigh seeking entry.

"Yes," she cried. "Yes, please…"

He responded by thrusting into the warm, wet hollow that closed around him.

Her head sank back against the planks as her legs wrapped themselves around him, hugging him to her. A rush an excitement overtook her. The feel of him, hard and potent, the savage thrusting of his hips, the taste of the salt and desire on his skin, the sound of the animal-like growls that came from his throat lit a fire in her blood that raged out of control. It seemed to go beyond anything physical, to something primal and much more elemental. It was like a dream, and yet not a dream, for she was fully awake and heard every groan and whimper, each cry of satisfaction that came from her throat and his. Somewhere in the mist of ecstasy that enveloped her, a fleeting thought tugged at a far corner of her mind, and she laughed at the crazy irony that the undead could make her feel so alive.

His shuddering climax was matched by her own that pounded over her like waves on a beaten shore. Only he could ravish her like this. Only he could make her feel violated. And only he could make her burn for every bit of it.

***

Nicolae lay very still, trying not to think, not even to breathe, lest the euphoric spell be broken and he would find himself catapulted back to the dismal reality of what he was and what he could never have. His gaze was fixed upon the beamed ceiling that stared back at him like a petrified forest, as dark and remote as the life he lived.

For him, choice was a non-existent concept. He'd had no choice in his making. No choice but to go hunting night after endless night, a lonely wanderer in search of the blood he had no choice but to drink. And the most dangerous choice of all, love, had been wrenched from his hands with the intrusion of this woman into his life.

Despite everything, it was easy to love her. She was pure and innocent, untouched by the evil that consumed him. The sexual appetite he had awakened in her was matched only by his own. She was beautiful, even if she did not think herself to be, which, ironically, only made her that much more beautiful to him. He wondered if there was a more perfect blue in the world than the blue of her eyes, like the cloudless blue sky he remembered from a time almost beyond reckoning when he had been human and had been able to gaze at its clarity without fear or pain. What need did he have now of blue skies when he had only to gaze into her beautiful eyes?

He had not planned on loving her, or wanting her as desperately as he did. It was, he supposed, another cruel irony in a life that seemed one long mockery.

It would have been so easy to grant her wish, no matter how foolish she'd been to suggest it. She was an innocent mortal with no idea of what her life would be like if he succumbed not to her wish but to his own hopeless need. She would hate herself for becoming a creature of the night and a slave to the blood thirst, just as he hated himself for it. But worse, she would hate him, and that was a chance he could not...would not...take. No, it was better to have her like this, a consenting mortal partner, for as long as it lasted. For the time would come, he knew, when she would feel for another man the love he wished she felt for him, and he would lose her. Then, too, she would grow old and die, as all mortals did, and he would be left alone in this dark abyss. But even that was better than her hatred. Besides, he thought with a flash of annoyance, one did not seek to become the undead for any reason, least of all out of some misguided sense of gratitude.

His body, cold to the outward touch, burned within like an inferno as he struggled with his emotions. A touch as light as a feather stroked the sleeve of his shirt, forcing the pragmatic thought that in their haste to satisfy their carnal hungers, they had not even bothered to completely remove their clothing. He tried to tell himself that this was the way he would take any common whore, inflicting his brutal lust in some back alley, tossing her a coin and then disappearing into the night without a glance back. But this was not some nameless harlot. This was Prudence, the woman who imagined she'd seen a soul in him.

A part of him wanted to get up and walk away from her and never see her again, while another part, this one stronger—or perhaps weaker—made him want to pull her into his arms and hold her tight against him, and protect her from everything, but mostly from himself.

He turned his head to look at her nestled in the crook of his arm and found her eyes upon him, the lazy look of fulfillment in the blue depths. Her voice, husky with satisfied desire, drifted like the chords of a sweet sonata to his ears.

"How can I thank you for all you have given me?"

A long, silky smile spread over his lips. "Your body speaks quite elegantly." Through the night shadows that filled the room he saw her blush. "Sweet Prudence, you are such a contradiction. Boiling over with passion one minute, embarrassed by it the next. When will you learn to embrace all the wonders of your body without shame or embarrassment?"

Lashes swooping down to conceal her eyes, she confessed, "When we are together like this, it is so easy to lose myself in the moment, to become something I never thought I could be. I feel like crying out to the whole world, this is me, this is the real Prudence Hightower, not that timid little mouse who was afraid to as much as squeak."

He caught her face in his hand. "You must never tell anyone about what we do together."

"I am not ashamed."

"Nor should you be," he said. "But the day will come when you will want to give yourself to another man, and men are, well, let's just say, possessive about such things."

She drew away from him into a sitting position, frowning. "But won't he know that he wasn't the first?"

"You can make something up. If he loves you enough, he will believe anything."

"Aunt Vivienne said the same thing."

"There, you see. It's entirely possible."

The moonlight that whispered through the garret room window fell across her milk-white breasts as she straightened her stays and tied what was left of the laces. "But it is not possible, for there will never be anyone for me."

Nicolae swallowed hard at hearing her bleak pronouncement. "What makes you say that?"

"I am beyond the age at which most women marry. I am not beautiful. And thus far I have had appalling luck with men."

Nicolae scowled. "If you are referring to Edmund de Vere, you should consider yourself lucky that you did not marry that scoundrel."

"I am referring to Edmund and…to you."

"Me? How so?"

She heaved a dismal sigh, and said, "I will grow old and infirm and you will not want me like this any more."

There was no disputing the truth. "I want you now, Prudence. That will have to be enough for the both of us. Beyond that…" He lifted his shoulders in a careless shrug.

She bit her lip. "But if you were to make me immortal, then we could be together forever."

A slow dawning brightened his eyes to a fierce glow. "Ah, I see it now," he said, familiar cold, like ice, hardening his tone. "Your reason for wanting immortality has nothing to do with gratitude. You're afraid of being alone. If I don't turn your father into a vampire and he dies of whatever is slowly killing him, and if you never find a man who will love you for who you really are, you will be completely and utterly alone."

He got to his feet, buttoned his pants and stood now looking down at her. The pained expression on her face told him his words had cut deeply. She pulled in her breath in a sound of despair that should have made him feel bad, but it didn't. "I will not do what you ask just to save you from yourself. Life is a risk for all of us. Every night when I go out in search of blood I do so at great risk to myself. There could be a stake to my heart waiting around any corner. But I do it because I must. You will have to take the risk that no man will ever love you for who you are. And if you are not, well, believe me, there are worse things than that." Like loving and not being loved back, he wanted to say, but his immortal pride had sustained enough bruising at her mortal hands.

Her gaze dropped to the knotted planks as she toyed with the rumpled fabric of her dress. After a while, she said quietly, "Does it matter so much what the reasons are? You are lonely. I am lonely."

"Not lonely enough to damn you to this eternal hell."

She looked up at him, her eyes widening. "Back to being noble again?"

He turned and stalked away, unable to bear that accusing look in her eyes. "Damn it, Prudence, stop trying to see in me something that is not there. I am not noble. I have no soul. I am a man without convictions."

"That's not true," she said, scrambling to her feet and rushing toward him in a swish of ruffled skirts. "You saved me from the fire."

"I told you, it was for my own self-preservation."

He wished she would get angry. It would have made hurting her more palatable. As it was, his words left a bitter taste in his mouth. He whirled around to face her, staring at her long and hard and desperately. She looked so utterly pitiful. So utterly human. And suddenly, he hated her for it.

"You want to know what it's like for me? What you will become? Very well, my sweet little fool." He grasped her by the hand and yanked her toward the door. "Come with me. I have something to show you."

Chapter 23

The lamplighter was lighting the lamps along Hanover Square as Nicolae rushed down the street, pulling Prudence along after him. Her shoes clicked frantically against the cobblestones in an attempt to keep up with his ferocious pace.

He dragged her clear across town, past the fetid rookeries where cutpurses and cheaters dwelled and the stench of crime and poverty made her gasp. Past the bawdy-house door-keepers who called to them at the lurid pleasures that waited within, flaming her cheeks. Past packs of scavenging dogs that greeted them with bared teeth and threatening growls, and decrepit old watchmen lost in their immense coats. Down the winding alleys of the East End they went, splashing through puddles of muck and refuse, until they came at last to the wharf.

When they stopped, Prudence nearly doubled over in an attempt to catch her breath, but the stink made her hold her hand over her mouth to keep from gagging. The wharf was alive with activity. Watermen plowed through the dark water, fish were landed, colliers docked and ferrymen pulled against the tide.

He led her to a ramshackle building and pushed her into the shadows. "Wait here," he ordered, "and don't make a sound no matter what you see." These last words were spoken purposefully with a strong, threatening look until she nodded her agreement.

Pru watched him walk off with that silky smooth gait of his and disappear into the fog. After many long, disquieting minutes a figure emerged into the lamplight, not that of a man, but of a creature that walked on four legs with a loping gait.

She drew back in fear, her back pressed against the splintered wood of the building. The animal came nearer, then stopped and turned its magnificent head toward her. It was a bristling black creature, broader and more massive than an ordinary dog, with front paws that looked to be larger than those in the rear, and eyes of yellow-gold. Pru sucked in her breath. Those were not the eyes of an ordinary dog. A soundless word formed on her lips.

Wolf.

She watched with widened eyes as it loped off. Her eyes scanned the night searching for a sign of it and spotted it crouched at the corner of the neighboring building. What was it doing? Where was Nicolae? Oh God, why did she have this sickening feeling in the pit of her stomach?

Her fearful thoughts were disrupted by a sound from somewhere in the fog. She turned her attention toward it. A man approached, becoming more visible the nearer he came. He was whistling a tune from the Beggar's Opera. Had she really attended with Edmund and Aunt Vivienne in what seemed now like another lifetime? So much had changed. She had changed. Who could have guessed back then that she would find herself standing in the shadows by the murky wharf waiting for God knew what to happen?

From the corners of her eyes she saw a movement. The whistling stopped as another figure emerged into the sputtering light of an oil lamp. The two men seemed to greet each other. She was too far away to hear the words they exchanged, but there was no mistaking what happened next.

The whistler suddenly drew a knife from his coat and lunged at the other man who crumbled to the ground. Bending over his fallen victim, the whistler rifled through his coat. Then, looking about in all directions, unaware of the horrified blue eyes watching from the shadows, he stepped over his victim and continued on his way, his pockets jangling with the shillings he stole. Pru tried to scream, but before the sound could gather strength in her throat, another form flew past her in a blinding fast movement.

It was the wolf, fangs gleaming in the lamplight as it pounced on the whistler. The night suddenly filled with sounds of terror—growling, snarling, the shriek that faded into choked silence, a muffled cry, a protracted howl that split the night, sending violent shivers over her flesh.

She shut her eyes tight and put her fists to her ears to block out the hideous sight and sounds. She had no idea how long she remained thus, pinned to the wall of the building, quaking, her lips mouthing a desperate prayer. There soon came to her ears the sounds of the wharf—the fisherman loading their hauls onto the landing, the shouts of the ferrymen, the calls of the colliers. Familiar sounds. Safe sounds. Yes, it must have been a dream after all.

Sucking in a deep breath of air, she opened her eyes. A man stood in the foggy distance, a prostrate body hanging limp in his arms. He turned over his shoulder to look at her. His green eyes were molten with a viciousness that chilled her to the bone. His mouth was crimson-stained. Dropping the body to the ground, he stepped over it and wiped the blood from his lips as he came toward her.

"*That* is what you will become."

He reached for her hand and drew her out of the shadows. She followed without speaking, numbed by what she had witnessed.

***

For a long time Pru sat without thinking or speaking, just breathing. Her thoughts were trapped behind a wall of disbelief, her voice smothered beneath the weight of reality. The only emotion she felt was anger, at herself, at him, at the whole world.

She was only dimly aware of the glass held to her lips, the hand at the back of her head, the clink of crystal against her teeth, the full and heavy taste of the Oloroso that slid down her throat.

Gradually, the crazy, savage world into which she had been thrust returned. The color rose to her cheeks and she felt her heart beating again. She sat there, dismally contemplating what her life had turned out to be, and worse, what it would be if she became the thing she had witnessed on the wharf. She felt numb, and stupid, so incredibly stupid for thinking she owed him anything at all.

"You are revolted by what you saw, and well you should be."

At the sound of his voice, smooth and charming as if nothing had happened, she lifted her gaze and stared at him—at his angelic face, the green eyes so clear and innocent, the sensual curve of his mouth—and the truth of what he was hit her with sudden impact.

She looked away, unable to bear the contradiction of his physical beauty and the demon that resided within.

"You are truly an evil thing," she said.

He walked away and placed the empty glass of sherry on a sterling tray. "It's not I who am evil. It is the narrow-minded and the intolerant."

"You are a sin against all that is holy."

He shrugged elegantly. "After the fall of the Roman Empire, Islam and Christianity should have put an end to dark gods and blood rituals, but the church's use of demons to further its army of converts served merely to move me one step closer to humanity."

"You dare to compare yourself to a human? No human would have done what you did tonight."

"It was a human who plunged his knife into the heart of an unsuspecting innocent tonight. Humans fight wars in the name of what you call all that is holy. In those wars men are maimed and slaughtered, women raped, children butchered. You're right. I am much worse than that."

Pru clenched her teeth. "Your appalling sarcasm is more than I can bear. I hate you."

"Ah, but love and hate are all the same in the end, aren't they?"

"Do not presume to know what is in my heart, Nicolae. I will never love you."

His voice tightened. "So you have said. I will survive it."

"What you did tonight was reprehensible." Her voice reeked with disgust.

"What I did tonight was beyond my control," he snapped. "I am what I am. I have never pretended to be otherwise."

"That thing, that terrible snarling thing." With a shudder she recalled the eyes of yellow-gold and the fangs she imagined seeing once during their lovemaking, and the dog that chased the rats away in the distillery cellar. Only it wasn't a dog; it was something far more diabolical. It was him.

"Yes, well I do have the power to transform," he said, "but unlike you, I did not ask for this. I did what I did tonight to show you what you would become if I accepted your gratitude."

"I would become a…a…beast of the forest?"

"Only if I gave you enough of my own immortal blood to drink. Otherwise, you would become a common blood drinker."

Pru drew back and gasped softly. "Papa."

"I told you, he would not necessarily have to drain humans for his survival. Chicken blood would do. Or ox blood."

"Then why isn't chicken blood or ox blood good enough for you?" she charged. "Why do you kill innocent people?"

"Innocent?" he echoed. "You saw what that footpad did."

Was he trying to divert her attention away from himself? She shot him an appalled look. "I despise you," she said. "I was a fool for thinking I owed you anything, least of all myself for all eternity. You are a loathsome creature and you deserve to be alone."

A look of distress crossed his face, hidden in the next moment behind a careless smile. "I take it that means you do not want me to give your poor papa eternal life."

"I don't want you anywhere near him."

He spread his hands wide in a gesture of feigned helplessness. "As you wish."

"I would prefer that he die with some dignity than at your hands," she said with a huff.

"From what you have described to me, and from what I have seen with my own eyes, what dignity can there be in feeling your life slowly slipping away? If I did not know better, I would say he was the victim of something far more insidious than me."

"He is receiving the best possible care," Pru said defensively. "I do everything I can to make him comfortable, and Aunt Vivienne tends to him."

"You mean when she is not busy with one of her young lovers."

"You are being impudent."

"I am being truthful."

"I grant you she is headstrong and spoiled and given to having her way. She is flirtatious, and somewhat cunning, and her moods can be changeable. Nevertheless, I am lucky to have her." She spoke without much conviction in her voice, trying to convince herself as much as Nicolae of her aunt's attributes.

"She sounds like someone I used to know," he said.

"One of your former lovers, perhaps?" Even now, despite how much she hated him, she felt a twinge of unexpected jealousy.

"Hardly," he replied with a laugh. "She reminds me of Lienore. I told you about her. She, too, is spoiled and headstrong and flirtatious and given to having her own way. I wouldn't exactly call Lienore cunning, though. Devious, is more to the point."

"You mean the witch who was sacrificed for something, I forget what."

"For lying with her female lover in the bracken."

"Oh, yes, that's right," she said, not bothering to hide her distaste. "Well, Aunt Vivienne is nothing like your friend Lienore."

He ran a slender finger negligently over the fluted edge of the silver tray. "She is no friend of mine, I can assure you. It is said she hates music. Can you imagine a friendship between the two of us?"

Pru stared dismally at the floor. It had all been a foolish fantasy, a flight of her naïve imagination, to fancy anything remotely romantic about him. The tortured creature, part-man, part-demon, shut away from light and friendship for all eternity. The temperamental musician sunk in a remote and brooding unhappiness. She thought she understood what he was, and was willing to offer him the companionship he seemed to crave in exchange for the thrill of being in his arms. Until tonight, that is, when she witnessed him at his most brutal, and now she wasn't sure which of them she hated more, him for shattering her illusions, or herself for believing she had seen something human in him. And the music? Perhaps it was as he said. Just that. Music. Nothing more.

She squeezed her eyes shut at the awful disgrace she felt. When she opened them, he was watching her, a lazy smile on his lips as if he could read her shame. She stood up, smoothing her skirts. "Would you hail a carriage for me please? I would like to go home."

Chapter 24

*N*icolae paced the floor of the garret room, cursing himself and the world. He cast a scornful look at the violoncello that had brought her into his life. It was not likely she would want to see him or hear his music ever again, and it was just as well. He could do nothing but bring her harm.

Yet a part of him wept at the loss. He could find other lovers, even ones as inexperienced as she whom he could tutor in the ways of lovemaking as he had tutored her. But where would he ever find another as pure and guileless as to believe him capable of possessing a soul? With her departure went the last vestige of his humanity.

With a beleaguered breath he blew out the candles and sat down on the floor with his back pressed against the wall, legs drawn to his chest, staring into the blackness.

Inside of him was a great lonely space that nothing had ever been able to fill, save a timid Englishwoman with blue eyes, and then, only for a little while.

The loneliness bore down on him with a heaviness that threatened to suffocate him. If only it could. If only it could squeeze the air from his lungs and the beat from his heart until there was nothing left but peace and rest from the awful burden that was his life.

He wanted to cry, but could not. Tears were a thing of the past. In the decades after his making he had shed so many thousands upon thousands of tears that there simply were no more left to shed.

Without her, he would go back to the great nothing that was his life.

And what about her? What would her life be like now that he was no longer a part of it? Would she find the love she was seeking and bestow upon some lucky mortal the love she could not bring herself to feel for him? Would her womb swell with the children he could not give her? Would she and her beloved grow old together and reminisce over their vanishing youth? Would she look back upon this time and place as she drew her last breath and think of him and wish she had made a different choice?

Well, at least she was not alone like he was. She had the music master, for now at least, until he succumbed to whatever it was that was slowly draining the life from him. And she had her aunt, that frivolous woman whose dislike of him had been evident from the start, almost as if she could sense what he was, and recoiled from it.

Words spoken earlier in the evening came to mind. Headstrong. Spoiled. Flirtatious. Cunning. The words fluttered around him like bats in a dark cave. There was something about them that he could not quite put his finger on, yet which unsettled him. He tried to banish them from his mind and concentrate on his own self-pity, but they continued to haunt him.

Headstrong.
Spoiled.
Flirtatious.
Cunning.

He had laughingly compared Prudence's aunt to the witch Lienore. But now, looking into the dark, an impulsive thought began to take shape, growing in his mind to a frightening possibility.

Headstrong.
Spoiled.
Flirtatious.
Cunning.

Just like...Lienore.

***

Pru stood at the window of her bedroom, eyes raised to the moon, an aching in her soul. This was the same window before which her mother had sat at the loom weaving her silks what seemed now like a lifetime ago. Margaret had suffered from a melancholy that could not be explained, just as Pru herself was suffering now. Was she destined to meet the same fate? The only difference was that her mother had found a deep and abiding love, and until the inexplicable sadness had overwhelmed her, had been happy and content, whereas Pru was doubtful of ever finding the kind of love for which she longed.

Nicolae claimed to love her, but there was little comfort to be derived in that thought. He may not have pretended to be anything other than what he was, but he had conveniently neglected to mention that he was a brutal killer. Oh, how naïve she had been. He was a blood-drinker, for God's sake. His victims may have been thieves and murderers, but that did not make him any less of a killer. How could a man like that love anything at all? Well, he had done her one favor, at least. He had shown her what he truly was, although she doubted his reason for doing so had anything to do with her, but everything to do with him, selfish thing that he was.

What a fool she had been to think him capable of possessing a soul. He was self-centered, not given to regret, and possessing no conscience whatsoever. By all indications, he was void of anything remotely human. She was glad to be rid of him. Why, then, did she feel like weeping? A tear formed and slipped down her cheek and would have been followed by others, had something not captured her attention.

She saw a slight movement on the street below, and through a splash of moonlight she recognized her aunt's form. She expected to hear the front door close, but no such sound came. Squinting into the shadowy night, she saw the figure draw back and look up. For many long minutes Vivienne just stood there staring at the house as if she were deciding whether or not to enter.

Just then, the moon appeared through a tattered cloud, illuminating her aunt's face, and it was plain to see that she was looking up at Papa's room. Pru gasped and blinked hard. Was it a trick of the shifting light, or did she really see an expression of abhorrence on her aunt's face?

Pru turned from the window, feeling sick. She knew Aunt Vivienne had grown weary of tending to Papa, but she never imagined it had grown into such loathing as she had seen on her face just now.

Perhaps it was time to speak to her, to relieve her of her duty as caregiver and send her back to Paris where she could be as free and wanton as she liked. Surely, Papa would not mind. He had been begging her to bar Vivienne from his room, claiming there was something unnatural about her.

Pru pressed her fingers to her temples and attempted to rub away the headache that had only grown worse since leaving Nicolae's house.

A glance down at her dress revealed the truth she would have liked to forget. The hem was soiled with mud from the wharf, the bodice ripped at the hands of Nicolae's demon lust. Beneath it, her stays were broken, the laces torn. In the morning, she would go downstairs to the kitchen before Gladys arrived and toss them into the fire. For now, she undressed and shoved the soiled and torn garments to the back of the wardrobe and slipped a simple white linen shift over her head.

She glanced at her disheveled reflection in the mirror, and frowned. Sitting down at the dressing table, she withdrew what pins were left in her hair and let it tumble past her shoulders. With mechanical movements, and staring at nothing in particular, she drew the bristles of a rosewood hairbrush through the tangled tresses, trying hard not to think about Nicolae, but not succeeding.

What was it about that man that made her ache with conflicted emotion? She should have been glad to be rid of him, yet she knew she would never meet another man like him. He was a rake and a clever manipulator, a petulant and dangerous man, yet he was intelligent and passionate and blessed with a gift for music that few men possessed.

She could tell by the look of distress on his handsome face that the cruel things she said to him this evening had cut him to the quick. Not even the undead were immune to that type of injury, it seemed. She felt dreadful for it, yet he deserved it. She didn't fancy herself in love with him, yet what she did feel for him was something she could not define. Empathy, yes. Lust, oh God, yes. Damn him for causing her this misery.

She tugged the brush through her hair with long, angry strokes. The thought of his judgmental nature was too much to bear. Not even Aunt Vivienne was beyond the reach of his scathing comments. How dare he compare her aunt to that witch Lienore? The only thing they had remotely in common was their preference for young lovers, although Vivienne had claimed to have been in love with only two of them, the one she had married and divorced, and the one with whom she had laid in the bracken a long time ago. The bracken. Vivienne's own words.

Pru stopped brushing her hair in mid-motion and slowly lowered the brush to the dressing table. Something nagged at the back of her mind, causing a sensation not unlike a hundred pin pricks over her flesh.

The bracken. A long time ago.

How long, she wondered? Years? Centuries?

She laughed nervously at the preposterous thought.

Yet try as she might, she could not banish it from her mind. There were too many coincidences to ignore.

Papa had begun to grow weaker with Vivienne's arrival in London. He did not want her in his room. His own words rattled like sabers in Pru's mind. "Don't let her come."

There was Vivienne's dislike for Nicolae, as if she knew there was something unnatural about him. Who but another like he would have known what he was?

Then there was Vivienne's aversion to music which she tried to hide. Pru recalled the night of the concert. Had she really run off to meet one of her lovers, or had it been an excuse not to stay and hear the music? And the night she, Vivienne and Edmund had gone to see the Beggar's Opera, glancing over at her aunt during the production to see a repugnant look on her face. Pru had been too preoccupied with her own problems with Edmund to give it much thought. Until tonight, when she had seen the same look on Vivienne's face as she stood in the street beneath an oil lamp staring up at Papa's room.

This was outlandish. Her imagination was running away with her. Or was it?

Papa!

The brush fell from her hand. The flame flickered as she rushed past the candle to the door.

Her bare feet flew down the narrow winding stairs and across the hardwood planks to her papa's room. Hearing no sound from within, she opened the door and stepped inside.

She approached the bed cautiously and stood for several moments staring down at him. The gentle rise and fall of his chest and the soft wheezing sound of his labored breathing told her he was sleeping. Expelling a breath of relief, she backed out of the room on tiptoes and quietly closed the door behind her.

She was headed back upstairs, chastising herself for letting her imagination run wild, when a sound from behind another door caught her attention. A voice she did not recognize was coming from Aunt Vivienne's room. Had her aunt brought one of her lovers into the house? But wait. It was not a man's voice she was hearing; it was a woman's. Tiptoeing closer, she pressed her ear to the door.

The voice was chanting in a language Pru did not recognize, one moment crooning sweetly, the next filled with low, gurgling tones. She caught her breath. With trembling fingers she reached for the knob and gave it a turn, ever so slightly, ever so quietly, and pushed the door open, only an inch at first, ready to flee at any second. The chanting continued, luring her to push the door open further and peek inside despite every inner warning to turn around and run.

The room stretched before her like a great cave. The drapes were drawn, blocking out the pale moonlight. The only light came from the candles that sulked and sputtered from the gilt wood wall sconces set on either side of the bed. There was a smell of decay in the room, of something old and dead, that made Pru's stomach heave.

Through the fluttering shadows she saw a figure seated at the walnut dressing table that had belonged to her mother. It was Vivienne. But the voice that spoke was not her aunt's. It spoke in a dialect that seemed to come from another time and place, in soft, mournful tones.

"Goddess. *Mathair*. Why have you forsaken me and banished me from the Sacred Isle? Have I not kept the traditions? Lain with lovers to celebrate your union with the Sun God? Honored you in all ways? And still you punish me for one wrong coupling."

The voice hardened, the vehemence in it dripping like blood from an iron blade.

"Because I chose a maiden to love at the Beltaine feast I was hunted like a beast and my heart was cut out of my body on the stone altar. I called for you, prayed to you, begged you to save me, but you turned from me. Gods above, I did not make myself into that writhing thing in the bracken. *You* made me what I was."

Her head fell forward and for many long minutes she was silent. When she lifted her face, her mood swung again, this time to haughtiness.

"But what I became that night, when they danced around the stone altar to the music that haunts me to this day, was from the spell I wove. I needed no cauldron of smoke and fire around which to weave my spells. I was the daughter and granddaughter of witches. I had only to work powerful earth magic and speak the chant of immortality to cheat you of the death you ordained for me."

She threw her head back, whipping her thick hair about her face, and laughed.

"No one has rule over me. Not you. Not the old ones. I lay with whichever lover I choose and I take whichever body pleases me. What do you think of this one, *Mathair*?" She ran her hands over the opening of her dressing gown and drew out her breasts. Their fullness spilled over her palms and the nipples strained against the candlelight. "They are beautiful, are they not?"

Her hand moved downward to cup the mound between her thighs. "And this." Her breath quickened. "Welcoming all lovers like an open door. I was fortunate indeed to find this one, don't you agree, *Mathair*? She likes her lovers the way I do, many and young. Not like that other one. Gods above, but she was a troublesome one. Where such a willful nature came from, I do not know. It was just as well she threw herself from the bridge."

A gasp from the doorway spun her around with alarming suddenness.

"Prudence! How long have you been standing there?"

The color had drained from Pru's face, leaving it a pale oval in the sputtering candlelight. "Wh—who are you?"

She turned back to the dressing table. "Long enough, it would seem," she muttered to herself, answering her own question.

Picking up the hairbrush, she ran it through her tresses with leisurely strokes, deliberately prolonging Pru's mounting fear. "Don't stand in the doorway like a timid little mouse. Come in."

Pru took a cautious step into the room. She looked into the mirror and their eyes met. The person seated at the dressing table looked like Aunt Vivienne, with her handsome face glinting in the candles' glow and resplendent in her flowing silks. But there was a dark aura about her, wrapping a chilly hand around Pru's heart.

"Who are you?" she asked again.

The eyes that stared back at her through the mirror danced with mischief. "Why, who do you think I am?"

"I don't know," Pru answered tremulously.

"Oh," that sweet voice crooned, "but I think you do."

"Aunt Vivienne?"

"In a way, yes. And in a way, no."

Pru looked at the stranger seated at the dressing table and felt her anger beginning to rise. "I asked you a question."

"So you did." She placed the brush down deliberately and looked her. "Hasn't your friend told you about me?"

Somewhere in the darkest part of her soul Pru knew the answer. She groaned aloud. "Lienore."

"There, you see? He has told you about me."

Pru felt the floor slipping beneath her bare feet. It could not be. Not here, in this very house. She felt suddenly cold to the bone. She raised her eyes to meet the unwavering stare of the creature. "What have you done with my aunt?"

"She's right here," came the chilling reply. "As long as I choose to inhabit her, that is. Of course, when I decide to leave, she will die."

"What evil is this?" Pru burst out. "I should have guessed." Her fingers pulled at her shift. Her eyes were wide, desperate pools of blue. "How could I not have known?"

"We see what we want to see. Or, in your case, we don't see what we don't want to see. You're not such a clever little girl after all, are you?"

Rage began to flood through Pru. "Why are you here?"

"Why should I not be?"

"Why this house? This family?" Her voice cracked and broke.

"If you must know, I was wandering through this place you call London and heard the most awful sounds of laughter and music coming from this house. Gods above, the music was unbearable. I had to put an end to it, don't you see?"

The sound of her mother's laughter rang in Pru's memory, and suddenly, she understood. "You did that to her," she said accusingly. "You made her sad. Took all the joy out of her life."

"Nonsense," Lienore answered in sharp reproof. "I gave her reason to live. I offered her lovers, but she refused each one, preferring that insipid musician to the beautiful young men I brought to her. I chose her for her beauty. Such a stunning creature she was. But she fought me every step of the way. Willful natures will not do. I took from her what I could, and she threw herself from the bridge."

Pru closed her eyes in anguish. She would never forget that night the constable came to the door to inform her and Papa that Margaret had been found laying in a heap of broken bones in the river muck. The hurting was more than she could bear. Her mouth twisted painfully and one word emerged as a strangled groan. "Mother!" She would have collapsed had she not been held erect by blinding rage.

"Imagine my surprise when another one, just as beautiful but much more malleable, arrived from Paris." The woman, the creature, whatever she was, continued with her evil tale. "I thought at first that I would take you, my little mouse. But this one…" She paused to look again at herself in the mirror. "This one suits me better. In this body I can attract men like flies to honey."

"More like flies to dung," Pru spat.

Those eyes glowed ominously at her through the mirror. "Take care what you say, little mouse," she said warningly, "or you will find yourself in the Otherworld."

"Or perhaps it will be you who will be sent to the Otherworld."

Lienore laughed dismissively. "You cannot kill what is already dead. Surely your vampire told you that. Besides, if you harm me, you harm Vivienne."

"I will tell Nicolae about you," Pru said.

"That common blood-drinker has no power over me. I am a witch of the Sacred Isle. I practiced the healing art in the circle of standing stones before the ancient order of Druids inhabited this land. They turned a place of the living into the domain of the dead. It was Merlin who ordered the stones removed from the Sacred Isle and brought to the plain. Did you know that the dark lord, Uther Pendragon, sire of the king called Arthur, is buried within the ring of stones? I was there. I witnessed it."

She went on, talking to no one in particular as she spun her tale of sorcery and ancient kings. "It has been said that giants moved the stones from the Sacred Isle to Britain. But it wasn't giants at all. They were moved by ancient vampires, each one possessing the strength of a thousand men. When the stones were in place, they turned upon the mortals and killed them, drinking their blood in a great frenzy until the earth ran red."

Shaking off the memories like dust, she turned her face toward Pru. "Your vampire has no power over me. Now, shoo, before I squash you like a bug."

Pru's face turned as white as her linen shift. "You are not going to kill me?"

Lienore gave her a frozen smile. "Why should I, when I have another victim? I will admit that old man clings stubbornly to his miserable existence, but in the end, I will succeed in sucking the life from him. I always do. And then perhaps that infernal music will stop."

Realization slammed into Pru. "Stay away from him you bitch!"

Without a thought to the consequences, she lunged at the figure seated at the dressing table, fingers like talons aimed at that beautiful face.

Lienore raised her arm, thwarting the attack, sending Pru flying across the room and crashing against the door with a jolt that rattled her senses.

Dazed, Pru stumbled to her feet and grasped for the knob in an attempt to flee.

In a motion that was not seen, but felt, like a cold, dark wind rushing past, Lienore was at the door, slamming it shut with her palm.

"Vile little mortal," she hissed. "You will not keep me from destroying that old man."

Hands that were no longer beautiful, but gnarled and rough as tree bark, circled Pru's throat. The eyes of a demon glowed like fire from a face that had taken on hideous proportions. Gone was the beautiful visage of Vivienne. In its place was a face from hell, a skeletal thing of rotting flesh and sunken eye sockets. A stench of decay issued from its thin, bloodless lips when it spoke in a voice that was no longer recognizable.

"Now I am going to kill you."

The fingers tightened, squeezing the air out of Pru's lungs. She felt herself growing weaker as she struggled for breath. And then, the thing was lifting her off the floor. Her legs thrashed about, feet searching for purchase. Higher into the air she went. She couldn't breathe. Her vision was fading. The world was growing darker. In a far off corner of her mind one word grew fainter and fainter. Papa. Papa...

She was flying through the air. For a split second she was able to breathe again. One quick gasp of air was all she got before she crashed through the window.

Shattered glass.

Pain.

Falling...Falling...

Darkness all around.

One last moment of paralyzing fear before she hit the ground below.

Chapter 25

*T*here was a sound in the night sky. Not that of the rain which had begun as a gentle patter and was now a steady downpour, but of a rapid fluttering, as a small nocturnal creature winged its way toward the row of weavers' houses in Spitalfields.

When it reached the house in Folgate Street, it glided silently to the ground. For several moments it remained on the cobblestones beneath the glow of an oil lamp, the naked pads on its nose twitching to pick up the scent of blood, its pointy ears straining to detect sounds from within. Using its membraned wings as forelegs, it walked toward the front door, and as it did, a startling transformation began to take place. The wings grew longer, taking on the appearance of arms. The bony membranes stretched into fingers. The hind legs lengthened, forming flesh and bone. With each step it took it became more and more human-like until, at last, a man stood before the door, a man fully clothed and looking like any ordinary caller but for the red glow in his eyes and the lips curled back over sharpened eye teeth.

There was no time to wait for someone to answer his knock. The door crashed open under the force of his palm. His eyes scanned the receiving room. With its high plaster ceiling, dark painted wood walls and floor and no candles lit, it looked like a great hollow, empty and devoid of life. He sniffed the air. Something treacherous was afoot. He sensed it. He knew it.

"Prudence!"

He called her name into the darkness. There was no answer.

Taking the steps of the narow staircase two at a time to the second floor, he burst into the music master's room.

James Hightower lay in his bed, his face as pale as the bed linens, clinging precariously to life.

Nicolae rushed to the bed and knelt at its side. "Where is she? Where is Prudence?"

The old man was unable to speak. What life was left in him was fast slipping away.

"Oh, Lienore," Nicolae wailed. "What have you done?"

He should have known. He should at least have suspected. But he'd been so wrapped up in his own little dramas that he had not seen the evil that lurked in this very house. No wonder the doctors could do nothing to help the music master. What was ailing the poor man was far beyond anything their mortal minds could imagine.

He looked again at the old man laying helpless and dying. This was not what Prudence wanted for her beloved papa. He straightened and turned away. He couldn't do it. He wouldn't. Why should he, after the cruel things she had said to him this evening? Death, no matter how it came, was inevitable for mortals. Why should he interfere? Why should he care? His head began to hurt from all the conflicted thoughts that converged upon him. For the thousandth time he thought of the things she said to him. He was an evil, vile thing. A killer. A loathsome creature that deserved to be alone. He flinched, the words wounding him as much now as they had when she had flung them at him. And yet, they were true. As true as anything he knew to be true.

He closed his eyes and felt his self slipping away. All the old pain and misery tore at him. Old wounds festering under centuries of aloneness, of existing only for himself, of caring for nothing except where his next blood meal would come from. Oh, how he hated himself for this thing that he was. If only there was a way to redeem himself for the centuries of wrongs he had committed. He turned back toward the bed. Perhaps there was a way.

It took only minutes. The frail body in his arms shook violently and then collapsed against the down mattress. When Nicolae lifted his head, the linens were stained red. The music master's eyes were wide and blank and unseeing. At his throat were two wounds, like gaping little mouths from which no sound emerged.

The place on his own wrist, where he had punctured the preternatural flesh so that the music master could drink, was already beginning to heal. With the back of his sleeve he wiped the blood from his mouth as he watched the music master draw one final shuddering breath and then fall silent and still and…dead.

With the tip of his finger he wiped away the drops of blood from the corners of the music master's pale dead lips. Somewhere deep down inside he felt remorse. He stood over him, watching for the telltale signs that would come.

Suddenly, the music master's chest rose convulsively and his eyes opened. The pupils were dilated and as transparent as a pane of window glass. The puncture wounds at his neck quivered and gradually closed shut, erasing all trace of the violent act that had led to this.

It had not pleased him to do this deed, but Prudence had asked it of him, and he hoped now she would be happy.

His thoughts turned to her, and a feeling of apprehension gripped him anew. Where was she? Had she gone out for the evening, unwittingly leaving her father alone and at the mercy of the evil that was Lienore? He would have to tell her what he knew now to be the true nature of her father's illness and also about her aunt. He had saved her father for her, but there was no saving the aunt. Once Lienore knew they were on to her, she would abandon Vivienne's body and steal another. But for now, Prudence was not safe in this house. He had to find her and tell her of the danger she was in.

He left the music master's room and headed toward the staircase when something captured his attention, causing him to pause in the hallway. His head cocked to one side as a familiar scent drifted into his nostrils.

He would recognize that scent anywhere. It was sweet and powerful and infiltrated his senses like no other had ever done. It was the scent of blood, but not just any mortal's blood.

Prudence!

A bolt of alarm shot through him.

Lifting his nose to the air, his head whirled in all directions to determine from where the scent was emanating. There! Beyond that door. He rushed into the room, and stopped.

A solitary candle flickered faintly from the sconce, casting wavy shadows across the walls. There was a tension in the room, as if the air itself were stretching and straining. The smell of decay lingered in every corner, mingling with the rosemary used in a witch's brew.

Like a predator, his sulfurous glare stalked the room. It was empty, and yet he felt a distinct presence. He moved slowly to the side of the bed, then to the foot, and finally to the corner around which he could see to the other side.

A dark form lay crumpled on the floor. He moved swiftly toward it. Bending on one knee, he placed a hand on the soft, round shoulder and turned turned her upright.

A breath of sharp relief exploded from his lips. It wasn't Prudence. It was Vivienne. Placing two fingers to the side of her throat, his touch confirmed what he already knew. She was dead.

Dear God, what happened in this room to force Lienore to leave Vivienne's body and disappear? She was out there somewhere, searching for another hapless victim, if she hadn't already found one, wrecking vengeful havoc upon the mortal world.

And then, another thought, this one almost too horrible to bear, crossed his mind. What if the new body Lienore stole belonged to Prudence? The rest of the world might never know the difference, but he'd be able to tell whether it was actually Prudence or Lienore inhabiting those precious curves. He had to find her. He had to know. Then again, what if Prudence was merely out for the evening? He couldn't take the chance of her coming home and discovering Vivienne like this.

He knelt beside the lifeless body of the Englishwoman, contemplating what he would do. He would take her out to the forest and bury her there, and tell Prudence that Lienore had simply run off with Vivienne. Although it would pain Prudence, at least she would be spared the awful truth.

Reaching forward, he was about to lift the body into his arms when the candle fluttered, as if someone had opened the door. He looked up. No one was there. Yet the flame danced this way and that and the shadows swayed across the walls. A mocking night wind sifted through the window. He turned his head toward it.

Nicolae's heart groaned in his breast. For one treacherous moment all he could do was kneel beside the dead woman, frozen like a wolf in the forest.

The window was shattered. Shards of glass were strewn across the floor, glistening like a thousand tiny stars in the moonlight.

Slowly, he rose to his feet. Each step seemed to take a lifetime, when in fact it took less than a heartbeat for him to reach the window. He was mindless of the splintered glass that raked across his face as he thrust his head out into the night. His stomach heaved at what he saw.

There, on the cobbled street below, partly concealed by the fog, a figure lay face down in a rain puddle. Through the mist he could see dark stains on her linen shift, and he knew they were blood.

Before Nicolae could even will his body to move, he leaped from the window. He landed on his feet with the agility of a cat and rushed to her, throwing himself down by her side and drawing her up into his arms. A wild wail pierced his core, a sound of agony and rage and despair all in one.

No, no, no, no!

Don't leave me!

I cannot go through eternity without you!

He clutched her to him, pressing his face to hers. She was cold as marble. Not dead, but nearly so.

His astute sense of hearing detected the faintest of heartbeats.

Thump. Thump. Th—th—thump.

Dimming.

He could not lose her like this. She had given him the capacity to love, made him believe that he might actually possess a soul.

Slowing.

"I won't let you go!"

Dying.

In that instant, he knew what he must do.

He looked skyward. His lips curled back and raindrops glanced off the tips of the fangs that were bared in a hideous grimace.

"Forgive me, Prudence," he implored, as he brought his face to her neck and sank his teeth into the tender, almost dead, flesh.

The blood he had craved since the day he first met her now filled his mouth, sliding over his tongue and down his throat like nectar. It was as sweet as he had imagined it would be, as flavorful and tantalizing as any he had ever tasted. All he had ever wanted was within his grasp. She was his. His and no other's.

The thirst raged within him, tearing at his insides. But it was more than the mere drinking of blood to survive. He drank as if it were his salvation.

Dark, wet strands of her burnished hair spilled over his face as he sucked the blood out of her. He could smell the scent of rosewater that emanated from her skin. He could feel her heartbeat diminishing. She was dying, and he was killing her.

At the precise moment when he sensed that her heart had beat its last, he tore his shirt away, ripped open the flesh of his breast and punctured the muscle down to the heart.

Drawing her face forward, twining his hand in her tangled hair, he whispered, "Drink from my heart."

At first, hanging drenched and limp in his arms, she made no movement at all. But then her heart began to beat again, and her hands lifted to cradle him and hug him close against her face.

Nicolae closed his eyes to the sweet excruciating pain of it—the lips sucking at his open flesh, gently at first, and then becoming harder, greedier, hungrier.

"Oh Prudence, forgive me. Do not hate me. Love me as I love you."

For the second time this evening he offered his blood. He had given the music master only enough to be brought back from the brink, to become a creature of the night, yes, but with limited powers. But Prudence, drinking his blood now like wine, in great swallows until it ran out of her mouth and down her chin, mingling with the rain to stain her shift pink, Prudence with her fingers locked around his neck, unwilling to let go even when he tried to pull away, drinking far more than she should have. And still he let her, knowing that his blood would strengthen her beyond her own comprehension.

His chest heaved and a sorrowful moan escaped his quivering lips. "No more. No more." He grasped her by the shoulders and forced her away.

He looked at her through the rain. Her eyes were bluer than he had ever seen them. Her skin looked like porcelain with tiny cerulean veins showing just beneath the shimmering surface. The wounds he had inflicted on her neck were already closing. He removed a handkerchief from his pocket, and with trembling hands wiped the blood from her mouth, and then from his own.

Lifting her into his arms, he carried her into the house and brought her to her room on the top floor, where he placed her down on the cotton-stuffed mattress. He worked swiftly to remove the blood-stained shift, and tucked her naked body beneath the cover.

Her hair was a wet tangle against her pale face. After many anxious minutes she opened her eyes and looked at him. "Nicolae?"

"Yes, my love."

"She was here," she said weakly. "Lienore. Oh, Nicolae, it was terrible."

Worse than you know, he thought. "Don't think about that right now. You must rest."

"I know now it was she who killed my mother. And Papa. Oh!" She struggled to rise, but he coaxed her gently back down.

"Your Papa is fine," he said.

Sudden understanding flooded her eyes. "Did you—?"

"I have kept my part of the bargain."

She turned her head away and pressed a fist to her mouth, stifling her tears.

"Do not weep for him," he said. "It is as you wished it. He will play his instrument again"

"Will he become like that…that—"

"He will not become like that thing you witnessed on the wharf," he said, guessing her meaning. "He did not drink enough to become that powerful." *But you*, he could not help but think, *you drank more than you should have. God help the world when you come into your own.*

"Nicolae." She reached for his hand and grasped it tightly. "Aunt Vivienne is really Lienore. What will we do? We must find a way to stop her."

He drew in a breath, and replied, "I'm afraid there is nothing to be done. Lienore has fled, taking Vivienne with her. It is doubtful you will see your aunt again."

"Oh, no, it cannot be," Pru wailed. "She told me that when she leaves, Aunt Vivienne will die."

"Now, now, there's nothing to worry about. Apparently, Lienore is quite happy to inhabit your aunt. I'm sure she will continue to do so for a very long time. Trust me, Prudence, your aunt is quite safe."

The lie slipped easily from his lips and seemed to quiet her.

"Now, close your eyes and go to sleep. When you awake, you will see the world…" *and me*, he dared to hope, "…through different eyes."

The feather pillow cradled her face when her head sank back onto it. "I am tired. So very tired."

He touched her cheek. She was warmer now, pulsing with an infusion of his immortal blood. "Sleep. I will take care of everything." He thought of the woman lying dead on the floor below and of the neat little grave he would make for her in the forest.

"I had the most distressing feeling," Pru said. "Of falling. And then, I don't know, something more, something frightening was happening to me. Oh, I wish I could remember." She turned her face toward the window. "What was that? Did you hear it?"

It's only the rats in the alley, he wanted to say, amazed that her ability to hear what the human ear could not was already so pronounced. But then, she was no longer human, was she?

Chapter 26

Pru yawned and stretched her arms over her head, breathing in the fragrance of daisies and buttercups winking in the warm sunshine. Never before had she smelled the flowers as though they were blooming right outside her window. There came to her nose the scent of honeysuckle and moss, and to her ears the buzzing of insects and the rustle of leaves from some far-off meadow. She sat up and glanced around. Everything looked exactly the same, only something seemed different.

Throwing off the linen coverlet, she realized she was naked. Hadn't she donned her shift last night? She tried to see through the cobwebs shrouding her memory and sighed when she could not remember. These past days had been strange indeed.

Shaking her head, she walked across the room to the dressing table. She had traversed this floor untold times over the years and had never realized how smooth the hardwood planks were beneath her feet. Funny that she should notice something like that now.

Sitting before the carved gilt mirror, she ran the brush through her hair, thoughts scrambling to make sense of the strange sensations, for it seemed she could smell and hear every little thing. The brush moved through her hair with greater effort than usual, and looking at her reflection in the mirror, she was surprised to see that her hair looked to have grown longer and fuller overnight. And her skin. When had it taken on a translucency that made it look like marble? Why was her face so pale?

She leaned forward and peered deeply into the mirror. Her lashes were longer and darker, her eyes bluer and brighter than they had ever been. Yes, it was all very strange indeed.

Pondering whether her imagination was playing tricks on her, she went to the wardrobe. Reaching past the prim gray and brown Indian cottons, she chose instead the Mayfair shop silk, the one she had worn that first night with Nicolae, repaired to its former elegance. She wriggled into a shift, donned her stays and hoop, and without a second thought, slid the brown silk dress over her head.

At the window she drew the drapes aside and instantly threw her hand up to shield her face. The brightness hurt her eyes. She backed away, blinking and bewildered.

She left her room and descended the narrow staircase to the middle floor. At her father's door, she grasped the knob and entered quietly so as not to disturb him. The drapes were still drawn. The bed was empty.

Just then, the sound of the violoncello erupted from the music room, streaming upstairs and throughout the house. Someone was playing Papa's piece. Was it Nicolae? Last night's events were a mystery to her, locked away somewhere in a memory that was as fog-filled as a London alley. But something told her it had not gone well between them. What was he doing here now?

Her spirits were in precipitous decline when she reached the music room. Upon entering, her voice sounded strong and disapproving. "I'm sure that after last night—"

The words screeched to a halt on her tongue. The room was just beginning to brighten as the first traces of dawn seeped through a separation in the drawn drapes. Pru's mouth fell open. There was Papa, seated behind the violoncello, playing his beloved instrument as though he had never ceased to do so, his face calm and serene as she had not seen it in a very long time. For several moments she was unable to move as she watched and listened and prayed it wasn't a dream.

"Papa."

He stopped playing and lifted his head. His face was still seamed and worn, but there was a brightness about it, quite as though it were lit from within. The complexion that had been leprous white was now ruddy with color. The eyes that smiled back at her were no longer saddened and fearful but sparkling and bright.

Pru rushed to him and sank to her knees at his side. Great tears shimmered in her eyes that looked up at him.

He placed a hand on her head and stroked her hair. "Pruddy, my dear, isn't it wonderful? I am well. I can play again."

"Oh, Papa." She buried her face in his lap. How could she tell him that she had bargained away his mortality? "I have done a terrible thing."

"He told me you would blame yourself, but you must not."

She drew in a long shuddering breath and looked back up at him. "He?"

"Our young friend. He was here last night. He sat with me for a very long time after you were asleep and explained everything."

"Then you know what he is?" she asked tremulously.

He nodded. "At first I thought his story was preposterous. You must admit, it is quite a tale. But as he spoke, it all started to make sense. My illness began with Vivienne's arrival here. Each night when she came to my room, I knew without knowing that something was not right. Of course, I never could have guessed that the poor woman had been taken over by...by...well, I'm not entirely sure what it was, but I know now it wasn't of the natural world. Our friend tells me that your aunt and whatever it was have disappeared, probably never to be seen again." A wave of sadness washed across his face. "It is all for the best, I suppose."

Pru sniffed back her tears. "You don't hate me for what he has done to you?"

"Hate you? My dear Pruddy, you are my child, I could never hate you."

"But you said that immortality would come as a gift from Satan."

He cradled her face in his hands and wiped a glistening tear from the corner of her eye with his thumb. "I have always held hope that there is something after death," he said gently. "Remember the words Moses spoke to Joshua. 'The Lord himself goes before you and will be with you; he will never leave you nor forsake you.' If this is what I have become, then God willed it so, and who am I to question His judgment?" His gaze traveled lovingly over her face. "Our friend's faith has been tested and he has lost his way, but Pruddy, who among us is without sin?"

She stifled a chill at his cold touch and choked back the memory of the sinful nights she had lain with Nicolae, reveling in the shameful pleasure. "Has he told you what it will be like for you, now that you are a…" She could not voice the word. "…like him?"

"He has counseled me. It will take some getting used to." Glancing toward the drapes, he sighed, and said, "I think the thing I shall miss most is the light of day." His expression brightened when he turned back to his daughter. "But I have you, my sweet Pruddy. And I have this." He nodded toward the violoncello. "And an eternity of music to sustain me through the dark hours that are to come."

She wanted to cry out to him, *what about me, when I grow old and die? Will your music sustain you then? Oh Papa, what have I done?*

"You know, Pruddy," he said, "it's really not bad at all. On the contrary, it's quite extraordinary. I can hear things from far off. And I can smell things I never smelled before, like wild strawberries and buttercups."

He kept speaking, but she had ceased to hear. His words faded as she recalled having experienced those very sensations upon waking this morning. Even now she could smell the baskets of fish hoisted onto the wharf and the sea-coal brought to the landings and the mud of the riverbed at low tide. From far away a slow, sad roar began to pierce her consciousness. She rose on shaky legs and walked to the door.

"Draw the drape tighter for me, would you Pruddy dear?" her papa was saying. "The sunlight hurts my eyes."

She moved mechanically to the widow and pulled the drape, shutting out the little ray of sunlight that filtered into the room. The sound of the violoncello resumed, colliding with the terrible, desperate thoughts that were flittering like surprised bats in her mind. She walked numbly down the hallway, past the tall chiming clock, and stopped before the door to her aunt's room. Something, she knew not what, tugged her toward it. She placed her hand tentatively on the knob, and with fingers trembling, opened the door.

The room was quiet and still. A morning breeze billowed the draperies. Pru crept cautiously closer to the window. With one hand she drew the drape aside, and gasped. The glass panes were shattered.

Like a cold, dark wind a rush of memories suddenly overtook her—of Lienore admitting with gleeful cruelty what she had done to Margaret and Vivienne and of her horrible transformation into some cadaverous, hideous thing. Of the feeling of being strangled and the panic that came at being unable to draw breath. Of being hurled across the room toward the window. Of the sound of breaking glass. Of falling. And then…nothing. What happened between the time she went through the window and when she found herself in her bed with Nicolae standing over her?

Pru felt sick as she left the room. For several incomprehensible moments she stood in the hallway, afraid to put her suspicions into cogent thought. And then she began to run, as fast as she could, up the narrow staircase, to the room that had belonged to her mother and which was now hers. She raced to the dressing table and leaned forward to view herself in the mirror.

Her skin was as white as a goose feather and so transparent she could see the tiny blue veins that snaked just beneath the surface. Her eyes were as clear as glass, the blue pupils rimmed with black, making them look otherworldly. With trembling fingers she lifted her hand and touched her face. It was like ice to the touch, just like Papa's hand had been when he caressed her cheek, and Nicolae's hands when they made love and Lienore's merciless grip at her throat. Cold and dead. The terrible truth of what happened last night slammed into her with the force of a thousand runaway carriages.

As she looked, her reflection began to fade, until no image at all shown in the mirror. Oh God! It couldn't be! Oh God! No!

She screamed, and the world went black.

Chapter 27

*P*ru accepted the glass of sherry Nicolae offered, and sat back on the sofa.

"I never really noticed much about this room before," she said.

Her gaze traversed the dark wood walls, the heavy broadcloth draperies, the curved settee, a high-backed, winged armchair, a French oval tea table, the collection of paintings hanging about the walls, the bric-a-brac of alabaster and marble adorning the mantle. Her eyes fell upon the fireplace poker, her heartbeat quickening.

"You live well," she concluded. "The only thing absent is a clock, but I don't suppose you have any need to know the time of day."

"No, indeed," came his flat response. "Being a slave to time puts such restraint on things."

"What will it be like, living forever in darkness?"

"It's not so bad," he said. "The night is filled with wonder. And a cloudy day should cause you no harm."

"Will I be hunted?"

"Well, yes, there is that. But I will teach you how to stay one step ahead of the hunters."

"And the Sanctum?" she asked with a shiver. "The secret society you told me about? Now that Edmund is gone, will there be others?"

"I dare say there are other first born sons devoted to the task of our destruction, but I have managed to elude them for centuries, and you should be able to do the same. Oh, Prudence, don't look so grim. It's not all that bad. Look at the bright side. Now you can do what you will, take what you want, without consequence."

And be as miserable about it as you, she thought with a grimace.

"I've never seen you eat food," she said. "Do you?"

"Of course. I'm particularly fond of pigeon and sirloin of beef roast. Venison not so much. I like milk if taken from the cow immediately before consumption. And pudding and chocolate. Oh, and let's not forget strawberries. I find them most enjoyable."

The reminder of strawberries brought the color to Pru's cheeks and an instant warming inside which had nothing at all to do with the sherry. Why did she have to feel something like that now when she was hating him so thoroughly and plotting her revenge? It was all worked out in her mind. She knew precisely what she would do.

She glanced up at him as he stood before the fireplace, one arm resting casually on the mantle, a silhouette against the light of the candles, just enough luminosity on his face to define those pale, handsome features, his eyes downcast, candleglow glinting upon his lashes. She could do it now, she thought wickedly. Catch him unaware and make him pay for his crime. But a stronger impulse held the unspeakable act at bay.

"You know," she said, the seductive tone of her voice drawing his eyes toward her, "it's terribly warm in the room."

Placing the glass of sherry on the table beside the sofa, she reached up and began to take down her hair, letting the pins fall silently to the carpet. The braided coronet tumbled across one shoulder. With her fingers she separated the thick plait until it fell like cords of silk across the nape of her neck and down her back. She shook her head, fanning it loose.

His eyes stuck to her like hapless moths to a flame. "Shall I open a window for you?"

"No. I don't think that would help."

He came slowly forward, his shadow falling across the carpet, until he was standing before her. "Is there anything I can do for you?"

The candlelight glistened on her moistened lips. "Perhaps there is something I can do for you."

A crooked little smile crossed his mouth. "You are a contrary creature, aren't you?"

"Contrary? I don't think so. Creature?" She rose slowly to stand before him. "Would you like to see what kind of creature I am?"

As she spoke, she toyed with the laces at her bodice, twirling them around her finger, slowly pulling them open and pulling her dress down to reveal the smooth bare skin of her shoulders before pushing it past her hips to the floor around her feet. She heard the sharp intake of his breath and saw the green of his eyes brighten with anticipation. Sweeping her hair up off her neck, she turned her back to him, and asked sweetly, "Would you unhook me please?"

His fingers worked swiftly to comply, unhooking her stays. When the garment was loosened, she allowed him to grasp a handful of her hair and bring it to his face to breathe in its fragrance for a moment before turning back around to face him.

She slipped quickly out of the stays and pushed her shift down past her shoulders and elbows, forming a pool of fabric around her ankles. She bent forward to step out of the silk and linen at her feet, and as she did, her hair fell toward her face, cascading over her shoulders so that when she stood erect, it concealed her breasts beneath a blanket of dark burnished gold. With slow, purposeful movements, she swept her hair back to reveal the plump white mounds with their rosy tips. Her eyes never left his face as she cupped her breasts, pushing them together to form a deep, hidden valley, and then slid her hands slowly, provocatively down her sides to her waist and over the flare of her hips.

His eyes widened and his tongue darted out to moisten his lips when she cupped the downy mound between her legs with one hand while with the other hand she reached forward and without ceremony grasped the hardened bulge that strained at his trousers.

"Prudence," he said with a gasp. "What are you doing?"

"I am taking what I want," she answered.

He leaned forward and reached for her, but she pulled back. "You must first finish undressing me."

He obeyed, dropping to his knees before her. He cupped one calf, and then the other, as he lifted each leg to remove her buckled shoes with the small curved heels, then slid his hands up and down the white thread stockings before peeling each one off in turn while she balanced herself with her hands on his shoulders.

When she was naked before him, he rose and again advanced toward her, but she stopped him with her palm against his chest. "Not yet."

With deliberate slowness she unfastened the buttons of his shirt, feeling deliciously wicked at the heavy rise and fall of his breast.

Yes, she would get him exactly where she wanted him, and then she would make him pay for his evil deeds.

With two buttons left, she grasped his shirt in both hands and ripped it fully open, pushing it off his shoulders and down his arms and flinging it away to fall in a soft heap on the carpet.

She ran her hands over his bare chest, across the little nipples that pricked her palms like tender thorns, and over the taut muscles of his stomach, watching with wicked satisfaction as every caress was reflected on his pale face.

Bringing her face close, she licked the salty flesh. He made a rough, licentious sound when she drew one taut nipple into her mouth and tugged at it with her teeth. She could feel the heavy throbbing of his muscles, smell the scent of him mingled with the rich earth upon which he was obliged to rest, and it drove her further into her determination to subdue him, tame him, and destroy him.

She bit him, kneading his flesh with her fingers that were stronger than she had ever felt them, but he made no protest. His head tilted back, eyes closed to the ceiling in pleasure. The sound of his breathing was like the wind, growing stronger and more violent with every inhalation.

"Oh," he rasped, "you are a very naughty little vampire."

Glancing downward, she could see his manhood throbbing against his trousers. *Not yet*, she whispered to herself. She wanted him to beg for it. The way he had given her no opportunity to beg for her mortality.

Taking his hand in hers, she led him to the sofa and pushed him down on it.

Standing naked before him, she watched the rise and fall of his chest grow more erratic as his eyes traveled over her.

"Do not torture me like this. Let me touch you."

She moved closer, standing with her legs apart, her secret places now within easy reach. This time when he put his hand out, she did not pull back.

He touched her, forcing a gasp from her throat. She tried to concentrate on her purpose, but his fingers massaging her, teasing her, making her wet, forced the wicked plot aside in favor of pure, unadulterated pleasure. His hands were between her legs, forcing them wider apart as he slid forward on the sofa and brought his face to that spot of undisciplined desire.

Her fingers burrowed into his hair and she arched against him, panting and writhing. Looking down, she watched him as he pleasured her, his long dusky eyelashes fanning his cheeks, his lips suckling, his tongue teasing her to madness. His fingers pressed into the soft flesh of her buttocks, locking her to him. What would once have been immoral ecstasy was now sweet madness. The shame she once felt from such an act was now a wanton need. The embarrassment was gone, replaced by a desire to have him see and touch and taste and know every inch of her. White hot heat spread through her, making her nipples ache with fullness. Drops of wetness of her own carnal juices mingled with his saliva to trickle down the insides of her thighs, tickling the tender flesh.

With a sudden gesture, she grasped a handful of his long, silky hair and pulled his head back. He looked up at her, a mixture of surprise and relish brightening his green eyes, wetness upon his lips, but she just smiled dangerously and pushed him onto the sofa, pressing his back against the cushions.

She came toward him like a great cat advancing on its prey, and dropped to her knees, moving into the space between his legs. She eased the buttons of his trousers out of their slots one by one, slowly, until he finally reached for the last few and tore them open himself, sending them flying off into the air. His phallus thrust itself from the opening of his trousers with a defiant will of its own, red and rigid, blue veins pulsing at its sides and drops of dew glistening on its tip. Her gaze moved from his arousal to his face. His eager expression told her what he wanted. She molded her hand around his shaft and heard him suck in his breath.

"Tell me what you want," she whispered, her breath fanning his swollen member.

"You know what I want." His voice was a low, taut grinding sound, the kind a man makes when he can scarcely breathe with pent-up lust.

"You must ask me nicely for it," she teased.

He gave out with a short, strained laugh. "You would have me plead with you?"

Pru's fingers tightened. "I would have you beg."

For the barest moment he said nothing, his breath coming hard and fast, his member throbbing inches away from the pleasure she could give it.

"I have never had to beg for this," he said hungrily.

She moved her face away and placed her hands upon his knees as if to rise.

He swallowed hard between breaths and gripped her shoulders with cruel strength, holding her there.

Smiling up at him, she said, "How badly do you want it? Bad enough to beg?"

In a voice seething with anger and lust, he said, "I could snap your neck, you insolent bitch."

"But you won't."

For several moments their gazed locked, sizzling green striking cold, hard blue.

His grip tightened painfully at her shoulders as he pushed her head slowly forward. "All right, damn you. Do it. Please. I beg you."

Yes, she thought triumphantly, *beg for it. Beg as if nothing in the world matters except this.*

She touched her lips to him and felt his shuddering response. He groaned and splayed his long elegant fingers in her hair, twisting and twining the burnished tresses. He tasted of sweat and semen when she drew the shaft into her mouth, just the tip at first, swirling her tongue around the soft ridge, and then taking it fully, while her hands slid up and down the long muscular tightness of his thighs beneath the coarse fabric of his trousers.

His long lashes closed over his eyes, his back arched and his hips thrust in rhythm to her maddening strokes. He was at her mercy now, as she had been at his as she had lain in a mud puddle on the cobblestones. She was taking his will from him as surely as he had taken hers, leaving him no choice but to succumb to her desire.

Long before last night he had turned her into a wanton woman, made her crave the desires of the flesh as desperately as she craved life. But he had taken life from her, and there was nothing left to crave except this carnal pleasure and the insane desire to destroy him as he had destroyed her.

Drawing her lips from him, she rose and straddled his legs. Her hand found his wet and swollen member and guided its tip toward her opening.

He made a sound, part groan, part laughter, at the aggressive power of her body. His hips thrust upwards, seeking entry, but she hovered just above him, prolonging the agony.

"Let me fill you," he rasped.

She came down hard on him, her body tightening around him.

Placing his hands on her hips, he lifted her up and down, up and down, impaling her on himself. Her plump breasts shook with each thrust, the hardened nipples brushing his face. Tilting his head toward her, he opened his mouth over her nipple and sucked hard, drawing a moan from deep in her throat. Her hair fell forward, catching glints of candlelight along each strand, the fragrant waves washing over his face.

She had wanted to bring him to his knees, to make him feel powerless and defenseless. But she should have known better. It was she who felt helpless to withstand her own dark hungers. She who was defenseless against this desperate pleasure. She who no longer recognized herself. Decent. Reckless. Modest. Wanton. Alive. Dead.

Even her climax, when it came, was a betrayal. Wave upon wave of unbridled pleasure shook her to the very core of her being. There was no sense of triumph in it, only a stark reminder of what she was, what he had made her into—a creature of the flesh, of the night, of eternity.

Damn him for this. Damn him.

Chapter 28

"You know, Prudence, I think I much prefer you when you are hating me."

His voice, so damnably casual as he straightened his trousers, pressed upon her nerves. He was back to his old self now, arrogant, haughty, in full possession of his overconfident nature. For a few moments in time he had been an ordinary man quivering with sexual desire, but the figure that stood before her now was the cold, calculating vampire she had come to loathe. It only strengthened her resolve to do what she knew she had to do.

"We two make quite a team," he went on. "Rather like a pair of wild horses hitched to a runaway carriage."

"I never thought of myself as a mare," Pru said sourly.

He scooped up his shirt from the carpet and donned it. "Think of the times we will have. The things we will do. The love we will make. If tonight was any sample of what is to come, I thank God that I have the rest of eternity and you to share it with. You are quite the little tigress. I must say, being a vampire agrees with you."

Pru grimaced and got up from the sofa to go in search of her clothes. She pulled her shift on over her head and reached for her stays.

"Allow me," he said.

"I can do it myself," she replied, brushing away from him. "How do you think I have managed all these years without you?"

"As you wish." He backed away and went to pour himself a glass of sherry.

Pru hooked her stays in front and then twisted the garment around so that the hooks were at her back where they belonged. She slipped the shift over her head. With a rustle of silk she pulled the dress up over her hips and arms and laced the bodice. The candlelight glinted off the hair pins she retrieved from the carpet. With practiced hands, she plaited her long hair and wound it atop her head in a coronet. She glanced about the room, seeking a mirror in which to view her handiwork, and realized with a start that it would not matter even if there was one.

"Will I never be able to see my reflection again?" she muttered, unaware that she had spoken her dismal thoughts aloud, until she heard him answer.

"Not in a mirror, no. A puddle, perhaps, although not as clearly."

She whirled to him then, her face flushed with incomprehension. "How can you be so casual about it?"

"It is what it is," he said fatalistically. "I guess you can call me a pragmatist. It's a trait you too shall acquire over time."

"Did you never want to see yourself?" she questioned, appalled at his seeming lack of caring.

He shrugged elegantly in his shirtsleeves. "You learn to see yourself through the eyes of others."

"And if others see you as a monster?"

He arched a dark brow at her. "Are we speaking hypothetically? Ah, I can tell from the look on your face that we are not." He took a sip from the glass and allowed a bored sigh to escape his lips. "Oh well. As I said, it is what it is."

Pru did not trust herself to reply. If she did, her words might betray the thoughts hatching in her mind.

Still, tears of despair tore at the back of her throat as one question raged through her mind. She watched him from the corners of her eyes, so smug and self-assured, so overbearing as to think they were a team. Indeed! A team of what? Killers? Blood drinkers? Did he really imagine them as two merry vampires romping their way through eternity? She wanted to weep, to shout, to tear at him in any way she could.

She bit her lip, but the questioning words came crashing out. "Why did you do this to me?" she demanded desperately.

An impenetrable look darkened his eyes, and he answered warily, "You were dying in my arms."

Pru groaned. "You should have let me die."

"I could not," he admitted softly.

"It was not your decision to make."

His voice strengthened. "I felt you draw your last breath."

"You should have left my fate in the hands of God."

He placed the glass of sherry on the mantle and approached her, green eyes tense and alive. "To lay half dead waiting for your life to drain away at the hands of evil is worse than anything you can imagine. Believe me, I know. Ask your father. He knows. Did you not smell the stink of your father's dying spirit each time you entered his room?"

She stared at him in horror. The smell of the sickroom had not gone unnoticed, nor did the way poor Papa lay like a marble statue on his bed, his breath so shallow at times that she'd had to place an ear close to his lips to confirm that he still breathed. The doctors' pronouncements, each one worse than the last, had filled her with dread and sent her one fateful night to the bridge where she had first met the vampire that would change her life forever.

"You wanted him to live," he said. "To be free of his frail body and dwindling spirit, free to play his instrument again. I kept my part of the bargain and gave that to you. Have you considered the depth of pain your father would have felt had I carried your dead body into the house? Do you think an eternity of music would have mattered to him then?"

She shook her head angrily. "What you say is true, but I do not believe you did this to me for his sake, or for mine. You did it for yourself."

"Yes!" His bellow echoed throughout the house, shaking the walls and the floor beneath their feet and startling her. "Yes," he repeated, his tone softening. "I did it for myself. Because I could not bear to go through eternity without you."

Pru turned away from the dark and cruel look in his eyes, biting her knuckles and stifling a moan. There was an aching in her soul. But then, the worst possible thought came to her. Did she even have a soul?

Nicolae was at her back, close enough for her to feel his warm breath caressing the nape of her neck.

"Prudence, we can make this work for us. From now on, we will never be apart. You and me. Just us."

"Oh Nicolae," she cried, shaking her head, "There is no us."

Her heightened perceptions detected the dull ache in his heart. He leaned forward and whispered in her ear, "What do you think your life will be like without me?"

Despite his penchant for cruelty, she knew the taunt was meant to mask his true feelings. She turned then to look at him. There was such distressed confusion in his eyes that for a moment she was sorry she'd been the one to inflict more pain to an already over-pained life.

"You don't understand," he said, his eyes beseeching hers.

"No, Nicolae, it's you who doesn't understand. When I leave here, you shall never see me again."

He opened his mouth to speak, but the words came out a rusty whisper. "You cannot mean it." There was an expression of inexplicable pain twisting his handsome features, and his green eyes were dull, as if a light had been extinguished behind them.

Tears stung Pru's eyes. But who were the tears for? Him? Herself? She knew not. Another unanswered question bound to plague her for all time.

He turned away to stare rigidly into space. "I have waited centuries for you. It was ordained long before you and I were even born that we should be together." He laughed contemptuously. "I believe it down to the depths of the soul you think you see in me."

"I was wrong. You have no soul. And now, neither do I. Of everything you have taken from me, my virtue, my mortality, my happiness, that is the one thing I will never forgive you for taking."

"The soul is an overrated thing," he scoffed. "If it exists at all."

"It is the thing that made me human," she wailed.

"You still have a heart. I didn't rip it from your body, although I am beginning to regret not having done so."

"The heart pumps blood through the body," she said, dismissing his gibe. "No more than that. But the soul is the essence of a person. It is where the good resides, the kindness, the humanity. It is the principle of life and feeling and thought. It is what guides us through our lives."

"Then you should be glad to be no longer burdened with one," he said flatly.

She stiffened, holding his gaze for a long moment, before declaring, "We will never be together."

He rushed up to her, the candlelight reflecting the anguish on his face. "Why, Prudence? Why did you give yourself to me tonight as you never have before? I thought it was to be the beginning of something wonderful for us."

"I don't know why," she said, turning away, unable to bear the look in his eyes. "Perhaps it was because it was the end of something. My way of bidding you farewell."

His eyes narrowed with suspicion. "Or perhaps it was because you know that only with me can you experience such wild abandon."

"So what if that's true? It does not mean I want to go through eternity with you. There is more to life than the joys of the flesh."

A surge of resentment sharpened his tone. "You little fool. Don't you know you will never be able get away from me?"

In a weary voice, Pru implored, "Nicolae, be reasonable. You can have any woman you want. I cannot be that important to you."

"But you are," he said, sounding petulant and dangerous.

"Why? Because I thought I saw something in you that you yourself claim does not exist? No, Nicolae, you cannot use your words to sway me, nor your charm, nor your beauty, nor all your powers. You have made me into a vampire like yourself. With that curse comes the power to resist you, and resist you I shall, with every fiber of my being and every ounce of strength I possess."

"I will never let you go."

Pru tensed. Something in his voice made her turn around to look at him. By the light of the flickering candles his height seemed to grow nearly to reach the ceiling, throwing a tall, eerie shadow across the wall. His lips were curled back in a snarl, revealing the deadly white fangs. Before her loomed a supernatural force, something akin to a beast of the forest, something that could not be controlled, a dark, ancient threat with the power to rip her head from her body. Suddenly, she remembered the tale he had told of his making that terrible night in Transylvania, and how the Prince of Walachia had been beheaded by the Turks, ending his bloodthirsty reign of terror. Hadn't he said that decapitation was one way to destroy a vampire? As was piercing the heart.

She ought to have been afraid, and would have been, but for one thing. His eyes. His beautiful, mesmerizing eyes. Despite the hideousness of his visage, there was in his eyes a softness, a vulnerability, an aching need that transcended all else and made him seem, for a fleeting moment at least, almost human.

"You don't frighten me," Pru said. "And you aren't going to destroy me."

The sound of her voice broke the terrible tension in the room. The towering shape diminished, the fangs receded, and handsome Nicolae stood before her once again.

"No," he said, "I'm not going to destroy you. But I am going to have you. Whenever I want. Wherever I want. However I want. And nothing you do can stop me."

He sauntered back to the mantle where he had left his glass, picked it up and downed the sherry without ceremony. With his back to her, he said flatly and irrevocably, "You are mine. Now and forever."

"You underestimate me if you think that."

He turned around to find her standing there, the fire poker in her hand. He smiled a crooked little smile and was about to say something when she lunged at him with a cry.

His eyes went wide as the poker struck its mark. He let out a howl of pain and shock that reverberated throughout the house.

For several seconds nothing happened. And then, a warm trickle of crimson blood began to seep into the fabric of his shirt over his heart, spreading wider and wider like rings upon water.

He staggered toward her, but she leaped out of the way and watched in wild-eyed terror as he stumbled about, his hand clutching his breast, the blood pouring over and through his pale fingers, catching the glint of the candles like sherry.

Into her nostrils came the smell of fear, not hers, but his. She stood rooted to her spot, unable to move, watching him thrash about the room, knocking over tables and chairs. The crystal decanter crashed to the floor, shattering into a thousand shards and sending the costly Oloroso splattering over the carpet.

"Prudence!"

The cry of her name jolted her into movement. She ran to the door.

Looking back, she saw him crumble to his knees and then fall forward. His head was tilted to one side, toward the door. Those green eyes were looking at her, beseeching her. One pale hand lifted off the floor, palm up, reaching out to her. His eyes clouded and his breath came scarce.

"Prudence." This time his voice was a pale whisper.

With shaking hands, she reached for the doorknob and threw open the door. The night air slapped her in the face and the fog swallowed her as she raced down the steps.

The long, mournful howl of a wolf resounded through the night, bouncing off the worn timbers of the shops, echoing down the cobbled streets and through the mud-soaked alleys.

Pru stopped and looked back, her heart weeping.

It all came crashing down on her, the reality of it, the finality of it. She would never gaze into those beautiful green eyes again, nor feel the touch of his hand against her skin, nor hear the fierce splendor of his music. For the first time, the terrible consequence of what she had done registered upon her brain.

And then she heard it, a voice, the faintest of whispers, yet sounding like a deafening roar to her ears.

"Now and forever."

Horror seized her. With a cry, she began to run, faster, faster, so fast that her heart threatened to explode in her chest.

Away from the house in Hanover Square,

Away from the blood.

Away from the haunting beauty of his face and the magic of his voice and toward the only thing that was left.

Eternity.

http://www.nancymorse.com
Historical and Contemporary Romance
Where Love Is Always An Adventure

Printed in Great Britain
by Amazon

48157782R00155